The

by

Kerry J Donovan

©Kerry J Donovan, October 2016

The right of Kerry J Donovan to be identified as Author of this work has been asserted in accordance with the Copyright, Designs and Patents Act, 1988.

All rights reserved. No part of this novel may be reproduced or transmitted in any form or by any means, electronic or mechanical, including photocopying, recording, or any information storage and retrieval system without prior written permission of the Author and without similar condition including this condition being imposed on any subsequent purchaser. Your support for the Author's rights is appreciated.

All characters in this work are fictitious. Any resemblance to actual persons, living or dead, is purely coincidental.

Published by Human Vertex Publications, France.
Head shot image, David Ilic ©2015.

Dedication

To Michaela Miles, my editor, my web and social media guru, my hero, and my friend. Without her, I could not have finished this book, or any other.
I love you, my cariad. Hopefully, one day, we will meet in real life and not just in pixels.

Chapter 1

Friday 6th September

The early afternoon sun toasted the air inside Richie Juno's Ford Mondeo. He removed his tie, rolled it into a coil, and dropped it on the passenger's seat. Despite lowering all four windows, no air circulated. He couldn't fire up the engine to use the aircon, and the temperature inside the cabin rose to pizza oven intensity. A glug of water helped, but he needed to conserve his supply. No telling how long he'd be watching the house or tailing his man.

Richie yawned and checked his watch: 13:55. Time for his first report. He pressed the button on his Bluetooth earpiece. The communications system's voice recognition software would add a time stamp, his details, and store it in audio and auto-print files. On his return to the office, he'd only have to read the transcript and sign the bottom of each page to confirm its accuracy. No need for today's police officer to type field reports or witness statements by hand. Comms software took care of the grunt work and prevented typist's repetitive strain injury—the curse of the old-time plod.

The system bleeped in readiness.

"Detective Sergeant Richard Juno. Badge number 3-6-8-8-2-D. I'm parked outside the subject's house. Nothing to report since my arrival. That's twenty-five minutes of my life I won't get back. Wait ... there's movement at the front door. Yes, I see him. The subject is wearing blue jeans and a dark grey polo shirt, and is carrying a canvas backpack. His face is hidden by a baseball cap, but it looks like the target. I'm taking shots for the family album."

He hefted the digital SLR, drew in the focus, and held down the button. The camera's motor whirred and the shutter clicked. The subject, Sunil Pradeep, slid behind the wheel of the car parked on the drive, reversed into the road, and turned left, away from Richie.

"Subject is driving a midnight blue Renault Clio. Index number matches the one on file. Tinted windows all around, including the windscreen. Dark enough to be illegal. Hope a uniform doesn't pull him over or I'll never find out where he's going or who he's meeting."

He followed the Renault along the North Circular Road and tuned into Radio 2—low background music wouldn't interfere with the recording software. As was his style, he kept the system open and sang along to the music—deliberately off-key in case any of the minions at Eavesdropper Central decided to earwig him in real time. They hated his voice and kept telling him to stop, but he needed to appear normal. He needed to be Richie Juno, the upbeat family man who couldn't sing for crap, not Richie Juno, the suspicious cop, who searched for and found dark secrets.

Fuck it all to hell. Why did it have to fall on him? Suspicion was a crushing weight to carry alone—one he hated. He'd considered telling Billy, but his brother-in-law would have laughed and told him to cut the conspiracy theory bullshit.

Conspiracy!

Too bloody right it was a conspiracy, but how deep did it run?

He had no hard evidence, not yet, only suspicions and gut instinct, but he did have enough to take to the governor. Yes, Chief Superintendent Knightly would know what to do—after all, it was his bloody job to know—and it would take a load off.

He'd lay it all out to the big man first thing Monday morning. Meanwhile, he'd carry on with the grunt work. That, he could handle—grunt work was his speciality.

Traffic slowed to a stop-start crawl, and they didn't reach the Chiswick Flyover until 16:15. He lowered the volume on the radio and spoke again.

"Two hours to cover thirteen bloody miles. I ask you. Why would anyone choose to drive through London on a Friday afternoon? Bloody idiot. Where's he heading? The target's a city boy. Nothing in his file about him ever straying into bandit country."

To pass the time and entertain the minions, should they be listening, he started a running commentary.

"We're on the M4 heading west, repeat, west, towards Welsh-Wales, boyo. Here's a thought. If we cross the border, will I need a passport?" He winced as the Renault bullied its way into an impossibly small gap between a petrol tanker and an old Bedford panel van. The Bedford's driver blared his horn and flashed his lights. Pradeep gave him the finger and the Bedford closed to within a couple of centimetres of the Renault's bumper.

"Whoa. The target's driving like he's got a death wish. He'd better take it easy or I'll be scraping him out of a wreck. He's either spotted me, or he's as pissed as I am about the queues. I'm guessing the latter."

The nose-to-tail traffic, as far ahead as Richie could see, crawled along at less than ten miles per hour. He settled down to continue the long, boring drive, anticipating mile after mile of traffic jams and drivers with shortening tempers and overheating radiators, all going nowhere fast. The sun burned low through the side window on its rush to meet the western horizon. He dropped the aircon a couple more degrees, turned up the radio, and prepared for an excruciating evening.

Richie pushed his left foot into the floor pan beneath the brake and clutch pedals and pressed his backside into the base of the seat. A quick rotation at the waist, a shrug of tight shoulders, and the sciatic ache subsided a little. He relaxed his leg and rolled his ankle to ease the cramp in his calf. Scrabbling around on the floor playing with his boys was fun, but didn't do his back any favours.

He shot a glance at his spreading belly. With a crappy, all-hours job and a sprouting family, the time available for exercise had shrunk to the occasional jog around the park and the even more infrequent gym session. He regretted the loss of fitness and muscle tone, but wouldn't give up what he'd gained for anything.

The tense night he'd spent holding Laurel's hand in the maternity ward didn't seem all that long ago, but tomorrow the twins would turn four. Four! Bloody hell, where had the time gone? The little tykes would be leaving for university in no time.

Mile after mile, the M4 curved westwards and brought the evening sun full into Richie's face. The sun visor didn't help. He raised the seatback, stretched his neck, and found the welcome shadow. Blinking tired eyes, he tried to rub life back into his face.

He perked up when the DJ played Golden Earring's *Radar Love*, a song his father used to sing along to at the top of his voice. He smiled at the memory. Good times.

Ten miles ahead of Junction 15, the traffic thinned enough for Pradeep to bullet his Renault into the outside lane and tailgate a Mr Sales Rep in a Vauxhall Insignia. Juno had to react quickly to keep the Renault in sight and maintain his surreptitious tail.

David Byrne's superb *Road to Nowhere* segued into Queen's *Bohemian Rhapsody*. Juno hit the mute button on the steering wheel.

"Pretentious overblown drivel."

He eased into the overtaking lane as the traffic thinned further and their speed climbed into the eighties and then the nineties.

"Naughty boy, breaking the speed limit. Watch you aren't pulled over, little man."

Richie returned to the middle lane and kept at least five vehicles between his car and the Renault. They reached, and passed, Junction 15. With London a long, long way behind them, he needed to check in with Billy.

He double-tapped the button on his earpiece to break into the auto recording, said, "Base One, are you receiving me?" and only had to wait a couple of seconds for the reply.

"This is Base One. Call sign, please."

The voice was female and young. Richie struggled to attach a face to the voice.

"Call sign, Tinkerbelle," he growled. "Don't laugh."

"Hold please, Tinkerbelle."

The woman didn't laugh, but a smile lifted her voice and Richie finally remembered the slim brunette who'd given him the eye the last time he visited Eavesdropper Central. Nice-looking girl, fit, come-get-me smile. Back in his single days, he'd have made a move, but not anymore. Those times were long gone.

Ten seconds of buzzing and clicking followed before the system's encryption cycle allowed further conversation.

"Hello Tinkerbelle." Billy's snicker bubbled through the connection in a calculated wind-up. "So nice to hear from you at long last. Please make your report."

Richie grinned and wound up for the usual banter. "Tinkerbelle? I ask you, Control. Tinkerbelle? What's with the fairy call-sign? You got a problem?"

"Tinkerbelle. That's no way to maintain radio protocol."

"It is if you keep assigning me the codename Tinkerbelle. Arsehole."

Billy cleared his throat loudly. "Okay, Tinkerbelle, enough of the backchat. I see you on the tracking system. You're heading west towards Wales, yeah?"

"Yes. Unless the subject exits at Junction 20 and hits the M5. Any idea where he's heading?"

Billy paused for a moment before answering. "None. Just finished re-reading the target's dossier."

"Bloody hell, Control. You've learned to read?"

"Tinkerbelle, this conversation is being recorded. There's nothing in the files to suggest he has any contacts further west than the M25."

One more jibe ought to do it. "Ah no, I get it. You had Chloe read it to you, right?"

"Tinkerbelle, maintain radio protocol."

"Have to pass the time somehow, Control."

Four cars ahead, the Renault's indicator flashed a nanosecond before it dived into the inside lane a few hundred metres ahead of the sign for Junction 20.

"Hang on a minute, Control … Yes … target is heading for the M5."

Anticipating the Renault's next aggressive manoeuvre, Richie eased into the exit lane behind the Renault and allowed three cars to filter between them.

The sun kissed the horizon in a blaze of orange and moved out of Richie's eyes for the first time in over two hours as they hit the M5, heading south. He blinked hard and relaxed the tense muscle around his eyes.

He imagined Billy watching the road map on the electronic whiteboard. "Control, are you following me on the big screen?"

"Of course."

"Still no idea where he's heading?" Richie asked, wondering how far from home he'd end up that night. Missing the twins' birthday party had just become a distinct possibility.

"None," Billy answered. "Nothing out there but fields, farms, and holiday homes."

"Exeter International Airport's up ahead and I don't have my passport. If he heads for Departures, I'll have to pick him up."

"You're the one on the ground, Tinkerbelle. Play it as you see fit. Use airport security to help detain him, and I'll send Clint to help you bring him back home as soon as he's free. Happy with that?"

"That's an affirmative, Control. The traffic's light now. He's picking up speed. I'll need to concentrate for a bit. Keep following me on the big screen."

"Will do, Tinkerbelle. Drive safe."

"Always."

Cauliflower clouds bubbled up from behind the western hills and hid the sun, making Richie's life a little easier. The Renault's speed hovered around the 100 mph mark and they travelled forty-five miles in the same time it had taken them to crest the one-mile long Chiswick Flyover. Wide green fields flashed past on their left and dark woods whipped by on the right. Nothing but nothingness.

Richie sniffed.

"Control. You still there?"

"Where else would I be, Tinkerbelle?"

"Feeling a little agoraphobic here. I mean, where are all the buildings and what's that bloody smell?"

"It's called fresh air, Tinkerbelle. People are supposed to love it. Open spaces and big skies. Enjoy it while you can."

"Give me flat grey concrete and orange bricks any day. Hang on …"

The Renault crossed three lanes, apparently ignorant of the traffic. The indicator flashed twice before turning onto a slip road.

"Target's exiting the motorway at the Taunton Dean Services. Either he needs a piss or some petrol. Traffic's light. I'll have to take care."

"Okay, Tinkerbelle, message received and understood. Keep your distance and be safe."

"Trying to teach me my job, Control?"

"Somebody has to."

Richie had visions of the aggressive idiot, Pradeep, careering through the Services at motorway speeds, but the Renault slowed to a crawl and negotiated the single lane road with excessive care. The car ignored the left turn into the main parking area and headed directly to the petrol station.

"Control, it's a fuel stop. I'm running on a quarter tank. If I don't fill up now, I might lose him later."

Three of the six pumps were clear. Pradeep stopped next to pump number three, Richie chose pump number six, the one furthest away and on the diagonal.

"I'll be on silent running for a couple of minutes. Don't go away now."

He pressed disconnect on the earpiece and opened his door.

#

"Tinkerbelle, report please. Where are you?"

Detective Inspector William 'Billy' Hook eased away from the microphone and flexed his fingers. The high-def whiteboard attached to the wall alongside his desk flickered. Bloody thing had better not be on the fritz like so much else in this place. It was supposed to be brand new, top-of-the-range, but he'd seen better in PC World.

The screen showed an Ordinance Survey road map of southwest England. A stationary red dot, marked DSJ#1, flashed over a place west of Taunton.

"Chloe," he called to his junior officer six desks away. "Taunton Deane Services on the M5. They're on the motorway road-monitoring network, right? Patch into their surveillance cameras and put them up on the board. Richie pulled in for petrol a little while ago, and I don't like him being so exposed."

DC Chloe Holder nodded and attacked her keyboard with a speed Billy could never hope to achieve with his sausage fingers.

Richie should have called back by now. Acid reflux told Billy something bad had happened, and his gut rarely told him otherwise. He stared at the blinking red light and hit the press-to-talk button on the mic stand. "Tinkerbelle, come back. Where are you?"

Silence. The noise-cancelling electronics removed all hint of static.

"Tinkerbelle, report in please."

Still Richie didn't answer. Where the fuck was he?

"Chloe? Where's that bloody surveillance footage?"

She looked up from her monitor, still typing. "Nearly there, sir. Putting it on the big screen ... now."

The OS map retreated into the top-right corner of the screen, and was replaced by a black-on-yellow Moto-Cam location template. A horizontal slide bar crawled from left to right, and the percentage numbers climbed slowly: 45%-49%-52%.

Of all the things they'd promised Hook before he joined the National Crime Agency, lightning fast broadband and state-of-the-art equipment had been high up his list. Golden promises worth fuck all.

"Come on," Hook mumbled. "What's taking so bloody long?"

As if in response, the numbers jumped from 84% to 100% and the template transformed into a grid of six video windows, all active. The first three showed external shots of Taunton Deane Services' main concourse, the car parks, and the people strolling between the two. Two more showed inside the food hall complete with the obligatory shop front logos of Costa, McD, and Little Chef. Billy's eyes flitted over the images and skipped to the sixth window, which displayed an orange and red striped filling station—six pumps, three unoccupied.

"Chloe. Bring up camera six."

The window expanded to fill the screen. The digital index at the top right read: *Tntn Dene Svcs, Moto-Cam#6, Ptrl Stn.* Hook checked the time stamp below the text with that on his PC monitor. It showed a ten-minute delay from live.

Four minutes before Richie's most recent message.

The acid in Billy's stomach gurgled. He clenched his abs and the pain lessened. Billy pressed a different button on his desk intercom. "Bee," he said, "better get out here."

The office door behind him opened, and Beatrice 'Bee' Endicott rushed to his monitoring station, knee-length skirt swirling. She grabbed the back of a spare chair and rolled it into position at his side, bringing with her a waft of flowery soap and peppermint tea. She sat and leaned forward. "What's wrong?"

"Richie dropped off comms"—Billy checked the time again—"eight minutes ago."

She stared up at the big screen and frowned. "What's he doing in Somerset?"

"Surveillance. A minion in Eavesdropper Central intercepted a telecon this morning. One of Richie's suspects arranged an out-of-town meet. A drugs trafficking case he has on the back burner. I don't like it. He shouldn't have gone dark for so long. He's only filling the tank."

Bee leaned closer. "He's running the tail alone?" She kept her voice down, but the steel below the surface came across clearly enough.

Billy couldn't blame her for jumping all over him. If he'd screwed up and put Richie in danger … Fuck. What would he say to Laurel?

"Who's the target?" Bee asked.

"Small time dealer called Sunil Pradeep. I advised Richie to cancel the tail, but he went anyway."

Bee held his gaze. The blue eyes behind her designer glasses turned into diamond chips.

"Who's in charge here, Billy? You or your brother-in-law? You know the protocol. A minimum of two people on all surveillance operations. Safety first. I can't have a repeat of Basildon."

"That wasn't all Richie's fault—" Billy cut off his defence of Richie's error. The fuck up in Basildon was down to both of them, but Richie had taken the blame, as he always did. Billy raked fingers through his hair and concentrated on the screen.

"Bee, you don't know him like I do. Richie's got sommat on his mind but won't talk to me about it. I reckon he thinks Pradeep is more than a low-level bottom feeder." He waved his hand at the picture that showed a bright evening near Taunton. "Maybe I'm overreacting."

"Did he sign for a weapon?" Bee asked.

"No."

"God's sake, Billy." Again with the diamond chips and the quiet voice. "Neither of you had any idea where Pradeep would end up or who he'd meet."

Hook ground his teeth. Confession time and he'd have to drop Richie in the mire.

"If he drew a weapon he'd have had to return to the office to sign it back in and—"

"And he wanted to go straight home after the tail?"

Hook rubbed his stomach. "It's the twins' birthday tomorrow and nothing in Pradeep's file suggested he'd end up out in the sticks."

Shit. Now he sounded mealy-mouthed.

On the screen, a dark blue Renault Clio pulled up to the pump in the far right hand corner. Seconds later, Richie's Ford Mondeo stopped two pumps away.

#

The clouds peeled back and the evening sun, half eaten by the hills, returned.

Richie leaned against the car door, arched his back, and stretched his arms to the sky. Vertebrae popped in his neck and lower back. His knees had creaked when climbing out of the car.

"Christ, Richie," he mumbled. "How old are you, man? Forty?"

He took a deep breath of forecourt air—petrol fumes mixed with exhaust gasses—the taste of home.

The twins would be jumping up and down about now, excited for tomorrow, desperate to delay bedtime, and fighting over the bath toys. He didn't envy Laurel's job. Give him police duties and antisocial hours over homemaking any day.

He'd miss the boys' bedtime again though. Damn it.

Pradeep stood with his back to Richie—bent over, face still hidden by the peaked cap—filling the Renault with Premium Unleaded.

Richie followed his target's lead and the numbers on the petrol pump climbed fast. Twenty litres would do it and give him the chance to reach the kiosk first. He replaced the nozzle, locked the filler cap, and strode across the forecourt.

The Shell logo above the kiosk reminded him he hadn't taken the boys to the beach for weeks. Maybe next weekend if the weather cooperated.

#

The Moto-Cam angle came from a high position and faced the sun, but Billy had a good view. He, Bee, and Chloe watched in silence as Richie stowed the nozzle, replaced the filler cap, and headed towards the shop.

"Why doesn't he wait for Pradeep to finish?" Bee asked.

Hook relaxed. "It's an old trick. There's only one exit from the station. Richie's gonna pay first, drive around the corner, and wait for Pradeep to pass. Taking the lead position when tailing a suspect is a good idea if—"

"What's Pradeep doing?" Bee interrupted, pointing at the Renault.

The moment Richie showed his back to Pradeep, the suspect dropped the fuel nozzle and dived into the Renault. The car's rear end fishtailed as it took off, heading straight at Richie.

Billy screamed, "Look out!" even though he knew it was already ten minutes too late.

Richie spun, tried to dive clear, but the Renault hit him a glancing blow that punched him backwards into the kiosk's brick wall. He bounced forward and fell to the ground. The Renault increased speed and disappeared around the side of the building.

For Billy, the world stopped.

"Oh, God, no!"

Bee jumped to her feet. "Chloe, call it in. I want the bastard in the Clio found, now. Move girl! Move!"

The petrol shop's door opened. A woman and two men rushed out. The woman and one of the men, both in dark trousers and yellow sweaters, knelt at Richie's side. The other man—middle-aged, wearing a business suit—lifted a mobile phone to his ear and ran towards the exit, mouth moving in an animated conversation.

"Oh, Jesus!" Billy said, numb, senseless. "Oh Jesus Christ. What have I done?"

Chloe zoomed the camera tight.

The woman in the yellow sweater knelt and leaned close to Richie's crumpled body. She said something to her co-worker and shook her head. Blood spread in a dark pool around Richie's head.

"See that?" Chloe shouted, pointing at the screen. "His left hand moved!"

PART ONE

Mr Memory

Chapter 2

Thursday 12th September

Manda stared hard at me from her side of the breakfast bar, no doubt preparing to lay it on me. She'd been quiet all morning. I knew why, but didn't want to push. She'd tell me in her own good time. Although things had been a little fraught at home since my accident and I felt guilty as all hell, I'd been working on my mood swings and hoped she'd seen the improvement.

"We need some time apart," she said after finishing her bowl of muesli.

And there it was. Matter of fact, no hysterics. Can't say I was surprised. All I could think to say was, "Really?"

She nodded and started clearing the dishes. I snatched up my half-finished coffee in case she took that, too. My Manda doesn't like mess.

"Mum and Dad have hardly seen Paulie since the christening and it'll do you good to have some alone time."

"That's true," I said, lamely.

Then she kissed me and wagged her finger under my nose. "Only for the weekend, mind, so no wild stag parties. I expect the place to look exactly like this when I get back. Okay?"

We'd been playing a similar game off and on all our married lives. I grinned. "How am I going to cope for a whole weekend without you and my babies?"

She gave me her patented head tilt and knowing stare. "Think of it like this. You'll have the TV to yourself. Four days of wall-to-wall sport and no interruptions for CBeebies. It'll be heaven, won't it?"

She had a point. Despite still needing the walking stick, I could manage the stairs with a bearable slice of pain and precious little cursing. In real terms having the house to myself for a few days wouldn't be tough, and Manda had frozen enough emergency rations to feed the Villa supporters at half time. Mind you, the team's recent performances didn't exactly fill the Doug Ellis Stand anymore.

I moaned a bit and feigned disappointment, but no one could ever call Detective Sergeant Philip Cryer—possibly acting second-in-command of the Midlands Police's Serious Crime Unit—God's gift to the theatre. I have other skills, though, which might go some way to explaining what Manda sees in me.

Although I'd been slightly more upbeat following the improvement in my mobility, I couldn't really blame Manda for wanting a break. I helped her load the car and kissed them all a surprisingly teary goodbye.

As I closed the door on Manda and the little ones, I relished the quiet—for all of twenty seconds before my brain took over and started running its usual meta-analysis.

No doubt about it, I had been tense for a while, and the family did need a break from yours truly. Apart from the constant pain of knitting bones, some of my mood related to the 'possibly acting second-in-command' part of my job description. Although I'd retained the rank of DS so far, I couldn't return to active duty until the FMO, the Force Medical Officer, Dr Rosemary Kline—or as I like to call her, Rosa Klebb, after the Bond villain, thanks to her cold bedside manner, and wizened face—gave me the all-clear. Our next scheduled appointment wasn't for another month. That meant at least four more weeks off work. Thirty days of staying at home.

Ordinarily, I love being at home. But not twenty-four-seven and not while suffering constant, mind-crushing, throbbing pain.

Purgatory. For both Manda and me. Not that Manda ever showed it. She's a saint. Saint Manda.

And no, that's not sarcasm; it's the truth as I see it.

Recovery has been a complete and utter mare. Months of excruciating pain following two surgical procedures—one to rebuild the destroyed femur, and the other to remove the metalwork holding the bits of bone together—has turned me into a short-tempered, self-pitying, impatient lout.

Not that I can just forget the pain or every single detail of the accident, either. I never forget anything, me. Ever. My eidetic memory sees to that.

Despite what scientists say about the lack of empirical evidence to support its existence, my memory *is* eidetic. The term derives from the Greek noun *eidos*, or 'form'. Basically, I form an indelible memory of everything I see, hear, smell, and sense. What's more, I can recall these memories with a high degree of accuracy.

All I have to do is concentrate on an object or an activity and every detail is locked away inside my head. Music, films, books, police case files, mug shots, my brain treats them all the same way.

The first time I really listen to a song on the radio, I have it memorised note for note, lyric for lyric, phrase for phrase. That's why I don't bother with portable music players. I only wear earbuds to blend in with a crowd or to make phone calls when the background noise demands it. If I stay awake through a whole film—a rare occurrence when I'm not off sick—I can recite the dialogue, verbatim, the next time it's shown. Read a book, and I capture every word, passage, line break, and chapter heading. The only proviso is that I have to read the book properly. I can't simply scan the pages. After all, I'm not a bloody photocopier.

To the average bloke, this probably sounds great. Exhausting maybe, but great. In theory it is, but—and there's always a 'but'—in practise, there are drawbacks.

For instance, I'll never forget the exquisite pain of my first broken heart. Janet Middleton—Monday, May 25th 1989—primary school morning break, a grey day, overcast and drizzly. She poked her tongue out at me and held hands with Simon Pentecost, my former best friend. Or the time I broke my arm after falling off a swing—Saturday, March 13th 1992—a rainy, cold day. Or Staff Nurse Fiona Swann, who drew the sheet over my dead father's head—Monday, September 7th 1998—a sunny day, warm and still, but bloody awful.

Those particular memories are all available for easy access even though I'd rather bury them forever. I feel the pain of each physical and emotional injury afresh every time something happens to remind me of the incident.

There are good memories, of course. A form of compensation for the shite stuff, I imagine.

Manda is one example. Amanda Nicole Cryer, née Redfern. Dark hair, olive skin, brown eyes, a smile that can melt snow, and warm temperament to match. I've been in love with her since the second we met at Toby Vangelis' millennium party—Sunday, December 31st 1999, 20:13—I made a note of the exact time. She wore a slinky off-the-shoulder black number that knocked my eyes out and stopped my heart. Manda is and always will be utterly gorgeous. What she sees in me, I'll never know, but won't ask in case she sees the light and changes her mind. She's my rock, my partner, and the mother of my kids, Jamie and Paul.

I remember every second of their lives that I've been with them. The first breath Jamie took—Wednesday, September 13th 2006, 08:53—a happy joyous morning when I discovered parental love and terror. The maternity ward smelled of fresh soap and posters of Disney characters covered the walls. I'll always treasure the first time Paulie giggled—Friday, July 9th 2014—during his evening bath.

Although I try not to flaunt it, my memory's important to me. It defines me as a man and helps make me a bloody good cop.

It's no secret, but my boss, Detective Chief Inspector David Jones—never Dave or Davie—only accepted me onto his team because he recognised the value of my particular skill. For a start, it saves him having to work the Police National Computer, the PNC. I'm his walking encyclopaedia, his 'Mr Memory', but I don't mind. In return, David has taught me to be a better detective. Whether I'd still be a detective, or even a cop, after my impending consultation with the dreaded Rosa Klebb was up for debate, and added fuel to my miserable fire.

Bloody accident. Bloody injury. Bloody crippled leg.

And that's the absolute, unequivocal, indisputable downside of having an eidetic memory. No matter how hard I try, I can never forget falling through the rotten roof. I'll never forget the grinding, tearing agony of the moment that rusty metal spike punched through skin and muscle, and hacked a chunk out of my femur.

No. That joy will never diminish.

On my lowest days, when I'm at my most pessimistic, I run through the events in super slow-mo, as though it were a football replay.

In the weeks immediately following the surgery, I had no idea whether I'd ever walk properly again, let alone be fit enough to return to work. My useless leg—hideously scarred and throbbing with every heartbeat—was an agonising liability.

I finally made the decision to take rehab seriously seven weeks after the second operation—Sunday, 2nd June, 22:53—a warm evening after a hot, dry day. David Jones, the sneaky sod, sort of shamed me into it. He can be a calculating SOB when he puts his mind to it.

Manda had invited him for one of our irregular dinner parties. Just the three of us. For once, Manda, the incurable and hopeful matchmaker, hadn't invited any of her single friends to meet David. After the meal, we were sitting in the garden enjoying the air and sampling the rather smooth malt David brought with him, when he dropped his little bomb. He'd waited for Manda to turn in, to make sure I didn't have a support team to hide behind.

"Phil," he said, "do you *want* to come back to work?"

"Bloody hell, boss. 'Course I do. What made you ask that?"

His words slapped me in the face and stung worse than soap in fresh scar tissue.

He answered quietly. "I saw that letter from your physio on the hall table. You cancelled both appointments last week. I talked to Manda about it when you were tucking the kids into bed. She said you cried off because the sessions are, in your words, 'pure fucking torture'. That true?"

I read concern in his eyes and had no wriggle room. Too right the rehab was torture, but it took the boss to call me on it before I'd see my actions for they really were—pure bloody cowardice.

David let the silence stretch out for an age before sticking his devious boot in once again. "I can't hold your place on the team open forever. You know that, don't you."

It hadn't come as much of a surprise, but I'd expected the ultimatum in a letter from HR, not in quiet words from the old man. The shock of it seemed to flip a switch in my head. I had a moment of clarity, or one of those flashes the religious fraternity calls an 'epiphany'. I don't know how to describe it, but in that single moment, I made the decision and raised my glass. "Three months."

"Three months? What happens then?"

"Give me three months and I'll be fit to start work."

"Promise?"

"Promise. Can you keep my job open that long?"

David smiled. "Yes."

"Fantastic. And to prove my point, come back in six weeks to help me celebrate returning these bloody crutches to the outpatients' clinic."

We shook hands on the deal.

In my head, the following twelve weeks are like those flashy training montages from boxing movies. Apart from one early morning work-related incident, my days consisted of little more than sweaty gym workouts, harrowing physiotherapy sessions, a low-fat, low-cal, low-taste diet, and falling into bed every night, totally exhausted.

There's no way to explain how tough it was or how hard I worked, but I wasn't going to break my promise to David, or to myself. After making a decision, I always stick with it. No messing.

The rehab programme worked. Not only did I reduce my bodyweight and tone up—even regained my long-lost six-pack—I also made good on my interim commitment. Five weeks and four days after making the promise, I dumped the crutches and the boss came over help finish that nice bottle of malt.

I still needed the walking stick, but that was fine by me. The word 'walking' is the operative one. I could walk!

The exercise gave me a healthy appetite and meant I could sleep too—on the odd occasion Paulie designed to go through the night.

The work-related incident I referred to occurred during the third week of rehab. It began when David phoned in the middle of the night. God knows how many times he's done that to me over the years, but it never gets old. I pretended to be angry, but he needed my help, and I was secretly delighted.

"Philip, ah great," he shouted above the roar of his ancient Rover's engine. "Need your help."

After my garbled response, he asked, "Did I wake you?"

Really? At 04:33 the old man asked if he'd woken me. Gotta love the guy.

As it turned out, the technology gurus in London had closed down the PNC for a massive security upgrade and, thanks to regional penny-pinching, our local backup system was total garbage.

As I keep telling anyone who'll listen, you can't always rely on technology—or is it David who says that?

Twenty minutes after his call, the boss arrived to pick my brains.

A teenage girl had disappeared, and the old man needed background information on the prime suspect in her abduction—a sex offender named Ellis Flynn. I'd read Flynn's case file when working at the Juvenile Crime Unit and was able to point David to the nasty bastard's holiday home in Brittany.

At the time, I was pissed at being unable to join him, but I've since seen the pictures of what he found in Flynn's cellar, and, to be honest, I'm glad I didn't see it firsthand. I have nightmares enough, thank you very much.

So, there I was, home alone, churning through my recent past, stewing. Within fifteen minutes of my wonderfully patient family leaving home, I called a taxi …

…to take me to the gym.

#

After returning from a ball-busting, eye-watering gym session, I made a mug of coffee and a sandwich, and carried them to the front room on a tray. It wasn't easy to do one-handed, but despite female propaganda, some men *can* multi-task. With Sky Sports on the TV, I settled in for a pleasant, if solitary, afternoon.

There's no telling how long I'd been asleep but the doorbell woke me with such a start, I barked my knee against the coffee table, and screamed loud enough to risk scaring the neighbours. If Manda had heard me use the same language with the kids in the house, she'd have come at me with a bar of soap.

On TV, a panel of former professional footballers were discussing the upcoming weekend's Premier League fixtures, and I tried to clear my head. The door chimes belted out again.

"Okay, okay, I'm bloody coming."

We don't have a big house, but the hallway's a long way when you're dragging a throbbing leg and using a stick. Frowning fit to cramp the muscles in my forehead, I dragged open the door, hoping for Jehovah's Witnesses. A slanging match with a pair of wide-eyed God-botherers would have been massively therapeutic.

A tubby older bloke stood in the open porch. Early sixties, with grey hair cut short, he wore a dark suit, a cheery smile, and a Captain Birdseye beard.

"Afternoon, DS Cryer. Not disturbing you I hope?"

It took me a half a second to recognise the man out of context. Not surprising considering I'd only ever seen the bluff Yorkshireman via a video link.

"Superintendent Knightly. Good afternoon, sir."

As he raised a hand to scratch at the beard, his sleeve slipped down to expose a heavy gold watch. "Actually, it's Chief Superintendent now." His deep voice with its sharp Yorkshire accent sounded almost apologetic.

I leaned against the door, holding the handle for support, unable to speak. I mean, how often does a senior officer from the National Crime Agency—the nearest thing the UK has to the FBI—visit the home of a convalescing detective sergeant who lived in the middle of Birmingham?

What the bloody hell did he want?

Chapter 3

Thursday 12th September

CS Knightly stepped forward, offered his hand, and we shook. "Okay, lad? You look a bit flushed."

"Yes, sorry, sir. Banged my knee," I said, happy to say something that didn't come out mangled, stuttering nonsense.

"My turn to apologise, then. I read about your accident. Should have sent a card. Happy to see you're on your feet again."

"Thank you, sir. It's getting stronger every day."

"Good … good. I apologise for the unannounced visit," he said, rubbing his hands as though they were cold, but as it was at least twenty degrees outside, that didn't make sense. "Mind if I come in?"

Where were my manners? Still on the couch where I'd jammed my chuffing leg.

"Of course. Please do."

I stepped aside and showed him into the hall.

He'd parked his car—a seven-year-old Nissan—in front of the gate, blocking our drive. The age and class of the vehicle surprised me. A man of Knightly's rank on police business would have been entitled to an official motor and a driver. The aging Nissan made his visit unofficial, maybe even clandestine.

Colour me intrigued.

He hovered halfway down the hall, trying to decide which of the three doors to take. "Coffee, sir? Kitchen's first on the right."

"Any chance of a brew instead?"

"No problem, sir. We keep a stock of teabags for when the boss … I mean DCI Jones, visits."

"Teabags? For David Jones?"

I grinned. "You're right. He does prefer loose leaf, but will put up with bags when he has to."

"He must be getting soft in his old age."

"I couldn't possibly comment, sir."

Knightly and the boss had been friends from back when a pound note would buy you a round of beers in the pub and not just a packet of crisps—according to my dad. From time to time, Knightly calls on David for help, which is how I came to know him. We'd last met during a video call on the Sean Freeman case. Strange to see the big man in the flesh at last. His girth nearly filled the hall.

While I made busy with the kettle, Knightly stared through the window overlooking the back garden and made small talk. He knew his flowers and delivered complimentary noises about Manda's heroic efforts to add colour to a grey world. Me? I kill plants. Don't mean to, but that's what happens when I try to help.

"How do you take it?"

"Milk, no sugar, thanks."

I served. He sipped, smacked his lips, and said, "Champion."

"Can't offer you biscuits, I'm afraid. We're on a health kick."

He patted his overlarge midriff. "Not to worry, lad. I can afford to do wi'out."

We stood on either side of the breakfast bar, not drinking or talking. The silence dragged on, but I wasn't going to break it. Not my place, even though we were in my kitchen.

"I expect you're wondering why I'm here."

Ya think?

"You could say that, sir."

"How is the leg, Philip? May I call you Philip? You can speak freely."

The change in direction took me by surprise. He'd be asking me to call him Brian next. Yes, of course he would.

"Philip or Phil, either way I'm happy. And I'm on the mend. Be fit for a return to work within the month."

Did I mention I'm an optimistic soldier?

"Good … good. Excellent, in fact." He blew across the top of his tea before taking another sip. "Actually … I need your help," he said. "Or rather, the NCA needs your help … with a special investigation."

"Sir, I'm on sick leave. Not insured for police work. Health and Safety … you know."

Of course he knew. Everyone in the force knew the edicts of the dreaded Health and Safety Executive. Their rules hamstrung police activities as severely as government budget cuts.

His nod was slow and considered. "I know, but this is something only someone with your … gifts can handle."

"What use can I be? I can barely walk."

"I don't need you for your physical prowess, although I must say, you are looking somewhat leaner than when I saw you during that video call. I believe the modern term is 'buff'. Have you lost weight?"

"A little."

Knightly took a breath. "Have you been following the DS Juno case?"

Interesting change of subject. What was the old boy getting at? He was flitting around all over the place, and he seemed nervous. Well, if not actually nervous, uncomfortable.

"Shall we take these to the front room, sir? I need to sit."

"Aye, lad. Of course."

I led the way, but made the mistake of allowing him into the room first.

"Take a seat," I said, pointing to the sofa, but he had his back to me and the old bugger commandeered my recliner.

Knightly let out a huge sigh as he settled back into the most comfortable chair in Birmingham—not that I've sampled them all, of course. I didn't have the stones to ask him to move and reluctantly eased myself into the settee. It wasn't a patch on my chair, but I gritted my teeth, and rested my leg on the pouf. The throbbing diminished as soon as I took weight off the knee. A good sign. One of Manda's ridiculous throw cushions dug into the small of my back. I dragged it away and threw it on top of its partner on the other end of the sofa.

Knightly leaned forward and prompted me again. "DS Juno?"

"I only know what I've seen on the news and read online. Detective Sergeant Richard Juno, known as Richie. Killed last Friday in a hit-and-run incident at a motorway service station near Taunton. What's your interest, sir? If you don't mind my asking."

Knightly stared into his cup. "DS Juno was one of my officers. A member of the Organised Crime Task Force, led by DCI Beatrice Endicott. Do you know Bee?"

"Only by reputation. Highly thought of by all accounts. Useful spokesperson to put in front of a TV camera."

"Good … good." He nodded and fell silent again.

"What does this have to do with me? I thought the investigation was closed apart from the inquest."

"It is, officially."

"There's a 'but', right?"

"There is. I'm not happy with … a number of things."

Okay, now we were getting to the crux. I judged a prompt was in order.

"According to the Avon and Somerset Police, after killing DS Juno, the culprit, Sunil Pradeep, ran his car into a bridge support and died in a fireball."

Knightly looked up from his cup, his eyes narrowed. "That's what the evidence suggests, but I think someone took out a contract to have DS Juno killed."

My leg tensed in an involuntary spasm. Pain shot from knee to hip, and I rested my hand on the still-tender scar. Any number of questions rolled through my head. The chief one being, what did this have to do with a crippled off-duty Birmingham cop?

I took a moment to think before asking my next question. "What makes you think that?"

"A number of things, but before I say any more, you need more information."

I put down my mug and sat up straight, but kept my leg propped on the stool. "I'm listening, sir."

"On the morning of DS Juno's death, our communications surveillance unit intercepted a telephone conversation between Sunil Pradeep and an unidentified male. Pradeep was a minor member of one of the biggest drug cartels in London. A cartel that has an uncanny ability to predict the time and location of major police raids on its operations, I might add.

"It seems that DS Juno was the only man available to tail Pradeep at short notice." A shadow crossed Knightly's face that had nothing to do with the sun or clouds. "DS Juno followed Pradeep to Somerset and you know the rest. We have the whole incident on the petrol station's surveillance cameras. Pradeep's car deliberately ran over DS Juno. Of that, there is no doubt."

He toyed with his mug before pushing it away, still half full.

"Juno had a wife and two young sons, twins. I had to break the news to her. The very worst part of my job."

My senses tingled. Something didn't smell right. In fact, something stank worse than five-day-old road kill. "On camera, you say?"

"That's right. Why?"

Really? This had to be some sort of test.

"You know why I asked, sir."

"Humour me with your thought processes, DS Cryer."

No 'Philip' anymore? If he was slipping back into Chief Super mode, I'd have to revert to the role of junior officer. Hell if I was going to sit to attention in my own house, though.

"It's all very neat, isn't it. Suspiciously neat," I said.

"In what way?"

"Pradeep is clever enough to lure a police officer into an ambush, but he does it on camera? And then he screams off in a mad panic and ends up burnt to a crisp in a car crash?"

"Aye. That's what the Avon and Somerset Police investigators are saying."

"Begs an obvious question, though."

"Which is?"

"The body they found in the burned out car. Was it definitely Pradeep?"

"We're still waiting on the DNA results, but the dental records match. So, yes. Odds are the cremated remains belong to Sunil Pradeep."

"On the pictures at the service station, could you see Pradeep clearly?"

Knightly's mouth stretched into a tight smile. "David said you were smart. To answer your question, no. The CCTV only shows the driver from the back or in shadowed profile. We have DS Juno's voice on record saying he thinks Pradeep was driving, but he couldn't make a positive identification. The car he was following, a Renault Clio, was registered to Sunil Pradeep, but we can't be one hundred percent certain he was the person behind the wheel when the car hit DS Juno."

"That throws up another obvious question. If you're planning to kill a cop, would you use your own car?"

Knightly shook his head. "No, I wouldn't, but then again, I'd never plan to kill a police officer. Or anyone else for that matter."

"Are we thinking the same thing?"

"That depends, Philip. What are you thinking?"

Back to using first names. I must have passed his test.

"I'm thinking someone else drove the car and Pradeep was already dead before it hit the bridge and burst into flames. In which case, Sunil Pradeep was sacrificed to throw us off the scent."

"Then we *are* thinking along the same lines."

"Any idea who?"

"None."

"Can I ask another question?"

"Feel free."

"If everyone else is satisfied that Pradeep killed DS Juno and all the evidence points that way, what made you suspicious?"

Knightly crossed his arms and leaned back in my recliner. It squeaked in protest. "Armed with the same information, you became suspicious, too."

"Only because you're here and you raised the idea DS Juno was the target of a hit. Otherwise, I'd assume the facts in play were accurate. After all, the simplest explanation is usually the correct one."

"Correct. Like everyone else, I'd have been inclined to accept the findings of the Avon and Somerset investigation, but I have information they don't."

"Which is?"

"On the morning he died and about two hours before our communications team intercepted Pradeep's phone conversation, DS Juno called my office and asked to talk to me on a matter of extreme urgency."

"What did he have to say?"

"I don't know, I wasn't available to take his call. Under duress, my secretary made the next available appointment, which was last Monday morning."

"DS Juno didn't leave a message?"

"No. And he didn't go through the proper channels, either."

Jesus! No wonder Knightly's suspicions had been aroused. For a Detective Sergeant to contact a Chief Superintendent without going through the correct chain of command bordered on insubordination. It would be like a tourist knocking on the gates of Buckingham Palace and demanding an audience with the Queen.

"Christ Almighty," I said, "you think Juno was killed to stop him talking to you?"

"Aye, lad. That's exactly what I think, and the only people who could have known he wanted to speak to me were on my team. There's a corrupt officer in the NCA, and I need your help to find the bugger."

Chapter 4

Thursday 12th September

A dirty cop! Crap.

Police work is difficult enough without one of our own turning rogue. Anger bubbled up to replace my initial shock and sadness. And then frustration at my inability to do anything to help.

"Are you absolutely certain about this, sir? I mean, based solely on DS Juno's murder, you've decided there's a rogue cop working at the NCA?"

"Not quite. There's more to it than that."

"For instance?"

He'd placed a bomb in my lap and expected me to defuse it. I needed more information.

Knightly toyed with his beard before speaking. "Okay Philip, you deserve answers. Where to start ... A few months ago, one of the gnomes from the NCA's Crime Statistics Department gave me a presentation. According to him, over the past five years more important, well-planned raids have gone tits-up because of bad information than would be expected by random chance."

"Police work is difficult, sir," I said. "Things go wrong all the time. Stats aren't infallible."

"That's what I said to the gnome, but he was insistent. The little man showed me the numbers—what he called evidence—of raids going to the wrong location or being planned for the wrong date or time. I more-or-less dismissed him as you just did, but he's a tenacious little sod and pushed to make his case. He also said too many informants have died and too many witnesses have retracted their statements. Apparently it's been happening throughout London and the southeast—different towns, different police regions, different criminal organisations involved. He rattled off some numbers and showed me a bunch of charts to support his conclusions."

"Apart from your gnome, has anyone else noticed the same trend?"

"No, but before the formation of the NCA, no one collated or analysed the same information in such detail. This guy is a savant. Very keen. He ran the analysis in his own time. For fun, would you believe."

Stats for fun? Takes all sorts. But I knew how the gnome felt. I've been known to read other cop's case reports for my own amusement.

"So, you're basing this operation on one man's statistical analysis?" I couldn't prevent doubt seeping into my voice.

"And my gut instincts. I send him away with my thanks and platitudes, but his numbers had me worried and I couldn't let it go. I don't like so many coincidences." He leaned forward for emphasis. "Given that the analysis covered such a geographically widespread area, I asked myself a question ..."

He paused, probably for effect and to make sure I was paying attention. I obliged him with, "Which was?"

"Apart from our Statistics Department, who had access to information in all those cases? What answer do you think I came up with, Philip?"

"Bee Endicott's Task Force?"

Knightly's mouth stretched into a sad smile. "Exactly. And about a week later, DS Juno is murdered a matter of hours after he books a meeting with me? Another coincidence? I don't think so. This is wrong, lad. Bloody wrong."

Okay, he'd convinced me enough to ask more questions. I let his information sink in before asking another question. "Apart from tailing an apparently low-level dealer, what else was DS Juno working on?"

"Nothing to make him more of a target than any other member of the NCA. On Saturday morning, I sent an internal team to investigate DS Juno. Standard procedure, as you know. They looked at his activity, including his database access, in the weeks leading to his death."

Time for the most difficult question so far, the one I'd been putting off since Knightly dropped his bombshell. "Was he bent?"

"Absolutely and categorically no. We found nowt suspicious either in his working or private life. We looked into his close family members too, but they're all clean. In fact, his brother-in-law, William Hook, is a DI in the OCTF."

Interesting. Two family members working in the same police unit could be considered rare enough to raise eyebrows. "That must be hard on DI Hook. I suppose he's on compassionate leave?"

Knightly shook his head. "Refused to take it, and since the Avon and Somerset Police are handling the investigation, I allowed him to stay at work."

Even more interesting.

"You found nothing in DS Juno's workload or on the OCTF database to explain his request for a meet?"

"Nothing. Which means either there was nowt to find—"

"Or someone sanitised the files between DS Juno's death and the arrival of the investigative team?"

"Possibly."

"Tough to do that sort of thing without leaving a trace. Who has access to the system?"

"Apart from my management team and me, the only people with direct and unrestricted access to those particular servers are the members of the Task Force." His lips formed a thin line as he spoke.

"Okay. At least it restricts our initial suspect pool. How many active cases was DS Juno working on?" I tried to relax my voice and calm my breathing.

"A couple of dozen as part of the team but, in the month before he died, he accessed thirteen archived files, apparently at random."

"Interesting. It seems logical to assume that one or more of those cases will explain why he wanted to see you."

"Indeed."

"Did your team run a 'compare and contrast' analysis on the files and their backups?"

Knightly nodded. "Aye. The tech boys did that, but the files showed no signs of tampering. If anyone else was accessing them or hiding evidence, they did a bloody good job cleaning up after themselves and, truth is, I'm out of my depth when it comes to this technology stuff.

"To be honest, I'd like to close the system down and have a forensic IT team run a detailed analysis, but that'll likely spook the person responsible. Whoever it is, I can't risk him suspecting we're onto him or he'll scarper. That's why I'm here. I need your help to catch the bastard. Can't ask anyone else."

"You mean I'm the only police officer in the UK you can trust?"

Flattering it may have been, but unlikely.

"That's not far off. I'd trust David Jones with my life and the life of my family, but he doesn't have your particular talent. His memory's reasonable enough and his detection skills are off the charts, but I doubt he knows a bit from a byte."

I smiled. "That's true enough."

If there were a less IT literate person in the western hemisphere than David Jones, you'd be hard put to find them, but what he lacked in IT savvy he made up for in everything else.

Knightly stared at me for a moment, his eyes narrowed. "When you read a report, how does your memory work?"

He was back to his strange segues, but I figured he knew where he was headed and rolled with it.

"Don't know really. At a guess, it's pretty much the same as yours, only more so. I read the text and study the crime scene pictures. As long as I can make sense of it all, it sticks. It works less well with foreign languages and technical drawings. For that information, I have to concentrate hard and actively *try* to memorise it. In most cases, my recall rate is significantly above average."

I tried to make it sound matter-of-fact. I've been asked the same question a million times and it's difficult not to sound cocky.

"How fast do you read? Do you scan, take mental photographs? In the weeks leading up to his death, DS Juno accessed thousands of pages of case reports."

"Pretty fast."

The international average reading speed is around 250 words per minute with a comprehension rate of a little over fifty percent. As a kid, teachers measured my reading speed at over two thousand with an accuracy rate of ninety-seven percent.

In short, I'm quick, but not Hollywood rapid. Either way, Knightly didn't need to hear the details. I opened my hands in a shrug. My turn to ask another question. "What exactly do you expect me to do?"

"Read the files and see if anything jumps out at you as strange or inconsistent. If you do find something unusual, let me know and I'll take it from there."

To say I was sceptical would have been an understatement, but the big man had reached out for my help. Anyway, what else did I have to do with my mind but help Paulie sort his building blocks and Jamie with her homework?

"Okay. I can read the files in my home office. I'll make a start right now if you have the access codes."

Knightly looked around my part-decorated front room and shook his head. "Oh no. I'm afraid that's out of the question, lad."

"If it's a security issue, I could access the OCTF servers from Holton HQ. Although I'll need car and a driver. I've not been behind the wheel since …" I nodded at my leg.

"No. You're supposed to be on sick leave. If you turned up at work right now you'd raise eyebrows. The fewer people who know about this operation, the better. Besides, you're missing the point. If you access the system from outside, the person we're looking for will likely notice and bugger off. We need to find another way."

"In that case," I said without really thinking about it, "send me to London undercover and I'll find the bastard for you."

I seldom act on impulse, and never since falling through the rotten roof, but there I was, jumping into the shark-filled waters with both feet encased in heavy diving boots.

"Are you serious, Philip?"

A sensible man would have said, "No, I'm kidding," but I'm a moron and an overconfident moron at that. I could see plenty of challenges ahead—not least of which would be to convince Manda to let me go—but how could I sidestep an opportunity to put away a guy responsible for killing a cop?

Instead, I said, "I think so, but I can't do it without help."

"Whatever you need, just ask."

"The phone will do for now."

I grabbed my phone and punched in the boss' mobile number. Next shock of the day, he picked up halfway through the first ring.

"Jones here."

Honestly, his telephone manner is delightful. He rarely checks the caller ID and always answers as though the phone's going to bite his ear off.

"Hi boss, it's Phil, got a moment?"

"Philip!" With the single word, his voice rose up the weather scale from cold and frosty morning to sunny midsummer afternoon. "How the devil are you?"

"Fine thanks, boss. You'll never guess who's sitting in my chair."

Quick as a flash, he replied, "Goldilocks?"

A joke from the boss? Unusual.

"Oh, nice one. No, it's your old mate Chief Superintendent Knightly."

"Really? Am I on speaker?"

"No, boss."

"Good. Don't let him near your drinks cabinet. The man's a lush." He coughed. "Told me he'd be paying you a visit. Can I speak to him, please? You can put the phone on speaker now."

I hit the button.

"We're in my front room. He can hear you now."

"Afternoon, Brian. Was I right?"

Knightly looked at me before answering.

Realisation struck. They'd been working me. I crossed my arms, gritted my teeth, and waited for the explanation.

"As usual," Knightly said, "you were bang on, David. He volunteered all by himself. I didn't even have to ask."

"Told you he was a good man. Reliable. Didn't take as long as I thought it might."

"Glad I didn't take you up on that bet."

Yes, they'd definitely worked me. I'd felt something was up as soon as the old man made the Goldilocks quip. The only question open for debate was why? My hand reached down to touch the scar on my knee.

"Phil," David said, "are you sure you want to do this?"

"Not one little bit, but I did volunteer. You know all about the Chief Super's problem?"

"Of course. Brian would never approach a member of my team without checking with me first."

"Why didn't you arrive together?" I asked the question, but I already knew the answer.

"If I'd been there you might have agreed to the mission without thinking things through properly. I didn't want to add any pressure. Manda would never have forgiven me."

"Okay, boss," I said, adding a heavy sigh to show my annoyance, "you and I might have a little word in private when this is all over. Who else knows?"

Knightly answered. "At the moment, knowledge of this operation is limited to the three of us, your Chief Constable, my Director General, and the Home Secretary."

Bloody hell, I'd become part of a very exclusive club. No backing out now, even if I'd wanted to.

David broke the short silence. "Are you okay, Phil?"

"Not in the slightest, but right now, I need your help. Are you busy at the moment?"

"Always, but I'll make time for you. What can I do you for?"

Knightly shook his head. "We shouldn't talk on an open line."

"Boss, how soon can you get here?"

"This soon enough?"

The doorbell rang and I jumped. "You have got to be kidding me."

Chapter 5

Thursday 12th September

Knightly held up a hand. "Stay where you are, lad. I'll let him in, if that's all right with you?"

I threw up my arms. "Of course. Carry on. Invite the neighbours. Let's have a barbeque while we're at it."

The hell with police protocol.

Knightly shot me a understanding smile and made his way to the front door while I grabbed my stick and used it to help lever myself out of the chair. The worried thoughts washed back in, trying overwhelm me, but with the boss involved, I felt more comfortable with my decision. He'd have my back and would help me smooth things over with Manda—if that were possible.

The front door opened and the two old boys greeted each other like the long time friends they were. The boss, standing nearly fifteen centimetres shorter than Knightly, winced under his man-hug.

"Easy, Brian. I'm still recovering."

"Sorry, David. Forgot about that rib."

"Only hurts when I go swimming."

"When did you learn to swim?"

"I didn't."

David smiled and rubbed the left side of his chest as he strode down the hall to meet me. We shook, and he grasped my forearm with his free hand. "Good to see you, Phil."

"How long have you been outside?" I asked.

"A little while. Been catching up on some paperwork. Brian called me when he arrived and I drove from Holton." He pointed to the kitchen. "Any chance of a cuppa? I'm parched."

"Help yourself. You know where everything is."

I waved him and Knightly towards the kitchen door and looked up at the ceiling. Yes, no doubt about it, they'd been playing me like a guitar, and I could still feel the strings vibrating. I tried to relax my tight shoulders, but a team of masseuses working bonus rates wouldn't have helped. While the boss commandeered my kitchen, I retrieved the dirty mugs from the front room and loaded them into the dishwasher.

David did the honours with kettle and teapot, managing not to wrinkle his nose at the teabags. He found the extra large mug we keep to one side for him and added a dash of milk to all three cups. It looked as though we were in for one of his acid strong brews.

"What have you told him, Brian?"

Knightly cleared his throat. "Everything I know and everything I suspect."

The boss shot a quick look in my direction and I nodded. He poured the tea and reached for the biscuit barrel.

"It's empty, boss." I said, patting my flat belly. "I'm in training."

"So I see. I congratulate you on your efforts, Philip, but why should the rest of us miss out on Manda's biscuits because you're on a diet."

Ever since she'd first met him, Manda, the mother hen, had worried David didn't eat properly. It's not that he can't pop a frozen pizza into an oven as well as any confirmed bachelor, but she keeps saying how he needs a good woman behind him to make sure he eats properly.

To me, he looks healthy enough for an older guy. A little on the scrawny side, perhaps. Not exactly wizened, more wiry.

I've never seen him in action, he's more the cerebral type these days, but he'd let slip about physical things in his past, including a short spell in the army before joining the police. Alex Olganski, one of our DCs, told me how well he'd handled himself in Brittany, and I've seen the big blocks of granite he's shifted by hand during his house renovation. He's strong enough, for a little 'un. Small as he is, I'm not sure I'd have fancied tackling him when he was in his prime.

"She only bakes at the weekends these days. No cakes in the house means I can't backslide. Help yourself to some fruit." I pointed to the bowl of apples and bananas on top of the fridge.

He gave me that approving half smile I've learned to appreciate. "No thanks, I'll pass. Looks like you need to sit," he said, lifting the tray. "Shall we take these through?"

I rushed ahead of Knightly to bag my chair, forcing him and the boss to use the settee. Although the junior officer, we were in my home with my rules, and I wanted my special chair. Didn't use the reclining mode though. After all, there are limits.

"When did you two cook up this plan?" I asked David after we'd sampled his vicious brew. I could feel the stuff dissolving the enamel from my teeth and added more milk from the jug on the tray.

"What plan?" David answered, playing the innocent.

"The one to make me volunteer to play undercover cop."

"There was no plan. Brian told me his situation during a conference call with the Chief Constable yesterday afternoon when he asked permission to talk to you. I advised him to tell you everything and leave the rest to you. No plans, only hopes and a few expectations."

"You should have talked to me yesterday," I said, trying to gain some sort of control of myself as well as the conversation. "It would have given me more time to work the case."

Under normal circumstances I wouldn't have dreamed of questioning the old man's methods unless we were alone, but the situation had no precedent, and I took the chance.

David lowered his eyes to his tea and took another sip. "We needed to ... sort out one or two things in advance."

I didn't like the sound of that, or the way Knightly shifted in his chair.

"For example?"

More hesitation from the boss, but I waited him out.

After more than a few pulsating seconds, he said, "I needed time to discuss things with Manda."

"You what!"

I struggled to stand, but David beat me to it and held up a hand as though directing traffic. It wasn't difficult to imagine him as a youngster in uniform with those big white gauntlets you see policemen wear in black and white films.

"Easy, Phil," he said. "I had to ask her whether she thought you were ready to return to work."

His pale green eyes fixed on mine. When wearing his poker face, he rarely gave anything away. This time, I could tell he was sussing me out, checking my reaction.

"You were right out of order talking to Manda behind my back, and you know it."

Knightly, eyes averted, picked at some fluff from the sleeve of his jacket.

David nodded his agreement. "You're right, Phil. I understand how you feel, but an injury as serious as yours doesn't only affect the body."

"Christ's sake, boss. You were worried I'd lost my bottle?"

"No, but Manda knows you better than anybody. If she'd had any reservations, I'd have advised Brian to leave you out of this and choose another route."

I lowered my voice. "What did she say?"

He shook his head slowly and gave me the look of sad disappointment he usually reserved for the slow-witted. "We wouldn't be here if she thought you weren't ready. In fact she said you were climbing the walls and she couldn't wait to get you out of the house."

"Did she now?"

David tugged at his earlobe. "Not in so many words, but why do you think she's visiting her parents this weekend?"

"You're kidding? She wanted to clear the house for this meeting?"

"Exactly."

I couldn't believe it. Even my wife was in on the bloody setup.

"You didn't tell her anything about the case?"

"Of course not. She wouldn't have wanted to know, but I did have to promise to look after you. So, can I freshen your tea, Detective Sergeant Cryer? Would you like a cushion for that leg?" His eyes opened wide and innocent.

"No thanks, boss. You know I can take only so much tea." I deflated into my chair and—the hell with it—pressed the button to recline the back. "So, what's our plan?"

"I told you, Philip. We don't really have one." He turned to his friend. "Brian?"

Knightly scooted forward to the edge of the sofa and turned towards me. "Since I spoke to David yesterday, I've been laying the groundwork for you to replace DS Juno. It wasn't easy. There's been a recruitment freeze for the current financial year, but the Task Force is shorthanded and I've pulled rank. The only thing I've not been able to do so far is fill in the personnel details, but now you're on board, we can get started."

"Mind if I ask a question that's been bugging me?"

"Fire away, lad. Now's not the time to hang back." Knightly's Yorkshire accent was back, full-throttle now he had my acceptance and my undivided attention.

"Why not put the whole team on lockdown and bring in the Met's Special Branch. We're talking about a corrupt officer who's also involved in killing a cop. If DS Juno identified the dirty cop on his own, there's probably something in the files or in Juno's background that exposes him."

David smiled at me, but I frowned back. It would take me a while to forgive him for conspiring with Manda behind my back.

Knightly finished sprucing his jacket and leaned forward again. "There are a number of reasons. First, I want a watertight case against Alpine."

"Alpine?" David asked the question before I could.

"That's what I'm calling him. And for the present, we'll assume it is a 'him'."

"Why Alpine?" I asked that one.

"Brenda, my wife, and I have had to cancel our holiday to Switzerland since this thing blew up. We used to ski back when we were your age"—he looked sadly at his belly—"but can only walk the lower slopes these days. Alpine seems fitting enough, and when you identify him, I want to swoop down on the bastard like an avalanche." He coughed and shook his head. "Sorry. Not only do I want Alpine, I want anyone who's been helping him. And, if he's selling information, I want the buyers, too. DS Juno's death suggests there's something very wrong with DCI Endicott's team and I want to clean house."

"And there's more, isn't there, Brian?" David said, a knowing glint brightening his eye.

Knightly returned David's glance and nodded. "The Home Secretary has put her political weight behind the NCA. Both she and the NCA would find it hard to recover from a massive corruption investigation so early in its existence. My Director General insisted I investigate on the QT."

"So this has as much to do with politics as catching a criminal?" I asked.

Knightly clenched his teeth. Red blotches coloured the small area of his cheeks visible between beard and tinted glasses. I'd gone too far, and he was close to losing his temper. "It's about more than that, DS Cryer. Someone killed one of my officers, and I don't want that someone getting away."

My volunteer status would only allow so much latitude, and I drew back from the edge. "Sorry, sir. Didn't mean to step out of line. I'm only interested in getting a result. It's just as well I'm not planning a career in politics. Do you mind me asking how a bad apple passed your vetting process? I heard it was as tough as it gets."

A couple of my mates in the force, high flyers tipped for big things, applied to join the NCA when it first opened for business under a firestorm of publicity. The new organisation boasted impressive terms and conditions and a massive London allowance. Neither made it through the initial cull.

"Can't have been tough enough," Knightly answered bluntly. "Would you take it from here, David?"

"Boss, you're going to be closely involved in this?"

"As close as I can be, given my other work."

He gave me that look—the one that said he had unfinished business.

"The Ellis Flynn case?"

His jaw muscles bunched. "That has stalled for the moment. We'll discuss it another time." He shrugged and placed his hand against his ribs once more. "In any event, there's no way I'd leave you alone in this. Even though you'll be little more than a desk-jockey, undercover work can be dangerous. You'll need support from people you can trust, and I'll only be a phone call away."

Yeah, that's right. A phone call and about two hundred kilometres.

I suddenly felt very small and very alone.

Chapter 6

Thursday 12th to Sunday 15th September

David must have picked up on my doubts. He clapped me on the arm. "Not to worry, Philip. You'll be okay."

"Will I?"

"You're a damned good police officer. If I didn't think you could do this, I wouldn't let you. Trust your instincts."

"If I did that, I'd be running through the front door screaming for my mummy."

Knightly laughed and David grinned.

"There's one thing to remember when you're undercover."

"Only one?"

David fixed me with a steady eye. "Trust no one but your handler. No one. That's it and I know you won't forget."

"Understood. I trust no one except you and the Chief Super," I said, aiming for a confident-and-composed look. Somehow, I doubt I succeeded.

Knightly spoke next. "First thing we need is a foolproof legend for you, but it can't stray too far from the truth. According to your records, you have decent IT skills. How easy would it be for you to modify your personnel file? The most important thing is to remove all reference to your photographic memory. Right back to when you were a child. Might even have to lower your academic achievements, too. A first class honours degree from the University of Birmingham stands out among police CVs."

Knightly had done his homework. I didn't correct him on the photographic memory error, and David nodded his approval. As I said, the boss doesn't miss much.

"It's technically possible given the right access levels, but I'd have to alter my police, school, and university records, which, apart from being a huge job, is highly illegal."

"Don't worry about the legal niceties," Knightly said, cutting his hands through the air. "The Home Secretary has given me full authority to do everything necessary. Modifying your police dossier falls under that remit. Besides, it would only be temporary. We'll keep an offline backup and reinstate it good as new the moment we close this case."

"Can I give myself a promotion and a pay hike?" I smiled but was only half joking.

Knightly shook his head. "Sorry. You'll be replacing DS Juno, and you two are the same rank and pay grade. But you can expect a bright future in the force."

"Assuming I have any sort of future at all."

Nice one, Phil. Where did the big brave optimistic cop disappear to? I forced a smile and asked, "When do you expect me to start work?"

"Next Monday," Knightly answered.

"What? In four days?"

"We're hunting a murderer. No time to pussyfoot about."

Senior officer he might have been, but he didn't have a clue what it took to modify a person's online record and then sanitise the trail. Perhaps he made it into the David Jones camp of IT literacy.

"Not possible, sir. In that time I might be able to do enough to pass a cursory inspection, but it wouldn't fool an expert. I'm bound to leave a digital footprint. To do it right, I'd need more time. A couple of weeks might do it, but a month would be preferable."

David took a breath as though he was about to say something, but then he paused.

"Boss? What are you thinking?"

"Would the man who built Sean Freeman's cover be good enough to create a decent one for you in the time available?"

"No idea, but the question's irrelevant. We don't know where he is and can't exactly ask Sean Freeman."

"Why not?"

Knightly and I stared at the old man as though he'd sprouted horns.

"David? Explain yourself, right now," Knightly demanded, jaws clenched.

"I could ask Sean Freeman to put us in touch with his hacker friend. What was his name, Phil?"

"Corky."

"Corky, that's right. He built a background for the conman even you couldn't break."

"You know where Freeman's hiding?" Knightly asked.

David frowned and shook his head. "Not exactly, but I know how to contact him."

"You're kidding, right?" I asked.

"No, I'm not. Remember Freeman left one of those memory sticks in my house?"

"Yes," I answered. "And?"

"He also left a note telling me how to get in touch with him in an emergency."

"One bloody moment," Knightly said, stabbing his finger at David in time with his words. "There's a warrant for Freeman's arrest, and you have access to him, but chose to keep this information to yourself?"

David returned Knightly's stare unfazed. "Without Sean Freeman, you'd still be a Superintendent."

Knightly's mouth snapped shut, but his scowl told me he'd only shelved the conversation temporarily. I guessed the old friends would return to the subject at a later date.

"Boss," I asked, trying to clear my head, "have you talked to Freeman since he disappeared?"

"Not yet," he answered, staring right at me, "but ever since Brian ran this problem past me, I've been considering it." He turned to Knightly again. "Well, *Chief* Superintendent, what do you think?"

The Yorkshireman's shoulders sagged. He scratched at his beard again, his habit when deep in thought. "Freeman disappeared over a year ago. Are his contact details still valid? More to the point, can you trust him?"

"For the first question, I'll only know that when I try. For the second, yes. He's proven himself trustworthy. But we don't have to tell him *why* we want Corky to change Phil's background."

Knightly turned to look at me once more. "You're the one in the firing line, so to speak. What do you think?"

Bloody hell, that was a first. I mean, a Chief Superintendent asking the opinion of a mere DS? If I'd been a Catholic I might have written to the Pope claiming a miracle.

"If the boss thinks it's a good idea, I'm up for it. When I scoured Freeman's background information, it checked out all the way back to World War Two. A masterpiece. I have no idea how long it took Corky to build it, or whether he can do the same job by Monday morning, or whether he'll want to help the police. One thing's for sure though, he'll make a better fist of it than I would, and he can carry on refining the legend while I'm in London. On top of that, it'll give me more time to read up on your team. It's been a while since I've had to cram for an exam."

Knightly took a breath before nodding. "Okay, David. Contact Freeman if you can. We'll keep this between the three of us. The Home Secretary doesn't need to know the finer details. All she wants is a positive outcome."

"Phil," David said, standing. "Can you fire up your computer system and launch the internet browser? I need to send a tweet."

Without thinking, I laughed. "A tweet? You're going to use social media?"

He frowned at my question. "That's what I said, isn't it? I need to log on to my account."

Jesus wept. Had I heard that right? Two miracles in the same place on the same day? The Pope was going to come to me.

"Bloody hell! Not only do you know what a tweet is, you also have an account?" I made a great show of looking out the window. "Is the sky falling?"

Knightly snorted.

"Less of the sarcasm, DS Cryer."

The surprises kept right on coming. I raked my fingers through my hair. "How could you have opened an account when you don't own a PC or a laptop?"

"It just happens that my local village coffee house runs an internet cafe. When it's quiet, the barista is very patient with this poor old silver surfer."

"Well, I'll be bug—" In deference to seniority of the company, I didn't complete the expression, but stood and headed for the door. "Follow me."

We trooped to my office. A tap on the space bar brought up my screensaver—a shot of Manda, Jamie, and Paulie taken on the day we brought him home from the maternity unit. I entered the password and launched a public domain explorer.

"That was quick," David said. "The coffee shop computers take ages to boot."

Bloody hell. The boss knew the correct terminology. Impressed? I nearly fell out of my swivel chair.

"They'll be ancient units, boss. This one's state-of-the-art. Upgraded annually."

I hit the bluebird icon to launch the app and moved aside.

David signed in and then stepped back. "Mind if I dictate the message? You'll type it faster than me."

"What's Freeman's handle?"

"Excuse me?"

It hadn't taken long to find the limit to David's newfound technical mastery. "I need Freeman's ID."

"You're not going to believe it."

"Try me."

"SF-dot-Jewel-hyphen-Thief. One word, capital J, capital T."

"The cheeky bugger. How long does he take to reply?"

"No idea. As I've said, I've never contacted him before."

As David spoke, he turned his back to Knightly and double-hitched both eyebrows. He was lying and making sure I knew it. Strange. I planned to take him to one side later and grill him about it, but that wouldn't happen for a while. Knightly didn't look as though he had plans to leave us alone any time soon.

Entering Freeman's handle brought up the standard white-space holding page: black-male-silhouette; Tweets, 103; Following, 2; Followers, 0; Lists, 0. Barely enough activity to keep the account open.

"What's your handle?"

"DCIDAJones1. The name Freeman asked me to use."

I've always wondered what the 'A' stood for, but never asked. David's a private bloke. If we ever got hold of him, maybe I'd ask Corky to find out.

Nah, perhaps not.

"Did he give you any contact instructions, passwords, call signs?"

"No, just his name and the one I was to use. I'm guessing he's set up a slave address to forward the tweets to whatever device he's using."

What the fuck? Tweeting, internet cafes, and now slave addresses? I stared at the floor, wondering when the sinkhole would open up and swallow my house.

Things were becoming surreal. I'd planned a quiet weekend recuperating from the self-imposed torture of my rehab and learning how to survive without my family. Instead, not only had I volunteered to hunt a rogue cop, but David Jones, my technophobe boss, had started to sound like someone who actually lived in the Information Age. With the world turning on its head, I took a risk.

"Chief Superintendent?"

"Yes?"

"While we get on with this, you don't fancy making a cuppa, do you? I need a strong coffee and you know where everything is."

He lifted his eyebrows, said, "Good idea. Coming right up," and then headed out the door.

Stone me! I'd ordered refreshments from a Chief Super and he hadn't batted an eyelid. Forget the Pope and his double miracle, I should have bought a lottery ticket.

With Knightly out of the room, I leaned close to the boss and whispered, "You've spoken to Freeman?"

David raised his finger to his lips. "We'll talk about it later."

Twenty minutes after sending the tweet, and after Knightly's return with a tray of makings, David's mobile bleeped—caller ID withheld. He answered in his usual silky smooth way. "Jones here. ... Freeman? ... Yes, it has been a while ... Fifteen months? ... That's right. I am with friends."

After the initial forced pleasantries where the boss led the conversation, he listened for a few moments, silent and unsmiling, but looking right at me before he hit a button on the keypad. "Freeman, I've put you on loudspeaker."

"Okay, Mr Jones. Is Mr Cryer with you?"

"And Chief Superintendent Knightly. You know of him?"

"Of course. Good morning, Mr Knightly. Congratulations on your promotion."

Knightly gave a reluctant greeting. It might have been a 'thank you', but came out closer to a bulldog clearing his throat.

"And Mr Cryer, sorry to hear about your accident."

"You're well informed."

"I like to keep a weather eye open for my friends. How's your recovery going?"

"Fine."

"Sounds like a horrible procedure to me. The orthopaedic surgeon rebuilt the distal edge of your fibula, I understand?"

"Something like that," I answered, shocked he knew the details. The bugger must have hacked my medical records, or at least Corky had. "But I'm on the mend now, thanks."

Formalities complete, David took charge. "Thanks for answering my tweet, Freeman."

"Before I left the country, I did make the offer. Never thought you'd take me up on it, though. Things must be pretty bad for you to be contacting my sorry ass after all this time."

Freeman's familiar laugh made me smile. Say what you like about the locksmith-turned-jewel-thief-turned-whatever, he continued to be a happy bunny. In the months since I'd last seen him, he'd also developed a slight American twang. East coast, unless the phone's speaker distorted the sound too much.

"How's Angela?" I asked, referring to the innocent stooge Freeman used to dupe us into helping him.

"She and our son are wonderful, thanks for asking."

"Your son?" I asked, checking David for a reaction. There was none, which confirmed my suspicion that he and Freeman had been in contact recently.

"Yes," Freeman said, adding another chuckle. "We've called him Davie in honour of you, Mr Jones."

I gave him my congratulations.

"Wonderful," David said, his voice Sahara dry. "Do you mind if we move on?"

"It's always business with you, Mr Jones. How can I help the UK boys in blue, yet again?"

Knightly winced at Freeman's taunt.

David tugged at his earlobe, mouth twisted into a grimace. "Not sure you can do anything," he said, "but your … associate, Corky, might be of assistance."

"Corky?" Freeman's voice registered surprise. "This must be serious. He won't be keen to help the Dibbles. Very anti-establishment is my little computer whiz."

"Okay," David said, sighing loud enough for Freeman to hear. "I'd understand if you didn't want to help. There's nothing in it for you but my gratitude and helping me catch a killer."

"Don't be like that, Mr Jones. Never said I didn't want to help my favourite police officer, and I appreciate gratitude as much as the next man. Tell you what. I'll talk to him for you, but there's no telling how he'll react. Corky is … well, let's just say he's different. What exactly do you need?"

David gave Freeman the gist, and I chimed in when it came to the techie requirements.

When we'd finished, Freeman didn't respond immediately. Knightly opened his mouth to speak, but David shook his head.

"Is that all you need?" Freeman asked.

I couldn't make out sarcasm in his voice, but the tiny speaker might have masked it.

"Is it possible in the timeframe?" I asked. "And if so, can you persuade Corky to help?"

"You're kidding, right?" Freeman laughed. "You're giving him a free pass to play with the Police National Database and the personnel records of the Midlands Police? He's going to think he's died and gone to Valhalla."

The boss and I looked at each other. I couldn't gauge his reaction from his expressionless face, but from the doubt in Knightly's eyes I could tell he was worried he'd just opened the vaults to the nation's top secrets and allowed the digital Pixies in. David's lips pursed in a silent whistle. For my part, I tried to hide my excitement and fear. It wasn't easy.

"Give me a couple of hours," Freeman added. "Keep your phone charged, Mr Jones."

He disconnected the call and the boss finally gave vent to his feelings. "Cheeky bloody puppy. As though I ever forget to charge my mobile."

"Perish the thought," Knightly said.

I said nothing.

#

We spent the following two and a half hours with Knightly giving me the skinny on what was to become my new employer, however temporary. He walked me through the NCA's policies and internal protocols, and gave me a leader's view of the people in the team I was going to work with. As a board level officer, the only one he could discuss on a personal level was DCI Endicott.

"Here, take this," Knightly said, passing me a USB drive. "That contains the OCTF personnel files. Read, memorise, destroy. You know the drill."

"How many people on the Task Force?"

"Including Bee and DI Hook, ten. Won't take you long to absorb the information, will it?"

"Not long. Thank you, sir."

We moved on to discussing how I'd make my daily reports. Given the differences in our ranks, I could hardly pop into Knightly's office for a chat every day without raising suspicions. With the surveillance countermeasures in place at NCA HQ, internal phone communications were also impossible. Knightly came up with the answer which was efficient in its simplicity. Each evening I'd call him using burner phones over a VoIP service specifically encrypted by Corky—assuming he agreed to help.

David's mobile rang. He hit the speaker button.

"That you, Mr Jones?" asked a high-pitched voice, not Freeman's.

"Corky?" David asked.

"S'right. What d'you need?"

"Didn't Freeman tell you?"

"Sort of, but I want details. You there Mr Cryer?"

"Yep."

"So, you the guy what couldn't crack my creative background history on old Sean, eh?"

I tried hard not to scowl at the man's taunting, but didn't do a good job. Only the fact we were asking him to do us a favour prevented me having a pop.

"No," I said, "your fabrication was a masterpiece. Never seen anything so comprehensive. No doubt about it, you're the man."

Shovelling on the bullshit wouldn't hurt any.

"Yeah, I know. So what you need this time? A modest adjustment from DoB up to today?"

Buttering the guy up seemed to be working, and I continued the charm offensive. "We need you to modify my personal history a little. The basic facts can remain intact, but there can't be any indication that the file's been edited. You're the only one we know who is capable of doing the job at such short notice."

"When do you need it by?"

"Monday morning, oh-eight-hundred."

"You mean this coming Monday?"

"Can you do it?"

Hesitation, but not for long. "Yeah, no probs. I've already gained access to your data servers, but I'll need you available in case I have questions. We can video-call."

"Okay, I'm going nowhere."

"Yes you are. You're going to London to join the NCA."

Knightly spluttered into his tea. "Wha—"

"Who's that?" Corky asked. "Chief Superintendent Knightly, I suppose?"

"Aye, that's correct," he answered, wiping his beard with a hankie. "How do you know about the NCA association?"

Corky laughed. It sounded like a cat coughing up a fur ball. "Don't be daft, Mr Knightly. I've had nearly three hours. Plenty of time to run a little background check on you boys. I know what happened to Detective Sergeant Juno and that you have your balls in a vice. Only thing I don't know is how you're going to find the dirty cop what killed him. Gonna utilise that fancy eidetic memory of yours, I suppose, Mr Cryer?"

I considered throwing up the denials, but Corky beat me to it.

"Nah, nah, don't worry. It ain't none of my business. Your memory does help me in one way. At least I won't have to worry you'll forget the new history I create for you. You'll be surprised how long it took Sean to memorise his new identity. It's one of the main reasons people screw up when creating a new life. They forget the small things, but that ain't gonna be no problem with you, is it?" Again, the guttural laugh coughed down the line. "So, let's get down to work. You want I should remove all reference to your particular skill? Including your appearance on that game show back in the '90s?"

Christ! If he'd learned that after only three hours, what would he learn about me by the weekend? I could understand what victims of identity theft felt like.

#

By Sunday evening, Corky had worked his magic, and I had absorbed megabytes of information. That was the easy part; worse was still to come. I had to say goodbye to Manda and the kids.

In the bedroom in the quiet of Sunday night, I held Manda tight, making the most of our last few hours together. Her head rested on my bare chest, hair fanned and tickling. I loved it.

"Won't be for long," I said. "And I'll be back every weekend, unless there's an emergency."

"But you can barely walk. What happens if you get into trouble?"

"Don't be daft. I'll be on restricted duty, sitting behind a desk shuffling papers all day. Think of this way. It'll look good on my CV and won't do my chances of full reinstatement any harm. Not to mention I'll be a shoe-in for promotion after the next promotion boards."

"You're doing this for promotion?"

"I said you weren't to mention the promotion."

She punched my shoulder lightly. "Be serious for a moment, will you? Just take care, okay?"

"Always. You know me. Careful is my middle name."

"No, your middle name's Peter. And if you're so careful, what were you doing running over the rooftops hunting a crazed killer?"

"One time only deal. Never happen again."

She leaned up on her elbow and we kissed.

"Make sure you remember that."

"You know me, love. Never forget a thing. And by the way, when this is all over, you and I are going to have a little chat about your talking to David behind my back. Punishment might be involved. You know, whips and ropes, and stuff."

"Whips and ropes? Don't be getting any novel ideas, Detective Sergeant Cryer."

"Who me? Never had an original idea in my life, Mrs Cryer."

"Shut up and kiss me again, fool."

"Yes, guv."

I smiled and pulled her close again, suffering in silence as the movement jerked my knee and sent a knife thrust of pain into my hip.

PART TWO

The First Week

Chapter 7

Monday 16th September

London and I have never been close friends. Cool acquaintances at best. I hadn't visited for years, but the minute I stepped from the train, tasted the grit in the air, and smelled the fug of too much humanity in too confined a space, it all came flooding back. London, a noisome place full of bustling strangers heading who knows where and none of them seeming to enjoy the experience.

Shuffling along the platform with a walking stick in one hand, pulling a wheelie suitcase in the other, I felt a million eyes drilling into the back of my neck. Stupid really. On Euston Station's Platform 8, I was as anonymous as everybody else, which was just as well. Some of the criminals I've put away over the years hold deep grudges. When fit and healthy, I can handle myself well enough, but the injury put me at a disadvantage. I'd never felt more alone.

How long would the feeling of being in the crosshairs last?

At a pinch, I could have done without the stick, but I used it as much to ward off the bumps and nudges of the passing strangers as to help me walk. Leaving my emotional crutch at home would have been a step too far, too soon.

The digital clock on the arrivals board read 07:47. Despite being up for three hours, I'd still be late for my first shift. Not the best start to a new job. It would have been better if I'd travelled down the day before, but I wanted one more night in my own bed. One more night of normality. One more night to back out if my nerve failed. But it hadn't, and there I was, alone in a city of eight million lonely souls.

Echoing arrival and departure announcements, squealing train wheels, clanking carriages, traffic rumbling in the streets outside the main doors, and the click-click-stomp of a thousand footfalls combined into an aggressive white noise. I'd only been in the city a few minutes and already my head throbbed. I also found the smell of humanity, exhaust fumes, and grime intensely overpowering.

Welcome to London, Detective Sergeant Country Bumpkin.

Signs pointed me towards a bright morning and the taxi rank at the front of the station. It only took ten minutes in the queue to bag a black cab. My new job included a generous, if temporary, expense allowance, and I didn't fancy slogging through the Tube with the wheeled Samsonite. Not on my first day and not with a dodgy knee to slow me down.

The cabbie—the caricature of a wizened Cockney—jumped out and helped me with the case. Milking the sympathy vote was another reason I kept the stick.

Shameful, aren't I?

"Where to, guv?" the cabbie asked, smiling broad enough to reveal a gap between his front teeth and a gold right upper canine.

The smile unnerved me a little. London cabbies are supposed to be miserable, aggressive gits, but this one could have auditioned for a walk-on role in a stage version of Mary Poppins, except his accent sounded genuine. His grin made me wonder whether he'd mistaken me for a celebrity. Since losing the ten kilos of blubber, people have told me I could pass for Johnny Wilkinson, the former England rugby player.

The recognition thing was flattering, but inaccurate. Wilko is three years older than me and eight centimetres shorter. Although I have played rugby, at fullback, not centre, I couldn't dropkick a rugby ball between the posts any better than I could dropkick a thief into a holding cell. Still, Wilko's a good looking bloke and if people think we're similar, who am I to complain?

"Citadel Place, Tinworth Street, please. SE11."

"Certainly, officer." He jammed my case into the front footwell. "Hop in, seatbelt on."

"How d'you know I'm a police officer?"

He slammed the driver's door and fired up the big diesel engine. "There ain't nothing in Tinworth Street besides the NCA headquarters. You don't look like a criminal mastermind. Not in a suit that cheap." He winked at me through the rear-view mirror.

I took an instant liking to the little guy. Pity I'd never see him again.

"You anything to do with that business at Docklands overnight?"

"The bullion robbery?"

"Yeah."

"No, that's the Met's case. The NCA won't be involved."

"Evil beggars got away with millions. News report said they hurt a couple of guards. Nasty business, but the gold, hell. Wouldn't mind setting me minces on that lovely yellow stuff."

Minces? It took me half a second to work out what he meant. Mince pies—eyes. Why did they still insist on using the rhyming slang nonsense? Probably kept it up for the tourists in hopes of earning bigger tips.

The little Cockney wittered away for the rest of the journey. A few mumbled responses made me feel less rude, but I wasn't really listening; I had other things on my mind than gold bullion and sight-seeing. My heart trip-hammered away, and I wondered whether the driver could hear the bloody thing pounding.

After seventeen minutes of smooth progress, he pulled the taxi to a stop in a quiet back street. I handed over fifteen quid, pocketed the receipt, and took in the four storey grey brick and glass building—my workplace for the foreseeable future. Not a pleasant thought.

Unlike the world-famous New Scotland Yard building with its tower block, sleek lines, and instantly recognisable revolving triangular sign, Citadel Place wouldn't have turned any heads. Without the understated black on silver NCA sign at the end of the wall, the complex could have passed for the corporate offices of any multinational brokerage firm.

The compound comprises two tower blocks—the first for accommodation and amenities, the second for offices and admin—separated by a private gated road leading to a car park. I chose the second. Chrome railings guarded a gatehouse appendage that was bolted to the side of the building almost as an afterthought. An opening in the railings allowed access to four steps and a curving wheelchair ramp. I managed the steps without assistance, and I wasn't even grimacing when I reached the top. Progress indeed.

A white rendered wall housed a single, bomb-resistant door. I smiled into the security camera above the entrance for a couple of seconds before peering through the glass. If the NCA was worth anything, my security clearance would already have made its way to the striking receptionist sitting behind a highly-polished ebony desk. Late twenties and blonde, she wore a dark blue power jacket over a white blouse. The desk hid the rest of her ensemble, but I imagined a short skirt and shiny high heels.

The woman checked her PC monitor and the latch buzzed—I must have met the requirements. I pushed through the door and entered a single-person mantrap. One door wouldn't open until the other closed. I waited until the second lock clicked and the inner door opened with a vacuum pop.

The reception area was functional, if Spartan, and smelled as though the aircon had released an aerosol of 'countryside fresh'. Someone was trying hard, perhaps too hard, to create a welcoming oasis of calm.

The desk stood in front of a stark white wall that held two notice boards, where brochures proclaimed the latest NCA successes. On my right, a smoky glass wall—blast resistant—allowed a subdued view of Tinworth Street. To my left, a red brick wall housed a pair of brushed steel doors flanked by two rows of comfortable-looking leather chairs.

"DS Cryer?" the blonde asked, her voice cool, her accent refined home counties. The nameplate on the desk announced her as Ms Freya Brinkley. I knew her to be one of the civilian support staff.

"At your service, Ms Brinkley." I flashed a smile and my warrant card to supplement her security information.

"You're seven minutes late. Please take a seat"—she pointed at the leather chairs—"while I let someone know you've arrived. Finally."

Her dark blue eyes gave away nothing when she added the gentle barb, but I had the distinct impression she enjoyed playing the fiery gatekeeper. She hit a button on her telephone number pad and spoke quietly into a headset microphone.

The leather chairs *looked* comfortable, but were Scandinavian modern—ultra low and without arms. I remained standing. Arriving at a new job looking like a hospital reject was bad enough, but having to use a stick to help me stand again would have been too embarrassing. I'm a bloke, right. No way am I going to risk losing face.

While the attractive-but-stern Freya answered a phone call, an electronic ding and a red warning light pre-announced the opening of the brushed steel security doors. They slid apart like the doors of a lift, and I tugged my tie into position.

Showtime.

A tall, slim black woman, hair cut tight to her scalp, welcomed me with a bright smile. She wore a nicely-tailored dark blue trouser suit and a lilac blouse, the top two buttons undone. Shiny black leather shoes, flat heels. Elegant and professional.

"DS Cryer?" She thrust out a hand.

"That's me."

We shook.

"Hi, Sarge. Welcome to the NCA. I'm DC Chloe Holder, your welcoming committee and your new partner. DCI Endicott would normally do the meet-and-greet, but there's a panic on. She sends her apologies."

Her accent came straight from the cast of EastEnders and threatened to make my ears bleed. Twenty-seven years old, born and bred in Streatham, her grandparents had arrived in the UK from Jamaica as part of the Windrush Generation and settled in London.

"A panic?"

"Yeah, I'll tell you about it on the way." She checked her watch. "Trouble with your commute?"

"Train delay north of Luton. I should have come down last night."

"Not to worry. We don't punch a clock here. As you requested, Freya allocated you a temporary suite in the accommodation block across the way. Nothing palatial, but it'll suit until you find a place of your own. I'll take you over there later, when I give you the grand tour."

"Thanks."

She leaned close enough for me to catch a whiff of Dior's *Poison*. Manda uses it on special occasions. Expensive for everyday use, but it suited Chloe Holder. Maybe she wore it to impress her new DS.

"Nobody said you had a duff leg," she said, glancing at the stick. "That a permanent feature?"

Ouch.

A little brazen for my tastes, but I let it go. Can't be dressing down a junior partner on the first day. It's simply not done. Maybe they played things differently in the NCA, more relaxed. I kept my tone even. "Work-related accident. I'll be on restricted duties for the next month or so. The medics say I'm fit enough to fly a desk, though."

"Sorry, Sarge. I can be a nosy cow. Guess it's why I joined the force." She smiled at the receptionist. "Freya, you got the doings?"

Freya handed me a big buff envelope from a desk drawer. "Your care package, DS Cryer. Not to be opened until you're at your desk."

With the stick in one hand and the wheelie case waiting, I tucked the envelope under my arm and grabbed the Samsonite's handle. "Thanks, Ms Brinkley."

She didn't return my smile and that was fair enough. The law of averages says I can't win everyone over with my good looks and boyish charm. Yeah, 'boyish charm' and me a married man shuffling around with a walking stick. Who am I trying to kid?

"Come on," Chloe said. "The guys are keen to meet you."

Yeah, I bet.

She turned, and I followed her through the doorway. A line from Tennyson pushed its way to the front of my mind. I paraphrased it as, *Into the valley of death limped the Brummie copper.*

Chapter 8

Monday 16th September

My suitcase and I followed Chloe along a brightly lit corridor that smelled of fresh paint and floor polish. Our shoes squeaked on the shiny tiles.

Chloe entered the lift first and pressed button number three with a nicely-manicured finger. Short fingernails, clear varnish.

"Top floor's reserved for the brass who've got the dog's bollocks view of the river and the city. We're on the third. I'd normally use the stairs, but you'll probably prefer the lift." She raised her eyebrows and glanced at the stick.

First thought? Decent of her to be so accommodating. Second thought? She didn't really need to keep drawing attention to my leg. Okay, call me Mr Oversensitive.

"Thanks."

Not much else I could have said without appearing aggressive. We each took a far corner of the lift and the doors whispered closed.

"So," I said to break the silence, "what's this about panic stations?"

She looked at me hard. "You didn't see the news this morning? The bullion job?"

"Yes, the media's all over it. Read about it on the train. What's it got to do with us?"

"The Met boys have asked for our help."

Wow. A great day to start my new job. Excitement smothered my nervous tension. Things were about to get interesting.

"Okay, bring me up to speed."

"The blaggers made off with six hundred, one-kilogram ingots of 99.9% pure South African gold."

"Jesus."

The online news hadn't released those details.

"Yeah, 'Jesus' is too right, Sarge. A real bundle in folding money."

The last time I'd looked up the price of gold—purely out of interest—it had a value of around twenty-three thousand pounds sterling per kilogram. A quick calculation told me the robbers netted nearly fourteen million pounds. Huge, but not quite on a par with the 1983 Brinks Mat robbery , which in today's terms would have been worth nearly eighty million.

"What happened?"

"Reports are still coming in. Near as we can tell, five geezers armed with automatic weapons and shotguns used a bulldozer to ram the armoured car. They blew open the back doors with what looks like military-grade explosives and used one of them mini forklifts to shift the gold into a Mercedes Benz van. The whole thing was done and dusted inside of fifteen minutes."

I allowed the information to sink in for a couple of seconds before speaking. "Sounds like a professional outfit. Anyone hurt?"

Chloe grimaced. "Yeah. They shot two of the security guards. Both of them are in hospital. One's likely to lose a leg, and the other's touch and go to live."

Not that professional then. Most pros run a mile from actual violence unless they face real trouble. Nasty bastards these.

"What's our role in the case?"

43

"The Met asked for help with the intelligence gathering." She let loose another smile, this one half-hearted. "We've got the biggest and fastest criminal database in the country."

The lift stopped.

"And you're here holding my hand while everyone else is hunting a crew of armed robbers. Sorry. You must be pissed."

"Nah, no way," she said a little too quickly. "You're me new sergeant and I've been looking forward to saying hello."

"I appreciate it."

She wasn't a very good liar. Annoyance was written all over her darkly attractive face and something else—evasion in the way she refused to look at me when answering my questions.

The lift doors slid apart and she stepped into a bright corridor. The sun streamed through windows running along the outer wall. I stayed put and she turned to face me.

"Problem, Sarge?"

"What's wrong, DC Holder?"

Her eyes flicked away and she hesitated a fraction. "Nothin'."

"I detect an undercurrent." I raised the stick. "Does this bother you?"

She looked up and down the corridor before stepping back into the lift. "Nah. It ain't that at all," she whispered. "It's just ... well, I don't want to be speakin' out of turn. Not sure it's my place."

I had an idea what she was worried about, but played the dumb newbie and put on my serious face. "Chloe, if we're going to be a team we need to trust each other. Spit it out."

She took a breath. "Well, things are a bit fraught at the moment. Don't be surprised if DI Hook appears a little ... how am I gonna put this ... Don't be surprised if he's a bit pissed at ya."

Really.

I paused as though considering my response. "As far as I know, I'd never met a DI Hook so why would he be upset with me? Does it have anything to do with him not being part of the interview panel that approved my posting here?"

"No, it ain't nothin' like that." She kept her voice low. "It's more a question of who you're replacing."

"Oh, I'm replacing someone? I assumed the NCA was expanding. You—sorry, we—are the only law enforcement organisation in the country with a growing budget."

Chloe stared hard at me, eyes calculating. The lift doors started to close and I stuck my suitcase in the gap. One of the doors bumped against it and they both retracted in a huff. I kept silent, waiting for her to tell me what was on her mind.

"You really don't know?"

"Don't know what?"

"You're replacing DS Richie Juno."

"Who?"

I did that look-sideways-out-of-one-eye thing to show confusion and to suggest an internal struggle to access my long term memory. One-point-three-five seconds is the average human delay for dredging up unrelated memories. I waited twice that long for the tumblers to apparently click into place and release the information.

"Bloody hell," I said, allowing surprise to seep into my voice. "The officer run down by the suspect he was tailing? In Somerset, right? Week before last?"

She nodded again and made a face—a cross between anger and sadness. "Sunil Pradeep. We reckon he spotted Richie tailing him and decided to take him out. Bastard got what he deserved though."

An itch prickled the skin behind my left ear. I scratched it away. "I'm replacing him? Fuck. I had no idea DS Juno was with the NCA."

"We kept that information quiet. It'll come out in the inquest. Avon and Somerset Police are handling the case."

"Yeah. That's right. I'm guessing there's been an internal investigation?"

"It's ongoing. I've had the first interview, but I doubt it'll be the last. The brass want to lay the blame on someone and I hope it ain't going to be me."

"You were involved?"

"Sort of." She looked away. "If you don't mind. I'd rather not talk about it."

"Understood."

"Let's put it this way. We're all mad as fuck, but Hookie … I mean, DI Hook, is worse. For him it's even more personal. Thought you needed to know in case you pick up on the vibe. Right?"

"I can understand that. Must be hard for him to lose one of the men under his command."

Thankfully, I've not felt that loss firsthand yet, but I'm next in line for a DI spot—assuming I pass the exams—and will be responsible for a load more people.

She leaned out of the lift, eyed the corridor both ways, and lowered her voice. "Thing is, Richie was married to Billy's kid sister, and Billy was the one who gave Richie the job that got him killed."

"Damn, that's tough on him," I muttered, half to myself. "Tough on me, too."

"Why's that, Sarge?"

"It's just that I've been looking for a London posting all my working life and on day one I learn I'm stepping into dead man's shoes." Lying isn't a natural part of my makeup, but I'd have to get used to it. "Thanks for the warning, Chloe. Much appreciated."

"I reckon Billy thinks your appointment's probably a little previous. I mean, we ain't even had poor Richie's memorial service yet."

"I haven't missed it then?"

"No. It's a week next Wednesday. Official service, followed by a first class wake. We're all gonna get smashed in Richie's honour." The left corner of her mouth tweaked into a sad smile. "I gotta say, when Chief Superintendent Knightly announced your appointment last Friday, it came as a bit of a shock. The old boy rarely slums it with the other ranks."

"I met the Chief Super at my interview. Seems reasonable enough for a Yorkshireman."

She looked up at the roof of the lift and might have yawned if she'd known me better. "Don't know the bloke that well, but I'll take your word for it."

The lift doors slid across and nudged the suitcase as though asking it to get out of the way.

"We'd better get a shuffle on. Ready to meet the gang?"

"As I'll ever be. Lead on, Detective Constable Holding."

"Holder. I'm Chloe Holder."

I winced and turned it into an apologetic smile. "Sorry, Chloe. I'm not brilliant with names. Perhaps you can help me out if I get in trouble?"

Dear, dear. Such a liar. If needed, I could have recited every word of her personnel file from her date of birth—July 7th 1990—to her current address. I could have revealed her secondary school SAT scores and the balance in her current account—£256.53 at close of play last Friday.

"That's okay," she said. "No probs."

We took a right turn out of the lift and walked thirty metres along a corridor—grey-tinted windows on the right, bare white walls on the left. Another left turn at the end led to fifty metres of corridor. More windows on the right, but this time, black security doors broke the smooth line of the inner wall.

Spotless and new, the building gave off the vibe of a high security prison. Without the bright daylight blasting through self-cleaning windows, my old claustrophobia might have made a comeback.

Each of the black doors had a separate keypad entry system, and each was marked with the unit's designation: Economic Crime Command, Cyber Crime Command, Homeland Terrorist Command, People Trafficking Task Force. Finally, the *pièce de résistance*, the UK Protected Persons Service—the UK's witness protection program. The UKPPS is one of the most secretive organisations outside Spooks Central, otherwise known as MI5 and MI6. It shocked me to learn they'd put a nameplate on the door.

The UKPPS protects all sorts, from frightened and intimidated witnesses, to villains turning Queen's evidence. Some of them, real nasty characters you wouldn't want to chase across a knackered old roof. Unlike the brave—or possibly foolhardy—UKPPS officers, I doubt I'd ever have the balls to step in front of a bullet to protect a Supergrass. Life's too precious and my babies need both parents.

At the end of the corridor, we made another left, and reached the service area at the rear of the building. Double doors led through to the emergency exit. According to a sign on the red brick wall, a staircase allowed access to the rear assembly point. Below the sign, and out of sight of the building's other users, some bright spark had taped a photocopy of Edvard Munch's *The Scream*—the famous reflection on the madness of modern life.

Nice. At least someone within this lockup had a sense of humour.

We turned our backs to the screaming man and faced the entrance to my workplace for the immediate future.

Alongside another keypad-secured entrance, a steel cabinet bolted to the inner wall housed fifteen small security lockers. The door to each unit sported a digital display and all but five showed as *LOCKED*. Chloe pointed to one of the flaps marked *UNLOCKED*—top row, second from the right.

"That one's yours."

I opened it. The internal space was tiny. A thirty centimetre cube, each wall ten centimetres thick. After reading the design specs when the units first came out, I knew exactly what the lockers were for, but asked anyway. "Too small to hold much. What am I supposed to put in there?"

"The office is fitted with shit-hot security countermeasures. These lockers are shielded to protect our personal electronic devices from the EMP scan."

"What's an EMP?"

"Electromagnetic pulse. Take any electronics into The Cage and the EMP will erase the memory."

"The Cage?"

So many questions for which I already had the answers. As a newbie, the whole place should have been strange to me, and I played it as such.

"You'll see why in a sec," she answered and nodded to the open locker. "Put your wallet in there too or the magnetic strips on your bank cards will be wiped. Do you have a digital watch?"

"No." I showed her my Citizen analogue. "Anniversary present from my wife."

"Good. You can leave that on. The lock code is on the display inside the door. Don't forget it or you'll incur The Wrath of Freya. She's forever having to reset the lock codes for idiot cops with the memory of a guppy."

"I'll try, but numbers and me don't really see eye to eye." The lies, they just kept coming. "How often do people forget?"

"The numbers, or forget to protect their stuff?"

"Both."

She smiled again. She had a great smile, one that would make a camera sigh.

"Once or twice," she said. "Recovering the lost information is a pain in the butt. As is replacing all your credit cards."

"I can imagine."

With the reluctance of a smoker giving up his last fag, I stuffed my phone and tablet inside the locker together with my wallet. My empty pockets made me mourn the temporary loss of my electronic babies.

I made a great show of closing my eyes and mouthing the combination a few times—8-9-5-2-7. The flap closed, making a loud metallic clang, and I pressed the trigger button. The *UN* part of the display blinked out, leaving the word *LOCKED*. I wondered how secure the system really was. Someone, I guessed Freya, would have a general release code. She seemed to have taken on the mantle of the building's go-to girl, which married with the information in her personnel file.

"C'mon then, Sarge. Let's give you your first glimpse of The Cage."

"What about my case? I have an e-reader, razor, alarm clock ..."

"There's a bigger locker in the bogs. You'll need a pound coin for the lock. Follow the signs. I'll wait here." She pointed to the emergency exit.

It took a couple of minutes to store the Samsonite in one of ten changing room-type lockers.

When I returned, Chloe pushed through the OCTF door and another mantrap—this one large enough for four or five if they didn't mind not breathing—barred our entry. A screen on the wall announced the initiation of the small-scale EMP and counted down from fifteen, presumably to give a forgetful soul time to abort the sweep and save their electronics—and their blushes.

"Ready?" she asked.

"For what?"

"You'll feel a tingling and your hair might stand up a little. People with long hair normally tie it back."

She glanced up at my wavy blond mop. Truth is, I wear it too long, but Manda likes it that way. I'd have to remember to bring my comb to work.

An alarm sounded, my neck hairs tingled, and then it ended. No harm, no foul. Over the weekend, I'd looked up the physical effects of regular doses of EMP waves on my chances of fathering another child. According to the existing medical evidence, the jury is still deliberating.

The things I do for the job.

The lock on the inner door disengaged. Chloe pushed it open and there I was. DS Phil Cryer—a tiny goldfish in an aquarium containing at least one ruddy great big piranha.

Chapter 9

Monday 16th September

Chloe led us through an open plan office about the same size as the SCU briefing room, but that's where the similarity ended. The blue-grey industrial carpet prevented our shoes from squeaking, not that the squeaks would have registered above the background drone of the room.

Aircon hummed, keyboards clicked, the members of the OCTF chattered either to one another or into telephones, but overriding it all, the fizz crackle of static electricity dried the air. Each time I inhaled, my nose hairs stuck together and made me want to reach for a tissue. The little hairs on my arms stood on end—the place literally made my skin crawl. I could taste the supercharged ions in the atmosphere.

Windowless and harshly lit by overhead strip lighting, two doors broke the smooth line of the right-hand wall. Each wore a nameplate: DCI Endicott, Head of Unit; and the Data Acquisition and Storage Facility. So many new acronyms for the newbie DS to remember, but I'd probably manage.

Twelve desks, four unoccupied, had a clear view of a wall-sized interactive whiteboard—no making do with easels and paper flipcharts in the NCA. No one turned to watch our progress. The members of my new team concentrated on the difficult work of finding the gold bullion bandits.

The walls not covered by whiteboard, shelving, or notices, were painted in magnolia and strung with a net of thin, signal-disrupting wires—hence the name, The Cage. Anti-eavesdropping chic, the netting covered the ceiling as well, and would also have been woven invisibly into the carpeting.

Overcautious? Probably, but in these days of directional telescopic microphones and electronic surveillance technology, such countermeasures were essential. As CS Knightly warned me, the OCTF was serious about its privacy.

Chloe saw me scrutinising the wire and winked. Despite remaining on my suspect list, I marked her as a potential ally in my drive to fit in with my new team. No doubt I'd need all the help I could find.

She led me to DI William 'Billy' Hook's desk. It faced all the others and gave the place a schoolroom feel. He looked up as we approached, glowering at me as though I'd been personally responsible for his brother-in-law's murder.

Not guilty, Your Honour.

The photo in his personnel file didn't do justice to his broken-nosed brooding menace. At one metre seventy-four—seven centimetres shorter than me—Hook weighed in at eighty-five kilos of prime Essex beef and had the build of a cruiserweight boxer. Dark brown eyes bored into mine as though he wanted to boil me alive from the inside before they slid down to take in my walking stick. The glower turned into a sneer.

Subtle, he wasn't.

"Billy," Chloe said, gracing him with one of her knockout smiles, "meet DS Cryer. Sarge, this here's DI Hook." She gave me a look that said, 'Seconds out. Round One', and took a pace back.

I smiled, too. No harm in being friendly. "Morning, sir. Sorry I'm late. Won't happen again."

The rude bastard ignored my outstretched hand. Fair enough, be like that then. I allowed my smile to fade.

Hook nodded at Chloe. "Thanks. Get Bandage to fill you in on where we are with the bullion case. There's a state of play briefing in fifteen." He waited for Chloe to leave before deigning to acknowledge my presence. "Wait there, Detective Sergeant." He growled my rank as though it were an insult and headed towards DCI Endicott's office.

A glower, a sneer, and a growl? A wonderful welcome. And there I was thinking the job would be difficult.

Hook knocked on the DCI's door and entered without waiting—a man on a mission. His exit left me twisting in the wind, and I turned to the remaining eight people, none of whom had reacted to Hook's performance.

Chloe was talking to DC Harvey Poltous, an ascetic, college professor type—midfifties, half-moon glasses dangled from a chain around his neck. She said something and they both looked at me. He nodded a greeting, which I returned, and then carried on with his briefing.

Standing still for any length of time still makes my knee ache, but rather than take a load off uninvited, I picked out the character with the most open body language and wandered to his desk. With bright red hair, clean shaven, mid-twenties, the young man smiled as I approached.

"DS Phil Cryer," I said, sticking out my hand.

"Aye, we know, Sarge. Freya sent a global email last Friday. I'm DC Andrew Mackay, but everybody calls me Drew." He took hold of my hand and pumped twice before letting go.

"Pleased to meet you, Drew." I nodded toward the DCI Endicott's office. "Nice welcome."

Drew screwed up his face. "Don't take it personally, Sarge. He'd no' be keen on anyone taking over from Richie. You heard about that?"

I jerked up my chin in a nod. "Chloe told me on the way up. Losing a family member can't be easy."

"You could say that, but at least the killer didn't live long or prosper."

Drew Mackay, a Star Trek fan? That nugget hadn't made his dossier. What else had Knightly's information pack missed?

I nodded sagely and changed the subject to one less sensitive. "I'm getting a Scottish accent. East coast, maybe Edinburgh? Been in London long?"

"Well spotted. I'm frae Auld Reekie and proud o' it. Been in London a wee bit over a year now."

Yep, that tallied. Drew had arrived in London after serving three years as a uniformed cop in Edinburgh. It put him in the clear as far as being Alpine—unless my target had been busy recruiting a support team. Unlikely, but not completely out of the question.

"Enjoying London?"

"It's no' bad. Bloody expensive, mind. Want me to do the introductions?"

"Yes, please."

He named two DSs and five DCs in turn. Each greeted me with a different level of reserve and suspicion, checking out the new guy with the walking stick and the limp. I gave them my undivided attention and repeated their names as though needing to drive them into my long-term memory.

Drew finished with, "And saving the worst 'til last, the big monster's none other than DC Clint Schneider." He pointed to a giant of a man, blond hair, blue eyes, thick neck, small head, wide smile. "My advice?" Drew continued, leaning closer but not lowering his voice. "Don't offer to shake hands unless you enjoy having your fingers crushed in a vice."

The big man nodded and waved a hand the size of a small shovel. I waved back but didn't offer to shake.

Schneider smiled. "Don't take any notice of him, Sarge."

So there we were. A Scotsman, an American, a Jamaican, a Frenchman, and the rest English. I'd either landed a job in the UN, or it was the opening line of a very old joke. The most difficult part of my morning was going to be pretending not to remember their names or recognise who they were.

With this and other less official information—courtesy of Corky—I probably knew the OCTF members better than they knew each other, Freya included.

For example, the impeccably dressed DS Ian Cruikshank—'Rob' due to the first part of his surname—had recently left his wife to move in with a woman a mere ten years older than his daughter.

From her desk in the far corner, DC Hannah Goldstein—short brown hair, horn-rimmed glasses, brown eyes—blushed as she half-whispered a shy, "Hello."

DCs Harvey 'Bandage' Poltous and Freddie Bowen smiled at me and nodded, but said nothing.

The Frenchman, DS Xavier 'X' Delasse, wore leather trousers, white T-shirt, and motorcycle ankle boots. With a gunmetal-blue five o'clock shadow, dark blue eyes, and that French accent, he could probably make the ladies swoon from a mile away. As a biker, he acted as the team's point man on most of the inner-city tailing jobs. He'd been unavailable to follow Sunil Pradeep to the West Country on the day Juno died. Whether by luck or design, only Alpine knew. It wouldn't be diplomatic to ask. Not then. Maybe later, when we were all firm friends.

"What's your ride?" I asked, indicating the leathers.

"For work I use a discreet Honda CBR, but on my own time I have a Ducati Monster 1200 R. So beautiful, she could be a woman, you know." He grinned and the striplights dimmed in shame. "You are a biker, Philip?" He pronounced it 'Felipe'—real smooth. Manda would have be so impressed, I'd have had to mop her brow with a cold compress.

"Back in my single days. Had to give it up when I got married. My wife doesn't ride pillion and I don't do sidecars."

X gave me one of those mocking Gallic shrugs that suggested he'd never allow a woman to dictate his mode of transport, and I turned to Drew. "Which one's mine?"

He showed me to a clear desk next to where Rob Cruikshank sat. The office layout became clear. Three groups of three for a DS and two DCs, a couple of spares, and Hook's stand-apart teacher's arrangement.

"My advice?" Drew said, lowering his voice and hitching his thumb over his shoulder. "Keep well clear o' that one until Hookie gets used to seeing you around the place."

The desk he indicated, overflowing with the detritus of a copper's work—files, PC monitor, and family photos—clearly belonged to the late and much lamented, Richie Juno.

"Thanks again, Drew."

"Nae bother, Sarge."

I dropped the folder Freya gave me on my desk, draped my jacket on the back of the chair, and sank into it, stifling a sigh.

The chair wasn't too uncomfortable, but the desk was one of those metal, stamped-out-by-a-machine things. It was all sharp angles and minimal legroom that bites the knees the moment you slide the chair into the nook. Cold, unglamorous, and soulless, and in keeping with the rest of The Cage.

Chloe's desk faced mine. She kept it litter free, files in a tray, PC monitor squared away, and a photo of her parents. Nothing more.

With my back to the wall and desk facing towards the office, my view of the room couldn't have been better—except for the fact they were all looking at me. Clint Schneider nodded at my stick. "Hey Sarge, what happened with your leg?"

In the high-tech, European setting, his New York accent—softened by a decade of living in England—reminded me of something out of a British crime movie from the '70s. Back then, film producers often drafted in fading American stars to boost their box office.

I rested my forearms on the desk and made an apologetic face. "I don't like talking about it. Maybe later, over a beer."

Schneider nodded, and then, calm as you like, asked, "You fit for duty?"

His face was a mask, mine felt warm. My two fellow sergeants, Rob Cruikshank and X Delasse looked on in silence. The other DCs averted their eyes. No doubt about it, we were having what my mum would call 'a moment'.

The police isn't a military organisation; not quite. We're much more relaxed than that, especially when out of uniform, but we do have a hierarchy. I outranked Schneider and his question came perilously close to insubordination. If we'd been in a cartoon, he'd have been teetering on the edge of a cliff, rotating his arms anticlockwise, and hanging on with the nail of his big toe.

I didn't have long to decide how to play it.

Two options. Shrug it off and play the easygoing newbie trying to ingratiate himself within the team, or jump down the nosy Yank's throat. As a DS, one step away from promotion to inspector, I wasn't going to let the insult pass.

"Who do you think you're talking to, Detective Constable Schrödinger?" I didn't raise my voice, but the effect was the same as if I'd screamed.

Schneider's eyes widened. He snapped to a seated attention.

I stared at him until he squirmed, and then said, "Inquisition over now?"

He smiled awkwardly. "Sorry, Sergeant Cryer. I can be a nosy asshole sometimes. Meant nothing by it."

"Do you have any work to be getting on with?"

"Yes, Sarge."

"Don't let me stop you."

Red-faced, Schneider swivelled his chair around to face his desk and lowered his head. His shoulders no longer seemed quite so wide. Half hidden behind his computer monitor, Drew Mackay grinned and hid his thumbs-up from Schneider behind his monitor. The others were less subtle. Hannah Goldstein covered her mouth with a hand, her eyes bugged. Rob and X looked at each other and nodded, Bandage and Freddie returned to their work. Chloe smiled her encouragement.

Test passed? Time would tell.

Before I had time to open Freya's care package, Hook's raised voice from inside DCI Endicott's office marked a climax of their conversation. A barely muffled, "What the hell am I going to do with a bloody cripple?" made its way through the closed door. I toyed with the idea of marching into the office and joining their conversation, but how would that help me identify Alpine?

Chloe said, "Bloody hell," in sympathy, but I waved it away. I had other battles to fight, and DI Hook had a point. What *was* he going to do with a cripple? As a desk-bound DS, I'd be little more than a paper-shuffler until the NCA's medic gave me permission to hit the streets.

Moments later, the DCI's door opened and Hook marched out. He left the door ajar and returned to his desk.

"DS Cryer," he said without looking at me. "I don't have time for babysitting. Complete your housekeeping paperwork, keep your ears open, and catch up in your own time. Any questions, ask your partner." He waved a dismissive hand at me and graced Chloe with his full attention. "Chloe, over to you."

Chapter 10

Monday 16th September

I'd never seen anything quite like it. What a way to welcome a new member to the team. To say I was a little miffed at Hook's arrogant dismissal understated my reaction, big time.

Ordinarily, I'd have taken him to one side and had a 'quiet word' irrespective of the difference in our ranks, but creating a fuss wouldn't have helped anything. Instead, I said, "Thank you, sir," and hooked the handle of my stick over the arm of my chair.

"The rest of you, gather around and concentrate," Hook continued, and hit a button on his keypad.

The others turned to face Hook's desk and the huge screen on the wall behind him filled with thirty-six mugshots, some black and white, others in living colour. All but two were men, but I had to concentrate hard to tell the difference. Notes alongside each photo gave a brief bio: name, physical characteristics, distinguishing marks, last known address, major convictions, warrants outstanding, and recent suspected activity.

It didn't take me long to study the line-up on the whiteboard.

They were all hardened, violent offenders with extensive criminal records. Each had links to organised crime, were currently at large, and based in the Greater London area. And each had the credentials to form part of the bullion gang.

"Rob," Hook said, turning to the well-dressed ladies' man. "Where are we with the phone taps on the Martindale Crew?"

The Martindales occupied the top row of the grid. Six faces, each bearded, and each uglier that the last—including the matriarch, the fifty-nine year-old Rita Martindale, and yes, she did have a beard. None would make the cover of a beauty magazine, unless it happened to be published by the Farmer's Union. On the other hand, the man in the second picture, the battered and broken-nosed Roberto Martindale, stood a chance of winning Best Bulldog at Crufts.

DS Cruikshank answered. "Slowly, guv. I'm waiting for a magistrate to sign off on the documentation …"

While the team discussed the thirty-six villains on the e-board in order of possible involvement in what had become known as the Airport Bullion Robbery, or ABR, I opened Freya's welcome package. The envelope contained an A4-sized folder holding a thick wad of papers. A big red notice stamped at the top of each page read: Do Not Remove From Facility.

As though I would. Jesus, how much spoon-feeding did people think I needed?

The information on the sheets gave me my system access codes, a plan of both NCA buildings, and directions to my room in the accommodation block, the gym, and the refectory, which less pretentious organisations would call a canteen. It also held the usual pieces of paper required to complete the official housekeeping: annual leave application form; expenses chits; overtime forms; doctor's address; the next of kin contact details in case of injury; and a form demanding my inside leg measurement.

Okay, I made up the last one, but you get the picture. They really should have all that stuff online by now, but public servants love their paperwork.

"Sarge?" Chloe said.

"Yep?"

"You said to give you a hand with names. It's Clint Schneider, not Schrödinger," she said, pointing to the big American, huddled around Hook's desk with the rest of the team.

I winked at her. "Thanks, but I know. Perhaps I was being a little catty."

She frowned at me for a moment then folded her arms again and leaned back. "Oh, I get it. Schrödinger's cat. You was putting him in his place, right?"

"Couldn't help myself. But, that reminds me, I'll need to take notes to keep up. Got any paper?"

She took a fresh notepad and a cheap ballpoint from her desk drawer and handed them across. "You'll need to run a requisition past Freya. She's responsible for stationary—"

"Along with everything else around here by the sound of things. Thanks for this. I'll replace them soon as I can."

She paused again and I had the impression she wanted to tell me something but didn't know how I'd take it. A new partnership always takes time to bed in.

"Something you wanted to say?"

"The notepad, Sarge. You're not allowed to take it out of the building if it contains sensitive information."

"Chloe," I said, leaning forward and staring into her dark brown eyes, "let's get a few ground rules sorted before we start off on the wrong foot, eh?"

She stiffened and placed her hands flat on the desk. I guessed to avoid making fists. "Yes, Sarge?"

"I may be new here, but I'm not so green I'm cabbage coloured. I do know how to treat official information. Okay?"

"Yes, Sarge."

"If there's something I need to know, spit it out. I don't bite and I'll always listen to advice. Don't necessary follow it, mind."

She nodded.

"How long have you worked here?" I asked.

"Since they opened the building. I'm a fixture."

She slid a glance towards Hook that would have told me nothing had I not already known the DI had blocked her promotion to sergeant six months earlier. His evaluation report stated—in bald terms—that she was not yet ready to lead a team and might never be ready.

"So, you know where all the bodies are buried?"

She chuckled. "There ain't no bodies here but there's plenty of skeletons in plenty of cupboards."

"Great, perhaps we'll get to the bones of the matter over lunch," I continued over her groan. "Meanwhile, show me how to navigate this system. For example, where d'you keep the active case files?" I pointed to my screen.

"One sec, Sarge."

Still seated, she walk-rolled her chair around to my side of the desk.

At the desk beside us, Bandage told Hook about another potential candidate for the ABR crew, Frankie 'Spider' MacManus, an expat Geordie and second-storey man—hence his nickname. A known associate of the Martindale crew, Spider had dropped out of sight and hadn't used his mobile phone for the best part of a week.

Hook considered the information significant and gave Bandage and Hannah the urgent task of finding the aforementioned Spider. Desk research only, mind. No point schlepping around London until they had something definite to work with.

I kept one ear on their ABR investigation as Chloe walked me through the system architecture. To keep up the pretence, I asked loads of idiot questions, took plenty of notes, and spent far more time than I needed to familiarise myself with the access protocols. I wanted to gauge her technical expertise as much as hide my own. Hers was pretty good, close to expert.

"What are those green flags all about?" I asked, referring to thirteen file names on the screen.

She cut her hands over my keyboard. "Wouldn't go anywhere near them until you was invited."

"By whom?"

"Bee, I mean DCI Endicott."

"What's so special about them?"

"They're random files Richie opened before he ... you know. They've been sequestered. Standard, procedure when a cop dies in the line of duty. Bee would go ape-shit if she found you reading them. If you want my advice guv, stay well clear."

I leaned closer to her and lowered my voice to a near whisper.

"Don't call me guv or boss. In private, I'm Phil. In public, I'm Sarge. Okay?"

"Righto."

"So, what cases are we working? I'm guessing DCI Endicott has allocated us a bunch of crap to cut our teeth on?"

Chloe shook her head emphatically and turned again to look at DI Hook. "Billy deals out the case assignments. As you can tell by her absence now, Bee don't usually involve herself with running the Task Force day-to-day. She takes more of an overview role and runs interference between us, the brass, and the peasants."

Chloe couldn't hide the embarrassed blush. Heat beat off her in waves.

"Peasants?" I said. "You mean the regional forces, like my old muckers in the Midlands Police?"

She played with a ring on her right pinkie finger and scrunched up her face. "Yeah, sorry, Sarge. Don't mean no offence. It's a term of endearment really."

I turned my attention back to my screen. "No need to feel uncomfortable, DC Holder. I don't suppose the NCA's nickname is any less offensive."

"Really? What they call us in the sticks?"

I looked at her sideways and kept my face straight. "Arrogant, over-resourced arseholes," I said and added a shrug. "Still. I'm one of you now, so 'peasants' it is."

She smiled again, big and wide.

"Talking about Bee," she said, "I'd have expected her to be all over something as high profile the ABR case."

"Maybe she's liaising with the Met."

"Could be. She knows loads of faces over at The Yard. I expect she'll come out of her office soon enough."

"While I finish my housekeeping"—I lifted Freya's pile of forms—"you might as well earwig the ABR operation."

"Thanks, Sarge, but I've been doing that anyway."

She returned to her desk and I made busy with pen and paper. It didn't take long for my right hand to tire. I don't often resort to writing.

By twelve-thirty, Hook had referred to me as 'The Gimp' twice, and he did so without bothering to lower his voice too much. The hell with office discipline and the proper chain of command, if he did it one more time, I was going to limp across to his desk and ram my walking stick up his arse.

Or perhaps not.

I had a job to do and being arrested for assault with a deadly weapon on my first day wouldn't help me complete the task. On the other hand, the mental image of Hook skewered on the end of my walking stick like a pencil eraser made me feel a whole lot better.

At one o'clock, Chloe stood and tapped her watch. "Don't know about you, Phil, but I'm starving. Fancy a spot of lunch?"

I lowered my pen, flexed cramping fingers, and put on my serious face. "DC Holder, it won't take you long to learn that I'm always hungry."

Again with the quick smile, she said, "Don't expect much, but as far as canteens go, ours ain't bad. Hot, filling, and inexpensive."

"What more could a poor overworked and underpaid cop want? Lead on, Detective Constable. Lead on."

I grabbed the would-be skewer and made it to my feet with the fluid grace of a pensioner taking his first yoga class.

As Chloe and I walked towards the mantrap, I was surprised when the others rose and joined us, grabbing jackets, and chatting about the latest moves in the ABR investigation. In a similar situation at the SCU, we'd have eaten at our desks. The OCFT was proving to be an interesting change of pace.

The big American fell into line beside me and cleared his throat. "Sarge, you know what I asked earlier? I was being an asshole. I apologise. Are we cool?"

"Yep, we're cool, DC Schrödinger. It's already forgotten."

I waited for him to correct my naming error, but he didn't, and I allowed Chloe to explain while we waited for Rob, X, Hannah, Drew, and Freddie Bowen to suffer the escape procedure.

By the time Clint, Chloe, and I had received our EMP exposure, the others had collected their things from the lockers and were making their way along the corridor. All bar Hannah and Freddie had noses buried in mobiles, no doubt checking for missed messages. How they avoided bumping into each other, I'll never know.

The last one left, I keyed my numbers into my locker pad, but substituted '4' for the final number. The display changed from green *LOCKED*, to red *FAILED*, and bleeped a sarcastic alarm.

"Damn it," I said and tried again with the same result.

Schneider smiled and shook his head. "Don't worry, Sarge. I did the same thing myself on my first day."

"What's the drill?" I said, forcing a forlorn expression onto my face.

"You need to go sign a requisition form and hope Freya's still at her desk."

"And if she isn't?"

"You'll have to wait until she's back from lunch."

"But my wallet's in there and I'm bloody hungry."

"No probs, Sarge," Chloe said, her grin sympathetic, "I'll stump up … this time."

I mumbled a chastened, "Thanks", and followed them to the lifts and then to the ground floor and across to the canteen in the other block, happy to be the butt of their merriment. We caught up with the rest of the team and stood behind them in the lunch queue.

As with every police canteen I'd ever been in at feeding time, the place heaved with noisy uniformed and plain-clothed officers. While we shuffled towards the serving counter, Schneider told the tale of my naming *faux pas*.

"Schrödinger's Cat," said Bandage, laughing. "Brilliant. Why didn't I think of that? What do you reckon, guys? Clint's got himself a new handle. Howdy, Cat."

He slapped the big guy on the shoulder and that was that. Schneider accepted his new nickname with good grace—not that it mattered. The rules of moniker creation don't allow people to choose their own.

We took a long table at the far end of the room next to a window with a lovely view of the rail tracks. Trains thundered past at regular intervals, but the triple glazing did a reasonable job at deadening the noise.

In keeping with my new and hard-won health regime, I chose the chicken salad option, a large bottle of water, and added a banana and an apple for dessert. Yum. When Chloe paid for me, the Cat explained why, to the sarcastic and ribald amusement of the others.

Hook didn't join us in the canteen, which neither surprised nor upset me. Whenever possible, the aggressive DI spent his lunchtimes in the gym pounding bags and throwing weights around. I planned to spend some quality time working out, but in the evenings and without an audience.

"What's an American doing working for the UK's version of the FBI," I asked while Schneider attacked his double-burger and fries.

"Long story."

Some of the others gave up huge theatrical yawns and continued eating and keying mobiles while the Cat started in with his life story.

"My folks split up when I was still in junior high. Mom worked for the State Department and accepted a job in the London Embassy. I sort of fell in love with the place and settled here permanently. Wanted to be a cop since I was a kid. Thought carrying a gun would be cool. Ha, go figure."

Drew, sitting next to the American, stopped chewing his cheese and tomato sandwich long enough to say, "Go on, Cat. Tell him the whole story ye big softie."

Schneider grimaced and hesitated. I took a sip of water, giving him time.

"Aw, hell," he said. "I fell in love with a British gal. We got married when I was nineteen. Couldn't up and leave her, right?"

"She didn't fancy going back to New York with you?"

"Nope and I don't blame her. New York ain't London."

He had two kids about the same age as mine and commuted to work from Pinner, north west London. A one-way trip of nearly an hour. Didn't fancy that, which is one of the many reasons I'd never actually apply for a job in London. On a bad traffic day in Birmingham, my drive to work takes less than twenty minutes.

Accompanied by the bored groans of the rest of the table, Harvey Poltous explained that his handle, Bandage, came from the word poultice—a traditional remedy. Evidently, in the days before high street chemists, people would boil herbs and bran, wrap up the porridge in a cloth bandage, and use it to reduce soreness and inflammation. Who knew?

While the rest of us chatted and got to know each other a little better, Hannah and Freddie Bowen sat at the far end of the dining table eating a green salad and a toasted cheese sandwich respectively. They barely said two words the whole time. Fair enough, they smiled at the right times and responded to direct questions, but neither led the conversation. Hannah's reserve could be put down to shyness, but Freddie's quiet and sad-eyed demeanour had an altogether different origin. If my forty-five-year-old wife had been diagnosed with early-onset Alzheimer's, I'd be miserable too.

I'd just peeled my banana when a huge roar from the far corner of the refectory silenced the rest of the crowd and made us all turn towards the noise.

A large dark-haired constable sitting at one of the tables below the wall-mounted TV pointed up and shouted, "Hey look, it's Robby and Tel!" The officer on his right threw a piece of bread at the screen, and the men flanking them cheered.

The TV image showed a rear view of two uniformed police officers disappearing through the main entrance of the Old Bailey—the Central Criminal Court of England and Wales. They escorted a civilian who hid his face behind a folded newspaper. A female reporter spoke into a mic sporting a BBC News label. I couldn't hear what she said, but the tickertape banner running along the foot of the picture told of the latest events in the Trojan Horse Case, the so-called Trial of the Century.

> *"For security reasons, Judge Driscoll is hearing the case 'in camera' ... The jury will be sworn in today ..."*

"What's going on there?" I asked Chloe.

Eyes wide, she asked, "You ain't heard of the Trial of the Century?"

Rob chimed in with, "Don't you get the BBC in the frozen north?"

"Yes, and these days we have electricity and indoor plumbing, too," I said, staring hard at him. "The Trojan Horse Case. A hitman turning Queen's evidence to expose five of his high-profile clients. The media's in a feeding frenzy. What I meant was, why is the NCA involved in the Met's biggest case for decades?"

Rob leaned closer. "UK Protected Persons Service," he said tapped the side of his nose. "Say no more."

I nodded. "Okay, understood."

After lunch, I separated from the team and headed for the ground floor where Freya did the business with my locker code. She didn't gloat about my forgetfulness half as much as the rest of the team had done over lunch.

I fixed a patient smile in place while she gave me a quick lesson in memory mind mapping—and how to memorise things by creating a journey and using visual cues. I thanked her and promised to try my best in future.

Chapter 11

Monday 16th September

Shortly after regaining my seat in The Cage, DCI Endicott beckoned to me from her office doorway.

She had shoulder length grey hair tucked back behind her ears, no earrings, blue eyes. Dowdy and in her late forties, she wore a loose-fitting but expensive trouser suit, and would blend into most crowds. She pointed me to one of two visitors' chairs and took her place behind the desk—shiny white laminate top, ultra modern, and far more expensive than the ones in Cage. Had she bought it herself, and if so, did that tell me anything about her? Not sure.

She smiled and we shook—hand small, grip firm.

"DS Cryer. Sorry I couldn't do the meet and greet this morning, but you understand why?"

"No worries, ma'am. Chloe's been looking after me." I deliberately passed over any reference to DI Hook.

We sat and I avoided sighing with relief as the pressure on my knee eased.

The office was larger than I'd imagined from the outside. A large window overlooked the red brick buildings on the other side of Tinworth Street. Bookshelves lining the far wall were filled with the reading material required of senior officers: reference books; procedural manuals; hardbound copies of the Police and Criminal Evidence Act 1984; and text books of differing subject matter. I'd read most of them and they all look well-thumbed.

A whiteboard attached to the wall beside her desk sported a holiday calendar, reminder notes, and an organisation chart. Curiously, she had yet to remove DS Juno's name, which piqued my curiosity. Had she left it as a mark of respect, or was it an oversight? More to the point, what did DI Hook think when he saw the name each time he entered her office?

To me, it smacked of a lack of empathy, or absent-mindedness.

David would never have been so thoughtless as to leave the name in place. He'd have removed it and, as a mark of respect, would have made a ceremony of the process.

The DCI hit enter on her keyboard. The light reflecting from the monitor highlighted her crow's-feet and puffy skin. She narrowed her eyes while reading. A visit to the optician was in order, but no way I'd suggest it during our first meeting. Not my place to offer advice to a superior officer unless they specifically asked for it.

"Any developments with the ABR case?" I asked to break the extended silence.

She sat up straight. "Not in the past hour. My phone's been ringing hot all morning. The Met hates asking us for help and hates it even more when we don't come up with anything rapid-quick. They're facing a serious grilling by our friends in the media, and I've been asked to attend the press conference."

"Good luck, ma'am. I don't envy you that pleasure." I threw a sympathetic smile.

"I'd love to be able to give them something more than platitudes. Can you think of anything we've missed?"

More interesting information for my data bank. She didn't know Hook had sidelined me from the case. How to answer without making it sound like a complaint? Not a good idea to moan about the DI on my first day. A platitude seemed in order.

"Not at the moment. I'll have a ponder, ma'am."

"Phil, when we're in The Cage, we can be less formal. Call me, Bee. Ma'am makes me feel so old."

"Yes, ma'am … Bee. Was there anything else?"

"How's it going so far?"

"Not bad. Won't take me long to pull myself up to speed. I'll stay late and read up on the active cases. Nothing better to do in the evenings, so I might as well spend them here."

She rested her hands on the arms of her chair and stared at me in silence. I waited.

"What exactly are you doing here, Phil?"

"Excuse me?"

Uh-oh. I didn't like the direction she was heading but tried not to let it show on my face.

"It's a simple enough question. From what I've read of your file, you and DCI Jones were pretty tight. It seems you were in line to fill the vacant DI's job in the SCU. What happened?"

After a second's pause, I sighed, rubbed my knee, and frowned—using only a fraction of my acting skills. After we'd locked up Alpine, I'd consider applying for an Equity card.

"The accident happened."

"But you're on the mend according to your medical records. And faster than anyone expected." Her eyes turned to her screen again, which I imagined showed my personnel file—my Corky-doctored personnel file.

I pointed at the monitor. "Have you read the report on the Raymond Collins arrest?"

She nodded.

"Then you'll know that I disobeyed DCI Jones' direct order when I climbed out that window and started clambering over the rooftops."

"And?"

"Well …" Hesitating for effect added to my dramatic range. "DCI Jones is a stickler for the rules. The minute I was out of medical danger, he all but told me to sling my hook and find another job. Said he couldn't trust me anymore but would still give me a bang up reference."

Her eyebrows twitched. "That's a little harsh."

"Agreed, but DCI Jones interpreted my actions as insubordination. Which, technically, they were, but in the heat of the chase, I couldn't let Collins escape. He was going to kill again."

"Collins is in Broadmoor Hospital now?"

"Yep. The judge promised the victim's family he'd never see freedom, but you and I both know that's a crock. The murdering arsehole will probably be out in a few years. Excuse the language, ma'am."

"Not to worry. I've heard worse." She swivelled her chair and faced the screen again. "Okay, let me pull up this file."

She tapped on the keyboard and read something before looking at me again. "According to HR, I'm required to give you the full one-hour welcome spiel, but you can read a brochure as well as anyone, and I have other things to do. The NCA's Charter will be in the welcome pack Freya gave you. Read it. If you have any questions, my door is always open, except when it's shut."

Nice one. I didn't expect a sense of humour.

"Thanks, ma'am."

"In a nutshell," she said, "our job is to target serious and organised criminals who present the highest risk to the UK."

"No different to every other police force in the country, then?" I said, adding what I hoped was a disarming smile.

She ignored my comment and moved her mouse. "I see you don't have a firearms certificate."

"No. I leave the shooting to the action men and women. Falling through the roof was a cock-up I don't plan to repeat."

"I see," she said and her brows twitched again, too subtle to call it an actual frown. "That's not a problem. We've plenty of ongoing cases you can help out with until the FMO signs you fit." She paused and turned to face me again. "Chief Superintendent Knightly suggested I allocate you DS Juno's caseload, but I thought that would prove ... impolitic."

"DI Hook did send out a few—how can I say this diplomatically—negative vibes."

"Give him time. He's a damn fine officer, but he's hurting at the moment."

"Yes, ma'am."

From what I'd seen of DI William Hook so far, the description 'damn fine officer' didn't exactly spring to mind. He'd have to work bloody hard to prove his worth as a leader after the way he'd treated me so far. I'm a reasonable enough guy, but don't come to me for any of that turn-the-other-cheek bollocks.

"At least he and DS Juno's family have had some closure. Sundeep Pradil won't be hurting anyone else."

"Sunil Pradeep," she corrected.

"Yes, that's right. Sorry, Bee. I'm not brilliant with names, but I'm working on it."

"Try harder. No one here's going to forget that man's name in a hurry." She blew her nose on a tissue taken from a box on the shiny desk. "DI Hook has teamed you up you with DC Holder, I understand."

"That's right."

"Excellent. Chloe's a good, steady officer. Ask her to show you around the IT system."

"She's already done that. Your database isn't all that different from the PNC or HOLMES2. Maybe more up-to-date and a little faster, but it won't take me long to familiarise myself with the layout."

She read from her screen again. "It says here that you have a reasonable grasp of IT. I imagine that's why your application was fast tracked. Richie was pretty good, too."

That nugget hadn't made it into DS Juno's personnel record. I filed the information away in my think-about-it-later folder. Had he found something on the system to point him toward Alpine?

"Any particular case you'd like me to start on?"

"Actually, there is. Spend a couple of days reading up on a man called John Dryden Carney."

I jotted the name in my notepad. "There's a case file on him?"

Bee's eyes hardened. "It takes up some space on the servers. Carney is pond scum, but we've never been able to pin anything serious on him. According to the man's official company records, he owns a couple of dozen buy-to-let properties along the south coast from Brighton to Margate. He's converted most of them into what he calls hostels and bedsits, but they're little more than slum dwellings set up to house immigrants and asylum seekers. Believe it or not, East Sussex Council pays rent on some of his rooms. He even pays taxes on them, but that's not the part of his business we're interested in."

She straightened her shoulders and took a breath before continuing.

"John Carney's a people trafficker. He preys on the weak and the vulnerable. Everyone knows it, but we can't find the proof. With hundreds of thousands of displaced persons in transit camps around Europe these days—Africans, Afghans, Syrians, as well as economic migrants from Eastern Europe—there are rich pickings for unscrupulous operators like Carney. Many of the people who pass through his hands are young and most are unregistered. Some disappear altogether.

"In the past eighteen months, we've helped organise four separate joint operations with the Sussex and Kent Police Forces. We found nothing more serious than a few health and safety violations. The man didn't install enough smoke and carbon monoxide alarms. He earned a few thousand pounds worth of fines, damn it. The man's laughing at us."

The depth of anger in her voice surprised me. Carney had certainly pushed Bee's buttons. She must have picked up on my reaction because she continued with more control.

"When our last raid with the Sussex Police drew a blank, Carney set his solicitors on us claiming harassment. They threatened a lawsuit and the IPCC agreed he had a case. They warned us off Carney. Bloody idiots. Officially, we can't touch him. Unofficially, it's another matter."

The reason for Bee's anger became clear. The Independent Police Complaints Commission must have issued an official warning to the OTCF, which had humiliated her, and hamstrung future operations against Carney.

She leaned forward and fixed me with a fierce glare. "That's where you come in, Phil. Read the Carney files and see whether you can come up with something we've missed, but keep it quiet. Understand?"

"I do."

"It was one of the cases Richie Juno and Chloe Holder worked on together. They came up empty, and that's why I want you to cast fresh eyes over the file."

My senses tingled. Bee was giving me permission to access to one of Juno's cases, despite Chloe's dire warnings of Hook's reaction. The situation couldn't be better. She'd given me something to sink my investigative teeth into while I become part of the scenery and did my other stuff in the background. Perfect.

"I'll do my best."

"Perhaps you can find out why Carney's leading such a charmed life."

Bloody hell. She'd opened another door. It would have been rude of me not to step right in.

"You think someone's tipping him off?"

"Local police, you mean?" She wagged her head from side to side. "It's possible but we couldn't find any obvious suspects. And believe me, we did look."

"Okay, I'll keep that in mind while reading the file."

"Excellent. Thanks." She nodded towards the door. Interview over.

I left Bee's office relieved at having dropped her to the bottom of my suspect list. After all, if she were Alpine, would she really draw attention to the possible existence of a dirty cop? Of course she wouldn't. One suspect down, nine to go.

The relief didn't last long. By the time I closed the door behind me and took in The Cage once more, the doubts set in. Had I just witnessed a clever example of bluff and counter-bluff? Reluctantly, I moved Bee back to the top of the list.

Damn.

In the job half a day and the only thing I knew for certain was that I knew nothing for certain.

Chapter 12

Monday 16th September

On the way back to my desk, I scanned the e-board with its thirty-six mugshots and associated bios, looking for changes since the morning. There were none, but the screen's layout reminded me of a card game my Gramps taught me called *Pelmanism*. I've also heard it called *Concentration* or *Memory*.

It's simple enough. Shuffle a deck of cards, lay them face down on a table, and players take turns to flip two cards at a time, searching for pairs. At first, it's a random game of chance, but later on, becomes a game of memory. After turning over all the cards, the player with the most pairs wins. Everyone soon got bored when I kept winning. Gramps and I only played the game a few times, but all the while, he wore this strange expression, and kept calling me his 'little genius'.

The point to my trip to the past is that early in my recuperation from the operation, I spent a load of time locked in my home office reading internal police reports from all over the country. Some people do crossword puzzles, others read books, I study police files. Most people would find it boring, but I love it. So sue me.

As I said, the mugshots were laid out like a game of Pelmanism, and I tried to form matching pairs. It didn't work, no maps formed even when I added snippets from my memory banks. Something was missing.

The top row contained the aforementioned Martindale family, the ones who wouldn't need prosthetic makeup to form the cast of the latest zombie flick. They held no immediate interest and, to begin with, I ignored them.

In the second row, I recognised two faces from national police notices. Based in north London, Tony Bennett—no, not the singer—and Alfie Knowles had form for armed robbery. They worked as a team and neither had an aversion to using extreme violence. In the summer of 2011, the Hertfordshire Constabulary gathered enough evidence to make a case against the pair, but had to drop the charges when three witnesses recanted their testimony. The investigation team claimed witness intimidation, but couldn't prove it.

Here's where the Pelmanism thing came into play.

Alfie Knowles had gone to school with the youngest Martindale boy. This fact surprised me for two reasons. First, for either of these bozos to have attended school would stun anybody who knew anything about them. Second, if there was such an obvious association between the two gangs, why hadn't the computer searches flagged the link?

Moving on.

A round face on the fourth row belonged to Harry Hardiman, aka 'Hard' Harry, whose main claim to infamy was as an importer of illegal arms. He specialised in finding new homes for Eastern European weaponry: Kalashnikovs, Tokarevs, and Makarovs, among others.

Another mugshot proved interesting—William Wallis, suspected of fencing high value items, including jewellery and bullion. Yep, that's right, bullion.

On the same e-board, we had a family of thugs, a pair of armed robbers, an arms importer, and a dealer in gold bullion. The potential links slapped me in the face so hard, I nearly jerked my head back and shouted, "Eureka!". Instead, I stayed silent.

And there you have it, the human element. Say what you like about the value of technology, but as the boss says, no one should ignore the human factor.

All I'd done was complete a quick scan, add a little background information, mix in some intuition, and I'd come up with a potential association with five of the thirty-six faces.

Something didn't smell right.

If I'd spotted the pattern so quickly, why hadn't anybody else? More to the point, why hadn't the NCA's top-dollar, bells-and-whistles database found the same thing?

The whole mental process had taken me no more than a minute or two. The rest of my new team were so engrossed in their own worlds, I doubt any of them even noticed that I'd stopped to look at the e-board.

Ask detectives why they do the job and most of them will tell you they love the thrill of the chase, and I'm the same. With more than a trace of excitement accelerating my heart rate, I sauntered to my desk and navigated to the SCUD's search template. The Serious Crime-Users Database—SCUD. Oh, how the geeks love their acronyms.

It's relatively easy to design search algorithms to identify associations and patterns, but they only work if the links are clear and the basic data used is accurate. There's an old IT acronym, GIGO—garbage in, garbage out. How true that is.

Human error.

It happens all the time, even in police work. Or perhaps, especially in police work. All it takes is a simple typo and you can lose the association between two criminals. Lose one link and the pattern dissolves, and without the pattern you lose the trail.

Human error.

Yep, a simple little transcription error—a typo.

Someone somewhere had changed the metadata label on the file ID from William Wallis to William Willis. The header page and bio remained unaffected, but deep in the bowels of the SCUD, the typo fractured the links and the searches came back with nothing more than a few vague associations. Not enough to ring any alarm bells or light anyone's fire.

But was it really human error, or had I just found my first trace of Alpine doctoring the records intentionally? I'd have to think on that later, when I had more time.

With a few simple keystrokes, I made a temporary correction to the typo, and ran a new search. Starting with William Wallis, I added 'recent activity', 'known associates', and 'telephone surveillance' to the string. Within seconds, the SCUD spewed out a stream of information and all of it pure gold bullion.

Pardon the pun.

The telephone surveillance records were particularly informative. I filtered the information down to a smaller list of possibilities. After another glance at the e-board, I added the name Viggo Martindale to the search template and bingo, I'd found a direct trail to, and a potential location for, 'Hard' Harry Hardiman. Simple as that. It had taken me less than an hour to work a breakthrough in a case I had nothing to do with.

The next part wasn't so simple. How could I deliver the information to DI Hook without him knowing it came from me? That proved much trickier.

Of course, I could have just walked up to the guy, tapped him on the shoulder, and told him outright. But he'd have asked how, in the tens of thousands of names flying around the system, I'd noticed one typo when nobody else had.

A conundrum.

It took almost as long to work out the way as I'd taken to find the trail, and the answer came in the guise of one of Manda's favourite actors, Mel Gibson. No accounting for taste, I suppose. Either way, I have to give dear old Mel full credit for showing me the way through my maze. My new Scottish friend, Drew Mackay, who occupied the desk next to Chloe, also played his part.

I returned the database to its earlier condition, complete with the typo, and logged out. Later, when I had the place to myself, I planned to erase my audit trail from the system, but that would have to wait. Meantime, I trusted to luck that no one would spot my interference. Nothing in their personnel files suggested that any of them had the requisite IT skills. On the other hand, personnel files could be massaged, if you had the same skills. A circular argument I couldn't answer at the time.

Time to act.

"Chloe," I called, "do we have direct access to the DVLA database without having to jump through any legal hoops?"

She looked up from her screen. "Yep. What info you looking for? I'll find it for you."

"If you do that, how will I learn to do it myself?"

She leaned forward as though preparing to stand, but I waved her back down. "Stay there, I'll come to you. Need the exercise."

I swivelled my chair, reversed around to her side, and 'accidentally' bumped against Drew's chair.

"Sorry, Drew," I said, "I need a licence to drive this thing."

The young Scot sucked air through his teeth and rubbed his elbow. "No bones broken, Sarge."

Chloe shifted her chair along to give me room, and I took my place beside her, facing Hook's desk and the e-board.

Subtle stuff. Sometimes I surprise myself.

"How's it going?" I asked Drew, just to be polite.

"Not well. Odds are that at least one person on that screen is part of the ABR crew, but proving it's no' easy."

"The Dirty Three Dozen?"

That seemed to tickle the young Scot. He smiled. "Nice one, Sarge. DI Hook's talking to the Met and Rob's trying to get a warrant for a phone tap on the Martindales' land lines, but the magistrate's holding out on us. Fucking jobsworth." His cheeks, naturally red as though he'd recently stepped out of a sauna, deepened a couple of shades. "Sorry, Sarge, it's just so bloody frustrating."

"I guess he quoted 'due process' and 'burden of proof'?"

Drew nodded. "Something like that."

Still looking at the e-board, I asked, "Are they all part of the same gang?"

"No, Sarge. The Martindales are the ones on the top row. The others are random best potential fits for the crime."

"So what did Braveheart do to deserve his place on the list?"

Drew frowned. "Braveheart?"

Chloe looked at me and then up at the board.

"Bottom row, second from the left, William Wallis. He was that famous countryman of yours, yeah? Beat the English at the battle of Culloden or some such?"

I sat back and watched Drew's mobile face change as he worked through the problem. The film in question, *Braveheart*, was released in 1995. At the time, Drew would have been about six, but I doubt there's a red-blooded Scotsman alive who hasn't seen the film at least once. No doubt, I was on safe ground.

Chloe's expression remained quizzical, but Drew finally made the connection. "Ah, I see what you mean, but you're wrong. Braveheart was Sir William Wallace." He spelled the name for us. "W-A-L-L-A-C-E. That there is William Wallis. He's English and look at him."

I did. This William Wallis was bald, had three chins, and looked less like a Scottish military hero than my grandmother. Mind you, get between Nan and her grandchildren and you'd see a warrior through to her bones.

"See what you mean," I said. "My mistake."

"Aye. We gi' ye Sassenachs a full-on drubbing that day," Drew said, in his element. He winked and shook his head at the picture. "As though that guy could ever be mistaken for Scot, the fat-faced hoon." Drew straightened his tie and sat up straight. "And by the way, Sarge, William Wallace defeated the English army at the Battle of Stirling Bridge, in September 1297. Culloden was four hundred years later."

"Is that right?" I said as though it were news to me. To be more precise, the Battle of Culloden took place four hundred and forty-nine years after Stirling Bridge, and the Scottish lost that one big time, but I kept that knowledge to myself. No value in antagonising the young Scot.

"Thank you for the history lesson, Simon Schama," I said.

"Who?"

"Exactly. Get on with your work, DC Mackay," I said, smiling and turning my back to him.

I'd sown the seeds. If they took too long to germinate, I'd have to add a little water. Certain information—like Hard Harry's potential whereabouts—had a shelf life and I couldn't afford to have the gun-runner on the loose for too long. No telling what mischief he and his illegal arms business would foment.

The time on Chloe's PC showed 15:17. I gave Drew an hour.

"Okay, Chloe, the DVLA."

With the patience of Saint Monica, Chloe walked me through their access to the vehicle licence number search routine. I hated playing dumb, but it was necessary camouflage. After a thorough briefing with me trying to avoid looking at Drew and giving him a prompt, I thanked her and returned to my desk. Time to take an interest in my own caseload. Once again, I signed into SCUD, called up the John Carney case file, and started reading.

It didn't take me long to realise the Carney case wasn't going to help me find Alpine, but the bastard did need stopping, and deserved some of my time.

#

A full nineteen minutes before my arbitrary deadline—Drew shot back in his seat and yelled, "Oh my God!". He raised a hand and waved at Rob Cruickshank. "I've bloody found them."

Every head in the room turned to face the young Scotsman, mine included.

"Found who?" Rob asked.

"The ABR crew. At least, I think so."

"What you got there, Drew?" Hook shouted, his voice easily carrying over the background thrum of The Cage.

"A typo, guv. I swear to God. A bloody typo. Here look." He tapped at his keyboard and the mugshots on the big e-board faded away. He hit a few more keys and five photos appeared at the top of the screen; Viggo Martindale, William Wallis, Tony Bennett, Alfie Knowles, and Harry Hardiman. Below each, an extended bio emerged.

I listened to Drew's explanation with sense of pride. My boy was playing a blinder.

Drew spoke quickly, excitement speeding his words. He had a willing audience and took everyone through the timeline. "Once I noticed the typo and reran the search, it became obvious."

As he progressed the story, he added other documents to the screen to build his case. I'd seen the trail before, of course, but allowed his enthusiasm to carry me along.

"Look," he said, putting a telephone call log up on the screen below Harry Hardiman's photo. "Last Saturday at 17:53, Hard Harry phones the Palm Frond Pub on the Bell End Road, Northfleet."

Bandage and the Cat snickered at the name of the road, but Drew ignored them and carried on.

"The call lasts sixteen seconds. We can't tell what was said, because we didn't have phone taps in place. Anyhow, twenty minutes later, Tony Bennett"—Drew brought up another call log and placed it beneath the man's picture—"receives a call from the Palm Frond that lasts a little over three minutes. GPS tracking on the mobiles shows that Hard Harry, Bennett, and Knowles meet at the same pub and guess who joins the party?" Without waiting for an answer, Drew brought up yet another phone log and added a triumphant, "William Wallis and Viggo Martindale!"

Next, he dragged a street map onto the screen and traced the route—on fast forward—each mobile phone took for the rest of that Saturday night. Four of the signals never strayed far apart and ended up at an NCP car park three miles from London City Airport. At that point, midnight, each trace disappeared. The fifth trace, from Wallis' phone, ended up at his lockup beside the Thames.

"See that?" Drew said, almost shouting, "all four mobiles go dark at the same time." He paused a second and looked at each of his team. He had everyone's undivided attention and obviously loved it. I doubt he'd held the floor often in his short life. "And guess what happened four hours later?"

Hook answered first. "The Airport Bullion Robbery."

If Drew's smile had been any wider, his face would have split. "Exactly. We have three known armed robbers and one gun-runner within three miles and four hours of a gold bullion heist. And there's more." Once again, the Scotsman paused.

"Come on, son," Rob Cruikshank said. "Stop milking it."

"Sorry, Sarge." He didn't look sorry. "Before I found the typo, nobody picked up the relevance of the original meet, the Palm Frond."

"What about it?" This from Hook again.

With the flourish of a stage magician pulling his scantily-clad assistant out of a box, Drew enlarged the map and zeroed in on the pub, or more precisely, the industrial estate *behind* the pub. He hovered his cursor over a large building and clicked another icon. A satellite street view of the area appeared on the screen.

"See that factory?" Drew said to the whole group. "It's owned by Miller's Metals Ltd. And you'll never guess what they do for a living?"

Chloe answered. "Smelt metal into something that don't look like gold ingots?"

With his job done and his story told, a self-satisfied Drew Mackay folded his arms and relaxed into his chair. "Not officially," he said, calm as you like, "but I'd love to go take a look at what they're working on right now. What d'ye reckon, guv? Have we got enough for a search warrant and a phone tap now?"

"Oh, I think so, Drew. I really do," Hook answered, and for the first time since my arrival, he cracked a smile. It wasn't a pretty sight.

The excitement in the room ratcheted up by the second.

Freddie Bowen spoke next. "Anyone have an idea how long it would take to turn six hundred gold bars into something else?"

I answered. "Depends on the capacity of the foundry and what they're making. Anyone ever seen that old film, *The Lavender Hill Mob*, where they melted ingots into Eiffel Towers? Took them all weekend. Probably be quicker these days, though."

"Christ," Rob said, checking his watch, "it's only been twelve hours since the robbery. You don't reckon they're still at the foundry?"

Chapter 13

Monday 16th September

Tension in The Cage overpowered the background static as Hook built his strategy, arranged to meet an armed unit from the Metropolitan Police, and left for Miller's Metals Ltd. It had taken less than two hours to arrange the logistics. Mounting an armed operation on the fly wasn't easy, but having a DCI involved in the planning overcame many of the procedural challenges.

Bee, Chloe, and I stayed in The Cage, monitoring the away team's progress via the screen and the comms system.

At 17:23 Freddie, the OCTF's other deskbound team member, stood. "Damn it, I'd love to stay, but I'm already late. Sorry, Bee, but …" He shrugged and hurried to the mantrap.

Freddie started the exit sweep and checked his watch while the EMP charged. "Chloe, if they mop up the operation before midnight, will you give me a call?"

"Will do, Freddie."

I allowed him to clear the mantrap before asking Chloe a question to which I already knew the answer. "Leaving in the middle of an armed operation? What's that all about?"

"Freddie's hours are fixed. He works quarter-to-nine until five-fifteen. Special arrangement on account of his wife's condition. I'll tell you 'bout it later."

The journey to Northfleet took Hook and his team ninety minutes from leaving Tinworth Street. We watched every second on the road map playing on the big screen. Seven red blips representing the guys' signal trackers crawled southeast from the city centre. They ran into heavy evening traffic on the North Circular, more at the Dartford tunnel, and resorted to their lights and sirens.

We also had a live video feed from cameras attached to Hook, X Delasse, and Rob's armoured vests. We saw what they saw via individual windows on the whiteboard.

The whole thing was a touch surreal and not dissimilar to watching one of those fly-on-the-wall documentaries that follow a police operation. The prime difference being, we saw the action in real time. This made it intensely tedious until the away team reached the outskirts of Northfleet, where they turned off their blues and twos and approached the factory on silent running.

Using a combination of satellite imagery and the online Ordinance Survey map, Bee transmitted the images of the layout on the ground simultaneously onto Hook's laptop and the big whiteboard. The team leaders' personal cameras showed how the buildings looked in the early evening sun.

In a word, grotty.

Miller's Metals Ltd occupied a quiet corner of a near-derelict industrial estate to the north of Northfleet. Surrounded on three sides by a brick wall—three metres tall and topped with razor-wire—the industrial estate was accessible by road only through a pair of wrought iron, spear-topped gates.

The foundry itself stood three storeys tall, built of red brick with a black tiled a-framed roof, interspersed with four chimney stacks, each five metres high. One of the stacks emitted a steady stream of grey smoke.

"The gates are open," Chloe said. "Shows there's someone around this late in the evening."

Bee pointed at the screen. "That chimney's pouring smoke. Of course there's someone around."

Dozens of windows in the front face, filled with glass embedded with wire mesh, gave the place the decrepit air of a Victorian workhouse. Peeling paint added to the sense of a once-thriving business fallen on hard times. A concrete apron jutted from the front of the building—one metre tall and broken by a wide loading bay. On the left-hand side, a large black door allowed worker access.

The factory's only new feature came in the form of shiny metal roller shutters that defended the opening to the loading bay.

The satellite images showed that the factory backed onto the Thames, but a two-metre high chain-link fence prevented direct access to the river. The original owners would have used the Thames to ship its goods both west into London and east towards the continent, but modern road transport systems and the Channel Tunnel made that method obsolete. However, just in case, I had an idea.

I rolled my chair closer to Hook's desk.

"Bee."

She turned and released the press-to-talk button on the base of the mic stand to mute the sound. "Yes?"

"Might be a good idea to send someone around the back to make sure they don't have access to the river. It's high tide and that looks like an old jetty."

I pointed to one of the satellite stills, which showed a rectangular object jutting out from the back of the factory and dipping into the water.

Bee relayed the information to Hook, who sent X and the Cat, both carrying handguns, and wearing helmets and full body armour, to scout the rear of the building. Meanwhile, Hook and the others spread out on either side of the front gates and awaited the arrival of the Met's Armed Rapid Response Unit, SC&O19.

It's an old adage, but you can tell a lot about people by watching them working under stress. Bee sat still, eyes fixed on the big screen, issuing calm instructions, letting the action unfold. I stayed in my new position beside Bee, twiddling my walking stick. Chloe paced the floor behind us.

The wait was excruciating. If not for my damn knee, I'd have been with them and it hurt just as much to be sidelined. The time passed with the speed of glacial flow—an average of four-point-one centimetres per hour.

Our wait ended at 19:54.

The roller shutters at the loading bay started rising. Chloe stopped pacing and stood in front of the screen, careful not to obstruct our view. Bee leaned close to the mic and hit the PTT button again. "Billy? What's happening?"

Hook answered. *"A diesel engine just fired up. Looks like they're making a move, guv. Might have finished the smelting operation. How far away are the Met boys?"*

Chloe rushed back to her desk and hit a few keys. The satellite image on the lower left-hand quadrant of the whiteboard changed back to the route map. Two blue dots, marked SC&O19 1 & 2, crawled along the same stretch of Watling Street that had held up our team.

"Still at least twenty minutes out," she said, voice tense, lips thin.

Bee relayed the information to Hook.

On the screen, X's comms signal flashed as he activated his mic. *"There's a boat here, but it is too small to transport the gold. I see two men but cannot identify them. I fear they might be making ready to leave."* Even over the deadening effect of the radio comms, the Frenchman sounded cool, unflustered. *"What should I do?"* he asked.

"Are the men armed?" Bee asked.

"Impossible to tell from here. They're carrying small bags. Do you see the images?"

"Not clearly," said Bee.

X's video picture swayed as he moved closer to the rear of the factory. He and Schneider kept a row of dumpsters between them and the jetty. At one stage, the image shook so badly, it broke up completely, but recovered after X stopped moving. The two men by the boat became clearer, but not clear enough to identify their faces. Orange life jackets stood out sharp against their dark jeans, dark tops, and dark baseball caps.

At the front of the factory, Hook and Rob's video streams showed the metal shutters reaching the top of the doorframe. A white Mercedes Benz Sprinter, low on its springs, drove through the opening, and stopped near the edge of the apron.

"They're on the move, guv," Hook said. *"Any instructions?"*

"You heard DS Delasse's report about the boat?"

"Yes. But I don't have access to his video feed. Can you co-ordinate our moves from your end?"

"Will do, but if these guys are the ABR crew, they'll be armed, and they aren't afraid to shoot. Things could deteriorate quickly."

"Okay, gotcha. But these arseholes aren't going anywhere."

I glanced at the roadmap. The Met's ARU teams had reached the A2 exit for Northfleet but were still at least eighteen minutes out.

On Hook's screen, a man wearing a dark boiler suit jumped out of the Sprinter's passenger side and ran back to the factory. He closed the shutters and returned to the van. The images were HD clear. I asked Bee's permission before leaning across her and taking control of the keyboard. I scrolled the film clip back, took a screenshot of the passenger, and zoomed in on his face.

"That's Harry Hardiman," I said. "See the scar on the side of his neck?"

Chloe looked at me. "How d'you know he's got a scar?"

I frowned at her and shook my head aggressively. She needed to learn the right time to question her DS, and this wasn't it.

Bee shuffled her chair away to give me more room. Stuff the low-profile undercover bullshit. I'm a cop. No way I'd keep quiet if I could help. She activated the mic. "Billy, we have confirmation that the passenger is one of our targets. Do you receive me?"

"You sure, guv?"

She caught my eye.

I nodded and said, "Definitely."

"Confirmed. They are our targets."

"Right. What are your orders?"

We had seven armed colleagues facing at four, possibly five, armed and desperate men who had already shot two security guards. My heart rate hit the stratosphere and my attention flicked between the three video feeds, the roadmap, and Bee. Which way would she jump?

She was a DCI, but did she have the stones?

"We have to stop them, Billy. I don't want them getting anywhere near a civilian population. Can you hold them there until SC&O19 arrives?"

I held up ten fingers.

"Their ETA is ten minutes. Be careful."

"Yeah. We're on it."

Without wasting a second, Hook gave Bandage his orders, and the picture from Rob Cruikshank's camera showed the university professor sprinting to the team's Ford Galaxy. Rob's picture then moved to the left-hand side of the factory gates and stopped. The brick wall obscured part of the shot, but no one would ask Rob to stick his head out further to obtain a better view. We could still see the Sprinter van clearly enough.

Rob kept radio silence, but the lower part of his video showed him check the load readiness of his Glock 26. The dull, black pistol in his steady hand made me glad to be safe and sound in The Cage.

Phil Cryer, the coward? Absolutely. I didn't volunteer to be on the receiving end of a bullet. They don't pay detective sergeants well enough for that kind of shit.

Bee activated her mic again. "Xavier, ready to move on my mark?"

"*Oui, sorry, yes.*"

Even the cool Frenchman felt the tension.

"Billy," Bee said, "any sign of movement from the van?"

"No. The driver and passenger are shouting at each other. Can't hear what they're saying though. Now would be a good time. While they're distracted. Bandage is ready to block the gates with one of our cars and I'm pissed off with waiting for the Met boys to get here."

If she were a film director, Bee would have shouted, "Action," but she was more controlled than that. "Xavier," she said. "On my mark."

She studied all three digital pictures and then looked at me, a question in her eyes. I nodded encouragement.

Bee shouted, "Go, go, go."

The following ten minutes are a blur of audio-visual input from three body cameras and seven radios. After the event, I had to sort them into cohesive reports—the official one for the NCA and the Metropolitan Police, and the unofficial report for Knightly.

Sometimes, even my memory struggles, but I did my best to make sense of the action, if only for my reports to Knightly.

Camera #1 – DI Hook.

Four red dots appeared on the Mercedes' windscreen, two held steady on the driver's forehead, the other two alighted on Hard Harry.

From the cover of the security wall, Hook screamed at the men in the van. *"Armed police! Armed Police! You are surrounded. Exit the van slowly and place your weapons on the ground. Do it now!"*

Camera #2 – DI Delasse.

X's video stream did that shaky camera thing art house directors use to hide badly choreographed action scenes. Fractured images showed a fast-approaching jetty and boat. The two men in dark clothing turned towards the onrushing police officers and looked at each other. One dived into the vessel, a rigid inflatable boat, similar to the ones the Coastguard use for inshore lifeboats—very rugged, very fast.

The picture shake stopped as X reached the first of four steps leading down to the concrete jetty. He had a perfect angle to see into the RIB. His arms came into shot, holding his Glock 26 in a two-handed grip. The picture rose and fell in time with his rapid breathing.

"*Armed police. Get off the boat. Get out of the boat!*"

The man on the left raised his arms slowly while the other tried to start the motor. He looked comical trying to pull the ripcord of an outboard motor that refused to catch.

Camera #3 – DS Cruikshank.

The picture moved to the left, the wall moved to the right, and the view of the factory and the Mercedes became clear. Rob raised his weapon and held it level. Drew's gloved hands appeared to the right of the screen; they, too, held a Glock 26. The gun's muzzle, rock steady.

Camera #1 – DI Hook.
"*Armed police. Exit the van. Do it now!*"

The last thing I expected was compliance, but being faced with apparently overwhelming odds, the bravest of men can lose their will to fight. Add the red light of laser sights attached to Heckler & Koch MP5 machine pistols to the mix, and they can also lose bladder control.

Instead of taking off like a drag racer and charging at the exit gates in a squeal of burning rubber, the van's doors opened slowly and Hard Harry and his driver jumped out. They threw themselves flat to the ground, arms stretched out to the sides, hands empty, faces kissing concrete.

The roar of an engine grew and then stopped. The shadow of a car darkened the picture—Bandage had blocked the exit.

"*Where are the others?*" Hook roared to the prone men.

In The Cage twenty-two miles away, I felt the power in Hook's voice. For all Hard Harry and the driver knew, the whole of the Metropolitan Police force was lined up outside the wall ready to shoot. The final scene of *Butch Cassidy and the Sundance Kid* took up a small part of my mental view screen, but I pushed the image away.

Five men had taken part in the robbery, but we could only account for four.

Hook repeated his question adding, "*You, the driver, answer my question.*"

The man's head lifted. He said something but Hook's radio didn't pick it up.

"Billy," Bee said. "What did he say?"

"*He said there are only two of them out front,*" Hook answered. "*The others are still inside the building.*"

"Okay. He probably thinks we don't know about the two in the boat. There might be another in the back of the van. Hold your positions until the Met arrives," Bee ordered. "No heroics, Billy. Understood?"

Hesitation.

"*Understood,*" he said, reluctance in his voice clear.

Bee held her shoulders stiff. Her body quivered with tension.

Camera #2 – DI Delasse.

Slowly, X descended the steps to the jetty. His camera caught an occasional glimpse of Schneider, walking to his left and slightly in front. They closed on the RIB. The first man, hands still held high, looked into the camera for his close-up. Memories tumbled into place. The nose, crooked after a fight during his first spell in prison, slight cast to his left eye—Tony Bennett. His thin lips curved downwards in the dejected frown of a beaten man.

The man in the RIB stopped tugging at the ripcord and slumped onto the side of the boat, empty hands loose on his lap. He, too, faced the camera—Viggo Martindale.

Schneider stepped forward, weapon drawn. He grabbed Tony Bennett by the shoulder, turned him around, back to the camera, and started patting the bullion thief down while X trained his weapon on Martindale in the RIB.

"Stand up," X ordered, and raised the muzzle of his Glock.

Martindale pushed his hands against his thighs and stood. The boat wobbled as he shifted weight. He threw out his arms to counter the boat's movements. Schneider, still searching Bennett for weapons, had his back to X, but turned to look at what was happening in the boat.

Martindale dived forward, scrambling towards something in the RIB. X shouted, *"Stop!"*

Bennett's left arm dropped.

Information surfaced from a distant part of my brain and screamed a warning.

I jumped up, slapped Bee's hand away from the mic, and jammed my thumb on the PTT button. "Clint, watch out! His belt buckle is a knife."

Tony Bennett screamed. His arm shot down towards his waistband and he spun around. Something in his hand flashed in the fading light. The arm swung upwards in a vicious right-to-left arc.

Chapter 14

Monday 16th September

Job done, Bee, Chloe, and I were relaxing in the refectory waiting for the away team's return from Northfleet. Chloe hadn't stopped smiling at me since the end of the raid. If I were less modest, I might have imagined a little hero-worship in her exaggerated compliments related to my role in the raid's success.

Bee raised her coffee mug in salute. "Nice work, DS Cryer—Phil. Welcome to the team. You saved Clint a whole load of pain."

I returned her gesture and took a sip of coffee—made from one of those little plastic pots. Not quite freshly-roasted, but delicious nonetheless.

"Didn't do much," I said. "His reactions were lightning. Dare I say, cat-like?"

Chloe groaned. Bee threw her a questioning look and changed it to a facepalm when Chloe explained the origin of Clint's new nickname.

"And that uppercut he threw nearly took Bennett's head off," I added to deflect the attention away from me. "Made me feel like singing my head off ... Tony Bennett. Singing. Get it?"

"That's awful, Sarge. Please stop," Chloe said. "And while that's true enough, without your warning, the blade would have sliced him open, and X might have been distracted enough to let Viggo Martindale reach his gun. Christ knows what would have happened then. Brilliant, Sarge. How'd you know Bennett hides a knife in his belt?"

I took another slug of my drink, drawing out my response.

"Come on, Phil," Bee said. "Out with it."

"No secret, guys. I read it in his case file while you were arranging the raid. The belt buckle knife is Bennett's signature backup weapon. I guess *Mack the Knife* is his theme song."

"Jesus, Sarge. Will you lay off the singing references?" Chloe pleaded, lowering her can of cola to the table. "You read all them files in a couple of hours? That's hundreds of pages of information on those bad boys."

Shit. I needed to play things down a little.

"Don't be daft. I scan-read the first few and got lucky when some of the information stuck."

Bee checked her watch and stood. "They should be back soon. I'm going upstairs to do the initial debrief with Billy. No need for you to come back up. I'll see you in the morning."

Chloe and I stood, too.

"No way, Bee," I said. "I want to be there to hail the conquering heroes. Besides,"—I winked at Chloe—"I left my case upstairs and need my pyjamas, not to mention my toothbrush."

"That's interesting." Chloe said, frowning.

"What is?"

"I never saw you as the pyjamas-wearing type."

I'm not, but Chloe didn't need to know that. We left the canteen—sorry refectory—and headed for the lift.

#

Hook and the rest of the team arrived a little after 23:30 in a boisterous mob of back-slapping and raucous laughter. It took two sweeps of the EMP screening before they all entered The Cage.

Clint rushed to me and started pumping my hand so hard I worried he'd tear it off at the shoulder. "Thanks, Sarge. I owe you, big time."

"Don't worry about it, Cat. You'd have done the same for me."

"How the hell did you know about the knife?"

Chloe must have sensed my unease. She dragged him away and answered for me while I listened as the team's conversations filled The Cage. Even Hannah joined in the post-match analysis. Bee took Hook into her office for their private chat. Thirty-five minutes later, her door opened again and the room fell silent, or at least as silent as The Cage's background thrum would ever allow.

Bee took centre stage with Hook at her side. She smiled and even Hook looked less like someone suffering with haemorrhoids.

"Billy and I have just finished a conference call with Chief Superintendent Knightly and the Met's Deputy Chief Constable. Needless to say, they are rather pleased with our part in the early closure of the ABR case."

"I should bloody well think so," Rob said. "We did all their work for them while they were stuck in traffic."

Bee waited for cheering to die down.

"Exactly. Although it's officially a Met collar, and we were only offering backup support, we'll have our names on the arrest report. We'll also be involved in the interviews. All in all an excellent result for the Task Force."

Everybody cheered at that. I joined in with the back-slapping and the glad-handing until Bee raised both hands for silence. "So, tomorrow, Billy and Rob will spend the day at Paddington Green Station assisting with the interrogations. Let's see if we can't help the Met find the missing gang member. The one who got away with the equivalent of forty gold bars. The best part of a million pounds."

"Isn't that obvious, Bee?" This came from Drew.

Hook's eyes narrowed. "You got something to say, son?"

The young Scotsman nodded. "Sorry for interrupting, but we know who the fifth man is, don't we?"

"Go on," Bee encouraged.

Drew's Adam's apple bobbed. "Well, Tony Bennett, Alfie Knowles, Harry Hardiman, and Viggo Martindale are all banged up in the Paddington Green high security lock-up, so what's happened to Braveheart, William Wallis? He has to be the fifth man, right?"

"Don't be daft, Drew," Bandage said and thrust out an elbow that caught the Scotsman a gentle blow on the upper arm. "Wallis is a fence. He wouldn't be anywhere near the actual robbery."

"What do you reckon, Phil?" Bee said. "You've read the files. Anything in there to shed any light?"

I closed my eyes as if searching my memory.

"Not sure. There was something about him doing a little enforcing in his youth. Wouldn't think it to look at his mugshots, but he was a bit of a tough nut back in the day. Then he opened his jewellery shop and went semi-legit."

Almost apologetically, Hannah coughed and raised her hand.

She shrank in on herself when everyone turned to look at her. How the heck did she ever pass the initial training? Perhaps she had hidden depths I'd yet to witness.

"Yes, Hannah?" Bee asked quietly, as though trying to coax a kitten from the branch of a tree.

"Viggo Martindale might have something to do with it."

"Go on, girl," Rob Cruikshank said. "Spit it out."

Hannah lowered her head. "Sorry. In 1989, William Wallis and Roberto Martindale, Viggo's father, shared a cell in Pentonville. The warders had to separate them after five months. Roberto lost an eye in a brawl in the exercise yard and spent weeks in the infirmary." She stopped talking and started playing with a large pendant dangling from a heavy chain around her neck. I couldn't make out the detail, but it looked substantial and shiny.

Hook broke the short silence. "What are you saying?"

"Well ... why would Viggo and Wallis work together if there was bad blood between them? Maybe there was a trust issue and Viggo forced Wallis to take part in the raid. And then maybe they had a falling out? It's possible?"

Chloe joined in the conversation. "You reckon we'll find Braveheart's body at the bottom of the Thames, weighted down by a couple of ingots?"

"Hardly," Drew said. "Why waste all that gold? They'd have more likely wrapped him up in one o' those rusty chains they had lying around the factory floor."

Hook and Bee exchanged a look.

"You think we ought to call in divers to search the river?" Bee asked.

Hannah tucked the pendant back under her blouse and shrugged.

I knew this story of course, and Hannah had it mostly right. Roberto and William actually shared a cell for seven months. Hannah's timing error was irrelevant, but her omission wasn't. The brawl in question had been started by members of a white supremacist gang. Wallis saved Roberto's life and became life-long buddies. The way I saw it, Wallis was more likely to have been part of the raid to watch after Viggo, the youngest member of the Martindale clan.

Here was another dilemma. Should I tell the team what I knew and poke my head above the parapet once again, or allow Bee to call in the divers and waste police resources?

The phone on Hook's desk rang. "Hold that thought," he said and answered, turning his back to the room.

Bee signalled for Hannah to join her and the rest of the guys moved slowly to their desks. The excitement of the raid, with its adrenaline-fuelled highs and lows, had taken its toll. Clint yawned wide and clapped Drew on the shoulder, nearly knocking the young Scot off his feet.

"Easy, big fella," Drew said. "It's been a long day and I don't have the energy to beat you to a pulp."

Clint, eyes wide, mouth still open, stepped back and raised his hands in surrender. "Sorry, ma wee man," he said in an attempted Scottish accent that ended up sounding like an Ulsterman in full-flow. "I only wanted tae say, well done, ma' wee laddie. You're a credit tae the force, so ye are."

"Do me a favour, Yank, and cut the crap."

Drew pushed the big guy in the chest and received a harsh rub on the head for his troubles. Bandage was about to join the rough and tumble when Hook called them to order.

"That was The Yard giving us a courtesy call. They have a covert observation team staking out William Wallis' home. It's just reported in. They've got eyes on our man. He's watching TV in his front room. Can't know we have his boys. They're sending a snatch team to pick him up."

Another cheer rattled the ceiling tiles.

Although he joined in, Drew's yells didn't have the same enthusiasm as the rest of us. In fact, his reaction seemed a little muted, and I could hazard an educated guess as to the reason.

Once again, Bee called for silence. "Oh, I forgot something important. DC Mackay will be joining Billy tomorrow to explain to the boys in the Met exactly how *he* broke the case. Drew, this is all down to you. Don't be surprised if there's a commendation coming your way down the line."

More cheers, and Drew's face glowed so red it could have stopped the traffic in Trafalgar Square.

Hook took over. "Okay, it's late. Off you go home, and those of you not down to visit the Met tomorrow can have two hours extra in bed."

Another roar, this one sarcastic. A two-hour lie-in hardly made up for the seven hours they'd spent in Northfleet. Still, nobody joins the police force if they want to work regular hours—Freddie Bowen excluded.

Ten minutes later, The Cage was empty except for Hook and me.

"Trying to suck up to your new boss, DS Cryer?"

"Bee's already left," I said, absorbing his sarcasm and spitting back some of my own.

"I suppose you're expecting me to thank you for saving Clint from a knifing."

"No, sir."

Actually, I was. Praising subordinates for a job well done is not only good leadership, it's also common courtesy. Hook was an aggressive bastard. No wonder his team's arrest record didn't stand up to close scrutiny. I'm used to working with the best, and DI Hook fell miles short of what I considered to be the minimum standard required of a leader.

"You reckon you're the dogs bollocks because you can read a police file?"

"Not at all."

What I really wanted to say was, "Why didn't you read it properly, you ignorant arsehole?" but didn't want to antagonise the son-of-a-bitch. He was doing a great job of climbing over Bee to reach the top of my suspect list, without me having to search very hard.

"Yeah, well, I do. Thank you I mean. Well done, Detective Sergeant Cryer. You saved the day, and no mistake." He tugged a forelock and his upper lip curled into a sneer. "There, happy now?"

"You've made my day."

We engaged in a staring contest for a few seconds. Childish, I know, but I wasn't about to back down to a bully.

He blinked first. "So why are you still here?"

"Nothing better to do so I thought I'd familiarise myself with the system."

"Really? It's gone midnight."

"Really."

He stood and dragged his jacket from the back of his chair. "Turn the lights off when you leave."

I should have left it there, but sometimes, I don't know when to stop.

"Mind if I ask a question?"

He started towards the exit. "Ask away."

"What's your problem with me?"

Hook stopped dead and turned to face me, anger boiled in his eyes. "I don't have a problem with you, Cryer," he said quietly. "None whatsoever. Just do your job and we'll get on fine."

I watched him enter the mantrap, face the exit, and wait for the EMP to cycle through its routine. He walked out and didn't look back.

The sod did have a problem. It couldn't simply be my replacing Richie Juno so quickly. It had to be something else.

If he were Alpine, as I suspected, he wasn't doing a very good job of hiding it. Perhaps my stint undercover wouldn't last so long after all.

Chapter 15

Tuesday17th September

Alone in The Cage at last, I should have rushed to my desk and dived straight into the online research, but I'd been up for twenty straight hours and had spent most of them staring at a screen. To be honest, I was exhausted and my eyes were stinging. Although I had done no exercise since leaving the taxi, the emotional stress of my first day back at work after the accident had turned my body to jelly, and my brain to mush. Five months is a long time away from an office desk.

The first yawn, when it came, was deep and satisfying. I didn't bother holding back and added an arms-above-the-head stretch for good measure.

I should have forced myself to scour the SCUD but doubted anything I read would register. It was time to call an end to my opening day undercover, but first, I had some housekeeping to complete. An undercover cop's work is never done.

It took twenty minutes to run Corky's history-erase program, which sanitised the footprints I'd left in the William Wallis file. After that, I powered down my system, closed my eyes, and scrolled through my memory banks to make sure I hadn't missed anything on my to-do list.

Something niggled in the back of my head, something between Freddie and Chloe. Yes, she'd promised to call him before midnight with an update but had left with the others in an excited scrum. Had she remembered to call? I didn't think it would do any harm to curry favour with one of my colleagues and checked the time before dialling the Bowen's home number.

"Hello?" Freddie answered, his voice quiet, barely above a whisper.

"Freddie, it's Phil. Not too late, I hope?"

"It is a little. I was about to turn in. Everything okay? How did it go in Northfleet?"

"Chloe didn't call earlier?"

"No."

"She must have forgotten in all the excitement. Thought you'd like to know we caught the ABR crew."

"That's fantastic," he said, relief flooding his voice. "What happened?"

I gave him the potted version, leaving out the knife-in-the-belt incident—no value in sounding like a braggart. The others could fill in the details in the morning.

"Thanks for keeping me in the loop, Sarge. I can sometimes feel a little isolated. You understand."

"No problem. Us desk jockeys need to stick together, right?"

He laughed quietly and I ended the call feeling as though I'd done a good thing. Pastoral care, an essential part of leadership. DI Hook clearly hadn't read that memo.

Smiling, I grabbed my stick and headed for the place that would become my temporary weekday home.

Freya's welcome pack had included a numeric code for my 'suite' in the accommodation block. Before she left, Chloe gave a health warning related to bed lice and damp mould, which I took to be a joke. No matter the quality of the room, any bed seemed pretty inviting right then. Truth is, I'd have been happy curling up on the sofa at the back of Bee's office.

I made it as far as The Cage door before Hook's desk phone rattled into squawking, strident life. Damn thing nearly gave me a coronary. Voicemail would have kicked in eventually, but I couldn't pass up the opportunity to learn something about my prime suspect.

"Hello, DI Hook's phone."

"Is he there?" The man on the other end of the line carried an authority I recognised even though I didn't know the voice. His accent rivalled Chloe's, but with an educated top coat as though he tried hard to hide his lowly origins.

"Afraid not, sir. This is DS Cryer, a member of his team. Can I take a message?"

"DCI Bartok here, from Paddington Green Station. Were you involved in the Northfleet operation earlier today?"

"Yes, sir."

In a manner of speaking. No lies or obfuscations needed so far.

"Wait a minute. DS Cryer you say?" A flash of genuine warmth coloured his words.

Fuck. Had he recognised me from somewhere? I'd have remembered meeting someone with that name.

"That's right, sir."

"Yes, I heard you saved the day with your warning about the knife. Well, done. Don't know what would have happened without you. The head of my ARU was most impressed."

"Thank you, but I did very little. DC MacKay broke the case. He's the one who deserves the credit."

"And he'll get it, Sergeant. No need to worry on that score."

"Excellent, sir. Can I pass on a message to anyone?"

"Ah, yes. Tell DCI Endicott and DI Hook we've arrested William Wallis. He was at home in his six-bed house in Battersea with his wife, two dogs ... and thirty of those souvenir telephone box miniatures they spent all day making and spray painting bright red." He chuckled at the last bit and added, "We found them in the boot of his Jaguar. They were still warm, would you believe?"

"That's good news, sir. We were worried there'd been a falling out and we'd find him floating face-down in the Thames. But you say Wallis only had thirty phone boxes?"

"Yes, I know what you're getting at. Each phone box weighs one kilo, and DI Hook's team found five hundred and sixty in the Sprinter van."

"Leaving ten bars unaccounted for."

"That's right," Bartok said, his voice smiling. "Any idea where we might find them?"

"Me? Absolutely none. All I can say is, I haven't left the building all day."

"I understand," he said, laughing.

Somewhere between the robbery in the Docklands and Northfleet, the ABR crew had offloaded ten gold bars, probably as a payoff to whoever organised the raid. I doubted we'd ever find the missing loot and didn't waste any time wondering who and where it was.

DCI Bartok ended the call, a very happy man, despite the missing loot. And quite right too. Deep in the high security bowels of Paddington Green Police Station, the Met had five armed robbers who'd been at large for less than a day. The only things to dull the polish on his achievement were the missing bars and the fact that the NCA had done most of the heavy lifting. Still, no doubt the Met's Press Department would spin the case in their favour.

I returned to my desk, fired up the PC, and emailed the information to Bee. She could distribute the news as she saw fit—I wasn't interested in keeping Hook informed. Housekeeping done, I headed for my new home.

Mantrap negotiated, I took three attempts to open my locker. As with the keycard operating systems in modern hotels, the NCA's system monitored anyone accessing their lockers. The mistakes were good camouflage.

Talking about watching the watchers, the paranoid undercover cop in me wanted to know whether anyone had tampered with my electronics while they were out of my possession. The minute I had the chance, I'd access the internal surveillance system and see whether anyone had opened my locker while I'd been in The Cage. Until then, I'd treat my phone and tablet as though they'd been bugged.

Complete again with the comforting weight of wallet and mobile in my pockets, I collected the Samsonite on the way, and the lift rushed me to the ground floor at express speed. Freya had long gone, but a sixty-something man with neat grey hair and nicely-trimmed moustache was keeping her chair warm. Watery blue eyes stared out from behind reading glasses. He gave me a tired but kindly smile.

The old fellow stood with a lot more ease than I had done when leaving The Cage. "Good evening, sir."

"Evening. I'm DS Cryer."

"Yes, I have you on the system. Congratulations on the bullion case."

"You heard about that already?"

He lifted his chin and stood tall. "Good news, it travels fast. Although not as fast as the bad."

He had a Mediterranean accent I couldn't place exactly. Italian possibly. Knightly's briefing notes hadn't included any of the night security guards.

"Is there anything you need?" he asked.

"I'm heading to the accommodation block which is …" I opened my hands to ask for help.

He pointed to the building directly across the access road. "Go through those doors, turn left and take the lift to the top floor. You room is three doors along the corridor."

I smiled. "You know my room number, too."

"I know many things, Detective Sergeant Cryer. It's my job."

Mine too. I'd check on the old guy's credentials later, after about ten hours sleep.

"It's too late now, but I'll be looking for a decent restaurant. Don't suppose there's one nearby?"

He lifted a bushy eyebrow and regarded me with the patience only the elderly can attain when they look at a silly young fool. "This is London, sir. Same as New York, it never sleeps. What do you like to eat? There's something called a Gastropub at the end of the road."

The way his lips curled when he said 'Gastropub' didn't count as a ringing endorsement, nor did it suit my purpose. I didn't want to eat within sight of Citadel Place, and since the old chap and I would share the main building late into the night and would probably get to know each other over the coming weeks or months, I took a gamble. "I've always loved Italian food."

He beamed and opened his arms wide. Had Freya's desk not separated us, I'm sure he would have drawn me into one of those European kissy-hug things. All I can say is, I'm English, and thank God for the desk.

"Good choice, my friend. I recommend *Gino's Ristorante* on Elm Street, no more than fifteen minutes walk from here." He stabbed his chest with a gnarly right thumb. "Tell him Paulo Dragoni sent you. And don't worry about it being on Elm Street. Eating at *Gino's* won't be a nightmare." A smile wrinkled his face and he barked out a loud cackle.

I grinned with him and had the impression he'd been telling that one for years.

"Thanks, Paulo. Call me Phil. I'll check out *Gino's* tomorrow night if I get the chance. Even if London doesn't sleep, I need my zeds. Are you on all night?"

"Eight-until-eight. Four nights on, six nights off. It's a killer for an old man's sleeping cycle, but it tops up my pension."

Paulo waved me off, hit the button on the portable TV hidden beside Freya's computer monitor, and settled back to his overnight viewing.

#

If you enjoy spending time in a 1970s Soviet Gulag, the NCA's guest accommodation would satisfy. Painted in five shades of grey, it contained angular metal furniture and was only slightly more comfortable than a police holding cell. No maid service, but I relished the solitude after being under the microscope all day.

A tray on the surface of the sparsely-fitted kitchenette contained a packet of dry biscuits and everything I needed to make two cups of coffee. No fridge, no cooker. The delights of the canteen would keep me alive for the duration, that, and *Gino's Ristorante*.

While the kettle boiled—late night coffee has never kept me awake—I explored my new part-time home.

A low cabinet in the corner opposite the kitchenette held a small flat-screen TV, and a brochure beside it promised the gamut of Freeview channels. If I ever spent time in the room, at least I'd have something to watch.

The rest of the five-by-six room contained a low coffee table surrounded by a double sofa and an armchair and a three-quarter sized bed with two bedside cabinets. As I said, Gulag chic.

A door beside the kitchenette led to a small wet room and toilet. No schlepping down the corridor in the middle of the night for a potty break like the dorms in police training college. Almost luxurious.

Although not 'Manda clean', the place was tidy enough for me. The bed linen was fresh and, hopefully, I wouldn't have to stay too long. All I needed to do was identify a murdering corrupt cop. How hard could that be? Find a cop clever enough to hide his— or her—activities for at least eighteen months, and one who knew their way around the NCA's IT infrastructure well enough to hide all trace of their activities. No problem.

Hang on a sec.

'Their' way? 'Their' activities? Plural?

Originally, I'd discounted Drew Mackay as a target for being too recent an addition to the Task force, but what evidence did I have for thinking I was searching for a single dirty cop? What if Alpine had recruited Drew *after* he'd joined the Task force? What if I was hunting a pair, or a trio? What if the whole bloody lot of them were in on it?

A conspiracy. A cabal.

OCTF could turn out to be one big sack of boiling, festering dog shit.

The enormity of the task struck me like a physical blow. A small pebble of doubt grew into a boulder, and the boulder lodged itself firmly in my guts. How the feck was I going to identify Alpine?

The task was beyond me. Impossible. A dark cloud of panic descended.

Only then did the soothing words come. "Easy, Philip. Take it one step at a time. You'll get there in the end."

They were David Jones' words, often used when I run away with myself during an operation.

I leaned against the back of the couch, its textured surface beneath my hands, comforting. Eyes closed, I brought up images of the kids lying in their cots, sleeping peacefully. And then Manda's face appeared, smiling at me from her side of the bed. My heart rate slowed.

An old trick that rarely failed.

I sank into the couch, took out my mobile, and dialled home. Manda lifted my spirits with news of the kids, but she'd had a long day, too, and we kept it short—fifteen minutes—finishing with our usual routine.

"Keep safe, Phil."

"Will do. Love you."

"Me too."

"You love you?"

"Yes," she answered.

Soppy, I know, but we've been together for years and it's what we do.

I caught the hitch in Manda's voice as we ended the call and a lump formed in my throat. Okay, if I'm a big marshmallow inside, does it make me less of a man? If needed, I can still crush beer cans against my forehead.

Tired, but too wound up to sleep, I switched on the TV, selected the Midlands regional news, and turned up the volume to drown out the oppressive silence.

The familiar TV news anchor introduced a riveting article on local authority budgetary constraints. This one concerned a letter sent by the council leader to the region's librarians announcing a moratorium on buying new books. The letter blamed cuts in central government grants. The follow-up discussion questioned the need for local libraries in this day of home internet and e-readers. I let the he-said, she-said discussion run in the background. White noise for company.

After unpacking my clothes and stowing them in the minimal wardrobe space, I changed into sports gear and set to work: abdominal crunches and twists; single-leg push-ups; and stretches. The exercise routine—taught to me by a physiotherapist with a figure to drool over, a sunny smile, and the soul of a sadist—had me sweating a puddle onto the kitchenette flooring. Another side-effect was the deep dark ache in my leg, which would have made a weaker man cry, but these days, I'm made of stronger stuff.

The shower water started off hot enough, but low pressure propelled it through the sprinkler head with the force of summer rain in the Sahara. It took longer to wash off the soap than it had to generate the lather in the first place. I also discovered how long the shower took to run cold—around twenty-three seconds.

The towels were scratchy, but did the job, and I collapsed into a firm and surprisingly comfortable bed. I don't remember turning off the TV or the bedside lamp.

Chapter 16

Tuesday 17th September

I spent a frustrating Tuesday trying to concentrate on the Carney file, but had to suffer the constant distraction of overexcited teammates as they kept rehashing the events in Northfleet.

Hook's absence—he spent the day in Paddington Green with Rob and Drew—allowed the team to blow off steam, which wasn't a bad thing. Major success in our line of work is rare, and despite the interruption their rowdiness caused to my work, I couldn't begrudge them their celebrations. It was a hell of a bust.

Clint Schneider's response to me when he arrived midmorning bordered on overwhelming. Throughout the day, he kept singing my praises, and refilling my Villa mug—the one Manda bought the day I made detective and was given my first permanent desk—with extra strong coffee. He even used the good stuff reserved for important visitors.

More embarrassingly, he insisted on paying for my lunch. It became so over the top that by the middle of the afternoon I had to take him to one side.

"Cat, take it easy, eh?" I said, keeping my voice down "It's embarrassing."

He nodded. "Sorry, Sarge, but where I come from, someone saves your life, you owe them. How you doing for coffee?"

The big guy wouldn't take the hint. I clapped his shoulder and smiled. "Couldn't drink another drop, but thanks all the same."

"Don't forget. You ever need anything, I'm your man."

He sidled over to X Delasse's desk, where the Frenchman and Bandage were discussing the likelihood of Bennett having recovered from close contact with Schneider's flying fist. The Cat laughed and demonstrated how to increase the power of an uppercut by levering with the shoulder and twisting the wrist right before contact. I couldn't help but smile at the big man's ability to repeat the same action all day without getting bored.

Freddie caught my eye and I drew up a chair beside him. As a fellow deskbound detective, I considered us kindred spirits and felt more than a little sorry for the man. Bee had given him the task of coordinating the team's written statements. The old boy had been on the receiving end of every blow-by-blow account of the ABR crew's takedown more than once.

"How you doing, Freddie?"

"Not so bad, Sarge. Thanks again for calling last night. A nice thing to do. I'd love to have been there ... but, you know."

"You and me both, mate. Did you get home in time last night?"

His face creased. "Missed my train by three minutes. First time ever. Had to take a taxi at the other end. The day nurse kicked up a fuss." He paused for a second and cast a furtive look around The Cage. Tears glistened in his eyes. "Between you and me, Sarge, I don't know how long I can keep this up. Imelda, my wife, her condition is ... deteriorating so quickly. I thought we had a few years, but ..." He blew his nose on a tissue. "Sorry, Sarge, you don't need to hear this."

My family is my life, and I honestly don't know how I'd cope if Manda took ill. I touched his shoulder and spouted a platitude along the lines of, "Let me know if I can help," as though I'd ever be able to do anything useful, and returned to my desk.

By the end of the afternoon, the guys had calmed down enough for me to concentrate on my reading, but I didn't get far into the Carney papers before the previous day's activities took their toll. I could hardly keep my eyes open and the words soon started to swim on the screen.

Bee had been away all day briefing the Director General and handling media interviews. She wasn't expected back. Half an hour before knocking-off time—18:00 for most of the team—Hook called X Delasse with an update from Paddington Green. The Met had yet to charge the ABR crew. Still searching for the missing gold bars, they had been playing the crew off against one another, hoping one of them would crack for a lighter sentence.

He, Rob, and Drew would be staying to 'help the Met with their enquiries' for as long as they remained welcome. X ended the call and jumped to his feet. "I don't know about you guys," he said, wringing his hands, "but I have had enough for today. Is anyone available for a small celebration?"

Stupid question to ask a room full of cops.

"I'm game for a couple of sherbets and a ruby," Chloe said, standing and reaching for her jacket.

"Sounds like a plan," Bandage said. "What about you, Phil? You up for a quiet night out?"

The Cat stood and threw open his arms. "Yeah, c'mon Sarge. Let me buy you a warm English beer."

"No thanks," I answered to hoots of derision from all but Hannah.

"You sure?" Schneider said, his massive shoulders sagged.

The others looked at me as though I'd kicked a cat, which, given Clint Schneider's expression, I probably had. I relented. "Make it a lager, and I'm in."

"Now that's what I'm talking about." The big American smiled and we headed for the exit to join the others in the mantrap.

I should have cried off and taken the opportunity to start my private research, but fatigue screws with my memory as much as anyone's and I'd have achieved little. Besides, studying my new teammates in a social environment couldn't hurt, could it?

The night passed without incident. The lager was cold and the curry hot and spicy. I didn't learn much more than the team's taste in curry and liquid refreshment. Bandage preferred beer and chose beef madras. X Delasse preferred red wine—*quelle surprise*—and erred on the side of caution with a chicken korma. Hannah liked G&T, but only had two all night, and drank water with her egg salad. Chloe drank lager to start and white wine with her lamb vindaloo.

For a big man, Schneider couldn't handle his lager very well, and we had to pour him into a taxi well before midnight, but only after he'd polished off an extra large serving of burger and fries.

As for my search for Alpine, the excursion had been a total bust.

Chapter 17

Wednesday 18th September

I slept well and reached The Cage early on Wednesday morning keen to make a fresh start on the Carney case.

Now, I don't want to come across as God's gift to police work, but sometimes a fresh pair of eyes on a case really can see things other people miss. If those eyes happen to be attached to a memory like mine, there's expectation over hope.

John Dryden Carney is a bastard, and I use the noun advisedly. He's a bastard both by birth and inclination. He's also a murdering paedophile. Probably.

Tuesday's interrupted reading told me the SCUD held gigabytes of information on Carney, including hours of surveillance film of the failed raids on his various buy-to-let properties. At first, I ignored the videos and plunged into the reports. They didn't make good reading. The further I delved into the case, the angrier I became and the more I wanted to close down his operation.

Bee had undersold the man's case history.

Between 2010 and 2013, seven separate police raids on Carney's properties had turned up nothing but a few building code infringements. When the NCA stepped in to offer its support, it found even less. Carney's solicitors issued their harassment complaint after the most recent raid—a joint operation led by the Kent Police and supported by the NCA. And I already knew the outcome of that.

The so-called investigators at the IPCC—in the main, ex-police detectives who should have known better—couldn't find their way to the toilet without uploading a GPS app to their mobiles. As a result of the IPCC investigation, the Kent Police suspended the senior officer on the case, a DI Bilic, pending a disciplinary hearing. In effect, Carney had been given a free pass. No wonder Bee wanted the man stuffed and mounted.

And so did I.

But that wasn't the worst of it. A number of illegals who had escaped Carney's clutches claimed to have witnessed his predilection for young boys. According to the harrowing statements, Carney would pay particular attention to prepubescent orphans, many of whom would disappear after his visits. Whether he'd killed the boys, or sold them on to others, was unclear. I suspected the former, but for no other reason than the gut instinct of a father who'd die to protect his kids.

I pored over the witness statements and the subsequent police investigation, and I wasn't impressed. One officer, a DCI from Surrey Police, suggested the witness' claims were little more than a desperate attempt to support their asylum applications. This opinion gained credence when most of the witnesses recanted their statements—presumably under duress—and were subsequently deported. None of the sexual assault claims were verifiable and the investigations were dropped.

In short, the police had made a total Horlicks of the Carney case from day one. In the harsh light of The Cage, I found it difficult to believe the fuckup as anything other than intentional.

Carney had help. Of that, I had no doubt. I thought that from the moment I started reading the file and nothing since had changed my mind. To make matters worse, the perceived lack of due diligence by the police went a long way towards the IPCC's ultimate verdict.

The whole thing smelled worse than Paulie's morning nappies.

Chloe arrived three hours after I'd started. Bright-eyed and smiling, she looked none the worse for our evening on the lash. Her elegant dark grey business suit shouted class and the pink blouse added a subtle touch of colour. On Chloe, the look worked well, but it did nothing to lighten my mood.

"Mornin', Phil," she said after draping her jacket on the back of her chair. "You're an early bird."

"Nothing better to do," I snapped, staring at a photo of the bruised face of an Afghani boy who'd been interviewed by Kent Police after one of their failed raids. When questioned through interpreters, the thirteen-year-old claimed to have fallen down a flight of stairs. His advanced age had probably saved his life. Carney preferred his playmates younger—damn his eyes.

Chloe's smile faltered and I felt bad for taking my anger out on her.

"Coffee?" she asked, holding out her hand for my mug.

"Please. And sorry for snapping."

I handed over my Villa mug. It was still warm from my last brew but I needed a refill.

"White, no sugar, right?"

"Thanks."

Before my recent health kick, I took my coffee with three sugars, but now use sweeteners. Not quite the same, but you can get used to almost anything if there's a big enough incentive.

Chloe did the honours with the kettle and a jar of instant, and I hit play on a time-and-location-stamped video of the most recent Carney raid. The picture came from a patrol car's dashcam and showed a grey day, lashing with rain. The car followed an unmarked vehicle and a police Transit van, and the convoy stopped in front of a seedy-looking five-storey building in the centre of Hastings.

DI Hook, Bandage, Chloe, and two plainclothes men I didn't recognise, climbed out of the unmarked car. Six armed officers in full riot gear filed out of the Transit and took up a 'forced entry' position by the front door of the building. Two uniformed officers exited the patrol car—the video image shuddered as the car's suspension settled—and stood guard in the street.

Hook raised his arm in preparation to start the raid, but before the entry team could react, the front door opened, and a sneering JD Carney greeted them. He wore a smart pinstripe suit, collar and tie done up tight, although the video timestamp showed the time as 05:36. No doubt, he'd been waiting for them. His words of greeting weren't recorded, but after a few seconds, and calm as you like, Carney stepped aside to allow the armed officers inside. Hook and the other detectives followed.

Chloe returned with the coffees and took in the pictures, her mouth set firm.

"John-fucking-Carney," she said. "That animal has dead eyes. Sometimes when you look at someone you just know they're evil. You ever had that?"

"Once or twice."

She handed me my mug, still looking at the screen. "The inside of that house looked and smelled as though they'd had the cleaners in all night. Carney was so bleedin' smug. Offered us all tea and biscuits."

"Bee reckons he's receiving tip-offs. What do you think?"

She walked her coffee around to her desk, a look of resignation on her face.

I took a sip and tried not to grimace. She'd made the coffee so strong I worried my teeth would dissolve. At some stage, I'd have to teach her how I like it, but for a while, I could cope.

While Chloe considered my question, I rewound the video, stopped it at a specific image, and zoomed in. Streaked by the rain falling on the patrol car's windscreen, Carney's flabby, self-satisfied face engulfed the monitor. Dark hair, dark eyes, hairy mole on his chin. He grinned at me through a pair of uber-fashionable specs that had to have cost him a couple of grand, easy.

And they say crime doesn't pay.

"Yeah," Chloe answered after due consideration and a sip of her drink. "The bastard has help. No doubt in my mind. All them police raids and no one found nothing? I know he's guilty. Could feel it oozing out of him like stale sweat. Being close to him made me want to march him into an interrogation room and get to work on him with a lead pipe, you know? But we didn't have nothing concrete to attack him with. Nothing but unsubstantiated rumours and them recanted witness statements."

"I haven't reached that part of the file yet. Read me into the case from your perspective. Who planned the raids? What happened?"

Her briefing confirmed what I'd read and supported my interpretation. No two raids had been organised by the same team. Different forces, different divisions, different personnel, different locations, and no obvious associations anywhere. When the NCA joined in the fun, they brought in their team of forensic accountants to work with tax inspectors from HMRC. They shredded the man's paperwork and found nothing untoward.

Of course, we could all be wrong, Carney might have been an innocent businessman offering a helping hand to his unfortunate tenants. Yeah, and the Syrian president loves sunlit walks on the beach, breeds puppies, and gives millions of dollars to charity every year.

Total bullshit.

Everyone who looked at the Carney file knew he was guilty, but whoever was providing him with inside information was being bloody clever about it.

One thing was certain, though. As only the three most recent raids involved the NCA, I discounted Alpine as Carney's informant. Tempting as it might have been, I couldn't attribute every police failure to the same bent cop.

To keep Chloe occupied, and to allow me uninterrupted time to concentrate on the case file, I tasked her with updating the list of Carney's known associates. After that, she'd check the eavesdropper's logs for telephone calls made and received in the forty-eight hours before each raid. If we focused on his lieutenants, I argued, we might be able to find a way into Carney's organisation and a way to identify his information source.

#

Despite what Hollywood and TV would have you believe, police work is not all car chases, shootouts, and leaps of brilliant deductive reasoning. In fact, it's nothing like that. Our work mostly comes down to hard graft and sifting through reams and reams of paper, or these days, staring at computer screens for hours on end. My damaged knee and the odd assault aside, police officers' work-related injuries tend to revolve around sore eyes, RSI, and numb backsides. But every now and again, things come together like a well-drilled back row move at Twickenham, the Mecca of rugby union.

For me, breaking a case from the comfort of my office desk is every bit as exciting as running through the streets chasing a mugger. Hell, any time I don't have to endure a criminal's stinking breath or smell his sweaty armpits is a bonus.

The Carney case got under my skin so much, I skipped lunch, and that doesn't happen often. Off and on, I'd read the damned file for the best part of two days, found nothing, and had just about given up for the day when I lucked out.

The answer, when it came, had nothing to do with a bent cop or judicial incompetence, but everything to do with budget cuts, shared resources, and outsourcing to the private sector. Chloe's input helped too, inadvertently.

In the end, Carney hadn't needed to bribe or coerce a police officer, not when he had an employee working inside UK Telecoms Limited.

The scam was blinding in its simplicity.

In August 2010, three police forces in southeast England were married in one of those lovely civil ceremonies you keep reading about in the newspapers. The three brides looked stunning in their best dress uniforms, the grooms stayed sober, and all the guests had a wonderful time.

Yes, you're right, I am extracting the urine.

The deal was part of a massive cost cutting exercise where the Surrey, Kent, and Sussex Police Services signed a ninety million pound, Shared Network Services Agreement with UKTL. Under the terms of the government-sponsored deal, UKTL amalgamated three police data centres into a single regional hub, which it ran, and jointly operated with the police services in question.

The three Chief Constables and their civilian Commissioners sold the 'landmark' deal as a huge advance for inter-service collaboration. Their joint press release said it would enable the forces to connect and share information across a 'trusted and highly secure data network' suitable for the whole southeast region. As an added bonus, the contract would allow the organisations to outsource even more back-office roles to civilians, thereby freeing up uniformed officers for important frontline roles.

In a separate press release, a spokesperson for the telecoms giant claimed the deal would 'transform the region's communications infrastructure and save the police millions of pounds over its fifteen-year lifetime'.

Well, they would claim that, wouldn't they?

And everyone lived happily ever after.

Of course they did.

On the day they signed the contract, David Jones and I discussed the concept over a canteen lunch at the old Midlands Police HQ. True to form, the old man threw up his hands and harped on about the 'encroachment of omnipotent God of technology' the 'thin end of the security wedge', and 'the bigger the patch, the more difficult it is to police'.

In part, I happened to agree with him, not that I let on. When it comes to techie discussions, my role in our partnership is to play Devil's Advocate and to defend it at all costs.

In fact, I told David he was being his usual reactionary self and argued in favour of streamlining and improved tech support. In the end, we had to cut the discussion short to attend a road rage incident, where one driver took offence at the antics of a tailgater. He'd jammed on his brakes and forced the other guy off the road. The two fought, and the tailgater ended up stabbing his opponent in the eye with a ballpoint pen. A low tech crime, but just as damaging to the victim.

I'd never tell the old man he was right again, but by four o'clock, not only had I identified a prime suspect, but Chloe's list of Carney's known associates had pointed the way. This enabled me to give her plenty of credit and steer the spotlight away from me. A definite win-win.

Derek Black—one of the names on her list and a former school chum of Carney—is currently spending quality time in Her Majesty's Prison Winchester. A Category B prisoner, Mr Black was banged up in 2009, having received eleven years for computer hacking, identity theft, and tax fraud.

The man's surname screamed loud and pointed me towards the UKTL press release and their spokeswoman, Charlene Black, UKTL's Director of Internet Security for South East England.

Co-incidence?

Possibly.

Black isn't an unusual surname, but the prickling of excitement at the back of my neck spurred my interest. The terms of the UKTL-Police agreement allowed me easy access to their internal database. Information can flow both ways. Ironic really when you think about it.

Charlene Black's personnel file said she'd joined UKTL during the bidding process for the integration contract. It also listed her as: single, never married, no children. When I accessed Derek Black's prison records, it showed him as having married someone called Charlene Philippoussis in March 2006.

Another coincidence? Hardly.

These days, all prison visitors are photographed and fingerprinted. I checked Winchester's visitor photos of Derek's wife against the one on the UKTL corporate website and—drum roll please—they matched.

Have I said how much I love technology?

As so often happens, with the first crack made, the rest of Carney's defences crumbled.

Yes! I had the bastard. John Carney, I had him!

Keeping the news quiet was the most difficult thing I'd done so far as an undercover cop, but before moving onto anything else, I deleted my search history in the SCUD. Next, I worked the deception. It didn't prove difficult.

"Chloe, you're the IT guru. Help me out here, will you?"

She looked up from her screen, an end-of-the-day fatigue etched on her face.

"What can I do you for?"

"I'm trying to access the Kent Police's database, but the link keeps passing me through to a site with a UKTL badge. They want my user ID and system password. Is it safe?"

I manufactured surprise as she gave me story of the shared infrastructure before breaking in with, "Hang on a sec. Does everything in the southeast run through this single hub?"

"Yes. Didn't you know?"

"How would I know that? I'm from Birmingham. Has anyone looked for a connection between Carney and the guys running the network?"

She tilted her head and spoke as though I were a raw recruit needing a lesson in police procedures. "Of course. We looked at everyone. The police teams, the telecoms people, the guys who organised the transportation, everyone. And then we collated the names from all the other raids and ran a comparison analysis. We had a few hits, but none consistent across all the raids."

"And the UKTL people. They all checked out too?"

"All the ones working at the hub. Yes."

"You sure?"

"Positive."

If there had been any hesitation or doubt in her eyes, I would have left the idea to mature, but she was adamant, a closed book, and I had to give her a prod.

"What about the UKTL staff not working at the hub?"

This time she did hesitate.

"Sarge, you gotta understand. There was a shedload of data to filter and we had other cases to work."

"Tell me about it."

I leaned back, interlaced my fingers, and cradled my head in my hands, staring at the ceiling. It was a pose I'd seen David adopt when contemplating his next move in a case. I reckoned it made him look cool and in control. Hey, if it works for the boss, why not me?

"Okay, Chloe, fair enough."

My watch showed: 17:14. I waved goodbye to Freddie and yawned as though I'd spent another long day hacking away in the data mines which, of course, I had.

"Tomorrow, I'll want to look at UKTL's personnel records, but we'll probably need a search warrant. Let's pick this up in the morning."

Chloe sat up straight, the light in her eyes flicked back on. "No, you're dead wrong, Sarge."

"Probably," I said, "but about what?"

"We don't need special permission or a warrant. The UKTL contract includes an open door policy. We have access to all their records, twenty-four-seven. All I have to do is enter our ID and password into the hub."

I gave her a hopeful smile. "Don't fancy taking a quick look before you leave?"

She returned my smile and started typing. "Only if you make the next round of drinks."

"It's a deal," I said, the Villa mug already in my hand.

#

Chloe did her thing, slowly, and I kept reading the Carney file. The clock on the bottom of my screen kept climbing and the excruciating wait continued.

Frustrating, or what?

What was taking her so damned long?

Despite my prompt, it still took her nearly an hour to find Charlene Black, but when she did, I relaxed and enjoyed a celebration that rivalled the one Drew made when he broke the ABR case. Her infectious excitement and the rising voice she used when rushing me through the convoluted association attracted the interest of the others. They listened to her explanation as intently as I appeared to.

"You want to tell Bee, or should I?" Chloe asked when she'd finished.

I opened my hands. "Be my guest. You did the spadework. Go take the glory."

She reached for the phone but stopped when the main door opened. Hook, Rob, and Drew entered, looking tired, but Drew's boyish grin and Hook's missing scowl told a positive story. They waited in the mantrap for the all-clear.

Bandage called out. "How'd it go?"

Drew's grin turned into a Cheshire Cat beam and he raised both hands in a double thumbs-up. "Turns out Harry Hardiman isn't that hard after all. He broke down and cried like a wee bairn. We ended up charging the crew with aggravated robbery, ABH, and a load of other stuff. With the evidence we have against them, they'll all get life."

The EMP's high pitched whine did little to drown out the standing applause and cheers. Rob and Drew punched the air, but Hook barely reacted. What the hell was his problem?

"And the missing gold bars?" Schneider called as the noise died.

"Still missing," Hook answered. "Doubt they'll ever surface."

Bee's door opened. I gave her a few minutes to deliver the congratulations before catching her attention with a raised index finger.

She approached my desk. "Phil? Everything okay?"

"Perfect, thanks. Chloe has found something interesting on the Carney case."

I let Chloe take the floor.

After she'd finished. Bee tried to send Hook and Drew home for a well-earned rest but Hook removed his jacket and dropped it on his desk. He gave me a sideways glance that made me feel watched, and said, "If you think I'm going home to my pit when we've got a line on that slimy git, think again, guv. Rob, Drew, off you go, guys. Get yourselves some shuteye."

The young Scot shook his head. "Oh no, if you're staying, so am I. Cannae let you have all the fun."

Rob walked to his desk and called home to say he'd be delayed.

After Chloe and I ran a tag-team briefing, Bee stepped away to call the cyber crimes unit for support, which arrived in the shapely form of Amy Bradley.

Amy shattered any preconceptions I had that all computer geeks are chinless wonders who wear bottle-bottom glasses and had faces pockmarked by acne. With her full curves, high cheekbones, and perfect teeth, she could have passed for Cheryl Cole's prettier younger sister. She was bright, too. It took her less than two hours to find a block of errant code in the UKTL's operating system that was definitely not part of its original design specs.

"What does it do?" Bee asked, standing over Amy's shoulder and looking at the hieroglyphics streaming through the monitor.

"This is really neat," Amy answered with a voice as deep and smooth as a nightclub soul singer. From what I could see, every man in The Cage—and Chloe—would have loved to hear her croon. Drew's face was a study in scarlet.

"In what way?" X Delasse asked, standing closer to Amy than absolutely necessary, although she didn't seem to mind too much.

"See this part?" Amy highlighted a small section of the code. "It contains a self-modulating subroutine. Any time it recognises a string that includes the word 'Carney', it sends an encrypted signal via satellite to a specific IP address. Give me a second and I'll find out where it goes."

I read the timestamp, scratched my chin, and asked the obvious question. "Can you tell when the code was added and when it was last used?"

"It's been there since before the system went live, but hasn't been accessed since, give me a sec … since last May."

"Around the time the IPCC told us to leave Carney alone," Chloe said.

It was also four months before Richie Juno's death, confirming in my mind that the Carney case probably had nothing to do with the elusive Alpine.

"Can anyone tell you're looking at the source code right now?" Bee asked.

"No. I've taken a flash-copy and this screen is offline. Completely secure."

Rob Cruikshank sidled up close to me and whispered, "Sounds as though she knows her stuff."

"Dunno, mate. She lost me at 'self-modulating subroutine'."

"Me, too."

The techno-beauty traced the signal back to an IP address registered to a Bournemouth Travel Agency, and from there, to a company called Dover Holdings Limited.

Chloe took it from there and tapped at her keyboard. "Let's see who owns Dover Holdings." After a few seconds, she added, "Bloody hell, what a divvy."

She uploaded a screenshot to the main whiteboard showing a PDF downloaded from Companies House. The Annual Return form for Dover Holdings Limited listed one JD Carney as the Managing Director. The date-of-birth tallied with our man, too.

"How sloppy is that?" Bandage said. "You'd have thought he'd be more careful. Isn't this Charlene Black woman supposed to be an IT security specialist?"

Hannah joined the conversation. "Maybe they're getting overconfident."

"You want me to disable the interface?" Amy asked Bee, her index finger hovering over the enter key.

Before I could yell "No," Bee threw out her hand. "Of course not," she said. "Why don't we use it to catch ourselves a murdering people trafficker?"

She looked in my direction, and her expression told me she knew I'd been about to pose the same question. And with her action, Bee Endicott demonstrated how she'd made DCI.

Nice one.

Chapter 18

Wednesday 18th September

One hour after Amy found the illegal source code, Bee held court in front of the big screen. Everyone understood that we only had one chance to use the code to force Carney into the open. The message we sent had to be perfect or he'd ignore it and get wise to our intercept. If we caught him in the act of moving his 'product', we could tear his operation apart and, hopefully, expose his transport route both up and down the line.

This might sound corny, but at the front of my mind I kept hold of the idea that we'd be saving hundreds of innocents—we might even find some lost boys along the way. Carney wasn't the only people trafficker operating in the UK, but as the supermarket's slogan goes, 'Every little helps'.

One of the Communications Officers in the almost mythical Eavesdropper Central—a comms room in the basement I'd yet to visit—had located Carney's mobile phone. It showed the man at home and, like as not, sitting comfortably with his trophy wife and half-a-dozen bodyguards.

Bee asked for volunteers to sit on the house in Dover.

"Hang on a minute, Bee," Hook said. "Before we get carried away. What makes you so sure Carney's going anywhere near his victims? In my opinion, he's more likely to delegate the evacuation to the hired help."

I answered for her. "Nope. He won't do that."

"Oh yeah?" Hook said, a sneer curled his upper lip. "What makes you so certain?"

Still sitting in my chair I swivelled to look at him.

"Simple psychology. Carney's hands-on. He won't delegate anything this important. Remember the smug look he had when he met you at the front door of his place in Hastings. Offered you tea and biscuits, didn't he? He loved putting one over on the cops. There's no way he'll turn up the chance of rubbing our noses in the crap. He thinks he's bulletproof with the IPCC sanction on his side. I know his type."

Bee nodded. "I agree. So, back to the original question. Who fancies a trip to Dover?"

Rob Cruikshank's hand shot up. "Clint and I'll take that. A trip to the seaside will do the pasty-faced Colonial the world of good."

Schneider sighed. "Another night away from me nice warm bed and me nice warm wife. Blimey, the life of a British Bobby." He tried for Dick Van Dyke, the chimneysweep, but earned a loud groan from Chloe, the only true Londoner on the Task Force.

"I should join them," X Delasse said. "The motorbike will come in useful, I think."

"Okay, off you go. Although our telecoms are nothing to do with UKTL, from now on, no one says the word Carney on air. UKTL might not be the only carrier he's compromised. Oh, and we'll need a codename. Any offers?"

"He moves people around the country," Hook said. "We'll call him 'The Conductor'."

Bee cast her eyes around the group as though looking for an alternative before saying, "Yep, makes sense. Operation Conductor it is."

When they were in the mantrap on their way out, Bandage reminded them to drive on the left-hand side of the road. Schneider gave him the finger, said, "Up yours, asshole," but smiled when doing so.

No doubt about it, The Cage was charged with more than the usual background levels of static electricity. There's nothing quite like closing in on a criminal to make a roomful of cops happy.

#

The observation team had been gone nearly an hour when Bee approached Chloe.

"Found us a target yet?"

"Might have. There's three obvious choices, I reckon." She tapped enter on her keyboard and three photos flicked onto the big screen. "The first is the hostel in Hastings. The second is in Folkestone, close to the port, and the third is in Dover on the sea front. All three are big enough to house dozens of illegals. The rest of his places—the ones we know about—are small, little more than B&Bs." She enlarged the third photo and brought up an Ordinance Survey map of the surrounding area. "If it was up to me, I'd choose Dover. It's the largest"—she checked her notes—"ninety-three rooms and a load of outbuildings, garages, and the like."

Despite wanting to keep a low profile, I made a face.

"Phil," Bee said, "do you have something to say?"

"Remember Dover Holdings? You ask me, Dover's Carney's legitimate business address. It's close to his home and the last place he'd use to house illegals. If he's as cocky as we think, I'd put money on him making his alternative HQ in one of the properties we've already searched. Hastings would be my favourite. It's a former hotel and far enough away from the ferry ports to avoid interesting the Border Agency."

Chloe pursed her lips and hiked an eyebrow. "That's a good point, Sarge. One moment." She enlarged the photo of the Hastings house and bled in a different street map.

Bee turned to Hook. "You raided the place with Chloe. What are your thoughts?"

Hook threw another glare in my direction before answering. "DS Cryer makes sense." He spoke as though it hurt to give me credit for anything. "Odds are, it's either Hastings or Folkestone."

Bandage interrupted from his desk. "I've put two armed units on standby, twelve officers. We probably have enough bodies for two strike teams, although it might leave us spread a bit thin. What d'you think, guv?"

Bee shook her head. "If caught, Carney and his gang are looking at life sentences. They'll be armed. I don't want to weaken our forces."

Hook spoke again. "Instead of guessing, why don't we ask Davor?"

"Who?" Drew asked.

"Davor Bilic," Hook answered. "He's been on suspension since the IPCC's decision."

"He shouldn't be anywhere near the case," I said and immediately regretted opening my mouth.

"What do you know about anything?" Hook said, stepping forward and encroaching into my personal space. I stood and stared him down. Hook had to crane his neck to look me in the eye. It couldn't have been comfortable for him, poor man.

I took a breath before answering quietly. "DI Davor Mikel Bilic. His family fled Kosovo during the Balkans Crisis in 1999. They settled in the UK when Davor was still a teenager. He was with you and Chloe during your failed Hastings raid. Bilic lost his temper and attacked Carney, which is one of the reasons the IPCC came down so hard on him in their case review. If you hadn't pulled Bilic off, he'd be facing serious assault charges and not just a disciplinary hearing. How am I doing so far, sir?"

Hook took a step back during my speech, but his jaw muscles didn't stop bunching. "You know a fuck of a lot about this all of a sudden."

"Funny that, isn't it? You may not have noticed, but I've been sitting at my desk for the past two days reading the case file. You shouldn't be surprised to learn that DI Bilic's name came up once or twice. As did yours."

"Drop the sarcasm, Detective Sergeant Cryer."

I returned Hook's stare for a beat less than would have been considered insubordination. "Sarcasm, Detective Inspector Hook? *Moi?*"

Although, I kept my voice steady and tried to appear calm, I wanted to ram his dentures down his throat. Yes, dentures. Young Billy Hook lost his front teeth in a school fight when he was thirteen—before he took up boxing. The information's in his medical records.

Bee interrupted our little spat. "We're planning an operation here. Will you two boys please start playing nice?"

Hook lost our staring contest and folded his arms. "Not every piece of information makes it to the police file, Detective Sergeant." He turned to Bee. "Davor has a little spare time on his hands these days. He spends some of it taking in the sea air on the south coast. We've been keeping in touch. By landline and using the name Conductor."

He aimed the last sentence at me, probably trying to regain some lost authority.

"You mean he's been carrying out a private investigation?" Hannah asked.

Hook smiled at her and his shoulders relaxed. "That's right. Just like in the Dire Straits song."

"Who?"

"Jees, girl. How old are you?" Hook said, adding a loud sigh that released some of the tension from the room.

"Dire Straits," I explained. "Private Investigations, written by Mark Knopfler in 1982." Hannah's puzzled look made me add, "My father used to play their stuff all the time."

"Ah," she said, "Granddad rock."

"Exactly."

I winked, she smiled, and Hook walked to his desk to make the call.

Bee gave Hannah, Drew, and Chloe their pre-operation tasks—mostly paperwork—and showed me to one side. "What's going on with you and Billy? Didn't I suggest you tread carefully there?"

"You did, ma'am, but his attitude stinks. If you don't mind me saying, you need to think about making him take some personal time."

"My office, now," she said and stormed off in a huff of swinging arms and swirling skirts.

I followed her, feeling every eye in The Cage drilling into the back of my neck.

"Who do you think you are talking to me like that?" she started. Her cheeks flushed. When I didn't answer she shouted, "Well?"

"Sorry, ma'am. Thought it was a rhetorical question. You have to see what's going on with DI Hook. He's out of control. Shouldn't be anywhere near a police operation."

She took a deep breath and rested her rear on the edge of her desk. I stayed near the door.

"Next week," she said, "Billy Hook will read the eulogy at his brother-in-law's memorial service. He was in charge on the day Richie Juno died and he's feeling as guilty as hell. I'm giving him a little latitude. What would you do in my position?"

My immediate thought was that Billy Hook might have had every reason to feel guilty—if he was Alpine. Already at the top of my suspect pool, I mentally highlighted his name, made it bold, and underlined it for good measure. Now all I had to do was prove it to Brian Knightly's satisfaction and I could resume my real life.

The old-fashioned digital clock on her wall clicked over to 22:08 before I realised that Bee was still waiting for my answer.

"In my opinion you should send DI Hook home before he screws up—again. And you shouldn't allow him back to work until he's been cleared by a medic and a counsellor."

Before she had time to respond, Hook barged his way into the office without knocking.

"Sorry to interrupt, Bee," he said, sounding anything but apologetic. "Davor Bilic just pointed us to the hotel in Hastings."

He slid a glance in my direction. The cast in his left eye seemed more obvious as fatigue caught up with him. Late Wednesday evening and already the week had stretched out long and hard. Tiredness was having its effect on me, too. Thankfully, I didn't yawn in his face.

"Seems like you guessed right, Cryer. We'll have to start calling you Lucky."

Lucky? Bollocks. It had nothing to do with luck and everything to do with using all the information at my disposal.

On the other hand, I preferred 'Lucky' to 'The Gimp', but kept the thought to myself.

"How certain is he?" Bee asked.

"Near as he can be," Hook answered. "He's been watching the place off and on for the past two months. Says he has enough photographic evidence to prove Carney's a trafficker. He planned to present the photos to his Chief Constable during his disciplinary hearing next week and expected to have the case reopened. He demanded to be part of our raid. I agreed so he'd keep schtum. He's on his way to Hastings now. Going to meet us there."

"Christ," I said, "you didn't tell him about UKTL?"

"Of course not!" he growled. "I'm no idiot."

I stared at him hard, but said nothing. My mother would be so proud that her only boy had learned the difficult art of self-control. Sometimes, I surprise myself.

Bee stood and brushed past me on her way to the door. "Okay, boys. Let's go arrest John Carney."

"Right behind you, Bee," I said and followed her out.

Hook threw his arm out to block me.

"Not you," he said, the glint in his eye one of pure malice. "You're on restricted duty, remember? Stay at your desk, safe and sound, so you don't get in the way."

"Are you serious?"

"Deadly. You aren't insured for field work. The Health and Safety boys and girls would have kittens. It's my job to exercise a little control over you, Lucky." He showed his teeth in what might have been a smile, but to me looked more like a snarl.

Despite keeping my voice down, Hook must have heard what I'd said about him to Bee. Way to keep a low profile, Philip.

Chapter 19

Wednesday 18th to Thursday 19th September

For the second evening that week, I was forced to follow an operation I'd initiated from the confines of The Cage. This time, though, I didn't even have the benefit of comms traffic or a video feed. From the outset of Operation Conductor, Bee had insisted on a total radio blackout and I couldn't argue with her logic. Until an army of police techies ran a complete diagnostic sweep on UKTL's entire communications infrastructure, we couldn't be certain the errant code Amy Bradley found was the only one on the system.

When Bee confirmed my spectator status—to Hook's obvious delight—I threw a bit of a wobbly at being sidelined again. I did it for show. Keeping in character, I sat at my desk, fuming, while everyone else made their plans for a second night of adrenaline-fuelled action.

While the team co-ordinated the raid with the NCA's internal Armed Response Unit, the ARU—using the NCA's non-UKTL landlines—Chloe, Drew, and Clint threw me the occasional sympathetic smile or shrug. I did nothing to suggest it helped.

Before she left for home, Amy Bradley created a data package of messages culled from comms traffic recorded before each of the previous failed raids. The only modifications she needed to make were to the date, time, and the target for the mock raid—Dover.

As for me, I had a simple, if integral, role.

Once everyone was in place—the task force with its armed support at Hastings and X Delasse's team outside Carney's place in Dover—I'd send Amy's data stream to the system, which would send it to Carney. After that, we'd wait until he took the bait. If he took the bait.

It sounded good, in theory.

At 22:43, in a scramble of waving hands and raucous farewells, the team—Bee included—trooped off to the armoury to draw their weapons. From there, they'd meet the SFC at the collection point in the car park, and head south.

They left me alone in The Cage, at long last, and with a mighty bound, I morphed into Snoopercop. Not really, but close.

I typed in the command sequence Corky had built for me—all 283 lines of it, including my passwords—and bypassed the SCUD's firewalls and internal security. With those lines of code, I'd gained unfettered and unrecorded access to one of the most secure IT systems in the UK. The power made me giddy. At that point I could see how hackers got their jollies from 'sticking it to the man'.

First thing, I scoured the file registry to see who had done what since my arrival, but found nothing unexpected. Next, I confirmed that no one else had opened my security locker for the same period and that only Freya had accessed the day log for the locker's reporting system. Again, I found nothing suspicious. That left me free to open the thirteen files flagged in green. Over 9,000 closely typed pages, plus the ancillary folders containing forensics and surveillance reports, photos, and videos. Even at my reading pace, it would take weeks to trawl through them all, especially since I could only access the files while alone. Still, no one earns the big bucks if the work's too easy.

Where to start? Working in accordance with the law of 'it's always the last one you look at', I started with the file Richie Juno accessed last, which also turned out to be the oldest one, created in 2008.

The case concerned the activities of notorious artist, Barry 'Baz' Gurvitz, a minor celebrity who appeared on TV whenever a news editor needed an expert on the works of the old masters. Over the years, Baz had built a reputation for creating high quality 'genuine' fake paintings, but had never tried to pass them off as originals—officially. Baz disappeared three days before his fifty-seventh birthday and nobody had seen him since. The file had him as 'missing believed dead'.

The Essex Police marked the case as Open/Unsolved and passed the file to the NCA on the grounds that Baz might have upset a team of art thieves who had stolen one of his fakes. They argued that the case had a significant 'organised crime' element, hence their hurry to pass along the file and massage their crime figures.

According to SCUD's tracking data, Richie read the complete file a total of five times, the final access being two days before his death, at which point he'd looked at the investigating officers' closing statements.

I only needed to read it once.

The computer's clock ticked over to 00:01 and announced the start of my fourth day as an undercover cop. Should I have baked a cake?

The Task Force would be three quarters of the way to Hastings.

My eyes, dry from staring at computer screens and whiteboards for the best part of sixteen hours straight, started losing focus. My blink rate was in the carpet and my stomach, abused through lack of food and abundance of coffee, grumbled and gurgled. To make matters worse, the staff canteen had been closed for two hours and the vending machines didn't offer anything more substantial than crisps and chocolate bars. I called my Italian friend at the reception desk.

"*Ciao*, Philip. How you doing up there all alone while your team is having all the fun on the beach?"

His friendly voice was a real tonic.

"They told you about the op?"

"Not directly, but the young ones talked like excited children while passing by my desk. I think you would say they are 'up for it'. Is there something I can do for you?"

"What are the rules about ordering a takeaway meal? Are you allowed to accept a delivery?"

"No, but I can do better. Mrs Dragoni wants to fatten me up. Always packs too much food. Come down to reception when you are free and we can share some bruschetta and deep fried tortellini."

My mouth watered. "Sounds fantastic. Are you sure? I wouldn't want you going hungry."

"Not a chance. You'd be doing me a favour. I hate wasting good food."

"You're a lifesaver. I'll be down as soon as I've heard from Chloe."

I rang off and opened up the next green-flagged file, the 2010 suicide of long-distance trucker, Paul Harris, witness to a murder at Southend-on-Sea. His wife found him hanging from a rafter in his garage two days before his court appearance as the chief witness for the prosecution. Without Harris' testimony, the case collapsed.

The third case originated in June 2010. An apparently healthy millionaire hedge fund trader, Juan Da Costa, OBE, died of a heart attack while out on an evening ten kilometre jog. The medical examiner marked the case as 'natural causes'.

In short, Richie Juno's first three cases involved untimely deaths.

There may have been a deeper pattern, but I couldn't find a commonality within or among the cases. I needed more data, but reading on would have to wait until after I'd had a full night's sleep. I'd done enough for one day and still had to file my first report to Knightly, but that would have to wait. No way was I going to phone it in from The Cage or from any phone registered with UKTL.

#

Chloe made her first call from the backup car in Hastings at 01:35. Despite the lateness of the hour, they'd been held up by an accident on the A21. By the time they reached their destination, the Dover contingent, led by Rob Cruikshank, had been sitting on Carney's house for hours and reported no movement.

Through Chloe, Bee gave me the go-ahead.

Using a predetermined comms signal, I reconfirmed the status of both teams, sent Amy's data burst, and ... nothing happened for forty-eight interminable, excruciating minutes.

It's a good job I had things to do, or I'd have been climbing the mesh-covered walls, despite my crap leg. Unable to concentrate fully on the Juno files, I ran some Carney-relevant internet searches and found a number of interesting morsels before my desk phone rang again.

I snatched up the handset. "Hello?"

"That you, Sarge?" Chloe said, the excitement in her voice clear in its pitch.

"Who else is it gonna be?"

"Yeah, sorry. Thought you'd like to know we heard from Rob. Seems as though the Conductor left home in a convoy of three cars full of heavily armed minders ten minutes after you sent the chivvy-up messages. Raced off like the devil himself were giving chase, Rob said. They still have eyes on the target."

I waited for more, but she didn't add to the message.

"Well?" I urged.

"Well what, Sarge?" She chuckled, enjoying herself way too much.

"Stop pissing about. Where's the Conductor now?"

"Oh," she said, "let me think—"

"Chloe!"

"Sorry, Sarge, Couldn't help myself. The Conductor and his party is definitely heading to our preferred destination."

"Excellent!"

To coin a phrase, I love it when a plan comes together.

"I held off calling you until he got through Folkestone, 'cause we might have had to leave here in a hurry. Rob's giving us a running commentary." She paused to take a breath. "Of course, we could both be wrong. He might stop at one of the smaller stations along the route."

"Doubt it. The terminus is the one we anticipated. I can feel it. Did you hook up with our friend from Kosovo?" In keeping with the covert names protocol, I meant DI Bilic.

"Yeah, he's in the lead car with Hookie and Bee. Never seen anyone so happy to see us. Smiling his head off, he is. Bee promised to let him put the cuffs on the Conductor providing he behaves himself."

I let the warm glow soak over me for a couple of seconds, but until we'd bagged Carney and his troops, and released his captives, a hell of a lot could still go wrong.

"Bee briefed you all on what happens when you reached ground zero, right?" I asked.

"She sure did. Why?"

"What's the plan?"

"Oh, right. Simple really. We're gonna storm the house once the Conductor's inside. Catch him with his dabs over everything."

Alarm bells started clanging inside my head.

"God no, you can't let him get inside!"

"What you worried ab—"

I cut our connection and dialled Bee's number. Engaged. Next, I tried Hook. He answered. Murphy's law strikes again. Why did everything have to be so bloody difficult?

"DI Hook, who's that?"

"It's Phil Cryer."

"What d'you want, Lucky?"

He just couldn't avoid the sarcasm.

"Don't let the Conductor or his men into the hotel."

"Why not?"

I took a breath. If he screwed around we might still lose our edge.

"Look, forget whatever's going on between us and listen. If you let him inside, there's a chance he'll escape, and he'll certainly have access to hostages."

I expected him to tell me to mind my own effing business or cut the connection but he didn't say anything for a moment and the line stayed open. In the background, I could hear Bee talking quietly, possibly into her phone.

After what seemed like hours, Hook spoke again. "You think we haven't considered hostages? Listen, Lucky. The layout here is shit. Side streets, hedges and gardens, parked cars, bad sight lines, and plenty of cover for desperate men carrying guns. The head of our firearms team says they can't secure the area without scaring away the targets and we can't evacuate the neighbourhood in time, or quietly. You should have known all this if you'd bothered to check the maps, so what's your problem?"

"Instead of sitting here twiddling my thumbs, I've been doing a little reading. Since buying that property in 2009, the Conductor has spent over a million pounds rebuilding it. You don't spend that sort of money doing up a place just for holding … unwanted guests. He's done a load of excavation and structural work. He's added some extra rooms, maybe dug a tunnel. There could be an escape route."

"Don't talk bollocks. How d'you know all this?"

I took the risk that Carney's system couldn't listen to every telephone conversation going on in the UK and laid it out for Hook, almost verbatim.

"It's in his company's last three annual reports. We know he's an evil sod, but he's also a greedy evil sod. In 2010, he applied for a Brownfield Redevelopment Grant for seventy-five percent of the renovation costs. To comply with the funding regs, he had to submit fully-accountable plans and provide Schedules of Work and receipts. The bugger claimed for all sorts, including excavation and underpinning works. For all we know, he's built a bloody dungeon down there."

For a second, my mind dredged up the photos of the underground torture chamber David discovered in a otherwise-quiet farmstead in Brittany during the Ellis Flynn case. I shuddered.

"DI Hook, are you listening?"

"Yeah, I'm listening. You certain about this?"

"As certain as I can be."

"Fuck. You got any suggestions?"

A surge of hope rose inside me. Perhaps I was getting through to the numbskull after all. He needed one more prod.

"I might have. Tell Bee what I said and then put me on speaker. The Conductor can't be far away. We don't have much time."

I lowered the handset into its cradle, hit the speaker button, and pulled up the architect's plans of the Hastings building I'd uploaded from the grant funding database. Open government is a wonderful thing—as was my Corky-derived near-unlimited online access.

"Phil, it's Bee, we're on speaker. Hookie just told me what you said. Do you have an alternative in mind?"

"I think so. First off, you'll need to cut the power to the hotel to neutralise any internal security and surveillance. Also, do you have anyone in the team who can pick a five-lever mortise lock?"

"I can handle the lock," Hook said, "and we can see the main power line into the house from here. One of the firearms guys can make the house dark."

It was good to have Hook on board at last, however temporarily.

"Excellent. I'm sending you the architect's plans for the ground floor. It's dated 2010, but there's nothing on file saying they've made any changes since. The front doors open into a reception area about half the size of The Cage. Your firearms guys have night-vision goggles, don't they? Why don't you break in and wait for the conductor and his bruisers in the warm and dry?"

"Break in?" said Hook, his voice dripping with sarcasm. "Without a warrant?"

Bloody hell. What was his problem?

"Under Section 17 of PACE, we don't need one. I have the document open on my system if you need me to quote you the exact wording, sir."

I cleared my throat and pretended to read from my screen. "Section 17 states that a police officer does not need to apply for a warrant when entering and searching a premises—"

"Okay, DS Cryer," Bee interrupted. "Point taken. The second clause, 'To arrest an individual for a sufficiently serious crime', covers this situation well enough."

Bee had quoted the exact wording. It seemed she knew the PACE rules as well as I did. Quite right too, given her rank. Hook should have known the same clause, but somehow, his lack of knowledge didn't surprise me.

"So," I said, "are you going to lay on a nice welcome for the Conductor and his friends? You could maybe offer *him* some tea and biscuits."

Bee and a man laughed, it didn't sound like Hook, not that I'd ever heard the DI laugh. It might have been DI Bilic.

Hook said, "Lucky?"

"Yes?"

I waited for the snide remark, but he said, "I hope the arsewipe likes chocolate digestives."

Christ, did I detect the crackle of melting ice?

A few minutes later Chloe called again. She was breathless and kept her voice down. "The firearms unit has made entry. The rest of us are outside waiting to spring the trap."

"The Conductor?" I asked.

"Ten minutes out, but still heading in the right direction."

"Excellent. Keep in touch."

"Will do. You staying in the office?"

"Where else am I going to go? I've as much invested in Operation Conductor as anyone."

"Sorry, Sarge."

While waiting for news, I deleted Corky's command code and ran his scrub program. After it finished, anyone looking at my search activity for that evening—DI Hook or Freya, for example—would see that I did nothing but read the Carney file and trawl the internet following his trail. Oh, and that I'd read Section 17 of the Police and Criminal Evidence Act, 1984.

The program would disguise my activities well enough to fool all but the most skilled of computer bloodhounds, and if Alpine were such an animal, my chances of catching him were close to zero.

At 02:43, I set my phone's call-transfer option to Freya's number at the reception desk, left The Cage, and reclaimed my electronic toys from the locker. Then I rushed downstairs for my delayed midnight feast.

It might have seemed strange for me to leave my post, but I had two reasons. The first was tactical. Overnight, Paulo sat behind Freya's desk. If he had any idea how to run her system, he'd enter my suspect pool. I needed to gauge his IT skills. I also needed to make sure he didn't have a hotline to JD Carney. Suspicion is a terrible thing and an occupational hazard for an undercover cop. The second reason? My grumbling stomach.

It turned out that Paulo had about as much IT savvy as David Jones did. And that's despite the boss' recent tentative interest in social media. Paulo could control the CCTV monitors and interrogate internal security diagnostics, given time. He could even send and receive emails, but that was about all. Unless he had Academy-Award-level acting skills—and nothing in his background suggested he did—Paulo Dragoni was in the clear. And for that, I was extremely happy. I really liked the guy.

We spent a pleasant half-hour eating food so delicious Manda could have cooked it and listening to Chloe's ongoing commentary through the speaker-phone. It was almost as good as following a Six Nations match on the radio.

Okay, I'll admit it. I shouldn't have allowed Paulo, a civilian, to listen in on a live operation. It broke all the rules of procedure, but I never let him out of my sight until the ref, Bee, blew the final whistle on the action.

Paulo and I had finished eating when an increasingly excited Chloe announced that my plan couldn't have worked any better.

When Carney and his thugs entered the hotel's night-dark reception area, they were met by men in black quasi-military battle dress, pointing red dot laser sights and halogen spotlights, screaming, "Armed Police! Armed Police! Put down your weapons!" They were so stunned, neither Carney or his hired thugs had the time or wit to react. Chloe laughed when she reported that more than one of the so-called hard men wet themselves at the moment of capitulation.

The US military call the tactic 'Shock and Awe' and rightly so. God, I wish I'd been there to see Carney's face.

"Please tell me you took photos, Chloe," I said, laughing and bumping knuckles with a delighted Paulo.

"Sorry, Sarge, I weren't around, but the firearms guys captured every move on their helmet cameras. I'll nab a copy and we can watch it later with a tub of popcorn."

"Excellent. Can't wait."

"Gotta go now, though. Bee's calling for a room-to-room search. I'll get back to you soon as I can."

Paulo 'found' a half-bottle of red wine in his lunch pack, and we toasted the success with a mug each of a rather nice Montepulciano, which had a light floral note and hints of raspberry. Hardly in line with the rules of engagement, but I'd been officially off duty for hours and who'd to mind?

A short while later, a much more subdued Chloe called again. "Jesus, Sarge. These poor people. We found eight rooms in the cellar and sixty-four kids. Smells rank down here. Human excrement, sweat. It's a bloody dungeon. Setting them free ... Oh fuck. We've done a good thing here, Phil. A bloody good thing."

After a few moment's awkward silence, she added, "You played a blinder tonight, Sarge. I ain't letting no one forget it, neither. If we'd have tried it any other way, it could have been a bloodbath."

Once they had things under control, Bee handed over command of Operation Conductor to an instantly-reinstated DI Bilic. She also called in the Kent Police, the local hospital, and social services for the released captives.

By the time the first grey light of dawn brightened the Hastings morning, the media had arrived on scene, and Paulo and I had Sky News pictures to go with Chloe's commentary. Blue flashing lights confirmed the presence of the emergency first responders—police wagons, ambulances, fire trucks, and the unmarked vehicles of local officials. No doubt, the sleepy coastal town would be the centre of the world's press for some time.

For me, the highlight of the morning came when Bee, Hook, and the swarthy, unkempt DI Bilic frogmarched a handcuffed JD Carney into a secure police van. My day was done. I thanked Chloe for keeping me informed and told her to enjoy the rest of her morning off.

"I'll see you later on today," I said through a yawn.

"Sarge?" she said. "Mind if I say something?"

"Fire away."

"You haven't been here a week and already you've done more good than the rest of the team put together. I'm proud to be working with you."

Unable to think of anything more to say than "Thanks," I rang off and removed the call-forward option from my desk phone.

Although delighted with the outcome of Operation Conductor, I couldn't shake off the sense of worry. The first rule of the undercover cop is to keep a low profile and blend in with the crowd, and I'd done the exact opposite since joining the Task Force.

In future, I'd have to do much better.

At 06:38 I took my leave of Paulo, thanking him for the meal, and promising to repay the favour. I left the office and dragged my bones to my soulless room in the Gulag. And so ended my third day as an undercover officer, or was it my fourth? I didn't have the energy to work it out.

I collapsed into bed—no shower, teeth not brushed—and worrying thoughts flittered across my exhausted mind. In less than a week, I'd achieved loads in terms of actual policing, which made me feel good, but had done little in my hunt for Alpine. Hell, the only member of staff I'd cleared to my own satisfaction was Paulo Dragoni, and he hadn't really been a suspect in the first place. I'd yet to make my first report, but that didn't matter too much. Knightly could wait another day.

The short phone call home to the real boss helped me relax and Paul's content gurgling filled my head as I lowered it into the pillows. Jamie, my little princess, was still asleep.

I didn't set the alarm.

Chapter 20

Thursday 19th September

On Thursday morning, I woke with a throbbing headache and a mouth the texture of a pebble-dashed wall. In times past, a full three hours sleep would have been enough to refresh, but I don't shrug off the long days as I once did.

Christ, listen to Methuselah.

A shower, a shave, and a fresh set of clothes had me out of the flat with the enthusiasm of a husband searching for his wife's last-minute Valentine's Day card. The short walk across the access road between the accommodation and office blocks gave me the chance to absorb a bucketful of autumn rain. The air tasted of exhaust fumes and grit, but Freya's friendly welcome brightened my morning. Her smile—the first I'd seen—would have dimmed the sun, had dear old Sol bothered to make an appearance.

Unlike on previous days, she wore her shoulder-length hair down. A softer look, far less intimidating.

"Nice work last night, Detective Sergeant Cryer."

Finger on the pulse as usual, how did Freya know so much? I'd have to delve deeper into her background, but from where I stood, it wouldn't be too onerous a task.

"Nothing to do with me. I was stuck in The Cage all night manning the phones."

"That's not the way Bee Endicott tells it. According to her, you were pivotal to the operation's success."

"You've spoken to Bee?"

"She called half an hour ago from Maidstone."

"Maidstone?"

Freya leaned closer and nodded. "Kent Police headquarters. Bee and DI Hook are trying to smooth some ruffled feathers. Kent's Chief Constable is kicking up a fuss about his force being kept in the dark. He called our Director General, who isn't a happy bunny." Freya tapped her headset mic. "This thing's been glowing red hot all morning."

"Wait until they make the UKTL security breach public. Nobody's going to be pleased."

She shook her head and the golden tresses danced under the halogen spotlights.

"That won't happen," Freya said, spearing me with another killer smile. "The bosses will keep it quiet. Too many vested interests involved, including the Home Office and the Treasury. One thing's for sure," she said, leaning over her desk and lowering her voice, "it's strengthened our position in the game."

I edged closer to her and caught a fragrance I didn't recognise—sandalwood mixed with something citrusy.

"How so?"

"On Monday, the OCTF closed the bullion case. Yesterday, you broke a huge people trafficking organisation, made the IPCC look stupid, saved the blushes of the Kent Police, and closed a security breach in the communications system. Extraordinary. Loads of Brownie points."

"If you look at it that way, it does sound pretty impressive."

She leaned back and studied me through confident, deep blue eyes. "It most certainly does, and it helps cement the NCA as a major force in the UK policing. A win-win all around."

"You care about this place, don't you?"

She nodded. "I've been here since they opened the doors. We've had our share of detractors, but this is wonderful news. It'll help our cause and you played a huge part, at least according to Bee. She says you're an asset to the team. And Chloe thinks you're the dog's ... well, let's just say she has a colourful turn of phrase. I happen to agree with her."

"Steady, you'll be making me blush. I'm off upstairs before you ask for an autograph."

This time, her smile did falter. She lowered her eyes and started to say something, but seemed to change her mind.

"Did I say something wrong?"

She looked up, her pupils dilated. "Nothing ... I ... don't suppose you'll be free this evening? For a drink?"

"Excuse me?"

She tilted her head. "DS Cryer, I'm asking you out on a date."

"Really?"

"Not much of a detective, are you. I've been giving you the come-on since Monday."

I showed her a confused frown.

"Are you really that slow?"

Yeah, without doubt. I thought she'd been giving me the evil eye, not the glad one. "Not slow, just out of practise." I flashed her my wedding ring and an apologetic smile. "Sorry, but I'm taken."

"Your wife's in Birmingham isn't she? I thought you might be open to a little innocent recreation. Despite that broken nose, you're not bad looking. In any case, I'm not interested in a long-term relationship. No strings. This is the third millennium after all."

My hand automatically reached up to touch the offending beak. Manda had cried her eyes out when she saw the blood pouring from my smashed nose. I'd made complete hash of a tackle during what became my final competitive rugby match and ended up with an opponent's knee in my face. Not the nicest way to finish my playing career and, to cap it all, we lost a match we should have won. Sport can be so cruel.

"Well?" she asked when I took my time answering.

A woman as good-looking as Freya wouldn't expect to ask twice.

"I'm sorry, Freya. You're beautiful, and I'm flattered, but Manda and I ... well, you know ..."

What could I have said? 'I've loved my wife since the first moment I saw her and you can't hold a candle to her wondrous beauty'? No, I'd have come across like the male lead in a Jane Austen novel—a right wanker.

"That's disappointing, but if ever you change your mind you know where I am. Don't wait too long though."

Stiff-shouldered, she turned away to answer another call. The rain stopped and the sun came out as compensation. I doubted Freya received many rejections, and I hated the idea of upsetting her, but no doubt she'd get over it.

The canteen was empty, and I didn't have to wait in line for my scrambled eggs, toast, and coffee. I had a table to myself and took my time over a second cup of coffee to let the eggs settle before heading to the third floor.

All the signs on the lockers outside The Cage showed *UNLOCKED*, which was to be expected given Bee's instructions to make up for unpaid overtime. Few cops would turn up the chance of taking time off after the successful nights they'd had, and I'd already taken the measure of the OCTF crew. They weren't exactly the hardest-working bunch of cops I'd ever met.

I suffered yet another exposure to the EMP and entered a ghostly Cage wondering whether I could risk doing some daytime clandestine SCUD exploration, but decided against it. Probably best to stick with the regular work during the day. Given the shit storm we'd raised during Operation Conductor, I half expected the internal oversight team to swoop in and audit the investigation. Best to keep things simple.

Instead of reading the next Juno file, I completed my status report on the week's activities so far and posted it into the official record. I glossed over my part in both operations. A full and honest record of my activities at the NCA could wait.

I worked on my little pieces of minor fiction and kept an internet window open to BBC Online News. The early bulletins I'd watched in the canteen had delivered sketchy local reports of armed police activity in an unnamed residential area of Hastings. By mid-morning, Kent Police announced they'd make a full statement at one o'clock.

Near the designated time, the bright-toothed, grey-haired news anchor passed the baton to an excitable on-site reporter, who spent five windblown minutes reviewing the same information they'd been regurgitating all morning.

At the allotted time, Assistant Chief Constable Peabody—an angular fifty-something man in full dress uniform, including a chest full of medal ribbons—delivered the statement. He stood next to a tired-looking DI Davor Bilic, whom I recognised from the Carney file. Both ACC and DI squinted into the intense sun.

In a clipped, South Coast accent, the ACC kept a straight face through his address. His version of the truth made me laugh so hard, I had to stop typing.

Apparently, acting on information gathered by undercover officer, DI Bilic, an overnight operation led by the Kent Police, with minor support from the National Crime Agency, released dozens of individuals. The captives had been held by an armed gang whose names could not be released for legal reasons. The raid had been a complete success and, despite the presence of armed officers, no shots were fired and no one was injured. The rescued people, some of whom were children, had been held in horrific conditions and were suffering from numerous serious, but non- life-threatening health conditions. Some had been taken to hospital, the rest were being held under the care of the Social Services.

The ACC stopped talking and handed over the rostrum to Davor Bilic. Cameras flashed and dozens of reporters shouted simultaneous questions. Bilic stood still, arms crossed and mouth closed until they shut up. I admired his style. It reminded me of David's interview technique. Eventually, he pointed at someone in the crowd and the camera panned around to a well-known face.

"Robert Standish, BBC News. Are you the same DI Bilic who was suspended from duty in May pending a disciplinary hearing?"

Bilic waited for a moment, stone faced. "Yes," he said to a background roar of camera motors, "and that was part of my cover story. We wanted the suspects to think they were in the clear. My colleagues and I have had the gang under close surveillance for the past five months." Although his Balkans accent was strong, his grammar and diction were perfect.

More questions followed and more lies spouted. At one stage, I saw a thunderous-looking DI Hook at the back of the shot talking to Bee out of the side of his mouth. I could imagine how he was feeling. The words 'spitting nails' came to mind and for once, I agreed with the pugnacious DI.

Like Hook, I could see the heavy hand of career politicians at work.

In disgust, I closed the internet browser and rolled my chair away from the desk. My knee stabbed a complaint into my lower back—I'd been sitting still for too long. Time to stretch my legs and breathe some city fug. I returned to the front desk and Freya greeted me with another heart-melting smile.

"Changed your mind?"

"Sorry."

"Pity," she said, raising an eyebrow. "I won't ask again."

Good.

"Did you see the news conference from Maidstone?" I asked to change the subject.

"The whitewash you mean?"

"Made me angry. I need some air. See you soon," I said, heading for the front doors.

"Bye, Gorgeous."

By the time I stopped and turned to look, she had her face averted and was talking into the headset mic, smiling. If things were different or if I'd had fewer scruples … ah well.

I turned right out of the building, limped along Tinworth Street, and continued under the rail bridge. A train rumbled overhead, echoing against the grey brickwork. Once through the tunnel, I turned left and continued to a petrol station, where I bought a pre-charged, pay-as-you-go mobile. Then I retraced my steps and carried on to the Albert Embankment. Ten minutes later, still on the move, I removed the sanitised mobile from the box, and dialled Brian Knightly's burner phone. He answered immediately with, "About bloody time," and then kept quiet while I talked.

The call lasted seventeen seconds.

#

I bought a diet cola and a ham and tomato sandwich from a vendor cart near Lambeth Bridge and leaned against the Embankment wall to watch the dirty brown river flow past while I ate. Not quite paradise, but the rain had given way to a watery sunshine and I could think of worse ways to spend a lunch break.

Lunch break in a patrol car below Spaghetti Junction came to mind.

By the time I returned to Citadel Place after depositing the burner phone in my room, Freya had left her desk, thankfully. In her place sat a young guy in a grey suit and a hideous tie who checked my ID before returning his concentration to the incoming calls. I passed no one on my way to the third floor.

Strangely, the UKPPS door was slightly ajar, but I overcame my curiosity and carried on to the end of the corridor without risking a peek inside. I didn't fancy running afoul of the armed freaks who risked life and limb to protect turncoat criminals.

With wallet and registered phone deposited in their protective cocoon, I pushed through the door to The Cage and entered the mantrap. A thin round of applause broke out, led by Clint Schneider. The clapping built in volume and Drew started a chant of, "Lucky ... Lucky ... Lucky." The others joined in.

My face warmed and I flapped a hand at them to stop, but the applause increased in speed and the chant grew in volume. I considered hitting the button to abort the EMP sequence and turn tail, but their smiling faces labelled the welcome as genuine. I stood still and accepted my punishment.

Undercover Policing 101: Keep under the radar.

Nice one, Philip Cryer.

I scanned each smiling face in turn. Three missing. Bee and Hook, who were likely still in Maidstone, and Freddie Bowen, whose extended commute made half-day working impractical. Nobody would kick up a fuss at his absence; no one wanted to make the poor guy's life any more difficult than it already was.

The gauntlet of backslaps and compliments I received during the progress to my desk was great, if a little OTT. I dropped into my chair and Chloe presented me with a hot coffee.

"Thanks, Chloe," I said, taking the Villa mug. "What was that all about?"

Rob Cruikshank led the explanation.

"You saved our blushes last night, mate. If we'd let Carney and his goons inside the hotel first, we'd probably still be there scratching our arses, trying to explain to the Kent Police why we'd fucked up and let the bastards escape."

I took a sip of coffee and rested my elbows on the arms of my chair. "Go on, I'm listening."

All but Hannah rolled their chairs into a semi-circle around my desk. She stood in the background, apart, and wearing a shy smile.

Chloe took over from Rob.

"As I told you last night, Sarge. The basement were like something out of a horror movie. Cages, dozens of them, full of half-starved women and kids. Made me cry and I ain't cried for years." She paused to sip her coffee. "And you were dead right about an escape route. We found a tunnel through to the workshops in the back garden. We reckon it was used to spirit away the ones Carney singled out for special treatment. Boys mainly, from what the people we released told us."

"We found a goddamned armoury in there too," Schneider added. "Enough assault rifles, grenades, and handguns to equip a small army. Even if we'd blocked their escape route, they could have held us off for days."

X Delasse stood and raised his mug. "A toast is in order, I think. To Lucky Cryer, we are pleased to have you working with us."

They drank while I maintained a bashful silence.

The chat-cum-debrief continued until we'd finished our drinks and then we drifted back to work in a subdued silence for the rest of the afternoon. Reports needed writing, editing, countersigning, and filing. No one mentioned a celebratory after-work drink this time. What they'd seen in the Hastings dungeon had dampened everyone's appetite for a party.

#

By 18:30 I was alone again and hard at it. I absorbed another Juno file, the fourth.

First registered in January 2011, the case followed the disappearance of Emily Dickson, heiress and wife of banker, Sir Horace Dickson. On a beautiful crisp morning,

Emily, an Olympic-class sailor, set out from Havant to their holiday home in Saint Helier, Jersey, in her ocean-going yacht. She'd made the same single-handed voyage dozens of times, but neither Emily nor the yacht were ever seen again. The Coroner recorded a verdict of accidental death. Sir Horace had to wait the mandatory seven years to inherit Emily's fortune. Case closed.

Four Juno cases related to four premature, but random deaths. The pattern continued, but hell if I could see a connection.

At 21:15, with an appointment to keep, I scrubbed the system and braved the EMP once more.

My little swimmers were taking a pounding. If I didn't find Alpine soon, Jamie and Paulie mightn't be having any more siblings. Mind you, the way they helped Manda eat through our income, that might not necessarily be a bad thing.

#

Gino's Ristorante more than matched Paulo's recommendation. Mediterranean colours and subdued lighting created a welcoming atmosphere, and the mouth-watering aroma of garlic and sundried tomatoes hit me the moment I stepped through the front door. The only thing lacking to complete the ambience was Manda at my side—I hate eating out alone.

Paulo's name drew a warm smile from the man behind the bar who introduced himself as Gino and welcomed me to his establishment with a natural enthusiasm. Before long, a darkly attractive waitress in high heels, a red blouse, and a pencil skirt showed me to a quiet table at the back and handed me a leather-bound menu. I'd have loved to bury my nose deep into the trough, but I made do with a chicken salad, ciabatta—two slices, no butter—and a bottle of light Danish lager. With a full night's sleep long overdue, I didn't want to hit the hay carrying a heavy stomach.

The waitress left me with an open bottle. I called Manda and she fixed the gash in my heart. Although far too late to talk to Jamie, I did get to hear Paulie's contented gurgle again. The happy sounds lubricated my sleep-deprived eyes. Without making it obvious to Gino's other patrons, I dabbed them with a napkin.

Yeah, all right. Never said I was the big butch hero type. I've been known to cry at chick flicks—if I think nobody's watching.

Manda talked me through her day. Jamie played in the back garden with her best friend from school, Isla. They had burger and chips for tea—a special fast food allowance for a play date. The girls were upstairs fast asleep in Jamie's room, exhausted from the excitement of the day. My little girl on her first sleepover. During our conversation, Manda climbed the stairs and held the phone to Jamie's ear so I could say goodnight to her dreams. The tears threatened to return.

No doubt about it, I'm a pushover when it comes to my family.

"My food's arrived, love. I'll have to cut this short."

"How long are you going to be away?" Manda asked, the closest she'd ever get to quizzing me about this particular job.

"No way to tell," I answered, truthfully.

"We all miss you."

"Miss you too, love. So much."

The chicken, cured in a mixture of hot and sweet spices, made me consider ordering a pudding, but I made do with an espresso and moved on to the second call.

"DS Cryer?" Knightly asked.

"Yes. It's me."

"You sound tired."

"I've had about six hours sleep in the past three days. It's hardly surprising I'm knackered, sir."

"You've made an impact though, lad. The Director General is delighted with the OCTF's results, but you're not there to improve the crime stats."

"I know why I'm here, sir."

"What do you have for me?"

"Is the recorder on? I don't want to repeat any of this."

"It's running. Go ahead."

I talked without interruption for forty-three minutes before ending the call, paying the bill, and slipping the receipt into my wallet. With any luck, I'd have something more useful to report soon.

London and I were not best mates.

Chapter 21

Thursday 19th September

Billy Hook sat behind the leather-clad wheel of Richie's Audi A4, staring at the entrance to Citadel Place. From his illegally-parked position on Tinworth Street, he had a clear sight line to the Italian duffer sitting behind Freya's desk. The old boy pretended to monitor the security screens, but everyone knew he spent his time watching soaps on his portable TV.

The orange numerals on the dashboard clock glowed bright. "Nine-fifteen. Where the fuck are you? Don't you need any rest?"

Something about Lucky Cryer didn't ring true. Too bloody confident and calm for a newbie. And how did he know all that shit about Carney? Couldn't have read it online, not in the time available. And how fucking dare Cryer quote PACE regs at a DI?

Of course he knew Section 17. Knew it front, back, and sideways.

"Fuck."

Things had fallen apart since Richie's death. Billy couldn't think straight, couldn't sleep nights no matter how hard he tried.

He closed his eyes, slowed his breathing, and tried to forget the pain of Richie's loss. Tried to remember the good times. There were plenty of them, but it was difficult to see beyond the hurt, beyond the guilt. Too soon to stop grieving.

His fault. Everything had been his fault. If he'd made different choices, Richie would still be alive.

Jesus, when Billy thought about it, he could have screamed.

William Hook and Richard Juno—the Two Musketeers, the Two Amigos, the Dynamic Duo. They'd grown up together and had been solid mates since primary school. Friends for twenty-eight years. Only ever had one serious fight, and every time Billy replayed it in his head, his toes curled.

His short fuse had caused it, his anger issues. Everybody knew he'd always been a hothead, a screw-up, but never with Richie until that night eight years ago.

Growing up, they'd had the usual rivalries. Kid's stuff. Arguments over who had the best collection of football medals, or who was the greatest ever English footballer, Wayne Rooney or David Beckham, or the two Bobbies, Moore and Charlton. The nearest they'd ever come to falling-out big time was when Richie started supporting West Ham.

Why do that when everyone knew Spurs was the greatest team on the planet?

The Hammers, for fuck's sake! Forever blowing bubbles? What was that all about? A ten-year-old Billy had called his best mate a sell-out and only half in jest.

Even when puberty kicked in, they never fought over girls. They'd come to an understanding. Billy was the leader, the chick-magnet, and Richie acted as wingman, and bloody good he was, too. Everything was cool until the fight. And the fight was a doozy.

Billy hadn't seen it coming, but he should have, he really should. Showed what a fucking useless detective he'd become. Blinded by their friendship, he'd ignored all the signs, ignored his instincts.

It happened during a stakeout in Harwich Docks—a midsummer evening, stifling hot. They'd spent five hours sweltering in an unmarked police car, watching the containers being shifted after a tipoff pointing them to cocaine smugglers. When Richie dropped the bomb, Billy picked it up just as the fucking thing exploded.

He'd never forget his kneejerk sense of betrayal. He'd just taken a bite out of a sandwich when Richie, after minutes of silence building up to it, said, "Laurel and I love each other and we're going to have a baby."

Wham! Just like that.

He'd nearly choked on his ham and pickle and didn't hear the second part of Richie's announcement—that Richie and Laurel were going to get married first and that Laurel wasn't pregnant yet. But Richie was never exactly gifted when it came to speeches.

If he'd started with, "Laurel and I want to get married," Billy wouldn't have reacted as badly. No, the black curtain slammed down on Billy, the way it used to do every time he stepped into the ring.

He threw the coffee and sandwich out the open window and attacked Richie full-bore. Luckily for Richie, the inside of a car is never the best place to have a scrap—no room to throw a decent punch. Instead, they grappled.

"Get off," Richie shouted. "You never fucking listen. Stop ... let me explain."

At the time, Billy had one arm around Richie's neck and was throwing body blows into his ribcage. For his part, Richie held on tight, trying to smother the punches. He didn't throw a single one of his own.

When they talked about the scrap in the pub afterwards, both agreed three things. First, it had been the worst few minutes of their lives. Second, Billy should have listened to the whole story before overreacting. Third, from outside the car it might have looked like two men dogging. Ha, at least they could laugh about it later.

For his part, Billy made Richie admit that he hadn't helped his cause by launching into the subject with the, 'I've impregnated your little sister behind your back', approach.

From a professional point of view, the most embarrassing part of the whole affair came with the realisation that they missed the drugs hand-off and a gang of coke dealers had gotten away. Still, shit happens and they caught the bastards a couple of days later, so no real harm done.

When Billy had taken time to think about it, he couldn't have been more delighted with the news—once he got over the hideous idea that his little sister was having sex in the first place.

While straightening his clothes and rubbing the pain away from his bruised ribs, Richie promised to treat Laurel like a princess and he'd always kept his word.

Richie's confession made sense of a load of things that had been troubling Billy for months. The times when Richie cancelled nights on the booze without a decent excuse or fair warning. A sideways look when Billy talked about the mysterious new boyfriend Laurel refused to name or bring home. Richie's evasion when he missed meetings or arrived at work wearing the same clothes he had on the day before. The occasions when Richie would disappear for whole weekends without telling Billy where he'd been.

Bloody obvious when he looked back. Richie had been seeing Laurel and had been too embarrassed, or scared, to tell his best mate.

It turned out right in the end. Richie made Billy his best man and godfather to the twins when they arrived fifteen months after the wedding. The twins, the wonderful little livewires, now fatherless boys. What were they going to do without their dad?

All Billy's fault. All of it. The guilt settled over him like a heavy dark cloud.

And then, six weeks before Richie's death, it started happening again. Richie became nervous and withdrawn, the same as before their fight. The furtive glances, the missed appointments, staying late at work for no apparent reason. The suspicion in his eyes.

Laurel had noticed a difference, too. She called Billy and wanted to know what was happening at the office. She suspected an affair, and when Billy covered for Richie, she saw right through his lies. Laurel could always tell when Billy was being evasive.

Sisters. Strange creatures with paranormal gifts.

Billy deflected Laurel by asking about their finances. Were they okay? Things had to be difficult coping with a growing family on a DS's salary. Laurel said things were tough, but manageable. The boys went through clothing, shoes especially, faster than they devoured breakfast cereal, but she and Richie were coping better than most.

Billy squeezed the steering wheel tight enough to make the leather creak.

Richie had discovered something that pushed him off-kilter and, despite Billy's questions, refused to fess up. Billy should have forced the answers from his friend. Then maybe they could have worked things out and Richie would still be alive. Billy might have been able to protect him, but now, he had to live with the guilt.

"Fuck!"

One simple mistake had led to another and another and ended in Richie's death—his murder. Billy would have to carry that load for the rest of his life. The only way out was to get even, get some payback. He stared at the entrance to Citadel Place.

"Where are you, Lucky? What you up to?"

No, the arsehole wasn't fooling anyone with his walking stick and his stupid Brummie accent. He was Knightly's man. No doubt about it. No way would the brass have replaced Richie so quickly, not with the current state of NCA finances. And why was Cryer so fucking self-confident and so goddamned smart?

Billy knew how intimidating he could be, especially to people who didn't know him that well, and especially when he wanted to intimidate. But Lucky hadn't buckled. He'd stared Billy down and that had rankled. Fucking bastard had protection, and that had to come from on high.

Knightly.

It all went back to the bastard, Chief Superintendent Brian Knightly, but what could he do about it? He had to be careful. No charging in half-cocked as normal. This time, he'd play it smart.

What was Cryer doing in The Cage so late at night?

Searching? But for what? The same thing Richie found?

Jesus H Christ.

He couldn't discover what Cryer was up to in The Cage in the evenings. No illicit radio signals could get in or out of the place, which was the whole point, what the room had been built for. So Billy watched and he waited, and finally, at 21:27, the bastard showed his supercilious face.

The fucker spent ages schmoozing the doorman and then stepped out into Tinworth Street. What did they have to talk about so friendly-like if they'd never met before that week? And why the walking stick? Was it a prop, or did the tall, muscular bastard really have a dodgy knee as he claimed? Billy had intended to read Cryer's personnel file, but the week's events had overtaken things. He'd get to that soon enough. A friend in HR owed him a favour, but in the meantime, he'd watch and he'd wait.

Cryer limped along Vauxhall Walk, made a left, and then a right onto Black Prince Road. By the time he reached the junction with the Kennington Road, Billy guessed

Cryer's destination. Paulo Dragoni was forever pushing newbies towards his cousin's overpriced restaurant.

He took the gamble, doubled back to park the Audi at Tinworth Street, and grabbed his binoculars from the glove compartment. He jogged a different route to *Gino's* and found a decent vantage point before Cryer shuffled into view.

Even alone, Cryer still limped. Most probably a genuine injury, then. Either that, or the guy had a hell of a method acting coach.

Hidden in an alleyway across the street from Gino's with binoculars raised, he watched Cryer eat—green stuff on a plate with a couple of pieces of white meat. Had to be on a health kick to make himself eat that rabbit food. Cryer also made two phone calls. The first lasted about fifteen minutes and—given the smiles and the teary eyes—must have been to his squeeze. The second was altogether more interesting. It lasted nearly fifty minutes, and the final forty-odd consisted of Cryer talking uninterrupted and with his eyes closed. What the fuck was that all about? The hairs at the nape of Billy's neck bristled.

He was going to have to deal with Lucky Cryer and the bastard, Knightly. He didn't know how, yet. Didn't have that many options, but whatever he decided, he'd handle the situation with care. No jumping in with both feet.

Not this time.

Chapter 22

Friday 20th September

On Friday morning, I woke early and spent an hour in the accommodation block's gym throwing free weights around and sweating through abdominal crunches and curls. I worked upper body and core only. The legs would have to wait until I found a local pool.

In the canteen, I limited myself to a large bowl of muesli and two slices of toast smeared with that greasy stuff advertisers try to pass off as butter. Washed down with a glass of fresh orange juice and a mug of coffee, it filled a hole, and gave me a decent start to the day.

At 07:55, back in the empty cage, I hit the spacebar on my keyboard. My screen blinked once before expanding into the black-and-white logo—royal crown to the left, NCA lettering to the right. Very understated, very 'now'.

First order of the day, checking the schedules of my new colleagues. I hovered my fingers over the keyboard and looked at the empty desks around me.

The desk furthest away, tidy and clean, as befitting its owner, seemed a reasonable enough first target, and I called up Rob Cruikshank's desk calendar. He'd booked himself and his team, Hannah and Drew, on a trip to Liverpool, and had borrowed Clint Schneider from X Delasse for the day.

Why was the impeccably dressed forty-two-year-old with the highly polished shoes headed for Merseyside, where he'd stand out more clearly than Prince Charles in a betting shop?

The Cage remained ghost-like as I read the detailed and well-presented file; it took me less than forty minutes. If e-paperwork was anything to go by, Rob Cruikshank's note-keeping was as impeccable as his dress sense.

The case dealt with drugs trafficking in the north of England. Although based in Liverpool, the targeted gang's geographical footprint covered Blackpool, Chester, Wrexham, and Greater Manchester. Since the NCA's remit covered the whole of the UK and targeted organised crime, the Merseyside Police contacted the NCA, and the OCTF took the lead.

Softly spoken and well mannered, Rob Cruickshank struck me as the cybercrimes type who'd be at home presenting crime figures and arrest statistics to the NCA management team. I couldn't see him pulling sweat-stained drug dealers off the mean streets of Wrexham and feeding them into a police van, but perhaps I was doing the man a disservice.

Freddie Bowen hustled in at 09:12, looking harried and more dishevelled than usual. He sat behind his screen, head down, avoiding eye contact. I took the opportunity to work a suspect.

"Freddie?"

"Yes, Sarge?"

"Where is everybody?"

He searched his screen for a moment before answering. "Bee and X are still in Maidstone. Hookie and Bandage are in Paddington Green. Rob and the others are in Liverpool on a drugs op. I have no idea what's happened to Chloe."

"Liverpool? Nobody told me."

Freddie shifted uneasily in his chair. "They've been planning it for ages. I'm guessing nobody read you in on the op, what with you being the new boy, and … your leg an' all." He finished by adding a shrug and an apologetic half-smile.

"And you? What exactly is your role here?"

He scratched the bald patch at the top of his head which glistened under strip lights. In profile, he could have passed for a slightly slimmer version of my former colleague, DS Charlie Pelham.

"Me? I'm here to shuffle papers, even if only I do it electronically. I lend a hand occasionally with interviews and field work, but only if it doesn't affect my home life. The regular hours is why I transferred across from the Met. Had to give up my sergeant's stripes and revert back to DC, but there was no alternative. I need the salary."

Freddie seemed in an expansive mood and, as we hadn't had the chance to chat man-to-man before, I made the most of the opportunity. He took a breath and I dived in, hoping he'd open up a little more. "What were you doing for the boys from Scotland Yard?"

Freddie eased his chair away from his desk and made himself more comfortable. His smile relaxed the worry lines on his forehead and I had the distinct impression he relished the idea of reliving his former glories. Given his home life, I guessed he struggled for grown-up conversation, and bending the ear of the new boy would be an opening too good to pass up.

"Bit of everything really. You name it, I've done it. Started with cyber crime before it was called that. Spent a couple of years in vice, but didn't take to it. Then I moved into admin. My last job was with ATU27, the anti-terrorism unit. We were hunting home-grown hard cases. Disaffected Ulstermen, radicalised Muslims, anarchist anti-capitalists. You know, the sort of nutters who don't mind planting bombs on London busses and tube trains and killing innocent women and children. Some of them are funded through organised crime, which is why I'm of use to the OCTF, I suppose."

No bullshit so far. Freddie's account tallied with the information in his personnel file. I leaned forward and planted my elbows on the desk. "You were part of the 7/7 bombings investigation?"

Freddie nodded and the frown returned. "Not our finest hour. We let the bastards get past us. Horrible it was, all those dead bodies." He rubbed the creases from his forehead. "I was part of the team that spent days searching through CCTV footage. We found evidence leading to the Streatham raids. You remember the panic at the time, coming so close after 9-11?"

Did I ever.

"Yep, I do. There's a huge Muslim population in Birmingham and the local members of the English League were kicking up a fuss. Scary times for this fresh-faced beat cop." I dug a thumb into my chest.

"Try being in the thick of it, Sarge. Imelda and I lived in Tooting when the bombers struck. Tension was high."

He met my gaze for the first time. The sadness in his hazel eyes showed the effect of trying to hold down a job while his wife's mind disintegrated in front of him. The pressure must have been horrendous.

"Do you enjoy it here?" I asked, trying to bring the conversation up to date and move away from uncomfortable family matters.

"It's okay. The work's easy enough. I'm pretty good at data collation and police procedure. During my time in admin, I helped draft the latter versions of PACE," he said, puffing out his chest.

Freddie claiming to be one of the people responsible for writing PACE interested me a great deal. At fifty-eight, he was certainly old enough to have done so, but that fact hadn't featured in his NCA personnel records. Either he was resorting to hype to bolster his CV, or the NCA's files were incomplete. Neither of which options were completely out of the question. I salted away the factoid for later consideration.

"So you're the guy I turn to if I need help writing a search warrant application?"

His smile returned and took years off his face, but nothing from his weight. "Anything you need, just ask."

We had a twenty minute chat about codes of practice for stop and search, and arrest and detention.

After exhausting PACE as a subject matter, Freddie asked about Manda and the kids, which forced me to ask after his wife.

"Imelda is my whole life." He tapped his temple with the fingertips of his right hand, the hazel eyes filling. "She's still in there, you know. My darling girl, hiding, but every now and again she comes back to me, and I can still see the woman I married."

"Sorry, Freddie, I don't know what to say."

Which was true.

He shook his head. "Nothing you can say, Sarge. I thought Imelda and I would have a couple more years together before … but she's taken a turn for the worse recently. I don't know how long I'll be able to keep working here."

Chloe arrived, one hour late and full of apologies, and ended my bonding session with Freddie. Despite feeling sorry for the guy, I'd enjoyed his company. In different circumstances Freddie Bowen and I might have been friends.

I allowed my partner to settle in and finish her first coffee before dealing with my second order of the day. I opened with, "Chloe, you've been slacking."

She sat up straight. "Come again, Sarge?"

"I've been here a whole week and you still haven't shown me Eavesdropper Central," I said, keeping a straight face.

"That's a bit harsh, innit? What, with the ABR arrest and Operation Conductor, I ain't had a spare moment."

I grinned. "Kidding, Chloe. Care to give me a conducted tour?"

She sucked air through her teeth. "Terrible, Sarge. Plain terrible. I'll need to phone ahead or little Jimmy's likely to throw a fit."

"Who's Jimmy?"

The broad smile was back. "You'll see."

She reached for her desk phone.

A couple of minutes later, Chloe and I rode the lift to the sub-basement lair of the NCA Communications Centre—'Eavesdropping Central'. A cavernous pit in the bowels of the earth with subdued lighting, it housed dozens of Communications Operators—the 'minions'.

Entombed behind acoustic partitions, each CO wore a headset with an attached microphone, and sat in front of a large PC screen, tapping keyboards. The place reminded me of a call centre. The drone of mumbled voices, combined with the low-pitched hum of air conditioning units and server fans, formed an annoying tinnitus that drilled straight through my head. I couldn't imagine spending my working days in such a place. Drudgery apart, the white noise alone would have driven me nuts within hours.

Chloe marched towards the overseer, a red-headed, bespectacled man who wore a set of headphones and sat behind a desk set on a raised platform, facing the minions. Senior Communications Officer James Brand, according to the nameplate stuck to the back of his monitor, beamed at us, but turned most of his attention on my partner. He stood and thrust out his hand. We shook.

Brand handed us each a headset and waited. The noise-cancelling headsets worked a treat and lowered the decibel level to an almost acceptable murmur. The devices would have delayed my visit to the madhouse by a day or two. Maybe.

Chloe nodded and Brand hit one of a hundred buttons on an electronic desk unit that reminded me of a sound engineer's mixing deck. "You'll find it easier to hear with these on," he began, his voice as thin and high-pitched as I'd anticipated. "Needless to say, we don't encourage people to raise their voices in here. It would ruin the acoustics and make our jobs impossible."

After Chloe made the introductions, she asked Jimmy for the Cook's Tour. The little man's grin widened into a full smile, and he wasted no time.

"It's probably best to walk you through a specific example. I'll use something that came in this morning. Really interesting and typical of the work we perform." He waved a regal hand across his domain. "For the past five weeks, we've had a lawful interception—LI—in place on any communications pertaining to the activities of a man called, Arndt Wyzniki. He's suspected of importing illegal weapons from eastern Europe. The recording you are about to hear is between Mr Wyzniki and an unknown male, who called from Southampton. Mr Wyzniki is the one with the European accent."

Brand turned to his deck, pressed another button, and worked a slider to increase the volume.

The recording lasted less than two minutes and ended when the men arranged to meet the following day at a place called The High Heath Hotel. Wyzniki's voice, middle-aged, deep, and with a strong eastern European accent was clear and easy to understand. The second man, I found difficult, but not impossible to follow.

"Mind replaying it, please?" I asked. "But this time, increase the volume a touch, reduce the base, and boost the treble."

Brand obliged and we listened again.

Happy I'd heard both sides of the conversation correctly, I thanked him, and the little man turned his obsequious smiled on me.

"What happens next?" I asked.

"We transcribe the conversation. Here's a copy."

He handed us a buff-coloured folder each and retained one for himself. Mine contained two sheets of paper, closely typed and signed on the bottom of each page by Communications Officer PE Dainty.

"You're not Dainty," I said, although in pure physical terms, he most certainly was.

"No, sir," he answered, grin widening again. "That would be Patricia Dainty."

He pointed to one of the cubicles where a mousey, forty-something woman with glasses and stooped shoulders sat with forearms resting on the desk. Her face was illuminated by the backwash from the large PC monitor, and she talked quietly into her headset.

After taking my time reading the document, I waited for a reaction, but neither Chloe nor Brand offered one. Interesting. They'd both missed three subtle transcription errors—one homonym 'here' for 'hear', and two substitutions of 'we' for 'he'. Simple human error and nothing that changed the meaning to a significant degree. Few people would have noticed.

"How did you create the transcript?" I asked Brand.

The man's thin chest swelled as he took a deep breath in preparation for delivering what was no doubt his party piece.

"Well," he began, eyes alive and shining, "it's really very clever. From this one room, we can monitor tens of thousands of LIs using our state-of-the-art linguistic algorithms, which listen for certain audio cues. I'm rather proud of the part I played in developing the system." He paused for a second as though waiting for applause, but hid any disappointment, and continued. "If the system identifies one of twenty thousand or so target words and phrases, it shows as an amber warning on this panel"—he swept both hands over his deck, the proud father showing off his baby—"and I direct the call to the first available communications officer."

"And what do the COs do, exactly?"

Brand glanced at CO Dainty before answering.

"The COs listen to the whole of the recording. If they decide the conversation merits a closer inspection, they run it through VATA. That's our Voice Activated Transcription Application."

"What, like the voice recognition app in every modern computer operating system?" I asked.

Brand's eyes popped open. My question not only upset the little guy, it earned a snort from Chloe, who turned away, hand raised to her mouth.

"Not at all, Sergeant Cryer," he said with a voice raised so loud two minions lifted their heads, frowns evident. "This is a much more sophisticated system. It can handle nuance and accents, and cope with significant ambient interference. We have a transcription success rate in the highest percentile."

"As measured by whom, or what?"

Goading Brand might have been enjoyable, but it didn't present much of a challenge.

"We have an extraordinarily sophisticated transcription interface overseen by the most expensive and powerful HPC—that's a High Performance Computer cluster—outside of GCHQ."

"And the COs?" I repeated. "Their role is?"

"Ah, yes, I see." Brand nodded and dabbed at his shiny forehead with a hankie. "We are the human element in the equation. We form a failsafe check on the process. If a recording is too corrupted by background noise, or, say, if one of the callers has an exceptionally heavy accent, or a speech impediment—"

"Like a stutter?" Chloe asked helpfully.

"Yes, yes, exactly. A stutter. In that case, the CO can augment the transcription process manually by adding a voice prompt, or even typed script. It's a triple-redundancy failsafe protocol. In fact, that's what CO Dainty is doing right now. Would you like to hear her in action? It's really rather entertaining." His hand stretched out towards the panels again.

"No thanks. What happens next?"

Brand stiffened and took a moment to recover before continuing. "Immediately after their creation, we send both the transcripts and their source recordings to the investigative team who raised the LI. And we retain a copy here."

Brand turned his eyes on Chloe, their expression fond, almost longing. Her patient smile made it clear she hadn't missed it.

"Sarge, you seen enough?" she asked.

"I have. Thanks, Mr Brand. I appreciate the time."

Chloe returned her headset, threw Brand another smile, which the little man caught with the eagerness of an Irish setter fetching a stick.

The touching scene over, I removed my headset and the background noise seemed to thrum much louder than when we'd arrived. I hurried from the auditorium and only relaxed when we'd reached the lift.

"That was interesting," I said after the doors closed.

"Yeah, always is. Couldn't work in a place like that though. Bleedin' background noise would do my head in."

"Yep, I know what you mean. At least you've made a conquest."

"Huh?"

"Jimmy's smitten."

She snorted. "Yeah. Sad innit. Poor little bloke keeps asking me out. Not happening. He ain't my type."

Although I sensed she wanted me to ask, I didn't accept the invitation.

After a couple of seconds' silence, she added, "I prefer women," and kept her eyes fixed on the lift's display panel.

I nodded and let the conversation rest there. Her sexual preferences made no difference to me one way or the other, but I did like her. Under normal circumstances, I'd have been happy that she'd felt able to open up to me in that way. If I could clear Chloe from all suspicion, I might be able to introduce her to my colleague, Alex Olganski, who needed all the friends she could find since her wife's murder.

When we returned to The Cage, X, Bandage, and Freddie were grouped in front of the whiteboard reviewing a joint operation with the British Transport Police. The case involved e-ticketing fraud on the London Underground. The NCA's cyber crime team valued the fraud at around half a million pounds. Not quite the scale of the ABR job, and probably too small to interest Alpine, but I kept half an ear open to X's briefing in case I'd misread the situation.

#

As it was Friday, and I'd made special arrangements with Bee, I left The Cage mid-afternoon and took an early train home.

That night, my call to Knightly from my wonderfully cramped home office under the stairs didn't contain much more than a 'Hello', and a 'Nothing to report'.

His response, "Early days, Philip. Keep up the good work," seemed like little more than a platitude.

PART THREE

The Second Week

Chapter 23

Monday 23rd and Tuesday 24th September

Credited with time off in lieu, I didn't need to rush in on the following Monday. Instead, I helped Manda get Jamie ready for school and fed Paulie before taking the mid-morning train to Euston.

Filled with the sort of mundane things that make life worthwhile—shopping, afternoons in the park, family meals, bedtime stories—the weekend hurtled past with the speed of a Japanese bullet train. Short-lived but a complete delight.

Sunday afternoon, David and I had a long chat using burner phones—neither of which used the UKTL carrier service. He would have preferred to visit in person, but it didn't fit our cover story. The likelihood of Alpine having me watched was miniscule, but neither of us wanted to take the risk.

As a belt and braces security move, David organised surveillance from Section 14, the Midlands Police's covert operations unit. The 'obbo team' rented the vacant house across the road from us—three teams of two, working in eight-hour shifts. We kept it secret from Manda. No telling how she'd react knowing people were watching her every move. If necessary I'd tell her after the operation, but only if I could find a room with plenty of soundproofing and nothing hard to throw.

CS Knightly funded the shadowing team out of a special Home Office budget, but that wouldn't last forever. Time was most definitely not on our side. We had three, maybe four, weeks tops before the money ran out. If I hadn't found Alpine by then, we'd scrub the operation. No way would I stay undercover with Manda and the kids unprotected. David and I made it a condition of our agreement with Knightly.

"You're doing a great job, Phil," David said towards the end of our chat. "Mopping up those high-profile cases, I mean. Don't let the bright lights of London suck you in, mind. Birmingham needs good detectives, too."

"That isn't happening, boss. Can't stand the place. Unless you like museums, opera, and the ballet, London's pretty much a culture-free zone. You should see what footie supporters have to put up with. I mean, Arsenal, Chelsea, and Tottenham-bloody-Hotspur, for God's sake?"

"They do have Lords and The Oval as compensation."

"Cricket? Do me a favour."

David sent his love to Manda and the family and we ended the call. It had been great to hear from him and made me feel better somehow. More confident.

Manda dropped me at the station and tried hard to hide the tears during our parting kiss. Me? I'm a bloke. Granite hard and twice as dense.

Never cry, me.

#

I reached The Cage around lunchtime, no applause this time, but plenty of welcoming smiles. As I walked my first coffee back to my desk, Bee opened her door and summoned me with a wave. Freya must have informed her of my arrival. Hook stared

127

daggers at me from his chair, but said nothing. Chloe raised her dark eyebrows and nodded as a sign of luck or encouragement, maybe both.

Bee's office hadn't changed much. The organisation chart still graced the whiteboard, but she'd replaced Richie Juno's name with mine. A sign of acceptance perhaps, but it probably acted as a red rag to DI Hook's bull.

"Morning, Bee. You looked great on TV. Very distinguished," I said, which was true. It would have been a lie to claim she looked attractive, and she'd have seen right through the bullshit.

Over the weekend, Bee had been the NCA's spokesperson as more and more information from Operation Conductor reached the media. She pointed at the visitors' chair. I took my seat and waited.

"I thought it best to make sure the Kent Police didn't underplay our role in the case. They'd have happily ignored us entirely if I hadn't been there to state our case. And by the way, I'd have included you in on the interviews but didn't want to break into your weekend. Spending the week away from your kids can't be easy."

"It isn't, and thanks, but why would you want to involve me? I did very little."

She tilted her head and appraised me through her grey fringe. "Rubbish. If not for you, Carney would probably have escaped. And I had a chat with Chloe this morning after reading your notes. You did more than you're admitting to. What are you playing at, DS Cryer?"

Her question threw me and I needed time to answer. I let go of my stick. As it fell, I made a grab for it and spilled some coffee on my trouser leg. The stick landed on the plush carpet, barely making a sound.

"Damn."

I put the mug on a coaster and fumbled for a hankie.

Bee snatched a couple of tissues from a box on her desk and handed them over.

"Thanks," I said, dabbing at the stain. "Bloody stick's a pain in the … neck."

I rubbed hard enough for the tissue to disintegrate and dozens of little white pellets attached themselves to the damp patch, making a stain.

The next time I looked up, a thin smile creased Bee's round face, as though she was grading my performance. Most off-putting.

"Okay now?"

I nodded. "Just about. I'll need to find a dry cleaners."

"Ask Freya. She'll point you towards the nearest one. So, why are you hiding your excellent police work?"

Despite my efforts, she clearly wasn't going to let it drop.

"You want the honest answer?"

"Always."

I retrieved the stick. "It's this bloody thing. From the moment I walked in here, everyone's looked at me as though I'm a cripple and I've been given this job as some sort of favour. The restricted duty tag doesn't help, and I didn't like being called Gimp."

Bee frowned. "I understand they've been calling you Lucky since Wednesday."

"Yeah, bloody amazing, isn't it. It seems the harder I work, the luckier I get." I paused again before launching into the best excuse I could come up with at short notice. "It's like this. I figured by spreading the credit, I'd ingratiate myself a little. And I really didn't do much. You guys did all the heavy lifting in Hastings and in Northfleet."

I grabbed my mug and drained the coffee in two long gulps.

"Okay, fair enough. I'm sure it worked well. You've become a hero overnight. Most of the guys are singing your praises and Chloe seems very impressed. By the way, how are you settling in? Do you have everything you need?"

Yep, I had everything. Everything but Alpine's name.

"Yes thanks. Wouldn't mind doing something other than reading files and helping with the paperwork, though."

She nodded slowly. "I understand your frustration, but put up with it until the FMO gives you the all clear. Break the rules, and I'll write you up on a disciplinary, despite what you achieved last week. Your six months probation period can be ended or extended depending upon my recommendation. I'd hate to see a stain on your record."

Six months? The idea of staying in London six weeks turned my stomach, let alone six months.

"Speaking of Chloe, I have a question if you don't mind." I waited a second and continued when she didn't object. "Why is she still a DC? She's bright enough, and I'd have thought she'd be an ideal candidate for promotion, given her ... seniority and experience."

I was going to say 'gender and ethnicity', but thought better of it.

UK Police PLC is forever trying to show itself as an equal opportunities employer. For Chloe still to be a DC after eight years in the force and nearly two in the NCA would have been seen by the senior management team as a failure both on their part and on hers. Other than DI Hook's poor appraisal, nothing in her file suggested she'd screwed up.

"That," Bee said after an extended pause, "is confidential." She leaned forward in her chair. "I will just say this. Chloe Holder is a valuable officer and deserves more recognition, and if she could pass her sergeant's exams, she'd be in your place right now."

"Oh, I see. The sergeant's exams are tough. Took me two attempts."

There I was again, lying with a straight face—oh the shame of being a mere mortal.

Bee stared at me hard and said, "Keep that information between the two of us."

"Of course. In time, I might be able to help her on that front. I've developed a few coping strategies when it comes to written exams."

"I'd be delighted for DC Holder to pass the exams, but let her approach you. She can be a little touchy on the subject."

"Bee, discretion is my watchword."

And I wasn't kidding.

"Good. Excellent. Accommodation suitable? Eating well?" she asked, marking an end to the sensitive subject with a little pastoral care.

"All the comforts of home, thanks. And the canteen food's not all that bad."

She looked me up and down and gave me the benefit of an encouraging smile.

"Did you ever find *Gino's Ristorante?*" Her eyes latched onto mine and her smile grew.

Uh-oh. Surely she wasn't doing a Freya and giving me the come-on? The woman had fifteen years on me.

"Yes," I answered at length. "Paulo, the night security guard, pointed me to it. Good food. Not too expensive."

She nodded. "Haven't been there for a while. It's a little too close to work for me. The food's okay, though. Might join you one evening if you could use the company."

"That would be really great," I lied again.

Not a come-on then, thankfully, just a boss offering the hand of friendship to her new subordinate. All this lying. Shame on me. Much longer as an undercover officer, and the Gates of Heaven would be forever closed to this sinner.

Bee nodded, turned to her screen, and began typing.

Was that it? The early dismissal threw me. I pushed heavily on the arms of the chair, stood, and half-turned to leave.

"How is the leg?"

"Getting stronger every day. Thanks for asking."

"Glad to hear it. DI Hook and I will discuss your case allocation. Meanwhile, carry on with what you're doing. Familiarise yourself with the place, help where you can, and"—she looked up from the screen—"while you're at it, break a few more high profile cases. Do that, and we'll be best of pals."

"I'll try, Bee."

The second I slumped into my chair and pulled it close to my desk, Chloe leaned forward.

"What was that all about?" she asked, eyes narrow, head lowered in a conspiratorial dip.

"Nothing much. A bit of pastoral care."

"Huh?"

"She wanted to know how I was settling down. Accommodation wise."

"And?"

"And what?"

She leaned back, shaking her head slowly for emphasis. "How *are* you settling down, accommodation wise?"

"As well as can be expected thanks."

"Found anywhere decent to eat? Them guest flats ain't exactly well kitted out in the kitchen department."

"Last night, I found *Gino's Ristorante.*"

Chloe wrinkled her nose.

"Ever been?"

"Once. Bloody expensive on a DC's pay and I don't go much on Italian grub. Too bland. All that pasta, garlic, and tomato sauce? Curried goat it ain't. You coming for lunch?"

The clock on my PC screen read 13:25. Despite having just arrived, I needed to clear my head. I made my excuses and, while the others visited the canteen, I spent an hour in the gym trying to avoid DI Hook's silent aggression. He spent the time punching ten bells out of the leather bags and speed balls. I've no idea what the bags had done to offend him, but the way he stared at me between rounds didn't make me feel inclined to engage in friendly conversation.

What the hell was his problem? A more paranoid undercover cop might think Hook suspected *me* of killing Richie Juno.

On the other hand, it could have been a question of, 'Methinks the DI doth protest too much'. Why pick on the newbie if not to deflect attention away from his own guilt? Would the real Alpine be so obvious, or was it part of another double-bluff?

Being in my position could be so damned confusing, and I'd only just started in the game. I'd end up a jabbering wreck if I kept double-guessing every little thing.

I finished with the bench press machine, chose some free weights, and threw in a ten-set-rep of biceps curls, turning my back to Hook, but keeping an eye on him through the wall mirror. I followed with two five-set reps of triceps lifts.

Trust my instincts, David had said. Well, my first instinct told me to run. The second told me I'd never find Alpine. It told me to give up and go home, but if I did that I'd never be able to look the boss in the eye again, not that he'd blame me. He wasn't that kind of man. I'd blame myself. Instead, I chose the final option—take things one step at a time. If I kept working through the Juno files, I might stumble upon something of value. It had worked for the ABR and Carney cases, it might work for Operation Alpine.

So far, I'd read four of the thirteen files, thirty percent. Two more and I'd be on the downhill slope.

One step at a time. That was it.

Finish reading the files, look for patterns and inconsistencies, and see what turned up. If Richie Juno could find something hinky, so could I. Possibly.

Hook ended his workout before me and I continued throwing the weights around until he'd cleared the shower, feeling a great deal better for having the gym to myself and a plan, of sorts, to work with.

#

Shock news.

That afternoon, I didn't solve a major crime, nor did I save a colleague from being stuck with a knife. Instead, I passed the time reading, listening to other people's conversations, chatting with Chloe, and keeping my head down.

By 17:30, everyone had left but Chloe and me.

"Fancy a beer, Sarge?" she asked closing down her system.

"What, now?"

"Yeah. There's a Gastropub at the end of the road. They do an 'alf decent pie and mash. Or jellied eels if you fancy going native."

Although spending an evening in the pub with the pleasantly attractive Chloe Holder held some merit, the idea of eating anguilliformes preserved in their own fat left me cold. Besides, it wouldn't get me any closer to finding Alpine. With some reluctance, I shook my head.

"Sorry, Chloe. Tempting as that sounds, I rarely drink during the week and we've got Richie Juno's memorial on Wednesday. No doubt the booze will be flowing. I'll save my alcohol intake 'til then. Thanks for the offer, though. Another time?"

She stood and shrugged. "Yeah. Another time. Don't work too hard."

"I'll carry on with the Conductor report and then turn in early. See you tomorrow."

Alone at last, I started on the fifth Juno file. This one, the May 2011 murder of PC Lyle Thomason, who died of stab wounds while on foot patrol in a leafy suburb of Gravesend, Kent. No witnesses, no suspects, a massive local investigation, but no leads. The case remained Open/Unsolved. Yet another premature death without apparent reason. The pattern continued.

What had lit the fire under Richie Juno?

For twenty minutes, I sat at my desk, stared at the mesh-encrusted ceiling, and allowed my mind to wander.

Five random cases. Five untimely deaths.

No, that wasn't right. Three confirmed deaths and two people missing *presumed* dead. Did that make a difference? I sifted through all the information available: witness statements; the background history of surviving family members; inheritance issues. Who benefitted from the deaths? I worked through the usual things a detective considers during an investigation, but the ceiling didn't give me an answer. Other than Richie Juno having read them, the cases had nothing obvious in common.

At 20:05 I sanitised the SCUD and called it a night.

An afternoon internet search had pointed me to the local swimming baths, a bone tired place housing a thirty-three-and-a-third yard, five-lane pool. It occupied the ground floor of a Victorian building a fifteen-minute hobble beyond *Gino's*. On the way, I video-called home and spoke to Jamie in her bed.

In the pool, I didn't do much actual swimming, but jogged widths at the shallow end.

The theory is simple enough. The water makes the exercise low impact and provides a progressive resistance—the faster you try to move, the harder it becomes, and the greater is the therapeutic effect. Vets use the same process for racehorse rehab, but the champion nags have their own specially made plunge pools and flumes. They don't have to resort to public baths.

Yep that's me, Lucky Phil Cryer, the recuperating thoroughbred.

My return route from the Baths to Citadel Place took me past *Gino's* and I dropped in to eat and make my report. I mentioned the murder vs. the missing-presumed-dead puzzle and suggested Knightly to factor it into his thinking. He had access to the original case files and could do his own clandestine research.

#

In terms of excitement and success, Tuesday turned out to be a near repeat of Monday, except the atmosphere started off dark and ended up darker. But how light could the mood be on the eve of a colleague's memorial service? People were hardly going to be jolly.

On the plus side, Hook and Drew spent the day in Paddington Green following up on the ABR interviews, which lightened my mood a tad.

From a pure housekeeping perspective, I found dozens of transcription errors and typos, during my file reading. None turned out significant or suspicious, and I left them alone. It wasn't my place to act as the NCA's proof-reader, and I didn't want to raise any suspicions.

Chapter 24

Wednesday 25th September

Richie Juno's memorial service had always been high on my to-do list. I anticipated it as another chance to study the whole team in a non-work, non-pub environment. If they let their hair down, maybe I'd find out something interesting. After nearly two weeks undercover, I was no closer to finding Alpine than when I first read their personnel files. I needed a break.

It wasn't as though I had any choice in the matter. Active operations apart, the invitations made it clear that attendance was mandatory, and every member of the Task Force arrived in their best suits and frocks. The top brass arrived in full dress uniform, their medal ribbons adding bright flashes of colour to an otherwise drab and sombre occasion. The sun hid behind a sheet of grey cloud all day, and even the grass around the gravestones appeared more brown than green.

At least the rain held off. A deluge would have been too much.

Juno's wife, Laurel, slim and shaking, dabbed her eyes and nose with a hanky throughout the Anglican service. Richie's four-year-old sons stood either side of their mother, flanked by older, haunted-looking civilians I took to be Laurel and Richie's parents. Mourners in sombre civilian clothes filled the first three rows of foldaway chairs. The NCA contingent occupied the four rows behind, some in uniform, most in dark suits.

Apart from Freddie Bowen and me, members of the OCTF formed an honour guard around the grave.

Freddie sat on the end of the fifth row with his wife, Imelda. He spent the whole ceremony with his arm around her shoulders, whispering—keeping her calm, I assumed. Imelda, hands trembling, stared into the hole with confusion on her face, and very little behind her eyes.

Not having known Richie, I took a seat at the back, trying to remain inconspicuous.

Christ though, the scene was impressive.

Brian Knightly, Bee Endicott, the NCA's Director General—a sharp nosed, pinch-faced woman in her late fifties—and three other officers I didn't recognise stood at attention on a low dais at the head of the open grave.

Knightly, in full dress uniform, band of ribbons that would make most Christmas trees look dowdy, delivered a faltering and emotional eulogy. His emphasis on Juno's death in the line of duty, and his years of valued police service made it particularly poignant.

Chloe and Hannah couldn't hold back their tears as the funeral staff lowered the oak coffin into the dark hole. Even big Clint Schneider's lower lip trembled. Rob, X Delasse, Bandage, and Drew stood to attention, blank-faced, and staring into the distance. Knowing Drew, I expected him to blubber, but he proved me wrong. The Scot was made of tougher stuff.

Hook spent the ceremony either staring sadly into the grave, or consoling his sister and nephews. For once, he didn't even look in my direction.

After a lone bugler blew the Last Post, which had everyone in pieces—including me—the crowd stood in line to throw handfuls of soil onto the box. Not wanting anyone to see me shuffling up to the grave with my stick in hand and struggling to bend low enough to grab the dirt, I didn't take part in this.

#

As I've already said, these days I'm not much of a drinker. A beer or two at the footie, the occasional glass of wine over dinner, and a tot or two of whisky when David and the in-laws visit is about my limit. As a younger, rugby-playing fool, I'd boozed it up with the best of them, but the times of knocking back the falling-over water are long gone, except maybe Christmas.

Normally, I'd make my excuses and cry off a boozy wake with a bunch of over-emotional cops, but in the interests of research, I took a lift with Chloe. She followed the crowd and we invaded Richie's favourite pub, The Oak & Acorn. Around the corner from his home it was about five miles from the cemetery.

Laurel Juno, together with the twins and the rest of their extended family, made their excuses early and left for home. Hook and Bee Endicott went with them, leaving the rest of the crowd to lament the departure of a close friend and colleague.

After an hour's hard drinking in the crowded down-and-dirty bar, Brian Knightly called the place to order. He made a final toast, confirmed that the barman knew where to send the bill, and then he and the other brass took their leave. The minute they cleared the room, the noise ratcheted up in volume.

My anger bubbled below the surface. If I was wrong about Hook, at least one member of the crowd was complicit in Richie's death, yet he, Alpine, stood in the dingy pub shedding false tears with the genuine mourners.

He? Yes. Until something or someone told me different, I'd think of Alpine as a 'he', a bastard. If Alpine turned out to be a woman, she'd become a bitch.

Freddie and Imelda occupied a table in the quietest corner. I side-stepped my way through the boisterous crowd, holding my bottle of lager close to my chest. Freddie looked up and nodded an acknowledgement. Imelda, glassy eyed and trembling, huddled closer to him as I approached, hugging his arm tight to her chest.

"Who's he?" she asked, casting a furtive glance in my direction before burying her head in his jacket.

"Easy, darling," Freddie said. He lifted her chin gently and she looked at me again, blinking fast. "This is the new colleague I was telling you about, remember? Detective Sergeant Cryer. Say hello."

She pulled her head away from his hand and turned away again. "Don't like him. Scary tall. His hair's too long. A shaggy sheep."

Freddie smiled and patted her shoulder. "Don't be like that, darling. Phil's nice. You'll like him."

He looked up at me again and raised both eyebrows in sad apology. I nodded an okay at him. "Not to worry, Freddie. It's lovely to meet you, Imelda. Can I get you guys a drink?"

That's me, generous to a fault, when there's a free bar. Imelda's head lifted again and she looked at Freddie, a question forming in her eyes.

"Who's that man?"

"Imelda," Freddie said, patience itself. "Let me introduce you to Philip Cryer. He's just joined the team. Say hello."

She turned to face me full on, eyes narrowing. After a second, a wide smile broke across her face and the vacant stare disappeared. The smile took years off her and for a second or two I could see the beauty masked by her condition. At forty-eight, dementia was taking her mind and spirit, but leaving body intact.

A god-awful thing.

Her eyes, grey-blue and clear, showed recognition and intellect. She'd been a tax accountant before her condition had worsened, but according to Freddie, there were times when she could no longer add two numbers together.

I held out my hand and, with trembling fingers, she reached out to take it but missed her aim and grabbed thin air. She frowned and her lower lip started to quiver but I took her hand and we shook. She gripped hard, fingernails biting deep, as though afraid to let go. Her grateful smile made everything seem better—at least for that moment. I relaxed my grip but she held on, her fingers playing with my wedding band.

"You're married. Are you having much sex these days, Detective Sergeant Cryer? Freddie and I are like rabbits sometimes. I love sex. Do you?"

"Imelda," Freddie said, blushing, "would you like another lemonade?" He looked at me and formed another apologetic smile.

"Yes, darling. That would be lovely."

I released my hand from hers.

"I'll get them. What's yours, Freddie?"

"Half a shandy please. I'm driving."

It took a while to fight my way to the bar and I had to wait ten minutes to place my order. A pub with a free bar, one barman, and a boatload of cops isn't the best place to be if you're interested in prompt service. The group around me, none of whom I recognised, were trading Richie Juno war stories.

It didn't take long to learn that the men were from the Essex Constabulary, and knew Juno and Hook before they transferred to the NCA. According to them, Richie was fiercely loyal, honest, and a great man to have at your back in a fight. From his personnel file, I knew their fond memories were far from hype. DS Juno's record was exemplary and far more impressive than that of his brother-in-law. The main thing to hold him back from promotion seemed to be a lack of drive. He passed his sergeant's exams on the first attempt, but never sat the two-part inspector's test, the OSPREs. It appeared that he'd reached the height of his climb up the promotion ladder and had been content with it. Not everybody can reach the dizzy heights of Inspector. The force needs Infantrymen as well as Generals.

The man telling the story—a squat fifty-something WASP with a shaved head and a pot belly—told of how Richie had nearly collapsed when the letter came from the NCA accepting his application. At the end of his tale, the storyteller smiled and raised his whisky glass.

"To Richie Juno," he said, slurring his words slightly, "the best partner you could ever ask for."

The others in the circle knocked back their drinks in one. I lifted my bottle and took a sip of lager before returning to the Bowens, tray of drinks balanced in one hand, walking stick in the other. The return journey wasn't easy, and I nearly dropped the tray more than once.

In my absence, they'd been joined at the long table by the rest of the team, who sat drinking in largely quiet remembrance. As I approached, Drew jumped up and took the tray from me.

"Thanks, mate," I said and waited while the others scrunched along the L-shaped bench seat and made room for me at the end of the shorter arm.

Clint Schneider, wedged uncomfortably in the corner, took up most of the room on my part of the bench, and I had half an arse cheek dangling in mid-air. Didn't do my aching knee much good but I preferred to suffer in silence rather than show weakness. We were celebrating the life of a man who could no longer feel pain, and I needed to suck it up.

Freddie and Imelda sat opposite me on a separate table. Her eyes scanned the faces, the confusion and fear evident. Freddie kept talking quietly to her, trying to keep her calm. I wondered why he'd brought her, but guessed she needed to leave the house at times to stimulate her memory, or what was left of it.

X Delasse, sitting closest to Freddie, knocked back his wine and refilled his glass from a bottle sitting between them on the table. At his side, Bandage had his hands wrapped around a large tumbler of whisky. X reached across him and offered Hannah a refill, but she shook her head and placed a hand over her glass.

"I've had three already. That's my limit," she said, her voice straining to make its way over the noise from the rowdies. She flushed bright red and lowered her head.

"I'll have hers," Chloe said, thrusting her empty glass forward.

Hannah leaned back to avoid Chloe's touch.

As the crowd around us grew more boisterous, the guys relaxed and reminisced, swapping more Juno war stories. I nursed my drink and concentrated on their words but learned nothing to forward my investigation.

Bandage took the orders for the next round and Drew accompanied him to the bar. Schneider, whose American accent and sharp voice carried easily above the din, took the floor.

"A couple of months ago," he said, talking to his beer bottle as much as to the group, "me and Richie were on stakeout. Overnight. Remember, Rob?" He turned to Rob Cruikshank who shook his head and frowned.

"Sure you do," the big American insisted. "We were in the East End keeping an eye on that Jamaican crew, The Kingston Posse. Waiting for a drugs pickup."

Cruikshank raised his chin. "Yes, I remember. You sure you want to tell that story?"

Schneider's toothy smile showed he wasn't about to take a detour. "Surely do, Rob. Surely do."

Cruikshank shrugged. "I hardly think this is the time or place."

"Aw hell, you Brits are so goddamned uptight. All I wanted to say was Richie got taken short when the courier arrived at the drop and we had to tail the mother all through London. Poor Richie didn't have time to take ... what do you guys call it? A comfort break? You remember how tidy Richie was? Well, in the end, we couldn't stop and he just *had* to hit the head. Know what I mean? Used an empty soda bottle and left it on the back seat and you know what happened then, don't you Drew?"

The Scot returned from the bar run ahead of Bandage, carrying a tray full of drinks. "What's that, big man?"

"I was just telling the guys how thirsty it can get when you're on stakeout. And how much you like your soda."

Drew glowed so red, I could feel the radiant heat from five feet away. He lowered the tray to the table and glowered at the American.

"How many times do I have to tell ye, Cat. I didn't drink Richie's piss!"

"Only because he took pity on you and sounded the warning."

"Yeah, well." Drew, still frowning, took his glass from the tray. "He always did the right thing. Unlike some." He raised the glass, said, "Detective Sergeant Richard Juno," and half-drained the beer.

The rest of us followed suit, apart from Imelda Bowen, who stared blankly into space for a moment, and then her lower lip started trembling. Tears filled her eyes. She turned to Freddie, her head dipped, and said something I couldn't hear.

Freddie stood and gently helped her to her feet. He took a packet of wet-wipes from his shoulder bag and rubbed one of the cloths hard over Imelda's cushion.

"It's okay, darling. Not to worry. We'll go clean you up. I think it's time I got you home, anyway. Wouldn't want to miss EastEnders, now, would we?"

He put his arms around her slim shoulders and drew her into a hug. She buried her head in his chest once more.

"Accidents happen, my dear. Never mind."

Freddie spoke gently and Imelda calmed. He waved goodbye to us all and led her towards the toilets. From my position on the opposite arm of the bench seating, the damp patch on the cushion stood out clear and obvious. As a father of two, I recognised a 'little accident' when I saw one. X Delasse, who'd been sitting next to Freddie, shuffled uneasily in his seat. Next to him, Rob Cruikshank reached to the tray for his drink. Nobody mentioned the wet cushion.

Chloe and I exchanged glances. She tilted her head. I took it as a sympathetic nod to Freddie and to Imelda. Seeing firsthand what the poor guy had to contend with brought the horror home and put even more of a dampener on the afternoon than the funeral had. It was one thing to be told of Freddie and Imelda's troubles, but quite another to see them up close and extremely personal. I wondered how I'd cope under the same circumstances. The Bowens were childless, but I don't know whether that was a good thing. As it stood, Freddie suffered alone. He had no help.

It didn't take long for my colleagues—proposed by the big American and seconded by the young Scot—to decide that drinking the pub dry would be a worthy challenge and a great way to show Richie Juno how much they cared. They headed to the bar for refills. Chloe followed them, but took a diversion to the toilet, leaving a space between Hannah and me.

Hannah caught me studying the large oval pendant I'd seen her wearing in the cage. Silver and studded with grey stones, it stood out bright and shiny against her black rollneck sweater.

"That's impressive," I said, trying to strike up our first non-work conversation. "Unusual design."

She took the pendant, still attached to the chain, and rested it in the palm of her hand. Her fingers traced the worn markings. "Three interlocking love hearts. The stones are diamond chips." As she spoke, her eyes came alive, and for the first time, I saw personality burst through her shyness.

"Beautiful. Never seen anything like it, " I said, encouraging her to continue.

"My great-grandfather was a jeweller in Leipzig between the wars. He made this for my great-grandmother on their tenth wedding anniversary. She, in turn, gave it to my grandmother, who smuggled it out of Germany on the *kindertransport*. You know about that?"

I nodded. "The mass evacuation of children from Germany at the start of the last war, 1938 to 1940. Must have been terrifying times for a small girl. Can't imagine what she must have gone through."

"Nana Mathilde was only nine years old when she reached England. She took care of me when my mother became ill. This"—she raised the pendant to her lips and kissed it—"is the only memento I have of her. I rarely take it off."

I hadn't heard Hannah say so much in one go and wanted her to carry on, but the guys returned with the drinks, Chloe reclaimed her seat, and we lost our moment. I tried to engage her in more conversation, but the boisterous crowd became so noisy it made quiet conversation impossible, and further investigation pointless.

Two hours later, after another five rounds—none of which included a drink for me—I pulled a wobbly and ordered a taxi to take me back to Tinworth Street.

Work, work, always work.

Chapter 25

Wednesday 25th September

Apart from Paulo Dragoni, who greeted me with his usual warm smile and cheery wave, the NCA building seemed pretty much deserted.

I made it to the third floor without having to share the lift. My knee ached from all the standing around in the cold at the cemetery and from the jostling at the pub, and I limped along the corridor more slowly than normal.

Through the blast-resistant, smoked glass windows lining the outer wall, the sparkling lights of London glittered red, white, and amber, and I paused to rest my leg and admire the view. Spectacular it may have been, but it wasn't home. I pushed away from the window and carried on towards The Cage.

A voice boomed behind me.

"Cryer? Phil Cryer?"

I stopped dead. The movement jarred my leg and I buckled, using the delay to give the information time to surface.

Shit, shit, shit.

Name?

Stefan Stanislas—'Stan the Man'.

Who?

A DS working for the Met Police out of Scotland Yard.

How did we know each other?

Opponents on the rugby field. We played against each other four, no, five times.

Last time we met?

Moseley Rugby Club ground, Saturday 7th February, 2009. A dry winter's day, cold with a light easterly wind, good ball-handling conditions, firm underfoot but no frost. Midlands Police Rugby Club versus the Met's All Stars. We lost a close game, twenty points to seventeen.

Five years older than me and half as big again, Stan the Man was a monster. He scored a try late in the second half to rob us of the win. I still feel the impact of his knee crushing my nose as he brushed aside my flailing last-ditch tackle. Made me look a right chump. Took a fortnight for the bruises to fade. My nose still shows the results of the impact, as Freya so kindly mentioned during her proposition.

As far as I knew, Stan the Man still worked for the Met, so why was he at Citadel Place? More important question, was my cover shot?

No. Probably not. He never knew about my particular skill—memory doesn't play a huge part in rugby—and he couldn't be involved with the OCTF or Knightly would have mentioned him and his details would be on the database.

I straightened and turned to face the voice, and did it with the grace and poise of a ballet dancer with arthritic hips.

"Who's that?"

"Phil Cryer, it's me, Stefan Stanislas. It is you, isn't it? The flying fullback?"

I stared at him as though trying to put a name to a face.

"Bloody hell! Stan the nose breaker? Christ, man, you're looking old!"

I added a smile and limped towards him, hand outstretched, leading with the stick to ward off a rugby tackle. Wouldn't have put it past the big bruiser.

"Well bugger me."

"No thanks, Stan. Don't do that sort of thing anymore. Not unless money changes hands."

He laughed and shook my hand in a crushing grip that reminded me of my first meeting with Clint Schneider. Maybe I should have introduced the two of them to see who came off worse.

On the ruby pitch back in 2009, he'd been 125 kilos of pure beef on the hoof. Little had changed. Blond hair, now sparse on top, but nicely trimmed as opposed to the flowing locks I remembered flashing past me at Moseley. Straight nose, clear blue eyes, broad smile. He may have been a fraction softer around the edges and a fraction wider around the waist, but I still wouldn't have challenged him to an arm-wrestling contest.

No doubt about it, the years had been kind to Stan the Man. At forty-odd, he looked as though he could take to the field and inflict as much pain as ever.

"Jesus, Stan," I said, shaking the circulation back into throbbing fingers. You don't still play?"

He scrunched up his face and shook his head. "Not much. The occasional pub match and a game of sevens now and again. Too busy these days. So, how's the leg? I heard about your accident. Meant to give you a bell, but I've been … well, you know."

"On the mend, mate. Getting stronger every day." My standard response.

"Excellent, my man."

He pointed over his shoulder to the door marked UKPPS. He must have just come through it or I'd have heard him walking behind me along the corridor.

"You a part of the NCA now?" he asked, beckoning me to follow.

"That's right, OCTF," I answered, economical with the truth. "And you're with the UKPPS?"

No wonder his name hadn't come up during my research. The UKPPS database is standalone and has tighter security than the SCUD. I doubt even Corky could … no, hold that thought right there.

"Sort of. Still working for the Met, but we run joint operations out of this office. Cover the whole of the southeast of England. Want to come in and get reacquainted?"

He pushed the door and held it open.

"You sure I'm allowed in there?"

"Don't be daft, man. Nothing in there but a few desks and chairs. And you have to be security cleared or you wouldn't be wandering around the building unaccompanied."

"I wouldn't want to compromise an operation."

"Don't worry about it. Everything's squared away and I trust you not to steal the paperclips."

Still smiling, I followed him in to a pocket-sized version of The Cage, minus the mantrap, but including the mesh-covered walls. Brightly lit, eight desks laid out in a cruciform, no electronic screens on the walls, and no internal doors. Disappointing really. I expected a flashy room with a target range and shiny gadgets like the set they give Q in the Bond movies. Another illusion shattered.

He tidied a stack of papers on his desk and stuffed it into the pocket of a cardboard folder, but not before I'd seen the top sheet. Nothing important, random addresses and associated phone numbers.

"Take a load off."

He slumped into the nearest chair. I took the seat opposite and stretched out, laying my stick on the desktop.

"Drink?"

He opened a drawer and pulled out an opened bottle of Laphroaig and two large glasses. I scratched my chin, balancing the negative effects of yet more alcohol against the risk of offending an old friend. With no need to drive home, I nodded.

"I can manage a small one."

He poured two large measures, quadruples at least, and pushed a glass towards me. I had to stretch to reach, but the first sip made it worth the effort. It went down smooth and easy. Very nice. The boss would have approved.

We chatted for a while, replaying our glory days on the rugby fields of England.

"You miss the game?" he asked, staring at my leg.

"Not really. My giving up had nothing to do with the knee and everything to do with being too small. Kept getting hurt by all you big mothers." I brushed my dented nose with an index finger.

He grinned at that.

"In the amateur ranks, you were one of the best fullbacks I ever played against."

I took another nip of the whisky. "Less of the bullshit, Stan. I was adequate at best, but you were a class act."

"No way, my man. Don't get me wrong, I had the edge on you that day, but I was close to a full-time professional at the time, and you were only half fit. If you'd been serious about the game and added a little more muscle bulk, you could have turned pro. No bull. I know talent when I see it. Fearless under a high ball, fast, and you had that neat little sidestep. Good hands too. Still"—he took another sip and offered me a top up, which I declined—"times past. And you were married, right?"

"That's right. Manda and I have two kids now. One of each." I couldn't help smiling. "What about you?"

He took another sip, smacked his lips. "Never did marry. Too wrapped up in the game and the job."

"Talking about the job," I asked, waving a hand around the room. "What's the work like around here. What's it like protecting a bunch of scumbags who are trying to shave a few years off their jail time?"

He sniffed and took another sip. "We protect witnesses, too. Lot of intimidation going on these days, but you're right. I've played bodyguard to everyone from rapists to child molesters. One time, I babysat a stone cold killer just to make a case against the bastard who hired him. Sometimes we get it all arse-about-face."

Stan laughed and sliced his hand across the air in front of his chest to signal an end to the topic.

I remembered the incident in the canteen on my first day and snapped my fingers at him. "Bloody hell, you're not involved with that Old Bailey, Trial of the Century thing are you?"

"Come on now, Phil, you know I can't talk about ongoing cases." He coughed. "So, tell me, what you're doing here? I thought you were a Brummie boy to the core. Seems to me you and your boss, DCI Jones, were joined at the hip."

I sniffed, but before I could give him the same story I sold to Bee, the door opened and a middle-aged man entered. Tall, trim, and wearing a grey suit, he had an air of authority that crossed the gap between us. I sat to attention as he approached, but Stan kept his relaxed attitude.

The man stopped a couple of metres from Stan, but kept his eyes on me.

"Who's this?"

Stan introduced me to his direct superior, DCI Sergio Falconi. I hadn't come across his name before, but no reason why I should have. Falconi turned away from my walking stick and me and glowered at the whiskey bottle.

"I'm sorry to put an end to your party, DS Stanislas, but—"

"We're saying goodbye to DS Juno," Stan said, finishing his drink. He replaced the lid on the bottle and returned it to the drawer.

Falconi slapped the heel of his hand against his forehead. "*Merda*. DS Juno's memorial was today, wasn't it? I wanted to pay my respects but …" He looked at Stan and shook his head sadly before turning to me again. "My sympathies and apologies, DS Cryer, but you'll have to leave. There's been a breach of security at one of our safe houses. We're having to move one of our … clients."

Stan jerked upright. "Not that fucking Greek prick again?"

Falconi shot a sideways glance at me before glaring at Stan.

I slid my unfinished glass across the table and stood. "No problem, sir. Stan and I were just about done."

The lines on his Mediterranean face smoothed. "Fine. Now, if you'll excuse me, I need to arrange an escort and secure transportation."

He made his way to the desk at the head of the cross, picked up his phone, and dialled.

Stan shrugged. "Good job I didn't have another drink or I'd be in the shit right now. I'll be doing some of the chauffeuring tonight. Sergio's a bit of a tight-arse, but he's a good man and knows his shit." He stuck out a hand and I risked another crush injury. "We'll catch up soon, okay? You up for a bit of a reunion with my old teammates?"

The thought of boozing it up with a bunch of rugby playing diehards, made my throat constrict, but I could hardly admit that to the big guy.

"Sounds great," I said, freeing my hand and backing away, "but it'll be difficult to arrange. I'm at home weekends. Family. You understand?"

"Of course I do, my man. Of course I do." He gave me a conspiratorial wink, and added, "We'll have to make it a midweek bash, then. Right?"

Busted.

"Great. Can't wait."

He showed me out and closed the door behind me. I headed back to The Cage for an uninterrupted run at the database.

The sixth file on Richie's list was the unsolved murder of a small time dealer, Danny Savage in 2010.

The twenty-four-year-old Billericay man had been shot twice in the head up close, hit-man style, by a shooter using a silenced .22mm handgun. The small calibre bullets had rattled around inside Danny Savage's head and turned his brain into porridge. Ballistic examination of the bullet showed the weapon, a Ruger SR22, hadn't been used in a previous crime—at least not in the UK—and had never been found.

The Essex Constabulary's Serious Crimes Squad attributed the killing to a rival gang as part of a turf war. They didn't expend too much manpower on the case and marked it as Open/Unsolved after what I considered a slipshod investigation lasting less than three weeks. I use the word 'investigation' loosely. David would have had apoplexy if I'd filed a report with as many holes.

Was that why Richie read the file four times in the fortnight before his death?

After two hours, and with yet another case file checked off the list, I removed my digital size-tens from the database before taking a midnight stroll along the Albert Embankment with the mobile phone pressed to my ear. Forty minutes later, I headed back to the Gulag, chatting to Manda on the way.

Despite the long and tiring day and the relative comfort of my temporary bed, the new information kept scrambling around in my head—another gangland murder, the UKPPS, and their Greek 'client'.

By 01:30 I still couldn't sleep and, with reluctance, I threw back the covers and resorted to something I hadn't done for years. I grabbed a pen and paper and started writing longhand. David would have been so proud.

After filling seven sheets of A4 paper and locking the pictorial information in my head, I tore the pages into small pieces and flushed them down the toilet. It took three flushes to remove them all.

Even after all the doodling, I still couldn't join the bloody dots. I had nothing and, at 02:58, crawled back into bed. Maybe sleeping on the information would bring an answer to the surface in some form of osmosis.

Perhaps I'd come up with the lottery numbers at the same time.

PART FOUR

Alone Again, Naturally

Chapter 26

Thursday 3rd October

Half awake, Brenda Knightly smiled. The smell of toasting bread and the sound of Brian pottering away in the kitchen filled her with both delight and a mild foreboding. The last time he'd surprised her with breakfast in bed, she'd spent the rest of the morning tidying his mess. How could making tea and scrambled eggs on toast require every saucepan they owned?

Still, it was a nice thought. He meant well, always trying hard to please when he had a moment to spare. She hadn't thought it possible, but his new role as Chief Superintendent took him away from home even more often than before. Long hours, stress, and now a new case, so secret he couldn't even give her his normal two-sentence summary. It worried him though. She could tell from his furtive manner and the way he took late evening calls in the home office, speaking oh so quietly.

A national emergency? A terrorist threat to London? Anything was possible with her Brian, the nation's last ditch defender.

Whatever it was, his recent bouts of broken sleep worried her. A heavy sleeper who rarely moved in bed except to visit the bathroom—a more regular occurrence with the passing years—he'd usually hit the 'snooze' button at least twice before rising. Then he'd complain his way through his morning bathroom routine. For three weeks, he'd withdrawn from her. A dour version of the bubbly man she'd grown old with.

The change had started with DS Juno's death. A desperate blow, but the loss of a colleague in Brian's line of work, although mercifully rare, had happened before. This particular death, though, had hit Brian even harder and started his slide into partial insomnia. He'd developed an unhealthy pallor, too. Pasty-faced, he refused to go for walks on his rare spells at home. Instead, he'd lock himself away in his room, headphones clamped to his ears, but not playing music. When delivering his evening cuppa, she'd caught tinny snatches of a man's voice through the speakers, definitely not music. He'd bought a new computer, too. A strange-looking thing—a bare metal case without a maker's badge. Didn't have any of those sockets you plug devices into—what were they called? UBSs? When she'd asked him about it, his reply that a colleague had made it for him surprised her. And why did he lock it away in the wall safe after each use?

Strange behaviour, even for her ultra-secretive Brian.

And last week, at DS Juno's memorial service, he'd taken it so hard. She wished she could do something to help, but that too was beyond her. He hadn't let her attend and that was a first. Throughout their marriage, she'd always stood at his side during the bad times. She'd never missed an official service for a dead colleague before.

Why?

Why hadn't he allowed her to go to the memorial? She'd asked him, but his responses had been vague and unsatisfactory. When she'd repeated her question, he'd snapped at her and she'd recoiled in surprise. In all their years together, he'd never raised his voice to her, and the guilt in his eyes had been clear. He apologised instantly and she'd forgiven him. Of course she'd forgiven him, but her shock remained.

Poor Brian. Things must be so difficult for him.

She stretched her arms towards the ceiling in an extravagant, whole-body yawn. Her back and shoulders creaked in protest in a way they never used to do when she was younger.

A crash, horrendous and sudden, followed by a heavy thump, rocked the house.

Oh, Lord, there he goes, the great ham-fisted fool. What a wonderful way to start the day.

Fully awake, shocked and angry, she waited. Silence. No swearing. No yelled apology. No 'I'll clean it up, lass'. No cluttering sounds of a hasty tidy-up.

"Brian? For goodness sake. What have you done?"

Annoyance forced the words into a shout.

Bren threw back the duvet and slid her feet into fluffy slippers. She reached for the dressing gown lying on the stool and pulled the belt tight around her waist.

"Brian?"

A groan from the downstairs hallway flipped her annoyance into fear in a heartbeat.

Oh God, no!

She ran.

The sunny Thursday morning darkened into a nightmare of fractured images and dissonant sounds. Staring down from the top of the stairs, her body froze in an eternity of panic.

"Brian!"

He lay among the wreckage of destroyed crockery, toast, and crushed eggs. His legs rested across the bottom four steps, his back on the hall carpet, right arm across his chest, hand clutching his left breast. Eyes wide, mouth open, he fought to breathe. Blue lips trembled, trying to form words. Spittle ran down the corner of his mouth.

Bren hurtled down the stairs. Her feet crunched on shattered crockery wet with warm tea. A shard sliced open her foot, but she barely felt the pain. She reached his side, knelt, and tilted his head back to open his airway.

God, oh God. No, please no.

"Hold on, darling. I'm here."

Sweat soaked his pyjama top and bathed his face. His eyes, wide and searching, met hers, the pupils pinprick small. She pressed her fingers to his neck.

Heart beating fast, too fast, breathing irregular, panting.

She dragged him along the corridor, turned him onto his side, head resting on hands, knee raised, crossed over the other leg—the recovery position.

"Don't move," she said, sounding much calmer than she felt. "I'm calling an ambulance."

Leaving his side to fetch the phone was the most difficult thing she'd ever done.

The empty base unit in the hall was too much. The phone, where was it? She pressed the locate button on the cradle and waited forever. A merry chirrup in the kitchen made her cry out. She ran, scrambled, grabbed the handset, dialled 9-9-9.

Answer, please answer. Oh, God, where are you?

Her foot hurt. She looked down. A blood trail led from the kitchen back to Brian. Blood? Where had that come from? One foot bare, sticky with blood. She was bleeding! Somewhere on the staircase, she must have lost a slipper.

Stop it, Brenda. Not important. Concentrate.

"Emergency, which service do you—"

"Ambulance. I need an ambulance. Please hurry. I think my husband's having a heart attack."

The ambulance took days, weeks, months.

As she waited, Bren knelt at his side, checking for a pulse and making sure his chest still rose and fell. All the while, the operator spoke, kind words, soothing words, talking her through the monitoring process, giving her the ambulance's location.

Bren left him again to fetch a blanket. The sirens, when they came, were undulating wails of hope.

"They're here, Brian, They're here."

His eyes closed, chest stopped moving. She screamed, "Brian!" and rolled him onto his back. She kissed him, mouth to open mouth, breathing for her husband, for her life.

#

She rode the ambulance with Brian, watching, praying, crying, holding his hand when the paramedic allowed. They told her that from emergency call to arrival at her house, the automated system clocked the time as nine minutes. The trip from house to hospital took another sixteen. Brian, the fighter, survived the journey, hooked to wires and tubes, and clinging to life. Only when they wheeled him into the operating theatre did she have time to think.

What now? What next?

Brian's funny little ways. His smile, his easy, booming laughter. How would she survive if God took him from her?

What would she do?

She paced the sterile tiles in the waiting room, mobile phone in hand, staring at its blank screen. The sign on the wall—a mobile phone with the diagonal red line running through it—warned of dire consequences of its use. The children. She needed to call her babies.

"Mrs Knightly?"

A blue-starched nurse, impossibly young, stood in the doorway, a serious expression on her smooth oriental face, dark eyes clear and bright.

"Brian, is he ..."

The nurse nodded and stepped into the room. "He's fighting, Mrs Knightly. Please, take a seat."

She led Bren to one of the chairs facing a window that overlooked a well-tended garden. In the central square, water flowed up through a hole drilled through the centre of a large stone ball. Sunlight danced over the surface and sprinkles flashed. The flowing water, designed to calm, failed in its task.

Why did she notice the small things while Brian fought to survive? She looked up at the nurse. "What's happening?"

"Mr Furness asked me to speak to you."

"Who?"

"Mr Furness is our most senior cardiac surgeon. He is operating. You're husband is in good hands."

"Operating? Oh, dear Lord."

The nurse spoke perfect English. She had a wonderful soothing voice and lovely straight teeth, but Bren had difficulty understanding what she said. The words arrived, some stuck, but most flowed past her.

"...coronary graft ... triple bypass ... seven hour operation at least ... one week in hospital ... a minimum of six weeks recovery."

She felt so alone and her foot throbbed, but pain didn't matter.

Oh, Dear Lord, what would she do without Brian? A part of her, the part that made sense of the world, had gone missing. What was the nurse saying? Harry would understand. Harry would explain everything. She needed to phone him and the others.

"…canteen, Mrs Knightly?"

The nurse touched her arm. A belt of static energy zapped Bren into the present.

"Sorry?" Bren asked.

"Do you know the way to the canteen?" the nurse repeated.

"No. I can't leave Brian. Is he going to be okay?"

"Hopefully, but there will be a long wait. Another five hours at least. Is there anyone you can call?" She pointed to the mobile in Bren's hand.

Bren stared at the phone and the ridiculous, sparkling pink cover—a present all the way from America. Sent by Georgina last Christmas so Bren would find it more easily in her cluttered handbag. She looked down at her clothes and couldn't remember dressing or when she'd grabbed her handbag. Perhaps while the ambulance men were working on Brian? Yes, that was it. They'd bandaged her cut foot in the ambulance on the way. Such nice, helpful men. They'd been so professional. Should she bake them a cake?

Oh dear. Stop rambling, woman. Concentrate.

The buttons of her blouse. She'd fastened them in the wrong holes and must look a state. What must the nurse think?

The mobile.

"Yes, yes," Bren said, looking at the young woman—Staff Nurse L Wong, according to her name badge. What did the L stand for? "I need to use the phone. I'm sorry, can't seem to put my thoughts in order. Brian's going to be okay?"

The nurse nodded. "We are hopeful. You can use your mobile in the canteen. Call you children, perhaps? You have children?"

"Of course. Georgina, she's in America, working for a national television company. Doing ever so well. And Harry has his law firm. Geoffrey too, he'll graduate this … Oh dear, I'm sorry. Not making any sense."

"That's perfectly okay, Mrs Knightly. You've had a severe shock. … You know you probably saved your husband's life?"

"Really?"

"The paramedics told us what you did. Putting him in the recovery position and keeping him warm, and the mouth-to-mouth resuscitation. Very good."

"I did that? … Yes, of course I remember now."

Bren closed her eyes, took a deep breath, and stood. Staff Nurse Wong's kind words were just the thing she needed to hear. Clever girl. So young, too. Was she married? Geoffrey might like to meet her.

"I've been a first aider with the Woodford Women's Institute for twenty-three years. Never had to use it before except to treat cuts and grazes. Are you sure there's nothing I can do here? Do you have all the information you need? A full, what is it, case history?"

"Yes that's right. We have all we need for now. I *will* call you the moment there is any news. I already have your mobile details."

"Really?"

"You gave them to the paramedics. Do you need help to find the canteen?"

"Not now, thank you," Bren answered, feeling stronger by the second. 'Up for it', as Geoffrey would have said. "Along the corridor, turn left at the sign that says 'Canteen'?"

The nurse nodded and Bren hurried along, heels clacking on the tiled floors. She'd feel better after calling the children.

#

The intensive care bed seemed to buckle under the weight of all the life support equipment clamped to its rails and headboard.

Bren held Brian's hand, just about the only part of him not attached to a machine. Tubes fed him air and medicine, others allowed fluids out. Wires taped to his skin carried information back to the machines. She had no idea what all the numbers and squiggly lines meant. Bren never watched medical dramas on the television—too much blood and gore for her sensibilities. Give her a good wildlife documentary or a costume drama any day. The BBC did the classics so well.

Brian, poor Brian—pale skin, staples holding together the ten-inch long gash in his chest—barely looked alive. Were it not for the machines tracing the beats of his repaired heart and his shallow chest movement, Bren would have raised the alarm again. She'd done so once already that long, long afternoon.

Georgina had cried when she learned of her father's condition. She'd wanted to catch the first flight into Heathrow, but Bren told her to wait. There was no point rushing if Brian didn't …

Harry arrived half an hour after they'd finished operating. As usual he exuded an aura of calm, considered professionalism. He spoke with the medical staff and explained Brian's condition to Bren in easy-to-understand language. His barrister training helped him explain the unexplainable. They were lucky Dad was still alive. Very lucky. Only Harry's glistening eyes gave away his pain. He'd break down soon enough, but on his own terms, when he thought no one could witness his suffering. So like his father. So much like Brian.

And Geoffrey, on the train down from Leeds, not due for another hour still. He'd take a taxi from Euston.

Fingers moved against hers. "Brian!"

She stood and leaned over him.

Harry jumped out of his seat. "Dad?"

Brian's eyes moved beneath the closed lids. They flicked open and closed again. He tried to lift his head from the pillow. He groaned, face folded in pain.

"No, darling, lie still," she whispered, resting her free hand on his shoulder. "You're in hospital. Heart attack. Can you hear me?"

His eyes opened again, found hers, creased into a smile. He winked.

"Oh, Brian. You had us all so worried."

"Yes, Dad. Too bloody right. I had a tee-time booked for three hours ago— had to forfeit the match. Cost me a bloody fortune in green fees." Harry blinked back tears, lower lip trembling. "If you want me to come home more often you only have to ask. No need for all these theatrics. This is what I call attention-seeking behaviour, you daft old … bugger."

Brian released Bren's hand and removed the face mask. "Language, Harry. You're mother's listening."

His voice, though scratchy and weak, made Bren laugh. The London Philharmonic couldn't have produced sweeter music. She kissed his forehead and wiped away the lipstick smear with her thumb. "You silly, silly man."

"What's that for?"

"Mr Furness, the cardiac surgeon, thinks you've had three minor heart attacks over the past fortnight leading up to this one. Says you've been foolish to ignore the symptoms."

"Suicidal was the word he used," Harry added, wiping his eyes with a hankie. Egyptian cotton. One of his monogrammed best.

"Thought it was indigestion. Your rich cooking."

Bren kissed his lips and then replaced the face mask only for Brian to remove it again. His mouth opened, but he seemed unable to speak.

"What is it, darling?"

"David. Call David … he needs to know."

"Oh darling, you can't worry about work now. Wait until you're—"

"Bren … please?"

"No, darling. You need to rest."

"It's … urgent."

Brian's breathing grew shallow, more rapid. The bleeping on the heart rate monitor increased in speed and volume.

"Brian!"

The door burst open. A nurse in green scrubs entered, closely followed by another. The first one eased Bren aside and fiddled with the IV. The second lowered the top half of the bed.

She stepped back, watching as the medical staff worked. The wearying hopelessness made her shoulders heavy and her legs weak. Harry wrapped his strong arms around her, holding her up.

The first nurse rattled off some indecipherable code to his colleague, who injected the contents of a syringe into the valve arrangement at the bottom of a plastic bag suspended on a metal frame.

Brian's eyes opened, searched, and locked with hers once more, pleading. The message unspoken but clear.

Bren recovered from her momentary weakness, pushed Harry's arms away, and stepped towards the door.

"Mum, what's wrong?"

"Stay with him, darling. I need to make a phone call."

"To whom?"

"I'll tell you later. Stay with your father. I'll be right back."

Chapter 27

Thursday 3rd October

Jones slammed the Crown Prosecution Service report down on his desk, furious at their refusal to prosecute another case he considered winnable by any barrister with more brains than the average ocean sponge.

How many times would a pencil-necked fool with a law degree from a minor university rob a victim of justice? Three times he'd read the report's conclusions, and three times he'd failed to understand the CPS's decision: *Not in the public interest to prosecute a case with the evidence presented.*

A woman had been raped, beaten, and left in a pool of her own blood, and it 'wasn't in the public interest' to prosecute the man responsible? According to the report, the cost-value analysis didn't add up. Justice measured in the price of the court's time. Total rubbish.

Who the hell did they think they were?

That the victim was a prostitute and the accused man a fine, upstanding member of Birmingham's business community had no bearing on the CPS decision. Of course it hadn't. Not one bit of it.

He toyed with the idea of picking up the phone and laying into the spineless clown who'd signed the report, Leighton Rhys, Barrister-at-Law, but what good would that do? The weak-willed idiot would only pass him up the ladder to his boss, who would support his subordinate's decision. Of course she bloody would. He'd expect nothing else.

No, if Jones wanted the CPS to reconsider the case, he'd have to find new evidence, or present the same evidence in a more convincing way. He closed the folder and placed it in his pending tray. Alex could have a go. She'd have a different perspective on the crime. The original investigating team, DS Cruise and DC Gupta from the Special Victims Group would kick up a fuss, but they'd have to suck it up. Alex could teach them a lot.

He stared at the empty chair on the other side of his office—Phil's empty chair. Despite Manda's assurances, Jones fretted over the decision to send him to London. Had it been the right thing to do? Was Phil ready for a return to work?

Jones stood and crossed to the window. Nothing had changed since he last looked out. The grey rain-bearing clouds still headed towards Wales, pushed on a stiffening easterly wind. Below, the car park had already started to empty, a queue had formed at the exit as vehicles waited to join the nose-to-tail traffic on the main road into town. He glanced up and to his left. The wall clock showed 16:57. Why didn't they wait an hour and miss the rush? Anyway, this was a police station, not a bloody bank. They shouldn't be knocking off early—criminals never did.

His desk phone rang with the comforting double-chime of an old-fashioned land line—programmed by Phil. Jones picked up the handset and dropped back into his chair.

"Jones here."

"David, thank God, it's me, Brenda Knightly …"

#

Jones ended the call, his mind racing.

Brian in a hospital bed fighting for his life left Phil in London alone and unprotected. It also meant a probable end to Operation Alpine.

A darker thought occurred.

Plenty of medicines could bring on heart attacks. What if Brian's illness wasn't natural? Christ, what if Alpine had found out about the investigation and had Brian poisoned? Phil would be the next target.

Jesus!

Phil's mobile passed him straight through to voicemail. He cut off the message, dialled '0', and interrupted the operator's scripted spiel. "Put me through to the National Crime Agency's head office in London, please."

"London, sir?"

"Yes. It's a big place down south. The nation's capital!"

"Yes, sir. Right away, sir."

The operator sounded young. He instantly regretted snapping at her and apologised.

He stood and paced through one of the interminable announcements the NCA recorded for the benefit of the people who used to be called 'the general public' but were now 'service users', for God's sake. This particular message reeled off a series of statistics relating to the latest reduction in the crime figures. Listening to the numbers, the 'service users' might be forgiven for thinking they lived in the peaceful gardens of Nirvana.

"National Crime Agency, how can I help?"

Another young female voice, but at least this one didn't sound as though she read from a script.

"DS Cryer, please. He's in your Organised Crime Task Force."

"DS Cryer, sir? And you are?"

"Detective Chief Inspector Jones, Midlands Police. Put me through to him and get a move on. I don't have all day."

Jones winced at his own words and tone. Lack of civility was something he hated in others, but he had a role to play in the game. At the end of the case, he'd apologise to every innocent he upset.

"One moment, please," she answered, cold and sharp.

Another click, this time followed by an actual recording of Beethoven's Pastoral Symphony—the sixth, if memory served. Not bad, and a damned sight better than the electronic drivel he often suffered.

"DCI Jones?" The new voice had a French lilt that reminded him of his recent visit to Brittany.

"Yes. Who are you?"

"DS Delasse, sir."

"Give me DS Cryer."

Although too aggressive, his urgency was real.

"I am afraid he is away from his desk at the moment, sir. Can I pass a message?"

"Where the bloody hell is he?"

Hesitation. "I am not at liberty—"

"Not at liberty! Oh for God's sake. Why isn't he answering his mobile?"

"We don't allow mobile phones inside the office, sir."

"But you said he wasn't in the office, man. Who's in charge there? DCI Endicott, isn't it? Put me through to her."

"I can't do that. She's in a meeting. I will be happy to pass a message to DS Cryer, sir."

"Damn it. Okay. Tell him he's misfiled the file for the Alpine Case and I need it for court next week. Is that clear?"

"The Alpine Case?"

"He'll know what I'm talking about. Tell him to ring me right away. Got that?"

Jones dropped the handset into its cradle and tried to think. What next?

A dozen options raced through his head, and he dismissed each in turn. He searched his memory to find a London-based colleague he could trust enough to send to Tinworth Street, but dismissed the idea on the same grounds as he did the other choices. If he tipped his hand to Alpine before making sure of Phil's safety, it could make matters much worse.

After three quiet raps, his office door opened, and Alex entered.

"Boss? Is everything okay? You do not usually raise your voice."

"Sorry, Alex. Had to maintain the 'nasty former boss' persona."

"Nasty? You?" she said, adding a thin smile. "Not possible. Something must be wrong?"

"Long story. Are Ryan and Ben still here?"

She nodded. "In the main office."

"Excellent. I'm afraid we're in for a long night. Hope no one has any plans."

"Phil is in trouble?"

Despite her recent bereavement, Alex had lost none of her sharpness.

"What makes you say that?"

"He is on a special assignment. Manda Cryer and I are friends, and I can tell when she is worried. So, to repeat my question, you think Phil is in trouble?"

"Yes. At least, he might be."

"What can we do?"

"I don't know, Alex. I really don't."

Sick to his stomach, Jones ushered her through the door and along the corridor, but the ringing desk phone sent him racing back to his office.

"Jones here," he answered, breathless.

"DCI Jones? This is DS Cryer." Phil's stiff voice, as though struggling to remain civil, showed he wasn't alone.

Unable to contain himself, Jones covered the mouthpiece and turned to Alex. "It's him," he whispered. "It's Phil!"

Alex smiled and closed her eyes for a moment.

Jones sat on the edge of his desk and raised a finger to his lips before pressing the phone's speaker button.

"Cryer, that you?"

"Yes, sir. I understand you were trying to reach me?"

"About time you got back to me. Where the hell are you?"

"In the office, sir. One of my colleagues left a note to say you called."

Jones had to take care over what he said. No telling who at the NCA might be earwigging.

"Where did you put the photos from the Alpine Case? I need the originals, not the copies. They've brought the court date forward and I need them for next week. You and your bloody filing system. Never could find anything after you've had your hands on it."

Quick as a flash, Phil replied, "Ask Alex. She'll know where they are. Top drawer in the pending files cabinet."

"Damn it man, don't you think I've already asked her? I shouldn't have to waste my time sorting out your mess. What are you going to do about it?"

Phil gave out a loud sigh. "What would you like me to do, sir?"

"Get back here to Birmingham and find the damned file, man!"

Silence.

"Well? Are you still there? Answer me."

"Sorry, sir. I'm thinking."

"That's a first!" Jones said, hoping the angry sarcasm hadn't been a step too far.

After a few moments silence, Phil spoke again. "Sir, unless something important happens here, I'll be home for the weekend." He made his reluctance clear in the way he drew the words out slowly. "Suppose I could pop into the office if you don't find the photos before then. I … promised Jamie I'd buy the puppy a new lead and Holton HQ is around the corner from that new pet shop."

Jones smiled and winked at Alex who opened her eyes wide and shrugged. She didn't have any idea what was going on.

"Yes, well, I appreciate the offer," Jones said as though begrudging every word. "You can't come tonight? Doesn't the NCA deem real police work important anymore?"

"No, sir, I can't," Phil said, no doubt relishing his role as the put-upon former subordinate. "I've only been here a few days. Surely it can wait until tomorrow evening?"

Jones cleared his throat loud enough and wet enough for Alex to wince. He grimaced and raised his hand in apology.

"Right, thanks, DS Cryer. Suppose I'll see you tomorrow."

"When needed, I'll be there—as usual," Phil said and ended the call.

Jones felt the weight slip from his shoulders. He stared at the handset for a few moments trying to decide his next course of action, before returning it to its cradle.

"Boss?" Alex said after the silence dragged out. "Will you explain now please?"

He looked into her eyes, seeing both concern and mild impatience, and nodded. "What did you make of it?"

"The call? Role play, *ja*?" she said, her Swedish accent as strong as the day he'd accepted her onto his team.

"Exactly. Care to interpret?"

He ushered her out of the office once more and locked the door behind them. More relaxed now he knew Philip was safe, at least for the time being, he had some thinking to do and his team would help.

Alex stepped alongside him. "Phil and Manda Cryer do not have a dog. I guess he was sending you a message?"

"Absolutely. And he's onto something."

"He has found a lead? Hence mentioning the dog?"

"Very good, Alex. We'll make a detective of you yet."

"Thank you, boss. That is most appreciated," she said, arching an eyebrow. "Are you going to tell me why you were worried Phil might be in danger?"

"Yes, but I'll brief you all together."

He pushed the door open and allowed Alex through first. DCs Ryan Washington and 'Big' Ben Adeoye looked up as they entered. Jones took his favourite position at the head of the table, close to the whiteboard and the window.

"If you have any plans for the rest of the night please cancel them. Phil's going to call in a little while and you need to know what he's been doing for the past three weeks."

Alex turned her blue eyes on him. "Phil is calling tonight?"

Jones nodded. "Yes. When he said he'd 'be there as usual', he meant he'd make his report after work, as normal. When he does, I'll need you all familiar with Operation Alpine."

#

"Any questions so far?" Jones asked after speaking non-stop, refusing to be interrupted until he'd outlined the Alpine Case and Phil's part in it.

Alex, Ryan, and Ben had listened to his briefing, read the notes Brian Knightly had brought with him during his initial meeting at Phil's house, and knew as much about Operation Alpine as he did.

Ryan spoke. "Any idea what's on Phil's mind, boss?"

"Afraid not. He's been reporting directly to CS Knightly and I've been keeping my distance."

"Sir?" Ben raised his hand.

"We're not at school, Ben." Jones smiled. He'd said the same thing to Ryan not so long ago. "Speak up."

"You've had more time to read these personnel files." Ben pointed to the folders littering his desk. "Do you have any favourites?"

Jones tugged at his earlobe. He'd asked for their feedback and didn't want to sway their opinions, but did need to move the discussion forward.

"Okay, let's take it from the top. According to CS Knightly, the OCTF's success rate isn't the worst in the NCA, but it is bad enough to raise the concerns of the senior management team. He had intended to replace DCI Endicott, but when DS Juno's death pointed to a corrupt officer, he put the reorganisation on hold. Didn't want to do anything that might warn Alpine.

"The OCTF's drop in performance preceded the arrival of DCs Andrew Mackay, Clinton Schneider, and Hannah Goldstein. In all likelihood, that puts them in the clear. As for the others, they're all suspects."

Alex attached the OCTF organisation chart to the whiteboard with magnets, making sure it aligned with the edge in deference to Jones' idiosyncrasies. "Are their personnel files on our system?" she asked.

Jones shook his head. "Absolutely not. Alpine, or whoever he's working with, is IT savvy. We don't want any random search algorithm tipping our hand. And stop smirking, Alex. I know what an algorithm is—at least in theory."

"It was not a smirk, boss. I promise. It is good to see you coming over to our side."

"The Dark Side you mean?"

This time, she smiled wide and it was like seeing the old Alex.

Jones opened his hands. "Over to you guys now. Anything we can do while waiting for Phil's call?"

To give them time to mull things over, Jones helped himself to a drink from the water fountain.

Alex spoke first. "The hacker friend of Sean Freeman, do you trust him?"

Jones rolled the stiffness from his shoulders. His neck ached and during the previous two hours, some evil sod had sprinkled grit in his eyes. "No, not in the least, but I do trust Sean Freeman. Can't explain it, but I'm certain he's one of the good guys, and he assures me Corky's on our side in this. Why?"

"Would he be able to access the phone records of the OCTF members? We could use information on their mobiles and landlines."

Ryan joined in. "We could do it from here, but going through official channels would take ages and might set the red flags flying."

"Good idea. I'll ask him."

"You can contact this Corky?" Alex asked.

Jones took the burner phone from his jacket pocket. "Not directly, but before he dived undercover, Phil uploaded one of his applications onto this thing."

He dialled a four-digit number, added a double hash, and hit the speaker button. It took a few seconds for the call to connect.

"Afternoon, Mr Jones. Any problems?" Freeman answered, sounding tired.

"Were you asleep?"

"Yes, jetlag, but I'm awake now. What's happening with Mr Cryer?" He yawned loudly. Jones tried not to copy him, but failed, and the yawn rippled around the room. It stopped at Ben, who seemed immune to general fatigue.

Jones gave Freeman an update and finished with, "My colleague, Alex Olganski, has a request for Corky."

"DS Olganski," Freeman said, his voice subdued. "We've never spoken, but please accept my condolences. It might not mean much, but I'm truly sorry for your loss."

Alex lowered her eyes. "Thank you, Mr Freeman."

"Please call me Sean. Although Mr Jones refuses to do so, there's no reason for us to be so formal. Also, I congratulate you on your promotion. What can Corky do to help?"

"Two things please. We would like him to monitor the telephone traffic of each member of the OCTF. Is that possible?"

"No probs," Freeman answered without hesitation. "He's been doing that since Mr Jones first contacted us. I'll get him to forward you the spreadsheets within the hour."

"Freeman," Jones said over Alex's cough of surprise, "you really are something else."

"I'll take that as a compliment, Mr Jones. You didn't really expect us to ignore your investigation, did you? We promised to help all we could. Now, the other thing?"

Jones answered. "Are you aware of CS Knightly's medical condition?"

"Of course, and I'm sorry to hear it. How is he?"

"Hanging on, but we need access to the information on that standalone computer Corky built for him. I'll be taking over the lead on the Alpine Case during his convalescence."

"Excellent, I thought you might. No probs there either. Corky has the information backed up to his very own special cloud."

"But ... damn it man, that device was supposed to be totally secure. A standalone unit with no internet connection. No USB ports, he said. Just serial connections for peripherals. Whatever that means."

"And you believed him? Corky handles information for a living and you thought he wouldn't protect the data Mr Cryer is risking his life to gather? Shame on you."

"Yes, well ..."

"I'm sending the files to you—"

"How are you going to do that? I don't want anything showing up on the PNC database—"

"A courier is *en route* to you with the device itself. Should be there within the half hour."

"Christ's sake, man. You took it from Brian's house?"

The reason for Freeman's jetlag became clear.

"Ya think? I used to be a burglar, remember? Don't worry, I didn't steal anything. After all, the device is technically mine as I paid for its manufacture."

Jones bit back his immediate response and opted for the restrained approach. "Where are you now?"

"Close enough to help if you need me."

Jones paused to absorb the information. Once again, Freeman was marching a few steps ahead of him. Although more annoying than he'd care to quantify, he couldn't claim surprise. Alex and Ryan smiled. Ben didn't.

"If you're that much smarter than us, Freeman, don't suppose you'd care to share Alpine's identity, would you?" Jones asked, only half-joking.

"Mr Jones, you know how to hurt a bloke. Don't you think I'd tell you if I knew. I hate murderers as much you do."

"I'm sorry, Freeman," Jones said, yet again regretting his tetchiness. "Things are a bit tense here."

"I understand," Freeman said, with more seriousness than he usually exhibited.

Jones looked to Alex. "Do you have anything to add, DS Olganski?"

"No, boss," she said.

"Ryan? Ben?"

Both shook their heads.

Jones sent Ben to the ground floor reception to await Knightly's computer. Or was it Freeman's computer? Not that it mattered.

Freeman let out another loud yawn. "If that's all, Mr Jones, I'll go back to bed."

"Yes, that's all, and ... thanks for the help, Freeman. Despite my outburst, I do appreciate it."

"You're welcome, Mr Jones. Goodbye, DS Olganski. Great talking to you."

Alex smiled. "Goodbye Sean. I hope we meet in person someday."

"Forgive me for saying this, but I hope we never do."

Freeman laughed his irritating laugh and cut the connection, leaving Jones to fume quietly.

Chapter 28

Thursday 3rd October

I'm an idiot. An arrogant, conceited, fat-headed idiot. No doubt about it.

For David to call and spout that 'missing photos' guff meant something serious must have happened, something that put me, the operation, or both, in jeopardy. It begged the question, why hadn't CS Knightly passed on the message himself? It would have made more sense for him to have paid a 'Royal visit' to The Cage and 'introduce' himself to the new team member. Strange, but I couldn't exactly call him and ask what had gone wrong.

David's call had given me the perfect opening to end my undercover adventure, but did I take it? Did I heck. Not me. Not Snoopercop. Not the idiot.

If I'd had any sense, I'd have told David to call in the Met's Anti-Corruption Unit, quarantine the OCTF members, and tear the SCUD apart, but I didn't. Instead, I spouted some crap about having a lead when I had nothing.

No idea why I did it, but calling in the ACU would have meant admitting defeat, and I hate failure. The thought of giving up turned my stomach.

Bollocks.

When David called out of the blue, I hadn't been ready to call Operation Alpine a bust, and I still wasn't ready, but by refusing his tacit offer to pull the plug, I'd only delayed the inevitable. I'd given myself six hours at most to answer a puzzle I hadn't been able to solve in three weeks.

So, what did I have? An inkling, maybe, fragments of a picture, but no actual, honest-to-god leads.

For the rest of the afternoon, I stared at my screen, pretending to work, but, in reality, was mulling over all the available information I had from the Juno files. I'd finished reading them on Tuesday. The information rattled around my head and gave me plenty of questions, but no answers. Thirteen cases, all different, none apparently linked by anything apart from Richie Juno's interest in them.

I reread the files in my head.

Circumstantial evidence in three—a shooting, a hanging, and a poisoning—suggested contract killings, but as the MOs were significantly different from each other, none indicated a single perpetrator.

In eight of the others, the deaths appeared unplanned or accidental—a drug overdose, a double stabbing, two suicides, three road traffic incidents, one person lost at sea, and one disappearance—the art forger who might, or might not, have been kidnapped.

The final two files—the outliers—didn't fit the overall profile. The first, the 1976 bombing of a pub in Earl's Court, London, resulted in nine deaths. The second, a failed plot to blow up a London Underground train, took place in 1997, a few months before the British and Irish governments signed the Good Friday agreement.

Those outliers occupied my attention for ages, but I still couldn't see where they fit into the overall picture.

Thirteen cases, a total of twenty-one people missing or dead and, to use the jargon, I could see no 'locus of commonality'.

Richie Juno had spotted something so it had to be there. His personal knowledge must have shown him the way, but I didn't have a Scooby what that could be.

I needed more time.

#

At 17:08, with Freddie Bowen tidying his desk in readiness for his usual early departure, Bee announced Knightly's hospitalisation, and the reason for David's call became clear.

Freddie mumbled a few words of commiseration before hurrying away, three minutes later than normal and in danger of missing his train again. The rest of us received the news in stoic silence. After all, Knightly was a superior officer not a close colleague. After Bee returned to her office, we gathered around the coffee machine, and discussed the fragility of life.

"Bit of a shock, yeah?" Chloe said. "Who knows when the axe is gonna fall? Knightly was carrying a bit of extra lard around the middle, but he didn't look like he were a candidate for eating brown bread."

Drew nodded. "Aye. Brings it home, right enough."

"Didn't know the guy that well," Schneider said, "but he seemed okay. Put his hands in his pocket during Richie's memorial."

Bandage nodded, but said nothing.

From his desk, Hook clapped his hands. "This isn't a fucking wake and Knightly isn't dead. Knock off early. Then come back tomorrow and work on putting away some bad guys."

"Easy Billy," Rob Cruikshank said. "Give us a sec, will you?"

Hook threw a dismissive hand. "Catching bad guys is what Knightly would want, isn't it?"

Over the following half hour, The Cage emptied, but I had too much on my mind to relax. As for my upcoming call to the boss, I still had no idea what to do.

#

I took a light snack in the canteen, more for a change of scenery than to plug a hunger gap, then braved the rain and the cool wind, and schlepped to the Albert Embankment. Dusk fought its daily battle with daylight, but as usual, the city lights won.

A young couple huddling under an umbrella strolled past in the opposite direction, giggling to each other despite the rain driving into the pavement and bouncing up around their ankles. People hurried home or to the pub for end-of-work refreshments. Cars and delivery trucks rolled past, throwing billowing sheets of dirty spray at my hunched back. Water dripped from my hair and ran down my neck. I turned up the collar on my coat and wondered why I'd never invested in a hat—or a brolly, come to that.

By the time I reached the Embankment itself, the rain had eased to a fine mist. After checking my perimeter for watchers and listeners, I leaned against the concrete buttress, faced the river, and dialled.

"Jones here."

"Hi, boss. What's happening?"

"You heard about Brian Knightly?"

"Yes. How's he doing?"

"Still in intensive care. It's touch and go."

"Damn. Not good. The Chief Super and you go back a long way."

"We do. You have something for me."

"Do I?"

"You mentioned a lead."

"Oh ... yes. That, I'm afraid I might have been a little ... premature."

For premature, read 'out and out lie'.

"You don't have anything?"

"Bits and bobs. Nothing concrete, but I am close. I've finished reading the Juno files and ... damn it, there's something I'm not seeing. It'll turn up. I'm certain." Another lie, perhaps. "This afternoon, you sounded worried."

"Yes. Brian Knightly's incapacitation seemed a little, I don't know, opportune."

"For Alpine?"

"Exactly, but I spoke to his surgeon, a chap called Furness. There's no doubt. Brian's heart condition is chronic and formerly undiagnosed. The medic put it down to lifestyle factors and stress, not foul play."

"That's a relief."

"You could say that."

"So, where's that leave us, boss? What do we do?"

The boss took his time to answer. Neither of us wanted to make the obvious decision, or so it seemed.

"I spoke to the Home Secretary about an hour ago. Gave her the news on Brian. She asked that very question. Do you want to close down the operation or carry on?"

"It's my decision?"

"You're the man at the coalface."

At least he'd said coalface and not 'in firing line'.

"Way to put me on the spot, boss. What would you do in my position?"

"Can't answer that, Philip. Wouldn't be fair on either of us."

"Can you give me a moment?"

"Take all the time you need. I'm going nowhere."

That was David Jones to perfection. He wanted Alpine as much as I did, but he wasn't going to apply any added pressure. The decision was mine and mine alone.

I stared at the river rolling out to sea and the lights reflecting off its rippled surface. Knightly's coronary had given me an easy way out. No one could say I hadn't tried. I could walk away, head held high, and get back to my real life, my family, my friends, my home. The brass would have to let me return to the SCU. They had to. Despite the bad leg, nobody could say I hadn't proved my usefulness as a police officer—an asset to any team. Christ, I'd helped break two huge cases, from behind a desk. I could leave the undercover operation right there, but the only person to benefit would be Alpine. I'd be giving him the chance to run. He'd likely have ears in the Anti-Corruption Unit. Someone would tip him off.

"Boss, you still there?"

"Of course."

"Give me a fortnight. If I haven't found Alpine by then, we'll call in the Met's ACU, and I'll come home for good."

"Excellent," he said without pause, "I told the Home Secretary you wouldn't let us down."

David Jones, you gotta love the man. He knew which way I'd jump before I did.

"So, who am I going to report to now the Chief Super's unavailable?" I asked, hoping he'd give me the right answer.

"Me."

That was the answer I needed. Relief rolled over me like the mist from the Thames. It sounds ridiculous to say it, but with David and the team working the case alongside me, I somehow knew we'd make a breakthrough.

"What about your ongoing cases?"

"There's nothing that can't wait two weeks. If anything urgent occurs here, we'll handle it, but you take priority. Alex, Ryan, and Ben are ready to help."

"Fantastic. I feel better now we're back together."

Didn't I just.

"Do you have time to brief me now? I have a recorder handy."

As if to emphasise my relief, a heavy gust threw musty river air into my face. I grinned, pulled the zip of my jacket up to my throat, and started walking. "Nothing better to do, boss."

Half an hour later, I'd given David my appraisal of each member of the OCTF. It added precious little to what I'd known at the start, but at least now, I had firsthand experience of working with them.

"Want me to give you my bullet point reading of each Juno file?"

"That won't be necessary. I have Brian Knightly's special laptop."

"Bloody hell. That was quick. How'd you manage that?"

"Long story. I'll tell you another time, but we've enough to work with for now. Get some rest and call me tomorrow. We'll finish this together. And, Phil."

"Yes, boss?"

"Good lad."

"Thanks."

Big Ben struck nine times, and I headed back to Tinworth Street, mind whirring, but happier than I had been at any time since my move to London.

An Audi A4, the same one I'd seen parked near the Lambeth Bridge during my phone call, passed me slowly. It headed south along the Albert Embankment road, turned into the brightly-lit Texaco petrol station, and stopped at the first pump. The driver didn't get out. I couldn't see him through the tinted windows, but I did recognise the car's number plate. Either Richie Juno had risen from his grave to take a joyride in his flashy, night-black motor, or Billy Hook was following me.

No prizes for the answer to that one.

He'd left The Cage with the others, an hour before me, claiming to be heading for home, yet there he was, cruising the Embankment, watching me. Paranoia be damned. It isn't paranoia when someone is out to get you.

At the entrance to Tinworth Street, out of sight of the forecourt, I paused. I should have ignored the Audi and headed straight for the Gulag, but sod it. Spy on me? Damn him.

I took twenty-five hobbled paces towards the petrol station, before calming enough to see the irony of my being pissed at Hook for spying. Even though I had justice on my side and was hunting a killer, it's what I'd been doing to him and the others for the best part of three weeks. Besides, what would I achieve by confronting him? He'd already made it to the top of my suspect list and couldn't climb any higher.

After weighing the benefits of knowing Hook was following me, against the fact that he didn't know I knew, I stopped.

First thing in the morning, my whole attention, and that of David Jones' Serious Crime Unit, would turn on Detective Inspector William John Hook. I dialled the boss again.

"Better watch out, Billy Boy. We're coming for you!"

PART FIVE

Working Together Again

Chapter 29

Thursday 10th October

I'd done it!

It had taken the better part of a month, but I'd only bloody done it!

No, I hadn't identified Alpine for definite, but I did know how he operated, and I did know his next target—at least theoretically. The only thing left to do was catch him in the act. Or preferably, before the act.

Two hours after my breakthrough, the heart-thumping, blood-warming, jump-up-and-down excitement had faded, but it hadn't died. Even after thirty minutes of sitting in a rented car on my solitary stakeout at Radlett Road, Watford, my confidence remained high. With Alpine in my sights, I found it difficult to stop smiling.

The only down side was the deafening wall of silence thrown out by my mobile. It hadn't chirruped in so long, I kept checking the signal strength.

"Come on, boss. What's keeping you?"

At first, it hadn't gone according to plan. For a start, the failure of Operation Billy Boy had knocked my confidence for a while.

Working from the outside, the SCU and Corky had spent a week peeling back the layers of Hook's life. Apart from the occasional parking fine and a couple of late mortgage payments, Hook's phone records, bank statements, family background checks, and work records, showed him as near squeaky clean as a cop could be.

He had a few complaints on his personnel file, but no cop's record is spotless on that front, and Hook's had its fair share of blemishes.

It happens to us all. Villains love making mischief, especially for the cop responsible for their incarceration. Anyone reading my personnel file—the real one, not Corky's fictionalised version—would find the same thing.

"I'm innocent, your honour. DS Cryer fitted me up."

"DS Cryer never read me my rights, sir."

"See this bruise, doctor? DS Cryer hit me when I was minding my own business. Police brutality, that is. I want to press charges."

No mention of that particular arsehole attacking his wife with a carving knife and me having to wrestle him to the floor over it.

All such complaints are investigated. The vast majority are dropped.

As for my part in Operation Billy Boy, I maintained a close watch on his activity inside the OCTF, mapped his SCUD usage, and found nothing.

Despite the lack of evidence, or maybe because of it, I *knew* Hook was Alpine and refused to admit defeat. Things came to a head during my Wednesday night phone debrief with David—over tortellini in *Gino's*.

"We have other suspects, Philip," David had said after we'd been hammering it out for the time it took me to finish the main course.

"It's him, boss. I'm convinced of it. Why else would the bugger be following me?"

"You're certain it was Hook in the Audi last week?"

"Well, I didn't actually see him, but it was Richie Juno's car. I double-checked the registration with the DVLA the next day. And the way he's been acting around me … it has to be him."

"Would the real Alpine be that obvious?"

That made me think, but I didn't let it deflect me for too long. "If he's responsible for his brother-in-law's murder, maybe the pressure's getting to him. Perhaps he's finding it difficult to maintain control. Maybe he's losing it."

"It's possible, I suppose," David said, but the doubt in his voice was obvious. "Have you seen the Audi since that night?"

"No, but he could be using a different motor."

"There's no record of him owning or hiring another car."

"Bugger could be borrowing a mate's."

"Listen, Philip, I understand your feelings, but we're running out of time. If we haven't found Alpine by the end of next week, the Home Secretary's going to pull the plug on the OCTF and send in the Met's Anti-Corruption Unit."

I gave myself a few seconds to calm down before replying. "Okay, boss. You widen the search, and I'll do the same."

At the end of the call, I pushed my plate away and refused dessert. If I'd tried to eat any more, the ice cream would have stuck in my throat. I'd returned to the Gulag, checking for Audis and any other possible followers during my walk, and managed a fitful night's sleep.

I spent Thursday morning in The Cage collating some reports on a counterfeit currency case and then the magic happened.

It might have been the added pressure of David's ticking-clock ultimatum, but the information in my head that had rolled around for days, suddenly clicked into place.

It worked like one of those combination locks.

Click, click, click.

Questions I asked were answered, the numbers rotated, and the lock opened. A total buzz!

The first number fell when I asked myself the question I should have asked on day one, namely, what had triggered Richie Juno's interest in the seemingly unrelated bunch of cases he kept reading?

Nothing in his NCA caseload at the time gave the answer, but a *This Day in History* search pointed me in the right direction. My tension started to build, and I had to fight my emotions and maintain an outward show of calm. I didn't want my excitement to filter through to others in The Cage.

Juno had accessed the first archived file—the case of the missing art forger, Baz Gurvitz—the day after the start of the Trojan Horse Case, the so-called Trial of the Century. The trial that centred on a hitman—codenamed The Greek—turning Queen's evidence against five of his high-powered clients.

The Greek!

Click!

A hitman!

Click!

The information thumped me with the mechanical force of a piledriver.

My UKPPS mate, Stan the Man, had accidentally mentioned an obnoxious Greek 'client'. No way could it be a coincidence. The association had meant nothing to me at the time, because I'd yet to finish reading all thirteen Juno files.

Click!

Mention of a hitman brought to mind the 2010 murder of alleged drug dealer, Danny Savage. When the police investigation failed to find the killer, family members posted a

£10,000 reward for information leading to an arrest. Dozens of people called the CrimeBusters tip line, but only one pointed a finger at a hitman named The Baron.

A PNC, SCUD, and HOLMES2 database search threw up six separate entries for a contract killer with that handle. On a whim, I ran an internet search for The Baron and, apart from the peers-of-the-realm association, it came up with an almost-forgotten 1960s TV crime series of the same name. No help there, but my mind started wandering.

Here's the route it took.

There are five ranks of peerage in the UK. In descending order of importance, they are: Duke, Marquess, Earl, Viscount, and Baron.

Unless the killer was an actual Baron—and rarity value made that highly unlikely—why would he use the lowest rank? Why not, The Earl or The Duke? Hired killers aren't exactly renowned for their modesty. The greater their renown, the greater fees they can command. So, why call himself The Baron?

With no clear answer, my mind returned to the Greek thing.

Why had the Trojan Horse Case tweaked Richie Juno's interest?

The Essex Constabulary's online records gave me access to Richie's case records from before he joined the NCA. It didn't take me long to find a reference to one Theodor Dukakis, whose father owned a Casino in Southend-on-Sea. In 1997, young Theo applied for a drinks and gaming licence. In 1998, he applied for a firearms licence. The Essex Police rejected both applications due to a 1995 conviction for reckless endangerment and driving under the influence. No prizes for guessing the name of the officer in who rejected the applications—DS Richard Juno.

Click!

Dukakis is a Greek name meaning Son of the Duke, or Little Duke. Only an idiot hitman would give himself a nickname so close to his real one, hence—I assumed—Theo's alias, The Baron.

Click! Click! Clickety click!

By this time, I could hardly contain my excitement, and had to take a canteen break for fear of giving myself away to Hook, which is where I had a blinding piece of good fortune. Halfway through my afternoon coffee, a TV news bulletin announced that the chief witness in the Trojan Horse Case—the one I knew to be The Greek—would take the stand the following day. The judge expected his testimony to last at least two weeks.

If Theo Dukakis was the hitman at the centre of the Trojan Horse case, how valuable would his location be to Alpine's criminal contacts?

That was the absolute clincher. I had the whole story mapped out. Well, if not the whole story, at least a good part of it.

Stan the Man's Greek 'client' had led me to The Baron, who pointed the way to the Duke, and then to Alpine. Tenuous perhaps, but proof enough for me to call in the big guns.

Although I had finally worked out a direct route from some of the Juno files to Alpine, I still had no real idea what made Juno think a rogue cop operated within the OCTF in the first place. Perhaps Hook, whom I knew for certain was Alpine, had done something to arouse Juno's suspicions. Or maybe he'd overheard one of the UKPPS team talking about their new Greek 'client'. After all, that's how I'd learned the name. No matter, when I caught Hook in the act of trying to kill Dukakis, I'd bloody well ask. If necessary, I'd beat it out of him.

Although seeing what Hook could do to a punching bag, I might have been overestimating my abilities on that front.

The moment I put it together to my satisfaction, I made two phone calls.

Trying to keep the excitement out of my voice, I played the first call warm and friendly, and the second cool and professional. Not sure I managed it with the second one, but the first went well enough.

"Hey, Stan the Man, how you doing? It's me, Phil Cryer." I relaxed my voice, playing the old friend wanting to chew the fat.

"Hi, Phil. I was wondering if you'd ever get back to me for that drink. You didn't seem too keen when I suggested it."

"Are you kidding, I'm up for it right now. I'm having a crap week. Fancy getting leathered?"

"Sorry, mate. Can't happen tonight. I'm on duty. Can we do it next week?"

"Are you in the office? I wouldn't mind seeing a friendly face. The arseholes here are so goddamned miserable."

"Nah, sorry, I'm at home getting ready for an all-nighter ."

"Pity. Looks like I'll be drinking alone then. I'm sure I can manage."

Happy to have Stan confirm his whereabouts, I promised a rain check, ended the call, and then dialled again.

"Jones here."

"Boss, it's me, Phil. I've worked out Alpine's next target. How soon can you get down to London?"

"A couple of hours at least. Why?"

I told him what I'd discovered, gave him Stan the Man's location, and arranged to meet him there. It took a while to organise a hire car, but I'd been sitting outside Stan's place for two hours before David finally rang.

"Sorry, Phil," he said, "We're about to leave."

"You're still in Birmingham?"

"Afraid so. Still trying to arrange firearms cover."

Stan's front door opened.

"Hang on a minute, boss. I've got movement."

Stan emerged from his house and hurried to his car, a Ford Mondeo Zetec. Seconds later, the throaty engine fired up and the car pulled out of the drive.

"Sorry, boss. There's no hands-free in the hire car. I'll call when I have an end location."

"Take care, Phil. We'll be there as soon as possible."

#

Standard operating procedure for the SCU is to use at least two, but preferably three vehicles to follow a suspect—not that I considered Stefan Stanislas a suspect. Three vehicles give plenty of scope for interchanges, which reduces the chance of the mark spotting the tail. No way could I risk asking anyone on the Task Force to help in case they were as dirty as Hook. The same was true of taking Stan or any of his other UKPPS teammates into my confidence. Apart from David Jones and the rest of the SCU, I could trust no one in the Force.

Phil Cryer, alone in the big city and tailing a man with a gun—life had turned into a whole heap of scary shit.

Following Stan in the gathering gloom of an autumn evening turned into a nightmare of sweaty hands, rear-view mirror checking for tailing Audis, indicator watching, stomach-churning fear, tinged with—I'll admit it—excitement. I hadn't had so much fun, or felt so alive, since falling through the bloody rotten roof.

Were it not for the light traffic, I'd have lost Stan at the first junction. Not having driven since the accident, I'd almost forgotten how. On top of everything else, the hire car's automatic transmission wasn't configured for high-speed pursuit. Fortunately, the route he took—straight roads, few roundabouts, fewer traffic lights—made following easy.

After a right turn at a roundabout, we drove three kilometres along the A1 before joining the M1 at Junction 2, heading north.

By the time we'd settled into the motorway stream, sweat soaked my shirt, and I was hyped into twitchy awareness. I allowed five cars to fill the gap between Stan's Ford and my BMW, before cracking the driver's window to suck in deep breaths of cool air. The wind dried my face, and I soon started shivering.

Three chocka motorway lanes restricted Stan to the speed limit and gave me time to report my position to the boss.

"Sorry, Phil," David said, "it's taken longer than I expected to issue firearms to the team. Giles and the Armed Response Unit needs special authorisation to operate outside the Midlands. I can't risk the official paperwork, so it's down to Alex, Ryan, and Ben."

In all the years I'd know David Jones, I'd never seen him so much as touch a weapon. I'd never asked why he didn't have a firearms certificate either. If he wanted me to know, he'd have told me.

"Ryan?" I asked, moving into the overtaking lane as Stan put his foot down once the traffic eased north of Junction 4. "He passed his firearms course?"

"Last week. I forgot to tell you. His instructors gave him a good write-up but this'll be his first active shoot. Ben's going to look after him. Any idea where DS Stanislas is headed?"

"Sorry, boss. I couldn't risk accessing the UKPPS servers. No telling if anyone on Stan's team is compromised."

"At least you're heading towards us. It won't take so long to reach—"

"Hang on, boss. He's exiting at Junction 5. We're headed for Watford. Hell, I think I know where he's going. When you get there, leave the M1 at Junction 5 and head for the A41. I'll confirm the actual address when we stop."

Knowing David and the team were on their way made me feel better, but my knee throbbed and the sweat still poured out of me. I was so thirsty, my tongue kept sticking to the roof of my mouth.

Off the motorway, Stan turned west. Heavy clouds blocked the setting sun and made it easier for me to make out his distant Mondeo. We filtered onto the A4008, Stephenson Way, negotiated two roundabouts, and ended up on Radlett Road. A couple of minutes later, Stan turned into the narrow Ebury Drive, and I stopped at the junction under a 'No Through Road' sign. I couldn't risk going further. Stan would have to park or turn around. If he turned, he'd see me following him.

Still scanning the rear view for a tail, I powered up the car's built-in Satnav. It took an age for the system to lock onto its satellites before I could find and relay the co-ordinates to David. According to the boss, they'd reached the end of the M6 and were racing towards me at flank speed, blue lights flashing. The two-tone sirens wailed throughout our call, but they were still at least an hour away.

What to do?

Make a decision, smartarse.

I parked behind a Transit van and, in the fading light, I took a gentle stroll down Ebury Drive. The clouds darkened and the freshening wind knifed through my thin jacket. No doubt about it, I should have brought a bloody heavier coat. Autumn had arrived early.

Uneven and cracked paving slabs worked my knee hard and I had to concentrate on my footing to avoid the trip hazards. 1930s bay-fronted terraced houses flanked either side of a quiet road barely wide enough for two cars to pass alongside. Cars parked on either side narrowed the road further. With no gardens, the front doors opened directly onto the pavement. I felt exposed and very much alone.

My watch read 20:13.

I kept my stick tucked tight against my left leg and walked slowly to minimise the limp. No sign of Stan's Mondeo or of Hook's Audi.

Street lighting threw deep shadows and hid the pavement pitfalls. I concentrated on avoiding the dangers when, halfway down Ebury Drive, the road split in two. The right fork became Shaftsbury Lane.

I chose the left-hand fork, the footing improved, and I increased my pace. One hundred metres down Ebury Drive, it opened into an upmarket tree-and-hedge-lined avenue, and ended in a cul-de-sac, where a mini-roundabout allowed a tight turning circle. Stan's car and an identical dark blue Mondeo filled the drive of a modern semi-detached house—Number 153. Once more, my memory had served me well.

After scouting the best place to park where I could still see the safe house but remain hidden, I hurried back to my Beemer. I couldn't stop smiling. Things were looking good.

When I was still two hundred metres from the car, the rain started—great big ice-cold droplets a late English summer produces so often. Five minutes later, safely parked behind the stout trunk of an oak tree and diagonally across the road from the safe house, I settled down to wait for David and the gang.

Although my damp clothes steamed from my body heat, I was sorted.

#

The dashboard clock ticked slowly to 21:07 and I struggled to stay alert. I couldn't stop yawning. Sheets of wind-driven rain smashed into the mist-obscured windscreen and rippled the view beyond. Although rain reduced my ability to see the safe house, I couldn't use the wipers for fear of giving myself away. On the plus side, the angry squall also discouraged people from taking evening strolls, and my vigil would remain clandestine. I cracked the window to let in some fresh air, but the rain found its way in and I had to close it again.

Solitary stakeouts had to be one of the worst parts of the job.

No, check that. On reflection, there were far worse parts. Notifying relatives of a loved-one's demise ranked up there with watching a colleague fall under the wheels of a car. DI Hook had seen that happen to Richie Juno. Christ, he'd been responsible for it. What must that have been like? No wonder he'd behaved like a complete prick to the man sent to replace his brother-in-law.

On the pavement behind my car, a stooped old man, part hidden under a black umbrella, walked his dog—a sodden little white thing, more waterlogged rat than man's best friend. I followed his progress in the wing mirror as he approached my car and then passed, stopping once to let Roland Rat make a deposit in front of a garden gate. The man removed a bag from his pocket, bent to scoop up the mess, and continued his stroll.

For all the care he took with it, the white plastic bag swinging in his hand might have contained his shopping. I'd have treated the foul object as though it contained nuclear waste. Man and dog crossed the street at the end of the road and disappeared into a garden two doors up from Number 153.

If my logic held firm, the Baron's first day of testimony would likely be the most explosive, and whoever Alpine worked for couldn't afford any information to make it into the court's record. Ergo, the night before the first day's testimony had to be the optimum time for a hit. Touch and go, but I felt really smug that I'd worked out the connection in time—

The passenger door yanked open.

I snapped my head around. "What—"

A black hole.

A huge black hole pointed at my left eye—the muzzle of a bloody great big hand cannon!

Chapter 30

Thursday 10th October

For a second, I couldn't see anything but the bore of the gun muzzle, the edges of the rifling grooves, and its outer ring. I'll never forget it as long as I live. Of course I won't. The muzzle didn't move, but I trembled. Couldn't stop my raised hands shaking.

My vision pulled out and into focus. The square stock of a semi-automatic—a Glock. Front sight above. Beneath that, a ring the shape of a Polo mint—a black Polo mint—and the protruding trigger guard. Then the fingers, left hand wrapped over right. Trigger finger resting along the guard.

Along the guard! Not on the trigger.

I breathed again. Slow and steady. Didn't want to risk any sudden movements.

Behind the hands, the pale, battle-scarred face of DI William Hook, lips pared back in a snarl. His body bent forward, half inside and half outside the car.

I should have locked the doors. Why didn't I lock the bloody doors?

What a fucking rookie mistake, and one that would probably cost me my life!

Where had he come from? While I had my eyes fixed on the safe house, the fucker sneaked up behind me.

Stupid, Phil. Bloody stupid.

I tried to swallow, but couldn't.

Microseconds passed while I worked out the options. If he shot while steady and braced, I had no chance. But if the gun wavered when he entered the car—*if* he entered the car—I'd make my move. Grab the Glock. Suicidal perhaps, but what else could I do? My stick, on the back seat, might as well have been in the boot.

"I fucking knew it!" Hook said, lips barely moving. "You bastard."

What? What was that? *I'm* the bastard?

Kidding, right? Responsible for his brother-in-law's death, yet he had the gall to call *me* the bastard? I opened my mouth to shout, but the big black hole enforced my silence.

If he moved his trigger finger a centimetre and applied a couple of grams of pressure, I'd be dead. No doubt. No doubt at all. It took every particle of strength I had, but I dragged my concentration from the gun and stared into his eyes.

Only one thing to do. Wait. Wait for his move.

"Grab the steering wheel."

I hesitated.

The gun twitched. "Do it! I'm not telling you again, you fucker."

As I obeyed his instructions, he dropped into the passenger seat, and the car dipped under his weight. It was as though he'd read my mind. I foresaw my death at the hands of the dirty cop I'd been sent to expose. The leather covering the steering wheel compressed under my grip. At least it stopped my hands shaking.

Such a bloody waste.

The thought of never seeing Manda or the kids again made my heart ache and guts churn. I tried to calm my breathing. My grip became slick on the wheel. Sweat pasted the shirt to my back.

"Start the car." Hook's calm voice showed control.

"What?"

"Start the fucking car."

"Why not kill me now and get it over with?"

"What?" The vertical creases on his forehead deepened, the crow's feet too. "Shut the fuck up and start the car."

He aimed the gun at my belly. Not the way I wanted to die—slowly and in gut-shot agony. Hell, I didn't want to die at all. Not with the kids so young. They needed me. Shaking fingers found the ignition key, turned, and the engine caught, purred.

"Where to?"

"Do a u-ey. Make it smooth. Wouldn't want this gun to go off all accidental-like."

"Me neither," I said, sounding way calmer and more confident than I felt.

Bravado, the last refuge of the stupid man.

At least we'd be leaving the safe house. It gave David and the guys time to arrive, and the further we drove, the more options I'd have.

Delay him. That was it. Wait for an opportunity.

While I was driving, he couldn't shoot. The look in his eyes, angry, not suicidal gave me hope. At the end of Ebury Drive, I stopped at the give way sign.

"Make a left. Keep below the speed limit."

We headed south, towards London.

Where the hell was he taking me?

I kept the speed below thirty. My hire car had a built-in GPS tracker, they all do these days, so at least David would know where to find my body. Hook would probably take me to some wasteland and torch the car—deal with my corpse the way his lackey dealt with Sunil Pradeep's. The irony hadn't escaped me.

Such a stupid bloody fool. Why hadn't I ended Operation Alpine when given the chance? My poor babies. I'd never hear Paulie's first words. Never pace the floors waiting for Jamie to come home from her first date.

Oh God.

At least I'd given Theo Dukakis a reprieve, however temporary. Maybe David would arrive before Hook's friends did the deed. That was my plan as far as it went. Play for time. It wouldn't do me any good, but it might save Dukakis' life, not to mention Stan and his colleagues.

We made another left and joined a dual carriageway. The signs pointed to the M1, London bound. I eased the throttle forward and the Beemer picked up speed.

"Steady, Lucky," Hook said, the sneer returning. "Not so fast. These Beemers have nice big airbags. I'd probably survive a crash, but you definitely wouldn't."

He raised the gun to make his point.

"Bastard."

"Naughty, naughty. Don't antagonise a man with a gun."

I lifted my foot from the throttle, dropped the car's speed to a steady sixty-five, and kept to the inside lane. Light evening traffic gave drivers plenty of chance to overtake. None of them turned to look at us, but why should they?

Think, Phil, think. Hostage Negotiations, Beginner's Guide. What did the book say? Keep the hostage-taker talking. Build a rapport. Easy to write, difficult to do with a gun in your face.

"Slow down. Keep your distance."

The needle on the speedometer had inched clockwise again and we'd started to tailgate the white van ahead. How did that happen?

"Where are you taking us?"

"You'll find out."

"You'll kill me anyway so why not tell—"

"Kill you? Don't be so fucking stupid. Why would I do that?"

I chanced another look at him. Despite the darkness and the pattern of the rain-pitted window reflected on his creased face, his confusion was obvious. What the hell was going on?

"Why?" I asked.

"Huh?" His frown deepened.

"Why did you do it?" I asked.

"Do what?"

"Set up Richie to be killed. When did he find out about you?"

"What the fuck you on about?"

For the first time, the gun wavered. I watched the traffic and the barrel. Hoping for an opening. Any opening.

"He was your brother-in-law, you sick fuck. Why did you have him killed?"

"Shut up you bastard! Richie was my best friend."

"So why'd you set him up?"

"I didn't!" he yelled, spittle flying. "You and your fucking mate, Knightly killed him 'cause he was onto *you*!"

"What? What are you saying?"

The gun wavered again.

I lifted my foot from the accelerator. Our speed dropped. Hook looked at the speedometer. I spun the steering wheel sharp left, threw up my left hand, and smashed the gun upwards. It barked. The explosion, loud in the confines of the car, rang in my ears, the heat and smell over powering. Back-blast scorched my fingers.

"Stop, you bloody idiot! Stop!" Hook yelled.

The car bounced and swerved, pushing me against the door frame.

The gun. I had to keep hold of the gun!

Push it away. Anything.

He twisted the Glock downwards. I focused everything on my two hand grip.

Hook's fist came from nowhere. The blow connected with my chin, smashing my teeth together, cracking my head against the window. The Glock tore from my fingers.

Apart from the stars swimming in my peripheral vision, I saw nothing. Eyes squeezed closed, breath held, I waited for the shot that would end my life. Heart-stopping seconds stretched into minutes, hours.

I risked opening my eyes. The shock and fear on Hook's face told me he wasn't a killer. Told me he wasn't Alpine. I'd made a mistake. Another bloody mistake.

Hook wasn't Alpine.

Breathing hard, I let the revelation sink in for a moment.

Hook backhanded my shoulder. This punch didn't hurt.

"What the fuck did you do that for, Lucky? I could have killed you."

"Thought I was a dead man anyway."

"Bloody stupid thing to do."

My jaw didn't feel broken but he'd loosened a few teeth.

"Was that your fist? Felt like a bloody sledgehammer."

He still held the gun, but it pointed down into the footwell. His trigger finger rested back along the guard. No way I'd make another grab for it. The bugger was too bloody strong from pounding those flaming bags every lunchtime. With his free hand he pointed at the hole in the roof.

"That could have been in your bloody head."

"I know." I shuddered and thought of something inappropriate. "How am I going to explain that to the hire company? Bang goes my insurance excess."

Weird how the stressed mind works.

"Your problem. Not mine."

My shakes calmed to the occasional tremor, but my heart still raced. I swallowed the bile rising up my throat. So close. So damn close.

The car had rolled to a stop on the grass verge, canted at a sharp upward angle. Without thinking, I tugged the handbrake and turned on the hazard lights. The loud clicking fused with the ringing in my ears and my heavy breathing.

"Why did you stop? Get back on the road."

Hook's pale face still displayed shock but the hand holding the gun remained steady. We both knew how close death had been. No way was he going to shoot me. That I knew and it put me in the driver's seat—so to speak. My turn to ask questions.

"What was that you said about the Chief Super?"

"Huh? … Oh. I thought Knightly had you kill Richie because Richie was onto him."

"Don't be bloody ridiculous," I said, the post-battle comedown removing the fear and replacing it with anger and more bravado. "I've been on sick leave for the past five months. Until three weeks ago I had nothing to do with Brian Knightly or the NCA."

I tested my jaw. Sensitive and bruised, but intact.

"Knightly probably has more people on his payroll than you."

Knightly as Alpine? Ludicrous idea. Knightly wouldn't have initiated the Alpine investigation if he'd been dirty. Besides, both Corky and I checked his background before I dived undercover—behind David's back. Nothing on the Chief Super's profile showed him as anything other than honest.

"You're right, up to a point. I am working for Knightly. He asked me to investigate the Task Force, but only because DS Juno made an appointment to see him the morning of his murder. Knightly was suspicious of you. All of you."

Hook shook his head. "Richie contacted Knightly? I didn't know."

"That's why he sent me undercover."

"But I've investigated Knightly. The bugger's bent as a bloody corkscrew. His investment portfolio alone shows more than he could make on a Chief Super's pay."

Massaging my jaw didn't help. I stopped.

"How deep did you dig?"

"As far as I dared. Didn't want to show my hand. Why?"

"Did you look into his wife's family? The Courtleys?"

Again the frown, this time he coupled it with another head shake.

"The Courtley clan owns a huge portion of Sutherland County, in the north of Scotland. They still do, but in the fifties and sixties they sold a few miles of coastline for salmon farming. Made a packet and invested it well. Brenda Knightly's a multi-millionaire in her own right. Brian Knightly doesn't need to do anything dodgy."

That gained Hook's attention. I could almost hear the cogs in his head grinding. "What were you doing in Watford?"

"I followed DS Stanislas. He virtually told me he was part of The Greek's protection duty."

"The Greek? Who's The Greek?"

"The supergrass in the Trojan Horse case …" I told him the whole story, but kept it brief. "What were you doing there?"

Hook's sullen expression gave me the answer.

"Fuck's sake. You followed me again?"

"Yeah. I've been tailing you off and on since you started. That stick made it easy." He tilted his head towards the back seat. "I reckoned you were reporting to Knightly from *Gino's* and during your evening strolls along the river. When you reached Watford tonight, I knew you were up to no good."

"What took you so long to stick that canon in my face?"

He finally relaxed enough to show me what he looked like without a scowl. Still no oil painting, but at least he'd stop curdling milk.

"Thought you were meeting a contact. I waited a while to see who'd show. Then I noticed the two Mondeos in the drive and recognised them as UKPPS pool cars."

He'd identified the safe house from pool cars? So much for covert protection protocols. I'd have to mention that to Stan the Man next time I saw him.

Stan the Man—Fuck … the safe house!

What had we done? If Hook wasn't Alpine, we'd just left the safe house unguarded.

"Put the gun away."

"Why?"

"I'm pulling into traffic and that thing's making me nervous."

"That's the fucking point of it. Where are we going?"

"Back to Watford. Dukakis and the protection team are in danger."

With the hazard warning lights still active, I cut a hole in the traffic, ignored blaring car horns, and hammered towards the next roundabout.

Hook ejected the Glock's magazine and pulled the slide back.

"What are you doing?"

"Making the weapon safe. There's always a live round in the chamber after it's been fired, unless the magazine's empty. Christ, Lucky. You know nothing about Glocks, do you."

"I know enough to leave weapons to you hot shots. Fuck's sake, I nearly rear-ended that truck."

He reloaded and replaced the magazine before sticking the pistol into his shoulder holster. It made me feel so much better. My arms still trembled from the exertion and fear, and my guts still churned, but I was less likely to throw up than I had been a few moments earlier.

It took five endless minutes to reach and negotiate the roundabout. Neither of us had spoken since my decision to return to the safe house. I worked through the new information and concentrated on my driving. Hook, I guess, had his own riddle to answer.

"Where *were* you taking me just now?" I asked, to break the silence, if nothing else.

"Tinworth Street. Where'd you think we were going?"

When I told him, he laughed. Not a particularly attractive laugh, but it made a nice change from all the growling.

On the way, I filled him in on the remaining details of Operation Alpine. He took it well. I half expected him to push his fists through the windscreen.

"This whole thing's about keeping Dukakis from spilling his guts?"

"Tonight is, but Alpine's been operating for months, years even. No telling what the bastard's been up to."

Hook stared through the windscreen for a moment. "Any idea who he is?"

"You've been top of my suspect list ever since I started looking."

"Me? Why?"

"Your attitude has been piss poor. I reckoned you were overreacting to deflect guilt away from you and onto me."

"You really thought I'd set up my own brother-in-law?"

I didn't answer that one and pretended to concentrate on an overtaking manoeuvre.

The rain had eased to a gentle drizzle by the time we reached Radlett Road, and the automatic wipers slowed. I jammed on the brakes and turned into Ebury Drive. Two hundred metres later, I took the left fork and parked in the same place as before, on the right-hand side of the street, diagonally across from the safe house. Full dark, but with the streetlights bright, I studied the safe house. Was it still safe?

The place didn't look right. Something had changed.

"Shit."

"What's up?" Hook followed my gaze.

"The front door's slightly ajar."

"It's dark. How can you tell?"

"The reflections on the paintwork and the shadows are different."

"You certain?"

I gave him my most withering look. "I stared at that house for half an hour."

He took the message and reached for the door handle. I grabbed my stick and cracked open the driver's door, grimacing against the stiff legs and throbbing knee.

"Wait here," Hook said. "You're a liability when it comes to action. No offence."

"None taken," I lied and pulled my door closed again.

Hook got out, hurried around the back of the car, and fetched up next to me. He crouched, taking cover behind the Beemer. I lowered the side window. Raindrops falling from the oak leaves drummed on the car's roof and on Hook's head and shoulders.

"How'd you want to handle this?"

"Call it in," Hook whispered, eyes flicking down to my stick. "I'll go see what's happening."

"Is that wise? We should wait for backup. My team will be here in a few minutes."

He rubbed his chin with the back of his hand, staring at the safe house door. "Damn it. I can't stay here in the rain scratching my arse when people I know might be in danger. Call for help. I'm going in."

I had to give him credit for balls, if not sense.

"Who do I call? Can't trust anyone in OCTF. Not until we've identified Alpine. There may be others."

"Good point. Give Citadel Place a bell and ask the Italian for the Met's firearms unit, SC&O19. The number's on file."

I closed my eyes and searched my internal directory. "Don't worry, I know the number." I said, ignoring his look of surprise.

"Call them and ask for Inspector Gregor Fleeting. Tell him what's happening and that I said 'Bingo'. It's my old call sign. Got it?"

"Yeah. What do I do then?"

"Stay here in case someone gets past me."

He reached down to his ankle and pulled out a snub-nosed revolver, a Smith & Wesson.

"Bloody hell, a hidden backup? That's illegal."

"Arrest me later." He handed me the gun. "Know how to use one of these?"

"No," I said truthfully.

"I keep the first chamber empty to avoid accidents."

"Accidents. Yeah, right."

The weight of the thing surprised me more than anything else. Bloody heavy despite its lack of bulk. Mind you, with my level of skill, I'd have probably been better off chucking the bloody thing. There's nothing wrong with my throwing arm.

Hook smiled. "If you have to shoot, squeeze the trigger twice. You won't hit anything, but you'll scare the crap out of anyone not expecting it. But please don't shoot. Think of all the paperwork."

A joke? Who knew the guy had a sense of humour?

"Right. What a pain in the arse that would be."

"Two more things. First, don't point that thing at me."

"Okay. Even though I owe you for putting a hole in the roof and scaring me half to death." I smiled but was only half kidding. "The second?"

He shrugged. "Sorry for calling you Gimp."

"Now that, I can't forgive. Cry myself to sleep most nights."

Hook tilted his head sideways, thinking. "Okay, maybe I'll start calling you Cry-baby. DS Cry-baby Cryer. Love it."

"Fuck off, Nookie."

"Touché."

He pushed his hand through the open window and we bumped fists.

"Be careful over there."

"Watch my back."

I reached into my pocket for my phone and dialled. Hook drew the Glock and held it in a two-handed grip. He broke from the cover of the car and sprinted toward the house at a half crouch, his Glock pointing down and to the side.

A gunshot shattered the silence. Hook spun, staggered, and fell. His head bounced as it hit the road. The sickening dull crump made me heave.

A second *crack*.

The BMW's front passenger's window shattered, showering me with sharp-edged pellets of glass. I punched open the driver's door. Dived out. My knee smashed against a concrete paving slab. Paralysing pain exploded through my leg.

Silence fell.

Silence, save for pattering rain, the thumping of my heart, and the wheezing of my lungs. I lay in a shallow puddle and waited for the next shot.

The kill shot.

Chapter 31

Thursday 10th October

Crack!

A flash lit up the safe house doorway.

The third shot hit the road one metre from Hook's right foot. The bullet tore a chunk of tarmac out of the surface, ricocheted, and smashed a window in a car behind me. How could the shooter miss him? The low wall in front of the safe house must have been obscuring his view.

Crack!

The fourth shot hit something metallic. I couldn't tell what.

Do something, Phil. Shoot back. Make him think again. Squeeze the trigger twice. I had nothing in my hands but the mobile. My gun, the revolver.

Where was it?

Crap! I remembered.

A headlong dive to the ground. I hit the pavement hard—head, knee, elbow. The gun jolted from my hand and skittered away.

Where? Damn it, where?

Under the car. Out of reach.

No!

Rain hammered my head and neck, and ran down my collar. It chilled my back through the light summer jacket. I shivered, and not only from the cold.

How many shooters? One or two? Only one flash at a time. I had to reach Hookie, pull him to safety. I lifted my head to look. No cover between him and me. No, no chance for either of us. Shit.

The revolver. A slim possibility, but worth the risk. I edged forward, arm outstretched, reaching.

Crack.

The bullet thumped into the tree above my head. I scrambled backwards, into the deep shadow. Kissed the pavement again. Gravel crunched, knee throbbed. Helpless. Nothing I could do.

I'd never been so scared.

Hook hadn't moved since his head hit the road. Dead? He had to be dead.

Minutes passed. My breathing slowed, as did the rain.

Behind me, headlights lit the houses, and a squeal of tyres pierced the silence. I rolled onto my back and raised my head. At the far end of Ebury Drive, a big dark blue car—a Range Rover according to the headlight configuration—took the corner on two wheels, full beams blinding. The cavalry? The shooter's support team?

Alpine, what was he doing?

I rolled onto my front again.

A shadowy figure in the safe house doorway—very small, dark, crouching, a flash of red optics catching the glow of the streetlights—ducked back inside. The door slammed.

The shadow's outline looked familiar. The way it moved, carried its head. The slope of the shoulders. Oh God no, surely not? How wrong could I be?

"Billy!" I called in a stage whisper. "If you can hear me, don't move. Stay where you are and the shooter can't hit you."

The Range Rover screeched to a diagonal halt forty metres down the street, forming a barrier across the road. Its moveable spotlights bathed the safe house in blinding, dazzling white. Car doors opened, shoes slapped pavement and splashed puddles. Torchlight beams swung. One lit my face.

"Armed police officer! Don't move. Drop that phone."

Phone? What phone?

A distant, crackling voice said, "Hello? SC&O19, Tactical Support."

My phone still worked, even if my hearing didn't. I could have sworn the man shouting, "Don't move," was Ben Adeoye.

"Sarge? Is that you?" The torch beam moved away, leaving orange after-images on my retinas, circular and fading.

"Ben? It *is* you. Keep down. There's a sniper." I pointed across the road.

"I know, we picked up 9-9-9 calls on the radio."

"Where's the boss?"

"Right behind me. Who are you calling?"

I looked at the half-forgotten mobile.

"SC&O19. Give me a hand up and grab that gun, will you?" I pointed to the handle of the revolver sticking out from under the car. "But be careful, they'll be able to see you from the house."

Hands under my armpits pulled. I stood faster than I had in months but kept my head below the BMW's roofline. I slapped the phone to my ear as Ben scrambled for the revolver and stuck it into his jacket pocket. No way would he give it back to me, and I wouldn't have taken it if he'd offered.

I spoke into the phone. "Hello? Are you still there?"

"Yes, sir. Who is that?"

I gave the man my name, badge number, and the safe house address. "Send an ambulance immediately. We have an officer down. Gunshot wounds. And put me through to Inspector Gregor Fleeting."

"One moment, Sergeant Cryer."

A click, a pause. While I waited, David arrived, crouching low, keeping parked cars between him and the houses opposite.

"Phil, are you okay?" he asked, worry in his eyes. "Your cheek, it's bleeding."

The flying glass? I felt nothing.

I gave David the thumbs-up, changed it to a raised finger 'hold on a sec' sign, and activated the speaker key.

"DS Cryer? This is Fleeting. Who gave you my name?"

"DI Hook says, 'Bingo'."

"Right," Fleeting said and paused before continuing. "Jesus. You're in Ebury Drive outside the safe house?"

"That's right."

"We won't be able to reach you for … an hour at least. Can you contain the area?"

David stuck out his hand for the phone. Gratefully, I handed it over.

The boss introduced himself and gave his badge number. "Inspector Fleeting, I have cross-jurisdictional authority from the Home Secretary. Send us some locals to help contain the situation."

He turned away, describing the scene and issuing instructions.

Crouching as low as I could given the pain in my fucked-up leg, I stared at Hook. He still hadn't moved. So exposed. I spoke to Ben, raising my voice over the downpour. "We can't leave him there."

"We'll have to wait," Ben said.

Rain streamed down his shaven head and dripped from his chin. A former soldier with two completed tours in Afghanistan on his dossier, Big Ben had trained for urban warfare. He knew what he was talking about, but so did I.

"I'm not leaving him out there, cover me."

He grabbed my upper arm and squeezed. It bloody hurt.

"You're going nowhere, Sarge. Too dangerous."

"He's a fellow police officer. We're not leaving him out there. Stand down, Constable."

"And you have a family," he said, lowering his voice and casting a quick glance towards David. "Can't let you out there, mate. Not happening."

I tried to shrug him off, but Christ the man was strong.

"Listen, Ben. I know what I'm doing. See the house?"

Without releasing my arm, he turned his head. "What am I looking for?"

"It's a Category A safe house. Bullet resistant glass on all the windows, which don't open. There'll be a courtyard garden at the back, ten foot walls topped with razor wire. No way in or out via the roof and you'd need the combination to open the rear escape route."

Ben scanned the road and the houses opposite.

"You sure, Sarge?"

"Absolutely. The UKPPS safe house specifications are on the NCA servers. I read them this week."

"Is there a panic room?"

"Some have, some don't. Not sure about this one. Listen, I've had eyes on the place since DI Hook went down. The shooter's trapped in there, and see at that wall in front?"

"Yes."

"It means the shooter can't see Hook clearly from the front door or he wouldn't have missed twice. To get a decent shot he'd have to come out into the garden and you can persuade him not to. I'll be safe."

He released my arm. The blood started flowing again and I flexed my fingers to shake off the pins and needles. Alex and Ryan arrived, both wearing full body armour, and both carrying H&K MP5s and holstered pistols. I hadn't seen Ryan for a couple of weeks. The gun made him look older and much scarier. The spark in his eyes showed controlled excitement. Alex, as always, exuded coolness and competence. I'd seen her in action before and knew her capabilities.

David returned, handed me my phone, and said, "You three spread out and give me cover. We're not leaving DI Hook out there."

Big Ben flinched, but one look from David had him turn to face the house again.

David reached out to me. "Phil? Sure you're okay? You're still bleeding."

"It's nothing, boss. Flying glass. What are we doing?"

"Still remember how to hotwire a car?"

"Of course."

"See the Transit with the sliding side door?" David pointed to an old panel van parked fifteen cars back on the other side of the street, facing the safe house. "We'll use that. That's a Category A safe house, yes?"

I nodded. He knew safe house specifications as well as I did. "Alpine's in there and blind."

"Okay, we'll have half-decent cover." He turned to Alex. "You and Ryan watch the house. If the front door opens issue a warning and don't let anyone out. No one. Shoot if you have to. Understood?"

"Yes, boss."

Alex and Ryan took up positions behind my Beemer, and she raised a thumb to show they were set.

David signalled to Ben. "You're with Phil and me. Keep your eyes on the safe house. Ready? Let's go."

The boss took the lead, and Ben kept between us and Alpine. When out of sight of the house, we crossed the road and made it to the Transit van in good time and without any more shots being fired. My heart pounded. My leg ached like beggary, but it didn't let me down. Somehow, I still had my stick.

David and I hid behind the van, and Ben took up a position at the side where he could still see the front gate to Number 153.

"Wait there," David ordered, and sprinted the ten metres to the Range Rover. He ducked into the back, emerged carrying a spare ballistic vest, and returned barely breathing hard. "When you get into the cab, stuff this against the windscreen, and keep your head down."

In the daylight, with the proper kit, I'd have opened the Transit door in about fifteen seconds, and without scratching the paintwork. Sod that. I jabbed the pointy end of my walking stick through the driver's side window, bottom corner, near the lock. Not exactly clean or silent, but quick enough.

I was in, under the dash, and had the engine running in seconds. I opened the passenger door for the boss. He jumped in, slid between the seats, and made his way into the back.

"Go, Phil. The loading door on these things unlocks from the inside."

With first gear selected, I stamped on the clutch pedal and spears of pain shot along my thigh and into my hip. My left foot wouldn't move fast enough to work the clutch properly. The gears crunched. I gritted my teeth and the van crept forward.

Exposed as all hell, I ducked low and peered through the gap I'd left between the vest and the dashboard. It didn't take much imagination to see myself through the crosshairs of a sniper's 'scope. Big Ben walked alongside us, arms over the bonnet, his MP5 aimed at the safe house.

There wasn't much room to squeeze the van between the parked cars and Hook's supine body, but I managed to crawl past. David cracked open the side door and called down the distance to our target. "Three … two … one. Stop. That's it, Phil."

I stamped on the brake pedal, yanked up the handbrake, and threw the Transit into neutral. It took a while to squeeze between the seats, and I held my breath while David checked Hook's neck.

"There's a pulse! Ben, help me with him. Phil get back behind the wheel."

"Careful with his neck, boss," I called. "He hit the road pretty hard. Might have a spinal injury."

The image of Hook's head bouncing off the tarmac returned to flip my stomach again, and I split my attention between the safe house and the rescue. Alex's lips moved, but without an comms earpiece, I had no idea what she said. "Boss? What's happening?"

"No movement inside the house. Get ready to move. Won't be long now." His voice strained as he steadied Hook's head and Ben took most of Hook's weight. The van rocked under the load of two extra bodies. Ben stayed outside.

"Right, Phil. Take us out of here."

I reversed slowly to the Range Rover and waited for Ben to move it clear before carrying on and stopping well away from danger.

"Boss, how is he?"

David looked at me, a grim smile cracked his face. "Bullet hole in his right thigh. Plenty of blood and massive swelling. Can't see an exit wound. The bullet's still in there. Might have smashed his thigh bone. Nasty crack on the back of his head, but his pulse is strong." He put a finger to his ear, pressing the earpiece. "The ambulance is five minutes out. How far to the nearest hospital?"

I pulled up my internal map. "From here? I'll have to take it slow. Twenty minutes at least. Maybe half an hour."

Ben hurried back to us carrying a first aid kit. He tied a pressure bandage over the bullet wound and a second over the top when the blood stared showing through the gauze.

David frowned. I could almost see him making the calculations. "Best stay where we are. The paramedics can stabilise him. If he needs a cervical support, we don't want him bouncing around the back of this truck all the way to the hospital." He spoke into his handheld mike. "Alex? What's it looking like over there? ... Good. The local uniforms will be here soon to evacuate the neighbours and set up a cordon ... Keep that house locked down. Nobody out, nobody in ... Yes, he's hurt, but still breathing ... I'm sending Ben to back you up. Don't shoot him." He gave Ben the signal. "Hug tight to the side. Try to get close, but no forced entry. Holding action only. We'll wait until the rest of the armed boys arrive. I'll be with you as soon as the ambulance gets here."

Ben turned to leave but David held out a hand to stop him. "Alpine will be desperate. He's responsible for DS Juno's death and for shooting DI Hook, and Christ knows how many are dead inside the safe house if there isn't a panic room. Don't take any chances. I'll back your decision. Understand what I'm saying?"

Ben nodded, said, "Yes, sir," and hurried off.

Hook groaned, moved his right hand, feeling the bed of the Transit. I guessed he was searching for his weapon. As with the revolver, Ben had picked up Hook's Glock to add to his growing collection.

I returned to the back of the van. "DI Hook, Billy, can you hear me?" I asked, leaning close.

David gave me room.

Hook coughed. "That you ... Cry-baby?"

Relief had me grinning, despite the new nickname. Why couldn't he stick to the other new one? Lucky, I could live with. At least his memory was intact, which suggested no brain damage.

"Yeah, it's me, Nookie. You gave us a scare. How you feeling?"

"Call me Nookie again and I'll tear your ... fucking ears off."

"That's the old Nookie I've grown to know and hate. Seriously. How you doing?"

"Been better. Leg hurts like a bastard ... blinding headache. Apart from that, I'm embarrassed to hell. Letting myself get shot like that? Stupid rookie mistake." He tried to move, but I held him down by his shoulders.

"Easy, mate. Ambulance is on the way. Won't be long."

With eyes squeezed shut, face creased in obvious pain, he grabbed my collar and pulled me close. "Did you get the bastard?"

"Not yet, she's holed up inside the safe house."

"She?"

"Yes, I saw her when she ducked back into the house after shooting you."

"Who?" His grip tightened. "What you waiting for? Go fetch …"

"Can't. Worried about hostages. Unless Dukakis and the UKPPS team are dead already."

"Oh, yeah. Right. Not thinking straight. Panic room?"

"Dunno. Wouldn't they have called SC&O19 for assistance? Your mate, Gregor Fleeting hadn't heard anything from Stan or his team."

"Nah, SOP would be to contact his control, DCI Falconi. They're probably on their way now. Silent running … compartmentalised … complete bullshit."

During my chat with Hook, David's expression had changed from concern to thin-lipped, brow-furrowed anger.

"You know what this means?" I asked.

David nodded. "Whoever's in there doesn't have any option but to negotiate. Either the protection team is dead, or they're in the panic room which will be stocked with supplies. We can wait Alpine out for days."

"I could try calling the house. What d'you reckon, boss?"

"Don't tell me, you know their landline number?"

"Of course. DS Stanislas had a file open on his desk last time I was in the UKPPS office. I had to read it upside down, though. Took a while to unscramble the numbers and allocate them to the right safe house, but you know what I'm like. Enjoy a challenge. Mind if I try giving Alpine a bell while we wait for the ambulance and Inspector Fleeting's men?"

He took a moment to consider the options. "Can't do any harm, I suppose."

I raised my mobile again, keyed in the number, and hit the call-speaker button. Police and ambulance sirens drowned out the dial tones.

She didn't answer until after I'd reached seventeen elephants.

Chapter 32

Thursday 10th October

"Who's that?" she asked, and the two words confirmed my suspicions.

"Hello, Hannah," I said, tiredness and defeat dampening my voice to a polite tone when I felt anything but. "Is it lonely in there?"

David mouthed a silent, "Are you sure?"

I didn't need to answer.

"Hannah? You still there?"

"Where else would I be, Sarge?"

She sounded like an automated telephone message, bland and emotionless.

"Are you lonely?"

Being a cop, she had to know what I was asking. Had she killed Dukakis and the protection detail?

"Wouldn't you like to know."

"Yes, I would. C'mon, Hannah, don't be coy."

The boss looked at me and then studied the house, but I couldn't tell what he was thinking.

I waited a full minute for Hannah to answer. Nothing.

"Are you coming out?"

Scraping sounds on the other end of the line suggested she was dragging something heavy across a wooden floor. Building a barricade?

"Hannah?"

"Yes, I'm coming out, Sarge. Feet first."

I hit the mute key. "Hear that, boss? She plans to die in there. What should I do?"

"Keep her talking. Try calming her down. Give me time to think."

The siren's wails grew louder. Flashing blue lights circled the houses as an ambulance and five police cars pulled up behind the Range Rover. An Inspector and a posse of uniformed officers exited the patrol cars. Two paramedics jumped out of the ambulance, but the Inspector had one of his men hold them back.

David held up his warrant card and hurried towards them. I couldn't hear what he said, but the Inspector's attitude showed a willingness to hand control over to a senior officer—any senior officer.

"Who's that?" Hannah shouted.

"Don't worry," I said quietly. "That's only the ambulance and the local uniforms. They'll set up the usual perimeter. Let's end this now. Please?"

"No chance, Sarge. I'm going nowhere. It's too late."

"Hannah. It's never too late."

I hit the mute key to cut off her laughter.

Finished with the Inspector, David escorted the two paramedics to the Transit. One carried a large medical pack, the other a spinal board. Behind them, a beefy constable lugged a stretcher and propped it against the side of the Transit.

Mute key released, I tried again. "No need to be that way, Hannah. Let's talk this out."

"Who'd I hit?"

What could I say? The book on hostage negotiations told me I shouldn't give up information for free, nor should I lie. She'd have read the same manual. Hannah had to know she'd shot a colleague. The Comms room back at Holton would be recording this call, as would Eavesdropping Central. Whatever I said would be scrutinised, picked apart, and probably used in future training courses—or against me in a tribunal if I fucked up.

Either way, a crapshoot.

"Phil, who did I hit?" she said, her voice rising in volume and pitch.

"DI Hook, but—"

"Oh shit. I … Oh shit."

"He's still alive, Hannah. Hurt and pissed off, but alive."

"Liar!"

The metallic click of an automatic pistol's slide cocking and being made ready to fire sounded over the background noise of the paramedics chatting to each other as they worked on their patient.

"Hannah, no! He *is* alive. You can speak to him. Hold on." I held the phone to the DI's ear. "Speak to her."

"Hannah?"

"Hookie?"

"Yeah."

"I'm so sorry. Panicked."

"Apology not accepted. You always were a lousy shot and a useless cop. Go on, shoot yourself … you'll probably fucking miss."

David's eyes widened. "DI Hook!"

"She killed Richie. I want the bitch dead."

The boss glowered at the injured man, but I cut my hand across my throat to silence him. David looked at me as though I'd grown a second head. I waved an apology and whispered, "It's his management style."

The old man wrinkled his nose as though he'd walked past a cartload of rotting fish, but nodded in understanding.

On her end of the phone, Hannah sniffled a short laugh. "And you were always an arrogant, bullying prick." Her laugh dissolved into a cry. "Oh God, what have I done?"

Hook coughed and clamped a hand to his forehead. "Fucking bollocks," he said. Such an eloquent way he had with the English language. The second paramedic held out the spinal board to give me the hurry-up. I took my phone back and eased myself out of the Transit to give them room.

"Hannah? The paramedics are working on him. Why don't you tell me what's happening in there?"

"Fuck off, Sarge. I'm telling you nothing."

This Hannah, nothing like the mousey creature I'd seen in The Cage, ran hot and cold—in control one minute, crying and terrified the next. It was so goddamned frustrating. I had no idea which way she'd jump next and didn't know how to play the call.

"Phil?"

"Yes?"

"I'm so sorry." And there was the little-girl-lost voice again. "Give me five minutes to think will you? I won't do anything stupid, honest."

She ended the call before I could respond.

185

Honest. Yeah, like I'd ever trust Alpine.

David, standing in the shadow of a garden hedge, beckoned me to join him.

"Did you hear that, boss?"

"Most of it," he said, eyes turned towards the safe house. "What do you make of her? Really unstable, or play acting?"

"No idea. She's not the woman I'm used to."

I ran my fingers through my hair. Fragments of glass fell out and landed on the drying pavement. When had it stopped raining?

"You didn't have her down as Alpine?"

"No. In fact, Hannah, Drew, and Freddie Bowen were the only ones I tentatively discounted. Fat lot of good I am as an undercover cop, yeah?"

"You've only been on the case a few weeks. Don't trivialise your work."

David turned away and stared into the middle distance. He tugged at his left earlobe—a thing he often did when lost in thought. I waited. He'd ask his questions eventually.

"Why did you scratch DC Goldstein from your list?"

"Richie Juno's off-book investigation focused on cases from London and the southeast. Hannah transferred in from the South Yorkshire Police. I discounted Drew Mackay for the same reason. Why?"

"Nothing. I came to a similar conclusion," he said, still tweaking his ear.

No doubt about it, he'd pulled some facts together, but there was no point asking him to tell me until he was good and ready. The old man could be an annoying sod sometimes. While he mulled things over in his head, I turned my attention to what was happening inside the Transit.

The paramedics had finished strapping Hook to the spinal board. The first man, a dark-haired, broad-shouldered rugby player type, shone a penlight into Hook's eyes and checked his blood pressure, while his mate wrapped another compression bandage around the leg wound. Ben's double dressing was already saturated.

The rugby player turned to me. "We need to move him now."

"Okay, take him away, and there's no need to be gentle with the ugly mother." The paramedic's eyes bugged until I winked and threw Hook an evil grin. "He'll be dining out on that bullet scar for the rest of his career. By the way, where you taking him?"

"Watford General, it's the closest hospital with a CT scanner. We need to check that head injury."

"Hope their scanner's powerful."

"Sir?"

"They'll struggle to penetrate his thick skull." To Hook, I said, "Some senior officer with an eye on the media hype is bound to give you a bravery medal. Guess it's only fitting since they don't award them for stupidity. Get well soon, Gimp," I added, showing him my stick. "Want to borrow this for later?"

"Fuck off, Cry-baby."

As the rugby player and his mate loaded my former prime suspect onto the stretcher and carried him to the ambulance, Hook gave me the finger. I turned my back on them. David gathered close when my phone bleeped.

"Hannah?"

"Yeah. Where's Hookie?"

"On his way to hospital. He's going to be fine. Are you coming out?"

"You want my story?"

"Yes. And your contacts—it'll help your case. You can still make amends."

"Richie's death. I didn't want that … wasn't supposed to happen. The twins. His poor boys …"

She broke down again.

"Hannah, let me help you make it right."

Like that was ever going to happen.

"I can't face you all."

"DC Goldstein, this is DCI Jones, Midlands Police."

She sniffed. "Phil's old boss? The hard arse?"

David closed his eyes as I tried not to look sheepish. "Part of DC Cryer's cover. I'm actually a really nice man. Give to charity, kind to animals. You know the type."

I coughed. "He's right, Hannah. You can trust him."

"Listen carefully," David continued. "SC&O19 will be here soon and I won't be able to keep control. You know what they're like when it's about their own people. We need to sort things out before they arrive. Understand?"

A pause.

"DC Goldstein?"

"Yes, I hear you."

"And?"

"Can you come in here? I trust Phil, but I'm scared."

"That's not happening. Come to the door and throw out your weapons. That's the best we can do."

"Phil? I'll give myself up to you. Only you."

David cut both hands outwards across his chest. "No! Absolutely not."

For the first time since meeting David Jones, I questioned his order. He feared for my safety, and he wasn't the only one, but Hannah had information we needed and I wasn't going to let it go without trying everything possible. And there was still the question over the fate of Stan and his team. Despite his emphatic refusal, I could tell David felt the same way.

"How about I lead and DCI Jones comes with me? All you have to do is open the door and throw out your weapons. All of them. Then I'll come in and we can talk."

"Open the door and give up my gun? That all?"

"I'm unarmed, you know that, right?"

"Yes, yes, I know."

She spoke without emotion. I'd never heard her so lifeless. It might have been sadness or defeat.

"We're on our way."

"Right, okay."

After I ended the call, David held up his hand, and reached into the cab for the armoured vest. "You're going nowhere near that house without this."

I pulled the close-fitting gear over my head and tugged the Velcro straps taut. David checked the fit.

"Bit of a squeeze there, Philip," he said, "despite you losing all that weight."

"You could have brought me one built for an adult."

He smiled. "Last vest in the shop. Sorry. Give me a minute to brief the locals."

David walked back to the hastily-erected barricade and spoke to the Inspector before returning to me. "Right, Phil. Let's not keep your friend waiting any longer."

"That woman's no friend of mine."

We kept tight to the hedge, hugging the shadows, and took cover behind a brick wall one-and-a-half metres high. We were opposite my Beemer, ten doors back from the safe house. The wall offered some protection, but precious little comfort. Despite the armoured vest, I felt hellishly exposed. Dry mouth, racing heart, sweaty pits, the lot. In short, I was a terrified, babbling mess. Brain the size of a planet and I still put myself in danger. What an idiot. And God, did my knee hurt. I tried to hide the pain but couldn't stop grimacing. Without the stick, I'd have been immobile.

At my side and down on one knee, David was his normal calm self. One day I'll ask him if he ever gets scared. Then again, I probably won't. Why knock him off the pedestal I'd built for him?

Hidden behind my hire car on the opposite side of the road, Alex and Ryan trained their weapons on the front door. Alex nodded an okay to the boss. Ben had taken a position behind the oak tree and also had a clear view of the safe house.

A light came on in an upper window of the house directly across the street. The curtains drew back and the silhouette of a man appeared. He wore a dressing gown and held a mobile phone up to the window. In full view of Number 153, the idiot was taking home movies!

I waved at him to move away, but he either didn't see me, or chose to ignore my signal.

"This is lunacy," David muttered. "Civilians are going to get hurt if we don't end this soon."

I hit the redial button and Hannah answered almost immediately.

"We're near the front of the house now. Have you cleared whatever barricade you built?"

"Barricade? ... Oh yeah, you heard me moving stuff earlier. It's clear. I'm ready. Just you and DCI Jones. You promise?"

Again, her words sounded flat, lifeless.

"I promise," I answered, hitting the mute button and looking at the boss.

His eyes, normally unreadable, showed clear worry, as did his frown.

"I don't trust her, boss. She's not going for it."

"Yep. I think you're right. Any ideas?"

He was asking me? I didn't know whether to be proud or even more terrified. I opted for a bit of both.

"Actually, I might have. How good a shot is Ben?"

The old man answered without hesitation. "Marksman. Expert grade, according to his army and personnel records. I've not seen him on the range, but Giles Danforth vouched for him and that's good enough for me. Why? What do you have?"

Giles Danforth heads one of the Midlands Police Armed Response Units, and is one of David's closest mates. He trusts Giles as much as he trusts anyone alive—as do I.

"I reckon Hannah's going for the 'suicide by cop' routine," I said, "and neither of us want that, right?"

"Agreed. So?"

"Work with me, boss. I don't have time to explain. Call Ben over." I released the mute. "Hannah? We're on our way. How you doing?"

"I'm okay, Sarge. Hunky-dory."

I ended the call and put the mobile in my pocket. After a comms instruction from the old man, Ben and Ryan took a long detour, sprinted across the road fifty metres behind us, and arrived at our position, breathing hard from the weight of the body armour. The three of them knelt in a huddle. I crouched awkwardly. Ben held his MP5 diagonally across his barrel chest, the point of his elbow resting on his raised thigh.

"Ben," I whispered, "forget the rifle, use the revolver you took from me."

David looked at me, eyebrows hiked to the dark sky, no doubt stunned at the idea that I'd held a gun at some point that night. He probably wanted to check my sanity. As he stiffened, I read his desperation to retake command fight against his trust in my judgement. I badly needed to justify that trust.

Ben looked at the boss, who nodded. Then he turned to me.

Time for Phil Cryer to earn his paycheque.

"Hannah Goldstein is 165 centimetres tall and weighs about sixty-five kilos. If she does anything iffy, put a single shot right there, okay?" I jabbed my index and middle finger into my sternum, slightly to the right of centre. "Got it?"

"You sure?" Ben asked, checking the safety of his rifle before handing it to Ryan, who confirmed the weapon as safe before hanging it over his shoulder by its webbing strap, barrel pointing down.

"Consider that an order, DC Adeoye."

"Yes, Sergeant."

"And remember, the first chamber's empty."

"Not any more it isn't," he said, holding the revolver in the double-handed, cocked-and-ready position.

I turned to David. "Ready, boss?" My voice sounded dry, scratchy. Christ, I needed a drink, and water wouldn't do.

"When you are."

David smiled. He actually bloody smiled. I had the distinct impression of a proud father at his son's coming of age party.

"Keep two paces behind and one to the right."

"Yes, boss," David said, straight-faced. I couldn't detect any sarcasm. Well, maybe a grain or two.

"In position, Ben?"

Hidden behind another low garden wall, Ben knelt, braced his left shoulder against the brickwork. He nodded and whispered, "Just make sure there's a plenty big gap between you for me to see enough of the target."

Trembling inside, I took the lead and limped down the garden path, with all the confidence I could gather—precious little. I kept tight to the left and David took the position I'd assigned him. The rest was up to Ben and the accuracy of a pistol he'd never fired. My tight and heavy body armour restricted movement and made it difficult to breathe. The word terrified didn't do it justice, but I couldn't back out. This was my show, and I didn't have that option.

"Hannah!" I called, stopping two metres from the front door. Black, with a fresh paint job, windows reinforced with a barely-visible wire mesh, iron bars behind. "Throw out your weapons."

The door yanked open. Hannah screamed, "Bastard!" and aimed a gunmetal blue automatic pistol at my chest. Her finger tightened on the trigger. I flinched.

Fuck's sake, Ben. Shoot!

Chapter 33

Thursday 10th October

A single *crack* behind me—quieter than I expected—corresponded with a ripple in Hannah's leather jacket.

She squealed and fell backwards into the hall, mouth open, arms splayed. Her head hit the carpeted floor—it didn't bounce as high as DI Hook's had done—and she lay still.

Before I could scramble to my feet, David leapt forward, scooped up the Sig semi-automatic pistol that had fallen from her hand, and gave it to the onrushing Ben. He cuffed her hands together and only then checked the pulse at her neck.

I stumbled into the hall and let the wall take my weight. It had to, I couldn't stop my legs trembling and my knees—both of them—were jelly, the shakes, uncontrollable. Shit, I think the bullet might have grazed my sleeve, but I didn't want to look.

Hell, what was I like? After all, I'd instigated the takedown.

"Still alive, Philip," David said, grinning up at me. "Lightweight body armour. She'll have a heck of a bruise, but there's no blood."

I gave a little fist pump, but held back on the whooped, "Yes!" I wanted to scream at finally bagging Alpine. David's an old-school cop. Doesn't appreciate too many outward shows of emotion during work.

He stood and wiped his hands with a hankie.

"You know what that feels like first hand, eh boss? I've been meaning to ask how you were doing?"

"Only hurts when I laugh."

"There's an obvious cure for that."

He rubbed his chest where he'd been shot a few weeks earlier. The bullet had cracked one of his ribs and would have killed him had he not been wearing a ceramic vest. When I learned about the shooting, I read up on ribcage injuries and related ballistics. Precious little else to do with my time in my hospital bed. Goes to show, reading expands the mind and the knowledge can be useful. Despite that, I'd taken a hell of a chance.

"I'll want a good explanation for this, Philip, but we need to secure the house first. Make sure this one doesn't have any partners hidden under the floorboards. And then there's DS Stanislas and the rest of his protection team to consider." A shadow darkened his eyes at the thought of what sort of carnage we might find inside.

"If there is a panic room, it'll be in the cellar," I said. "It's easier to secure an underground space. You noticed the bricked-in basement window under the front bay?"

"Yes," he said, nodding. "We'll check there first."

He signalled for Alex, Ryan, and Ben to search the house and stepped aside as they pushed past us yelling, "Armed police, armed police!"

David knelt again and rapped his knuckles on Hannah's chest. The hollow knock of his fist on body armour confirmed I'd called it right.

"How'd you know she'd be wearing a vest?"

"After she shot DI Hook, I saw her in the doorway. The body shape and way she moved …" I shrugged. "Educated guess."

"She could have removed it."

"I was also banking on Ben's accuracy."

"Care to expand on that, Philip?"

The telltale sign of his growing temper, the deeper voice, the slower than normal delivery, and the staring eyes, made me rethink the drip-drip account.

"Sorry, boss. Give me a minute to catch my breath. This is the first time I've been involved in an actual shooting. Guns scare the crap out of me."

"Me too."

David ran his fingers though his unruly hair and we waited until Alex called from a room at the end of the hall. David indicated that I should stay with Hannah and rushed to join her. He returned with Alex a few seconds later, his face thunderous. The floorboards felt spongy as I anticipated the worst.

"There's a body in the dining room with a bullet wound to the head. Dark hair, slim. Looks about twenty-five."

Relief fought with despair. Relief won, but only just. "That's not Stan, so where is he? And where's Dukakis?" I asked, but before he could answer, Ryan and Ben returned.

Ben carried on past us and climbed the stairs, his weapon braced for action. Ryan stepped alongside Alex. He scowled at Hannah, who still hadn't recovered. "There is a panic room in the cellar, boss," he said. "I tried calling, but got no response."

"Thank fuck for that." I sighed, the relief making me giddy.

"Phil?" David asked.

"Sorry, boss. UKPPS-specific protocols. They won't come out until they have the all clear from their team leader or his proxy."

"Any idea who either of those individuals might be?"

"The team leader is DI Sergio Falconi. No idea who the proxy might be. Gregor Fleeting perhaps? He's the guy you talked to from SC&O19. They'll be here in"—I checked my watch. Christ, was it only 22:15?—"about twenty minutes."

"Fleeting's the proxy? And you know this how?"

Again, he gave me the knitted brow and the low growl. We'd arrived too late and another police officer had died. Not a good day, but I knew David. We still had work to do and would make time to grieve later.

"Educated guesswork. DI Hook told me, in a roundabout way. Hopefully, we can sort this mess out in time to have The Baron appear at the Old Bailey tomorrow. Although, I think we could offer the judge a pretty convincing case for a short adjournment."

Even as I spoke, the words sounded callous, but the dead officer had offered his life to ensure Dukakis testified. If David and I had anything to do with it, that's what the hitman would bloody well do.

Ben finished searching the upstairs and gave it the all-clear. After Alex checked the front room, the guys half-carried, half-dragged a groggy former-DC Hannah Goldstein in and dumped her in an armchair well out of sight of the bay-fronted window. The five of us stood guard over her, watching as she blinked hard, apparently struggling to recognise her surroundings.

"Okay, Philip. While we're waiting for this woman to recover, it's explanation time. The revolver?"

The fire in his eyes and the accompanying stern expression made it clear he wasn't in any mood for more delays.

"Not going to be easy, boss," I said, lowering my aching bones into the sofa across from Hannah's chair. My knee shot sparks into my thigh, but at least the flames had stopped. I straightened the leg and rubbed the scar through my jeans. "Bear with me here. It's a bit of a stretch."

"Come on, DS Cryer."

The weight of four pairs of eyes fell on me—Hannah Goldstein still didn't seem to know the time of day. I took my time. A fellow officer lay dead in a room along the hall and his loss weighed heavily on us all.

"Right, here it is. At eight metres—the approximate distance from Ben to the front door—the energy of a bullet from a .32 Smith & Wesson is about 150 Newton metres. Not enough to penetrate police issue body armour, unless the bullet is armour-piercing. I checked the shells when DI Hook gave me the gun. Standard police issue. The MP5 Ben was going to use packs a much heavier punch. I didn't want to take the risk of killing this"—I waved a hand in Hannah's general direction—"murdering bitch."

I took a breath and David broke the momentary silence. "Stop trying to blind us with the science. What would have happened if she'd removed her vest?"

"To be honest, with her having a death wish, I'm surprised she's still wearing the bloody thing. But there were two more factors in our favour."

"Go on, enlighten us," David said, still not relaxing his frown.

"See her leather jacket with all that quilting? Leather's strong and pliant and can absorb some of a bullet's force. As you can see, it didn't stop it completely, but I told Ben to aim at the sternum, which is a strong bone—"

"—at the centre of the ribcage," David interrupted to show he understood my reasoning. "And the ribcage is flexible enough to absorb the rest of the force?"

"Possibly, but as I said, a bit of a stretch. It's the theory I was working with, and then there's the pendant."

"The pendant?"

"Yes, she wears a big silver pendant. Family heirloom. Strong enough to stop a bullet—probably. Rarely takes it off, according to her. I reckon when the strip-search team removes that vest, they'll find the pendant directly beneath where the bullet hit the armour. Exactly where I told Ben to aim."

David tapped the place on his chest I gave Ben as the target. "And if your calculations were wrong, or Ben missed?"

"We'd probably have been left with a dead cop killer," I continued, ignoring Hannah. No one could have blamed me for my lack of sympathy. "But we'd have been able to tear her life apart and find out who's been buying her police intelligence. Now though, we have a chance for a little chat before the SC&O19 boys take her away. By the way, I'd like to know what DS Stanislas makes of her. Want me to try and talk him out of the panic room?"

"Better not. I wouldn't want to let him loose up here after what happened to his partner. You told me he played semi-pro rugby, yes? I'm not sure we'd be able to hold him off."

Hannah groaned. Head lowered, she stared at me through hooded, dead eyes.

"How you feeling?"

She didn't return my oh-so-friendly smile. It might have included bared teeth.

The couch, comfortable as it looked, hurt my lower back. I leaned forward, resting my chin on my stick.

David stood over her, intimidating. Fists clenched, red faced. I'd never seen him so angry. "Want to take first crack at her, Phil? You've earned the right."

"Thanks, boss," I said, easing a little closer to the edge of the sofa. "You broke our deal, Hannah. Why?"

"I'm so sorry, Sarge," she said, voice breaking. "I wanted you to shoot me. Would have been okay somehow. My gun wasn't loaded you know. Not at the door."

Ben broke open her Sig and showed us the empty magazine. He pulled back the slider. The chamber, too, was empty.

"Why the vest?"

She sniffled and her lower lip trembled. "Nice bit of kit. Top of the range. Light and comfortable, you know? Forgot I had it on."

"I'm very disappointed," I said. "Thought we had a deal."

"A bent cop in prison? How long will I last?"

"You should have thought of that sooner. What were you thinking? That man in the next room, just doing his job, and Richie ... his twins, for fuck's sake."

"I told you ...I didn't want Richie dead. It just ... happened."

"Just happened? You mean an accident? Don't give me that bollocks. You set him up, didn't you?"

Her face crumpled and she collapsed back into the chair, face in her hands.

"Who were you working for? One of the men who hired Dukakis?"

She closed her eyes, lower lip trembling, and nodded.

"Which one?"

"Does it matter? They're all going down if he testifies."

"It matters. Which one?"

Her big brown eyes, liquid and pleading, looked at me. "Not telling you. Can't tell you. They'll target my family."

I'd expected the sob story, the self-justification. She was playing for sympathy. It didn't work on me and I turned to the boss, but he just rolled his hand forward, urging me to continue.

Easing my leg to one side, I leaned closer, and lowered my voice. "How were you going to kill Dukakis?"

"What?"

"You couldn't have walked in here and mown the protection team down. They wouldn't have let you in."

"Yes they would," she said, eyes lowered. "I have the password."

"So why are Stan and Dukakis in the panic room?"

She stared down at her trembling hands and hesitated. Whether it was to give herself time to invent a lie, or because she was genuinely distraught, I couldn't tell.

"I didn't know the protection team has a failsafe. Apparently, if someone unexpected arrives, even if they have the right password, one of the team takes the client into the panic room while the other verifies the visitor's identity."

"That's when you shot the officer?"

"DS Rick Bagshaw. I didn't have the second password—the one for the panic room—and he'd seen my face. It was me or him. I'm really glad it wasn't Stan, though. He's a mate."

Fuck. Could she hear herself? To this day, I don't know what stopped me ripping her throat out.

"How did you get the first password?"

She shook her head. "Not telling."

Her narrow shoulders sagged and she folded in on herself, staring at the carpet between her feet. I needed something from her before she had the chance to recover from what must have seemed like the end of her world. I rolled back all the memories I had of the timid woman who ghosted around The Cage or sat in the corner of the canteen, taking everything in but rarely adding to the conversation.

Apart from the facts in her personnel file, what did I really know about her? University graduate with a good degree in Politics and Law. I'd seen her using her PC at work and her mobile phone in the canteen, but that was about it. She didn't type particularly quickly and used her index fingers when texting on her mobile, not her thumbs like most people. I'd never seen her with a tablet or tapping away for fun.

Oh, hell. Oh bloody hell.

The awful realisation hit me. I'd screwed up yet again.

"Hannah?" I said, trying to keep the worry from my voice.

She didn't answer, didn't even react.

"DC Goldstein!"

Her head jerked up and she blinked until her eyes found focus on mine. "Yes, Sarge?"

"How did you do it?"

She frowned. "Do what?"

"Exploit the SCUD to hide your activity."

She lowered her head again and mumbled into her chest. "Don't know what you mean."

I lifted her chin. She resisted, but I didn't take it easy on her. This time, she refused to make eye contact.

"Come on, Hannah. I know all about the way you've been manipulating the phone intercepts down at Eavesdropper Central. Very clever, but this afternoon, I worked out who's been helping you. We have her under surveillance. Ironic really. We're watching the watcher."

Hannah's breath caught when I used the female pronoun, 'her'. The unintentional body language had narrowed our search to a little over half—the female half—of Jimmy Brand's minions. When we finally handed the case over to the Anti-Corruption Unit, they'd at least have something to work on. For now we'd have to concentrate on members of the OCTF. No time for anything else.

"The telephone manipulation is one thing, but what about the data locked into the OCTF's servers. They're standalone. No one can access them from outside The Cage. Did you drop one-time-use-only codes into the hard-wired operating system? Or did you force a back door into the binary core bundle? Come on, answer me!"

David, as much a technophobe as any person I'd ever met, turned blank eyes on me. If I'd spouted something similar in our shared office back at Holton HQ, he'd have given me a bollocking for talking gobbledygook. In this particular instance, of course, he'd have been dead right.

"Wouldn't you like to know," Hannah said, twisting her upper lip into a sneer.

No triumph, but I heard something else in her mocking response. Hope? Relief?

Damn it.

Her reply turned my stomach. She didn't have a clue what I was talking about. I had it wrong. All bloody wrong. I turned away from the cop killer and faced the old man.

"Boss, we need to talk in private."

He nodded, signalled for Alex and the guys to keep eyes on the prisoner, and we found the kitchen—a grubby little room with a sink full of dirty dishes. I closed the door behind us.

"What's the matter?" David asked, focusing on me and not the crud in the sink. It must have been hell for him.

"Hannah isn't Alpine. She's a bloody pawn. A soldier. And a low level one at that. Fuck!"

As I've said before, David's old-school. I've rarely heard him swear and he doesn't take kindly to his team dropping the f-bomb without good reason. This time, he let it pass.

"How do you know? That nonsense with the binary core bundle?"

So he *had* been taking notice? A deep man, he never fails to surprise me.

"Yes. Always wondered about her lack of IT knowledge. Another reason she didn't register high on my suspect list. We know Alpine has good tech skills, but Hannah's almost as clueless as you are." I smiled at that and added an apologetic shrug for good measure. "Ergo, Hannah isn't Alpine."

"Good God. How many corrupt officers do they have in the NCA? Alpine, Hannah, and one or more of your so-called Eavesdropper minions. They've only been in existence a few years. No wonder Goldstein wanted to end it here this evening. She hoped to keep her partners safe."

"What do we do? She's unlikely to tell us anything else."

"Give me a moment to think."

He frowned at the overflowing sink. I half expected him to start tidying the place. David Jones is borderline OCD over mess, but it rarely affects him at a crime scene. No doubt he had other things on his mind.

"Do you think Alpine knows we've already arrested Hannah?" I asked.

"No idea. We'll have to work under the assumption they arranged a time for a meet or a message. Can we use that?"

"Don't see how. But I've just thought of something worse."

"Go on."

"If Hannah failed with Dukakis, who's to say the real Alpine won't have another go?"

"My thoughts exactly. Perhaps it's just as well Dukakis is still in the panic room."

The memory of a gun pointed in my face grew large and an idea struck.

"We should try talking to DI Hook. He's been investigating Richie Juno's death on the quiet. He might have something on Alpine we don't. Want me to give him a bell?"

"You could try, but the hospital's unlikely to put you through, especially if he has concussion."

"Crap," I said. "We need to send someone to look after him. If Alpine thinks Hook's a danger, he might want to clean house."

The old man looked up at the ceiling, perhaps for inspiration. "This is getting messy and we're short-handed."

"Boss?" Alex called from the hallway.

"In the kitchen," David answered.

I opened the door to her.

"The armed unit from the Metropolitan Police is outside."

"Excellent. Just in time to save the day."

I smiled thinly. David could be a sarcastic beggar at times.

"Should I allow them in?"

"How many are there?"

"Inspector Fleeting and five others."

To me, David said, "I think we have our extra staff," and to Alex, he said, "Show the inspector in here. We need to talk in private."

I made a move to follow Alex, but the old man held up a hand. "No, Phil, you can stay. I'll need your help."

"Got an idea, boss?"

"Not yet, but I have access to a couple of secret weapons," he said, giving me his patent-pending old-fashioned look. If he wore half-moon glasses, he'd have been peering over the top of the bloody things.

"Really? Do tell."

"A world class hacker and a man with an eidetic memory."

Before he could say more, a powerfully-built man the same height as David appeared in the doorway. The man wore full body armour, minus the helmet, and carried an MP5 slung across his chest. "DCI Jones?" he asked.

"Yes, and this is DS Cryer."

We flashed our warrant cards.

"Sorry for the delay, sir," he said. "Drawing weapons from the armourer takes a while and traffic's a pig even at this time of night. I see you have everything under control?"

"We do, thanks."

"On the radio I heard there was an officer down."

"It's worse than that. Much worse." David told him about DS Bagshaw and Hook, and added, "With that in mind, can I rely on you to protect the prisoner from, shall we say, overzealous fellow officers?"

Fleeting's eyes narrowed. "Sir?"

"The prisoner—a police officer—shot two fellow officers tonight and is complicit in the murder of DS Richard Juno. I'll need you to seal off this house and mount protection duty for the next few hours. Oh, and you might want to tell DS Stanislas he can come out of hiding now."

I checked the time: 23:08. After the adrenaline-fuelled buzz of the previous hour, I was starting to flag. Even though hunger felt disrespectful with DS Bagshaw lying dead not ten feet away, a coffee and a bite of something encased in sugar would have been handy.

"We're not security guards, sir," Fleeting said, and then wilted under the old man's contemptuous glare.

David had no patience with jobsworths even ones carrying assault rifles. I've been on the receiving end of a few of those looks in my time and almost felt sorry for Fleeting. Almost.

"I'm fully aware of your normal role and responsibilities, Inspector Fleeting," he said quietly, "but my people are detectives. We need to do some detecting, and I need someone trustworthy to keep the prisoner safe and incommunicado until we can sort out this God-awful mess. I can rely on you, can't I."

It wasn't a question.

Fleeting looked at me as though for inspiration. I gave him nothing. Served him right for arriving late.

"Who has jurisdiction here?" Fleeting asked. "I mean, who has ultimate responsibility for the prisoner in the longer term?"

"Good question," David answered and aimed a question at me. "Does the NCA have an Internal Affairs Unit?"

"Not as such. They're under the direct control of the Home Office, but the Met has first responsibility to investigate internal NCA disciplinary matters. After that it's sent to the IPCC as normal."

"That's what you get when politicians stick their oars in the water with their half-baked schemes," David said. "Okay, here are your orders, Inspector Fleeting. Under the authority I have from the Home Secretary, I'm assuming full responsibility. You and your men will take over here. Hold the prisoner under suspicion of the murder of DS Bagshaw, and the attempted murder of DI Hook and DS Cryer. Put her on suicide watch and secure her in the panic room once DS Stanislas and his people have cleared it. Do you have a female in your team to conduct a full body search?"

Fleeting frowned. "Yes, sir. The prisoner's a woman?"

"DC Hannah Goldstein."

"Hannah? Oh, Jesus."

"You know DC Goldstein?" David asked.

"Yes, sir. My unit's worked joint operations with the OCTF a few times. Hannah's ... well, so quiet. She's a killer?"

"Yes, she is. And she's also involved in the murder of DS Juno. Is guarding her here going to be a problem for you? If it is, I can call in someone from the Midlands, but it'll take them two or three hours to reach us and I don't have time to waste."

"No, sir," Fleeting said, blinking hard. "It won't be a problem."

"Excellent. After you've searched her and put her in isolation, I don't want anyone talking to her but me or DS Cryer. Is that clear?"

"Sorry, sir?"

"Make sure nobody speaks to her? No lawyers, no one. Understand?"

"Not even her supervising officer, DCI Endicott?"

David leaned closer and lowered his voice. "Let me make this perfectly clear, Inspector Fleeting. DS Cryer and I are investigating corruption and murder carried out by members of a senior unit of the National Crime Agency."

Fleeting stiffened. "Yes, sir."

"Nobody speaks to DC Goldstein without my express permission. And that goes for DS Stanislas and his men. If the Commissioner of Police of the Metropolis and the Home Secretary come here arm-in-arm demanding to speak to the prisoner, tell them—ever so politely—to bugger off. Refer them to me if necessary. Is that clear?"

"Yes, sir. Perfectly."

"And one more thing. This is a murder scene. Keep everyone out of the dining room until the Met's Scenes Of Crime Officers arrive. Okay?"

"Yes, sir."

David clapped Fleeting on the shoulder. "Excellent. If things go well, we'll have this investigation wrapped up by morning."

I hoped to God he was right.

"Deploy your people as you see fit," David continued. "And one more thing. Make sure DS Stanislas relocates Mr Dukakis to a different safe house. This one's a tad compromised. Is everything clear, Inspector?"

"Crystal, sir."

David turned to me. "Philip, reintroduce Inspector Fleeting to the prisoner while I have a word with the locals outside. They need to keep the neighbours and the media at bay."

The sparkle in his eye and his clipped, hurried delivery told me David had a plan and I couldn't wait to learn what it was.

As for me, the man with the memory of a High Performance Computer Cluster and the instant recall most people would die for? I had nothing but a headache.

Chapter 34

Thursday 10th October

After passing the safe house and Hannah into the tender care of Inspector Fleeting and his stone-faced troops, David gathered us at the Range Rover. I'd seen a devastated Stan emerge into the hall, but hadn't managed to say anything to him. Commiserations would come later. Right now, we both had other things to concentrate on.

SCU reunited. Fantastic. The relief brightened my mood no end.

We didn't exactly resort to high fives or a group hug, things were much too solemn, but the excitement of being among friends improved the atmosphere a little.

"Okay everyone," David said, "it's never easy to lose a colleague, even one we didn't know, but we're not finished yet. Ben, Ryan, take the Range Rover to Watford General. Stand guard over DI Hook until I can find someone to relieve you. Ryan, you did a good job tonight, but Ben's in charge of security."

Despite Ryan's seniority—he'd served five years longer as a cop—Ben's two tours of duty in Afghanistan trumped Ryan's time spent walking the beat in Birmingham.

"Understood, boss, but I'm driving. I've seen Ben behind the wheel. He's slower than my Nan."

Ryan grinned at Ben, who stared back and, as usual, gave nothing away.

"Fair enough," David said to Ryan. "If the doctors allow it, pump DI Hook for anything he has on Alpine. You can be in charge of driving *and* detection. How's that?"

"Yes, boss." He jumped into the driver's seat and Ben rode shotgun. The Range Rover shot off, made the tight turn at the mini roundabout, and exited the cul-de-sac in a spray of rainwater and a blur of flashing blue lights.

David and Alex followed me to my Beemer.

"*Kära gud*, Phil—dear God," Alex said, pointing to the front passenger door. "You were so lucky."

Two bullet holes in the door panel, a shattered window, and a rip in the driver's seat showed how close Hannah had come to adding me to her list of kills. I swallowed a gobbet of acid bile. The crown-shaped hole Hookie put in the roof didn't help improve my mood either.

"For Christ's sake, don't tell Manda."

"Never," Alex said, crossing a finger over her heart before opening the rear passenger door and sliding into the back seat.

"Boss?" I asked, arching my eyebrows.

"Of course not. This is an ongoing police investigation. And besides, those bullets would have missed everything but your backside. You'd have survived."

David winked, but his pale face told me how much my near miss and the events of the evening had upset him. He brushed pellets of glass from the passenger's seat, removed his coat, and used it as a cushion.

"Should have kept the Range Rover and let Ben and young Ryan take this wreck," he said. "With all these holes and this rain, we're in for a soaking."

"So," I said, after he'd dropped into the seat and closed the door, "you have a plan?"

"I do indeed." He turned to Alex. "Pass my laptop, please."

"Your what?" The idea of David Jones having his own laptop was perhaps the second most shocking thing I'd learned that night. "How long have you owned a laptop?"

He scratched his chin and I wondered when he'd had the chance to shave. My stubble had already started to prickle.

"Strictly speaking," he said, "it's not mine. Corky shipped it to me at the office along with Knightly's which is now undergoing forensic data analysis. He also preloaded this one with some—what do you call them—applications, and talked me through the logon procedure. And don't look at me like that, DS Cryer. I know 'logging on' has nothing to do with felling trees."

Alex took a logo-free device from her shoulder bag and passed it to the boss. Hyper slim and matt black, it could have passed for something out of a sci-fi movie. I wouldn't have been surprised to see it sprout a Corky-shaped moving hologram.

David flipped open the lid and the screen flashed into instant life.

"Usually, all I have to do is touch this icon and Corky's there, smiling at me in a God-awful Hawaiian shirt. Careful of your eyes. His yellow, orange, and green number can do serious damage to your retinas."

He hit the screen and the round-faced hacker materialised, looking exactly the same as the last time I'd seen him—on the monitor in my home office. Same fuzz on his chin, same dusty glasses, and yes, the same ugly-arsed shirt worn over a once-white vest—Sean Freeman's buddy and self-proclaimed hacking *Wunderkind*. He never did volunteer his real name and neither David nor I ever asked.

"Watcha, Mr Jones. How you doing?"

"Pretty well thanks, Corky. Anything for me?"

That's the boss all over. No mention of DS Bagshaw. Never volunteer information when not absolutely necessary.

"Of course. At this rate, I'm gonna have to start charging you consultancy fees."

"No problem. Send me your mailing address and I'll pop a cheque in the post."

Corky frowned for an instant before jerking up his chin in realisation. "Yeah, right. Very funny. Like that'll ever happen."

"You have the added information?"

"What's that, Mr Jones. No gentle wind up? Don't want me to tell you what I've had to do to overcome the firewalls and hack the carrier signals of five—count them—five telecoms companies. Just, 'you have the added information?'"

The boss sighed and crossed his arms. "Please may I have the data you worked so hard to obtain, Corky? Oh Magnificent One."

The hacker sniffed. "Now you're being sarcastic."

"We're in a hurry, Corky."

"Matter of life and death, is it?" he asked, apparent boredom flattening his delivery.

"Yes, it is."

David closed his eyes. I could almost hear him counting to ten.

"Okay, Mr Jones, okay. See that little green square at the bottom of the screen?" He pointed down and to his right and the new icon appeared.

"Yes."

"Hit that and you'll find the information you asked for. I've collated all the telecoms data you asked me to collect way back before Mr Cryer joined the NCA. I've sorted it into bite-sized chunks like you wanted and added a few bonus tracks for your entertainment."

"Such as?"

"Bits and pieces I found in my digital travels. Sound files, hire purchase agreements, mortgage contracts, private healthcare arrangements. Don't know if it'll help, but I sent the same package to Mr Cryer's phone and to the tablets of every member of your team."

"Excellent, thanks. Did you find any patterns in the phone records we should be aware of?"

Corky pulled away from the screen. "Bloody hell, Mr Jones. Don't want much do ya? You're the detective, not me. I just play with the zeros and the ones. Anyway, I'm done. Don't wanna work for you no more. If word gets out that I've been helping the Dibbles, my rep's in the toilet."

"You have a reputation?"

Wunderkind smiled and polished his fingernails on the front of the garish shirt. "Among my peers, Mr Jones. Not that there's many in my league. A woman in Japan comes close and maybe two blokes in the States—"

"Thanks, Corky, but before you go, can you locate DC Goldstein's car? It should have location tracking and be within walking distance of where we are now."

"You want even more from old Corky?" He sighed.

"Please."

"Just a sec." The hacker lowered his head and rippled fingers over a keyboard we couldn't see. "Yeah, you're right. Her Renault Megane's parked around the corner from you. Outside Number 237, Spencer Way. Take the first left at the north end of your road and then make a right. Can't miss it. And with that, I'm gone."

Corky's image dissolved into green, orange, and yellow pixels, and reformed into a 'V' sign.

"Okay, Phil. Let's go see if DC Goldstein left anything interesting for us in her car. We need to get a move on. The real Alpine might be thinking about shutting up shop, and I want the murdering sod before he clears out completely."

I fired up the Beemer and followed Corky's directions.

David touched a finger to the green icon and ten folders popped onto the screen—one for each member of the OCTF, excluding me. In the centre of each folder, he'd added a name, rank, and badge number—very nice. I could have been looking at the cover of an official police dossier.

"Apart from the stuff Corky added, what's in the folders?" I asked, giving way at the junction before turning left.

"After you called this evening, I asked Corky to collate the telephone records he's been collecting since we joined the Alpine Case."

"Bloody hell. It'll take weeks to trawl through that lot."

"Yes, but we can concentrate on the past couple of days for now in the light of the new information. I wanted all the data to hand in case we needed it."

I indicated right, made the turn into Spencer Way, and parked behind Hannah's Megane Coupé—black, sleek, and built for speed. An unexpected ride for the quiet cop I knew from The Cage. Talk about leading a double life.

"Alex," David said, pointing to the car, "let's go see if she's left us a trail of breadcrumbs."

"Sorry, boss?"

"Clues, Alex. We're looking for clues."

"Want me to open the car for you?" I asked. The Transit hadn't been much of a challenge, and I wanted to show off my car theft skills with a modern vehicle.

"No need, Philip." David raised his right hand. A set of keys with an attached ignition keycard dangled between his thumb and index finger. "DC Goldstein kindly offered to lend me her car for as long as I needed. Well, not in so many words, you understand. Why don't you rest your leg while Alex and I search the Renault?" He added, "You could pass the time by seeing if anything in those files pops out at you. Only if you get bored, mind. No rush."

"Thanks, boss. I'd never have thought to do that without your prompt."

He pointed an index finger at me. "Less of the sarcasm, Philip. Wouldn't take much for me to refuse your reinstatement back into the SCU. Then you'd have to stay in London and help rebuild the NCA's reputation."

I sucked air through my teeth. "Hell, boss. I'm good, but I'm no miracle worker."

Staying in a reasonably dry car rather than searching the Renault in the tail end of a summer storm suited me well enough, and I happily left them to it.

With ten folders on the boss' laptop, I needed a strategy.

Hookie had pretty much crossed himself off the suspect list by his actions and by being shot, but nine others remained. My fingers hovered over the icons. Which one first?

No contest.

Hannah's folder opened into a spreadsheet with a separate worksheet for each registered phone. Corky had no doubt garnered the numbers from her personnel file. Every police officer is required to register all their contact numbers, but nothing stopped people—Alpine, or anyone else—buying unregistered burners.

Although David and the guys had been studying the telephone files for a week, I hadn't seen them before.

Corky had organised the worksheets by calls received, the name and address of the caller, and an audio file of the conversation, complete with a transcription document. He'd done the same for the calls made. I read the list of names on each worksheet for the previous two days. None of them jumped out and shook me by the throat.

Her landline showed a brief call earlier in the evening from a telesales company probably trying to get her to move internet suppliers. Disappointingly, her work mobile listed nothing but calls to and from members of the OCTF—no help there. Her private registered mobile showed no activity at all for the previous two days. Meaning she almost certainly owned an unregistered burner, damn it.

Damping down a growing sense of hopelessness, I closed Hannah's folder and moved to the second on my list, the head honcho.

As with Hannah, Bee Endicott had a rarely-used landline and two mobiles—one for work and the other private. Her call log showed nothing of interest. She hadn't called Hannah once. Again, nothing to help my search. Bee's 'bonus tracks' included her mortgage contracts and bank statements, which I ignored. The Met's forensic accountants could delve into all the team's bank accounts later.

I started on Rob Cruikshank's incoming calls, but the numbers began swimming on the screen, and I paused for a moment to rest my eyes.

David slammed the Megane's tailgate and joined Alex by the driver's door.

"Anything?" I called through the Beemer's smashed passenger window.

Alex held something up but I couldn't see it in the dark.

"What's that?"

"The mobile from DC Goldstein," she said in that cute way she had of refusing to use contractions or possessives.

"What's the number?"

She searched the mobile's directory, read out the number, and added, "It has not been used tonight."

The phone matched the one on Corky's list. Yet another dead end.

"Boss," I called, "this is hopeless. Too much information here for me to take in at one sitting. If there's nothing of value in the Renault, I could do with your help. Time's motoring."

"Okay, Phil. Leave the BMW. We'll use this car. It's not as big or as comfortable, but it doesn't have the same ventilation problems either."

I locked the hire car, secretly hoping someone would steal the damn thing, and save me the trouble of reporting the damage.

"You'd better drive, boss. I can't use a manual box with this leg."

Once we'd all settled into Hannah's car, David turned to me. "Okay, Phil, what's the best way to handle this?"

Jesus, he was deferring to me again. Riches indeed. With only a slight hesitation to recover, I gave him my mobile. "Use this. I've opened Corky's email. Alex, are you ready with your tablet?"

"Of course. With which file should I begin?"

"Okay, forget DI Hook; he's in the clear as far as I'm concerned. Alex, you take X Delasse and Chloe Holder. Boss, would you mind doing Harvey Poltous and Drew Mackay? I've already been through Hannah and DCI Endicott's records. I'll finish with DS Cruikshank and then move on to Clint Schneider and Freddie Bowen. If nothing jumps out at us, we'll swap files."

"How far back do we go?" That from the boss.

"Keep this tight for now. Last two day's calls only. If we find nothing, then I reckon we'll resort to Plan B."

"Which is?" David asked.

"We call in the Met's Anti-Corruption Unit and pull in the whole team for questioning. What do you think?"

"Absolute last resort," he said. "Alpine—whoever he is—will be on his toes the moment we make this official."

"At least that will give us his identity."

Trust Alex to see the positive side.

"But he'll disappear and we'll never find him," I said, wincing as a knife thrust of cramp gripped the back of my knee. Damned tiny car. "His exit strategy will likely be flawless. He's had plenty of time to plan."

The boss stretched out his arm, squinting at the tiny screen on my mobile. "Any place we can print these files off somewhere?"

"Short of finding a local nick, we're stuck with these."

The light shower grew in strength until the raindrops exploded on the roof with the force of an artillery bombardment. With three of us in the close confines of a small car, it didn't take long for the windows to steam up. I tried cracking mine but had to close it again when rain hit the laptop screen.

A thirty-minute silence followed before David spoke again, raising his voice above the downpour. "This is hopeless. I don't see anything relevant here. Phil, you?"

"Nothing," I said, trying to stretch another shaft of cramp from my leg.

"Alex?" he asked, twisting in his seat to look directly at her.

"Nothing out of the usual. Monsieur Delasse is constantly on the phone. He seems to be juggling at least three female acquaintances. DC Holder is less active. Apart from work colleagues, she telephones the same three numbers regularly. Her parents, her brother, and a woman in Brighton named Adele. I think Chloe is like me, *ja?*"

From the moment she joined the SCU, Alex never hid the fact that she's gay. It's not a problem to any of us apart from poor Ryan, who fancies her something rotten. And why not, Alex has that Nordic Warrior Queen vibe going. Added to the powerful athletic build, she has high cheekbones, clear blue eyes, and knockout smile. Not that she'd smiled much since Julie's death.

I cleared my throat. "Yeah, I've just finished ploughing through Rob Cruikshank's call log. When not on the line to his daughters, who live with his ex-wife, he spends most evenings online, playing MMORPGs."

"Playing what?"

"Online role-playing games, boss. Sword and sorcery. Heroes and villains."

"Ridiculous. How old is DS Cruikshank?"

I grinned. Despite recent events, it was good to hear the old man in full flow. "It's serious stuff, boss. For grown-ups."

"I'll take your word for it. Nothing on DC Schneider?"

"Nope. Clint's in the clear as far as his calls are concerned. Work and family calls during the day. Precious few calls in the evening. What about Drew and Bandage?"

David consulted his notepad. "DC Mackay is never off his mobile—morning, lunchtime, and evening. The transcripts are pretty tedious, though. Conversations revolve around family, girlfriends, and football. Most exciting thing to happen in his private life is when he missed his flight to Edinburgh the weekend before you joined the NCA.

"DC Poltous is slightly more interesting. He's a member of a couple of pub quiz teams and has a reasonably full social life."

The full beams of an oncoming truck bathed the Megane's interior with a white light so dazzling I had to shield my eyes and wait for the after-image to fade before opening them again.

What was that about a missed flight?

"What did you say, boss?"

"DC Poltous has a full social life."

"No," I said, trying keep calm when I really wanted to punch the Megane's roof. "That bit where Drew missed his flight."

"That's right. He had to stay in London for the weekend. Why? Is it important?"

"Yes, it bloody well is," I said, unable to keep my voice down.

The information had tweaked something in my memory and nudged something else. I open the laptop folder again to double check the information.

Yes!

Bloody hell, I had the answer! I really did have it this time. A more demonstrative bloke would have slapped his forehead or jumped up and down in his seat.

"I'm such a bloody fool. Fire up the car, boss. Let's go pick up the real Alpine!"

Chapter 35

Thursday 10th October

David pushed the big red ignition button on the dash. The engine caught and growled before settling into a feline purr. "Are you sure?"

"Certain." I formed fists, desperate not to give him the hurry-up.

"Where to?"

"Berkhamsted."

"Who's in Berkhamsted? ... No. Hang on." He closed his eyes for a moment. "DC Bowen?"

"Yep. Freddie's been playing us all from the start."

David threw the Renault into reverse and grabbed the handbrake. "Okay, explain when we're on the way. Point me in the right direction and then plug the address into that thing." He nodded at the built-in Satnav.

"Pull a u-ey here," I said. "Take the first left. Follow the signs to Watford and head for Aylesbury."

David glanced in the rear view mirror, worked the gears, throttle, and handbrake, and had the car pointing the other way in a squeal of burning rubber and blurred movement.

When did he become a stunt driver?

Halfway through the turn, he found first gear, punched the throttle, and took off. The impetus forced me hard into the seat and pressed my head against the headrest. At the junction, he made a left. Two hundred metres later, with the Renault's engine racing, he took the first exit off a roundabout, keeping the revs high and slipping through the gears like a pro.

"Alex," he called, "phone Ryan. See what's happening with DI Hook."

It took a couple of minutes to program the directions into the Satnav.

"Alex? Any news?"

"Ryan has turned off his mobile and I am on hold with the hospital switchboard."

He flicked a quick glance at me before checking his wing mirror and overtaking a petrol tanker. "Okay, Phil. Tell me why you think it's Freddie Bowen. Take your time. According to this thing, we're twenty-eight minutes away from the Bowen's house."

The Satnav ordered a right turn at the next junction.

With Watford behind and the A41 under our wheels, David opened up the throttle. The Renault's engine roared, the speedometer hit 128 mph, and the countryside flashed past in dark streaks flecked with the occasional flashes of light and car headlamps. Rain continued to fall.

"Drew missing his flight to Edinburgh reminded me that Freddie runs a tight schedule. Always leaves the office at or before 17:15 to reach home in time to take over from the day nurse."

"This is all about DC Bowen's timekeeping?"

"It is."

"Come on, Philip. I'm getting tired of you dragging things out as though you're a game show host announcing the winner."

He dropped two gears and drove straight over the top of a mini roundabout; the car's wheels left the road as we hit the bump. My stomach lurched as we took air.

"The Bowens have a private healthcare package. The day nurse attends from 08:00 to 18:30, Monday to Friday. It's very expensive and only part covered by their private health insurance. Any extra time is billed at sixty pounds an hour, and a full hour is payable even if he's only five minutes late."

"How do you know this?"

"Freddie told me, and I've just confirmed it in one of Corky's 'bonus tracks'. He's included the day nurse's terms and conditions. I have to say, I'm impressed with his thoroughness."

"Yes, he seems to have thought of everything. Perhaps we should draft him onto the team as a full time civilian analyst." David pulled his eyes from the road for a second to glare at me before concentrating on the driving again. As we were travelling at eighty mph in a built up area, I was glad he decided to concentrate on his driving. He overtook a long row of nose-to-tail traffic and ducked the car back into our lane before we could be flattened by an oncoming truck. Some time ago we'd turned off the dual carriageway; I hadn't noticed.

"I've just finished reading Freddie's phone logs and I didn't twig it until you mentioned Drew Mackay's missed flight."

"What about it?" he asked.

I opened Freddie's folder on the laptop. Apart from his office phone, there were two numbers: his home landline and his work mobile. Unlike the other Task Force members I'd looked at, he hadn't registered a personal mobile. "For tonight, the Bowens' home phone shows two outbound calls; one made at 16:08 to Freddie's office landline, the second at 18:27 to the Pizza Palace in Berkhamsted. The second call lasted nine minutes.

"On his part, Freddie made two calls from his work mobile, both to his home landline. The first at 17:10—presumably to tell the nurse he was about to leave the office—and the second at 18:39. Each call lasted less than a minute. After that, there's no activity on either phone all evening."

"Any idea what was said?"

"Sorry, Corky hasn't included today's transcripts."

"Okay," David said, keeping his eyes on the road, thankfully. "That tells us the Bowens don't use the phones much and Freddie calls home during his commute. Nothing unusual in either of those facts. Not for a middle-aged couple."

"Good point," I said, holding back on my revelation. "Moving on. Freddie told me his evening commute takes at least fifty minutes, sometimes longer. That gives him precious little leeway."

We weren't far away now. The Satnav's ETA showed us as eight minutes out. Despite our stomach-churning speed and the growing traffic as we reached the outskirts of Hemel Hempstead, David turned to look at me. "And?"

"Who ordered the pizza?"

"Sorry?"

"Who ordered the pizza from the house phone at 18:27? The call that lasted nine minutes?"

"Surely that was DC Bowen. Did he leave Tinworth Street at the usual time?"

"More or less. So he *could* have called the pizzeria if he'd made it home on time, but why would he phone home on his mobile at 18:39 if he'd already arrived?"

"Perhaps the day nurse or a neighbour called for the food?" Alex asked, still waiting for her call to connect.

David flicked the indicator in response to a command from the Satnav and made a hard right that threw me against the passenger's doorframe.

"That call would have taken the nurse into overtime," I said, "and that's never happened. During the whole of the healthcare contract—nearly two years—there's never been a single added charge. Check it yourself. There's a copy of the payment schedule on the laptop."

"The logic's a little fragile," David said.

"Is it? The Imelda Bowen I met at Richie Juno's memorial service couldn't have been left alone for any length of time. If Freddie had ever been late, the nurse would have had to stay."

"No. Not now perhaps, but her illness is progressive. She could have deteriorated recently. Before then, she might have been okay to leave on her own for a short while."

"Perhaps. Anyway, how likely is it for DC Bowen never to have been delayed on his homeward commute? Not once in all the time they'd had that contract. No train cancellations? No 'leaves on the line'? No 'wrong type of snow'?"

My question sparked a memory. "Hang on a minute, I've had another thought."

I scrolled back through Freddie's spreadsheet to the day we arrested the ABR crew.

"Hell, will you look at this," I said, pointing to the screen. "Monday, the 16th of September—my first day undercover. Freddie delayed his departure from The Cage until the Met's armed unit arrived at Northfleet to take the ABR crew into custody. He clock-watched all afternoon."

I held the laptop up to show Alex while David concentrated on making like Lewis Hamilton or, given his age, Nigel Mansell.

"See the call logs for that day? Freddie didn't phone ahead to warn the nurse. No way he could have made it home in time, but the healthcare plan still shows a normal handover time. No overtime charges. We've got him. We've got the bastard!" I said, unable to keep the triumph out of my voice.

"Unless he made alternative arrangements," Alex said. "A friendly neighbour, perhaps?"

"Possibly, but it doesn't ring true and, according to his phone records, he didn't call anyone to make any arrangements. You know what I think?"

"Do tell, Philip," David said, and compressed his lips.

"Imelda Bowen ordered that pizza today to have it ready for hubby when he returned home."

David took a moment to think things through before nodding. "Based on your assumptions, agreed. But if she's mentally sharp enough to do that, what about the day nurse? Imelda would have to act senile for the best part of twelve hours every work day. Is it possible?"

I paused to consider the question. "Freddie did say Imelda had deteriorated recently. So much so, he was considering early retirement, but I smell insurance fraud. When we have the Bowens safely locked up, we can set the NCA's forensic accountants loose. All I know is, this whole thing stinks."

David stamped on the brakes and aborted a dangerous overtake.

"Jesus, boss. Careful. I've already seen one ambulance tonight."

"Yes, *boss*," he said, lifting an eyebrow. "Did I never tell you I competed in the RAC Rally back in 1974?"

"No, you didn't. How did you get on?"

"Crashed and burned on the fifth stage."

The banter showed David was deflecting his anger. We both knew it, but it was still comforting to have some semblance of normality.

"Don't worry, Phil. I've got things under control. This Renault's a nippy little thing," he said, frowning in concentration and negotiating yet another mini roundabout without reducing speed. "Never driven one of these modern sports jobbies before."

"Boss," Alex said. "Ryan tells me DI Hook is in surgery. When they finish operating on his leg, they will take him for a CT scan."

"Okay," David said. "Tell them to stay close. DI Hook's still a potential target. Alpine might want to clean shop."

He dropped the car into fourth, then third, and slowed further as we approached a *Welcome to Berkhamsted* sign. The Satnav announced we were eight hundred metres from our destination.

Thirty seconds later, he pulled the car to a stop on Tennyson Rise, outside a row of neat, detached houses joined together with attached garages like a string of square pearls. Sixties-built boxes for commuters and excruciatingly boring, they didn't look like the place a dirty cop would set up his base which, I guess, was the point.

The road dropped downhill and made a long sweeping left-hand curve. We had perfect view of Freddie's house—Number 13, ironically enough. It stood six doors down and across the road from us, bathed in the orange glow of a streetlamp. Badly trimmed privet, wooden gate, lights in a downstairs window. It appeared that Freddie and Imelda had yet to turn in for the night.

Alex scooted forward. "I have a question. If Mrs Bowen has been living a lie for the past two years, why did she make the mistake today?"

"Who knows?" I answered. "Perhaps it was her turn to make dinner and she got lazy. Maybe they've grown overconfident. Maybe they're making ready to skip town and she didn't fancy cooking. We'll ask her in a minute."

David turned to face us both. He draped an arm around the back of his seat and hugged the headrest.

"You know DC Bowen, Philip. What's he like?"

I puffed out my cheeks. "Quiet, friendly, helpful, if a little sad due to Imelda's condition—or so I thought. Actually, I quite liked the guy. Always seemed the least likely to be Alpine. Bugger. I hate being fooled."

David nodded. "You weren't the only one. He'd have to be pretty smart to get away with what he's been doing all this time."

"What do we do now we're here? Sit and wait, or knock on his door?"

David looked at Alex and then back to me. "I'm open to suggestions."

The dashboard clock clicked over to 00:12. Friday morning. With any luck, we'd have the Alpine case wrapped up by the weekend and I'd be able to hang up my undercover hat forever. I tried hard not to get ahead of myself. No experienced cop ever took anything for granted in police work.

"It's been what, over two hours since we arrested Hannah?" I said and nodded to Freddie's house. "If he's aware of it, would he still be here?"

David lifted his chin. "I doubt it. They'd be at the airport with false passports in hand by now. So, how do we use their ignorance?"

Alex answered. "Philip should telephone him, I think. Give him the news of DC Goldstein. Then we watch to see his reaction?"

"My thoughts exactly," I said, and grabbed my mobile.

David raised his hand. "Don't put it on speaker, the echo might make him suspicious. If you've forgotten his number, it'll be on the laptop." He delivered the line straight-faced. Whoever said David Jones had no sense of humour?

"Funny, boss. Very droll."

"You did say you were tired."

I gave myself a few seconds to gather my thoughts. Then I dialled.

Chapter 36

Friday 11th October

"Hello? Who's that?"

Freddie sounded calm, no hint of worry or breathlessness. No sign he'd been rushing around the house throwing clothes into suitcases.

"Freddie, it's me, Phil Cryer." I spoke quickly and added a touch of worry mixed with shock.

"Phil? It's very late," he said, lowering his voice. "I was about to turn in. Imelda's asleep at last. Can this wait until tomorrow?"

"Crap, is that the time? Sorry mate, but I didn't know who else to call. Did you hear about Hannah?"

A sharp breath. "No. What's wrong? Has she been in an accident? Is she okay?"

"No, no, it's nothing like that. Remember I told you I'm mates with one of the guys in UKPPS? DS Stanislas, you know, Stan the Man? ... Well, he just called me. Hannah killed his partner and tried to assassinate one of their clients!"

"What? You're ... kidding."

Genuine surprise, excellent. He couldn't fake it. David raised an eyebrow and nodded for me to continue.

"No, on my life. She walked into one of their safe houses a couple of hours ago and started shooting. It's bloody mayhem, apparently. Armed officers all over the place. They've taken her to Paddington Green and the client to hospital with a bullet wound. The man she killed was DS Bagshaw. Did you know him?"

Well, part of it was true, even if the wounded man wasn't Theo Dukakis, but Billy Hook.

"No, I didn't. Fucking hell!" Freddie said, recovering his composure and back to playing his part. "What's wrong with her? Did she have a breakdown or something?"

"No idea. But I reckon we'll all be interviewed by Anti-Corruption in the morning. They'll probably close the Task Force during the inquiry. You know what they're like. Throw enough shit at enough blankets and some of it will stick. I've only just joined the NCA and now I'm under the same cloud."

I paused for breath and to let the information sink in before twisting the knife.

"Sorry, Freddie. Just wanted to mark your card. You'll need someone to look after Imelda if their questioning goes on past your normal knocking off time tomorrow."

Heavy breathing. The first signs of panic.

"Christ, what a mess. I'll make emergency arrangements with the day care nurse. Thanks for the warning, Phil. I owe you."

"That's okay, mate. Sorry again to call so late. Thought you needed to know."

"Yes, yes ... I understand."

"See you tomorrow for the Spanish Inquisition."

Freddie rang off and I turned to the boss. "Did you hear any of his reaction?"

"Yes. Took it rather well, but I thought he might."

"Didn't lay it on too thick, I hope?"

"Nope. Struck the right balance between confusion and annoyance. Nicely done."

"So now we wait?"

David took a deep breath, let it out in a sigh, and twisted around to face the front again. He wiped away the mist that had formed on the windscreen with his hankie. "Yes, Phil. Now we wait. Alex, can you bring up an aerial photo of this street? I'd like to make sure there's no back way out of that house."

The idea of David Jones resorting to online maps rather than an actual search made me smile.

"What's the daft grin for, Philip? Wondering why I'm not sending you out on a scouting party? Think I've turned into a technophile in my dotage?"

"Thought never entered my head, boss."

"No, of course not. Look around. It's so quiet here, if any of us went out in this rain we'd be bound to draw attention to ourselves. Right now, I'm guessing Freddie Bowen's frightened out of his criminal mind. See his curtains twitching? He'll be looking for anything out of the ordinary and I don't want to take the chance he's got an arsenal in there with him."

"Boss, this is an online map," Alex said, tilting her tablet so we could all see the picture. "The rear garden abuts the one of the neighbour. There is no way out other than climbing over fences."

"Did you see that?" David pointed to Freddie's house. Another light showed beside the first, probably in the kitchen. "Activity. Doesn't look like Alpine's turning in any time soon. And, hello, there's movement at the garage."

An up-and-over door cranked open, showing us the front part of a lit garage, and a dark blue saloon. I couldn't see the manufacturer's badge, but the rake of the bonnet suggested a newish BMW. Someone inside the garage cast moving shadows. The driver's door opened and the same someone slid behind the steering wheel. The car's courtesy light blinked on and showed us the driver's face.

Imelda Bowen!

"Gotcha!" I said, unable to contain myself.

Alex grabbed my shoulder and squeezed.

David broke out his lopsided grin. "Nicely done, Philip. This'll look good on your arrest record."

The Beemer's engine fired up in a roar of souped-up, burbling exhaust. The bonnet started vibrating and an angry-looking Imelda Bowen drove it out of the garage and parked in the driveway. When I thought of the unfortunate woman I'd seen at Richie's funeral being led away in tears after soiling her dress, I wanted to rush over and clap her in handcuffs there and then.

"You going to fire up the motor and block their driveway?" I asked.

"I'm considering it." David's eyes narrowed. His attention flicked from the Bowens' car to the clock on the Renault's dashboard, and back again. "That's a BMW 3 Series. Does Bowen have it registered with the NCA?"

"No. According to his file, he owns that Fiat." I pointed to a muddy brown Fiat Panda parked at the side of the road in front of their house.

"Damn."

"Why. What are you thinking, boss?"

"If we go barging in, they'll clam up and we'll learn nothing. I'd like to find out where they're going in such a hurry. Is there any way we can follow them at a distance and be certain of not losing them? Most new BMWs have trackers, don't they? Can we set up a trace from here?"

"We'd need a licence number and access to my desktop systems. Couldn't be done in time. Not legally."

"And illegally?"

"That depends on a couple of things. First being whether Corky's still on the other end of this laptop."

"And the second?"

"Whether that Beemer's license number is real."

"Why wouldn't it be? Freddie Bowen's a police officer. He'd know better than to risk driving a car with dodgy plates."

I shrugged. "You could be right."

"Well?" he said, pointing at the laptop. "What are you waiting for? Give it a go."

I raised the screen and hit the 'contact me' icon on the keyboard.

Alex leaned forward and I caught a note of Jimmy Choo's *Eau de Parfum*. Manda tried some last Christmas and didn't like it, but on Alex it worked well. Different chemistry, I suppose, but what do I know? The nearest I come to perfume is the stuff the manufacturers put in my shower gel; I don't do aftershave.

"Can either of you make out the license number?"

The laptop's screen lit blue and I touched my index finger to 'contact me' icon. Corky appeared, this time wearing a plain white polo-shirt. Or it would have been plain and white but for the big tomato sauce stain down the front—at least it looked like tomato sauce. He didn't seem surprised or happy to see me.

"Mr Cryer, what part of 'I ain't doing do no more work for the busies' don't you understand?" he asked, a deep frown crumpling his shiny forehead.

"Sorry, Corky, we really are, but this is an emergency. It's difficult though. Time sensitive. You might not be able to do it for us."

"Too difficult? Yeah, right. What you want from old Corky-boy?"

Sometimes, it's too easy. I gave him the details of Freddie's BMW.

The hacker sniffed. "Difficult? Nah, piece of piss." His frown deepened and stared closer at his screen. "Oh, is that you, Ms Olganski? Sorry for the language."

"It is nothing, Corky, but we do need your help. It is possible?"

I think the hacker might have blushed but the low definition screen couldn't handle the contrast.

"Is the car moving?"

"No. It's parked outside a garage a few doors away, but it's about to."

"Don't go nowhere."

His head dropped and the screen faded to grey.

"Nicely played, Philip," the boss whispered. "Using his pride made sense, but he's going to blow us off. He didn't even ask where we were."

Oh dear.

Over the previous few weeks, it might have appeared that the old man had travelled a long way down the road to technical awareness, but in reality, he'd barely left his front door.

"Doesn't need to, boss." I lifted the laptop. "This has a built-in tracker. Corky knows exactly where we are. From this, he'll have worked out whose house we're parked outside and who owns the car. Now all he has to do is hack the DVLA database, find the car's VIN number from the registration document, and trace it back to the manufacturer. A BMW that young will have smart technology for fault diagnosis and a built-in informatics facility so the manufacturer can talk to it directly. After that he'll hack BMW's systems and pop the tracking data onto this laptop.

"It isn't that difficult. In fact, I could do the same thing from my desk in the SCU, but it would take a hell of a lot longer since I'd have to keep within the law and raise a warrant."

"Okay, point taken. But if the Bowens look ready to leave before Corky hacks that car's system, we're going to pull them in. Alex, you still have your weapon?"

She patted her right hip. "Of course."

"Good. They'll be terrified right now. No telling what they'll do or whether they're armed."

"I will be ready for them, boss."

He looked at me. "Okay then, DS Cryer. While we're waiting for our friend to work his electronic magic, tell me exactly how Alpine's manipulating the NCA database."

"It's simple really, I should have spotted it right away, but I was looking for something far more complex. You remember the bullion robbery I helped crack on my first day in London?"

"The ABR case."

"That's right. A misspelled name corrupted the search routines. At first, I put it down to human error, a typo. You'd be surprised how often things like that happen. Well, maybe not. People make mistakes. It's one of the things I had to learn when growing up. Could never understand why kids in my class forgot things when I never did. Over time, I discovered that *I* was the abnormal one and had to make allowances for transcript errors, typos, and just plain forgetfulness. Then Chloe showed me around Eavesdropper Central."

From their expressions, I could tell I had David and Alex's undivided attention.

"I witnessed the process first hand when one of the COs screwed up right in front of me. She misheard something in a telephone conversation and transcribed it incorrectly— a homonym 'here' for 'hear' and a couple of substitutions. Easily done, but the fact I noticed it and no one else did made me think."

I tried stretching the ache out of my knee but the Renault didn't give me enough room.

"I got to thinking it wouldn't take much for Alpine—Freddie—to manipulate the system in the same way. Change a date or time of a meeting. Alter an address. Tennyson Rise becomes, say, Tennyson Ride and presto, a police raid visits the wrong place and turns up nothing. And best of all, Freddie has the real data and can use it any way he chooses."

"Nobody would notice this?" Alex asked.

"As long as he didn't make it too obvious or do it too often, why would they?"

David nodded and asked, "You think DS Juno found out?"

"Reckon so. If you remember, Richie was murdered a few weeks after the Trial of the Decade story broke. What if it prompted a memory? The first few files he transferred from Essex were cases he'd worked on indirectly. One mentioned The Baron, AKA, Theo Dukakis. What if Richie saw or heard something in The Cage that worried him? What if he noticed discrepancies in the files but didn't know who to trust? Hell, we might never know what actually spooked him, but we can make a guess from his actions. Let's say he started suspecting Hookie. Maybe that's why he kept his investigations quiet until he'd talked to CS Knightly. What do you think? Make sense?"

"Theoretically," David said, "At least it's something to look—"

Corky's face appeared on the screen again. "If you're ready for the data link, Mr Cryer, tap the new icon."

"That was quick," I said.

"It's easy when you've already opened the back doors to every car manufacturer in the world. And with that, goodnight, good luck, and good riddance."

Before I had a chance to thank him, a black box with a plunge handle, like an old style mechanical detonator, replaced Corky's face. I touched the icon and it exploded into a large scale Ordinance Survey map of Tennyson Rise and its surroundings. A flashing red arrow corresponded with the Beemer's position.

"Superb," David said.

"Look." Alex pointed to the house.

The light in the ground floor windows went out, as did the one in the garage. Freddie appeared in the front door, carrying a large case, head swivelling, eyes darting up and down the street. At least he had the grace to look furtive and a little scared. Imelda didn't. She sounded the horn—a traffic offence at that time of night—and waved an angry hand to hurry him along. Boot opened, case thrown in, and Freddie slid into the passenger seat. He barely had time to slam the door before Imelda gunned the engine.

The Beemer shot out of the driveway, turned right down the hill and away from us, and picked up speed until reaching the traffic lights at the junction with Broad Street.

David interlaced his fingers, rotated his wrists, and cracked his knuckles. "I do hope she isn't stopped for speeding."

David glanced at the laptop screen. The red arrow blinked and showed the BMW turning right at the lights, heading south towards London. He punched the ignition button and the Renault turned over with far less fire and brimstone than the Bowens' Beemer had done. He followed them at a much more sedate pace.

"Where d'you think they're headed, airport or ferry? I'll take three-to-one odds on Heathrow."

"The Channel Tunnel, I would say," Alex said.

To be awkward, I offered a fiver on Gatwick.

Chapter 37

Friday 11th October

Two miles along Broad Street, the BMW took the first exit at a mini roundabout and joined Chesham Road. A couple of minutes later, it filtered onto the A41, eastbound. We followed at a safe three hundred metre distance, only able to see the target on the long straights. I navigated, and David looked relaxed behind the wheel.

"What's the plan, boss? When are we going to pull them over?"

"I'd like to see where they're going first. No chance of them disabling the tracker, is there?"

"Not without immobilising their ignition system. The tracker's hard-wired in. Part of the car's guts." I tapped the Renault's Satnav screen. "See how this is moulded into the dash? Not possible to remove it without the correct tools and definitely not while on the move."

"That's what I thought. So we keep our distance and move in only if they look likely to stop and change cars."

With traffic nice and light, we travelled seven miles in less than six minutes, joined the M25, and turned onto the North Orbital Road. Then we joined the M1 at Junction 6.

"Where the hell's he going?" I asked no one. "If he wanted Heathrow or Gatwick, he'd be better off staying on the M25 this time of night."

Not one to answer rhetorical questions, David checked his mirrors, moved into the overtaking lane, and closed the gap. He kept at least three vehicles between us and our target until the M1 terminated at Junction 1, but closed it to one during the short stretch of North Circular leading to Brent Cross Shopping Centre.

"What the hell?" I asked. "Don't tell me we've got it wrong and the buggers are out buying the weekend's groceries."

David looked at me for the first time since leaving the M1. "And Imelda Bowen's conveniently having one of her lucid days? No, they're meeting someone. Maybe for a final handover. They might have been holding some information in reserve for this sort of occasion. Do you both have enough charge in your mobiles and storage to take plenty of pictures?"

"I have," Alex said, "but the quality will be poor in this light."

"We'll make do with what we have. Damn it, I was hoping they'd head for an airport or the ferry port so we could draft in armed security."

A couple of left turns later, the Bowens entered the multi-storey car park and climbed to the top floor—the fourth—ignoring all the empty spaces on the lower levels.

"Not looking for a parking spot, then." I said unnecessarily, tension loosening my tongue.

David parked on the third level, next to the exit ramp. "Let's go see who they're meeting. Alex, give me your tablet. You need to be ready with your weapon in case there's trouble. Phil, stay behind us."

My fists clenched automatically, but I could see the boss' point. I wouldn't exactly be much use in a fight, or a chase. Fucking knee. Alex handed me my stick from the parcel shelf and showed me a sympathetic smile.

"Be safe," she said in a whisper. "I do not want to attend another funeral."

It's not that I minded being protected by a woman, I'm not that shallow. Alex is a mate, bloody capable too, but if the Bowens escaped because I couldn't pull my weight, how useless would I feel? Nobody would blame me of course, least of all the boss, but I'd blame myself. I gripped the handle of the stick and fell in behind. The boss and Alex led, and the useless bloody Gimp brought up the rear.

Lucky Cryer? Yeah, right.

Brightly lit and reeking of exhaust fumes and spent motor oil, the near-empty car park echoed to our footsteps and to the tapping of my stick. Thankfully, the few other shoppers on our level offered us some cover. Concrete support columns and a low wall hid our approach to the curved up-ramp, but we couldn't climb much higher without being seen by anyone on the fourth level.

"Boss," I whispered, calling him and Alex back to hide behind a column. "I can't go any further. Freddie's bound to recognise me with this bloody stick. Why don't you and Alex go on up as though you've lost your car and get close? You could easily pass for a couple in love. Freddie's never seen either of you, right?"

"Not as far as I know. That's a good idea. You?"

"I'll go back to the exit ramp and take some film with Alex's tablet. It's zoom facility is better than the one on my phone. Not to worry, I'll be safe over there out the way." I spoke the last sentence through partly clenched teeth.

David clasped my upper arm. "Good lad. Guard our backs."

With what, my stick?

Alex handed me her tablet, took David's right arm in a close hug, and rested her head on his shoulder. And there they were, every inch the loving couple out for a late night shopping spree. She kept her right hand close to her concealed pistol.

As they climbed the up-ramp, David started wittering about being sure they'd parked on level four. Alex, in turn, disagreed and made it clear she thought they used the third and had parked near the exit to the shops. I hurried the seventy-five metres back to the far end of the car park, trying to avoid making too much noise. For once, my leg played nice and the exercise loosened the cramp. It didn't feel too bad, either. Adrenalin is a great painkiller.

The exit ramp had a black-painted metal guard rail on the inner side between each concrete column and a curved brick wall on the outer side. Despite having no desire to meet a car travelling down as I walked up, I stayed close to the outer wall rather than risking exposure to Freddie and Imelda. Scrapes of paint where drivers had misjudged the turn and left mementos of their visits on the brickwork gave me no confidence in the driving skills of Brent Cross patrons.

I was exposed, vulnerable, and—I'm not too proud to admit—a little scared of being crushed by an onrushing car.

Thank fuck the place was near empty at one o'clock on a Friday morning.

When my eyeline reached the lip of the fourth level, I stopped, and disabled the tablet's flash facility. The Bowens' car stood out shiny and rain-washed beneath one of the striplights. Rain driven in by a stiff breeze dripping into puddles added to the background concerto of traffic, mall music, and the crash-rattle of shopping trolleys on lower levels. I shivered as a cold wind found the gap between my collar and neck.

Inside their car, Freddie and Imelda faced each other, locked in a hand-waving, finger-pointing slanging match. I zoomed in until the tablet's picture started to lose focus, pulled out a little, and selected 'movie mode'. In the good lighting, the pictures were sufficient to make it worth the price of hiring a lip-reader at some stage down the line. The Bowens' body language showed how much Imelda dominated their relationship. On the down side, Freddie faced away from me, and I had little more than footage of his rounded shoulders and the back of his balding head. This improved though when he turned to watch the loving couple stroll past, arm-in-arm.

David's, "I'm sorry, darling. I was sure we left it here," held the perfect balance of annoyance at his forgetfulness and worry that some bugger had stolen their motor.

I slipped further into the shadow as Alex stopped, turned to face David, and touched her hand to his cheek. He smiled, kissed her forehead, and they hugged for a moment before continuing their search. Sweet. It was like watching a spring-autumn episode of True Love. During their hug, Alex took a couple of selfies of her and the old man, no doubt making sure to include the BMW and its occupants to back up my videography. They turned away from me and headed back the way they came, towards the exit doors.

Headlights crawled along parking level three and the low rumble of a big motorcycle—750cc at least—cut through the ambient noise. A motorcycle? Christ, not X Delasse? Surely there couldn't be a third bent cop in the same NCA unit? I shuffled to the side and hid behind one of the columns, praying the answer was no.

The bike reached the up-ramp and rolled into full view. Its rider was about the same height as X, but a lot thicker around the waist and had broader shoulders. I relaxed a little at the sight of an old-timer trying to stave off the male menopause.

As the cycle approached and then passed them, David and Alex didn't break stride, but continued towards the pedestrian exit.

The biker crawled the cycle forward and slowed to a stop on the driver's side of the Bowens' car. He leaned the bike onto its side-stand, put one foot on the ground, the other on the foot-peg, and flipped up his visor. In the tablet's screen, I could see his eyes clearly—hazel with flecks of amber beneath bushy dark brows. The biker's head swivelled as he scanned the surroundings. Finding them to his liking, he killed the engine. Those eyes, I'd seen them before. In the distant past, but where? Damn. The answer wouldn't come.

Biker removed his leather gloves and stuffed them between the forks of the handlebars.

The boss and Alex reached the exit door and pulled. It appeared locked. David cursed and they turned in my direction. It was his way of maintaining watch for as long as possible but left little old me as the point man.

DS Cryer to the fore with his trusty cane.

I tried swallowing, but sticky phlegm is a bugger to get down. Spitting it out wasn't the answer either. Spitting is never an answer.

With the stick hooked on my forearm, I pressed in against the rough concrete pillar to reduce camera shake, and continued filming. A small part of me wondered why the pillar smelled of salt and urine. Who could piss that high?

Imelda wound down her window and held out her hand to the biker, fingers flexed, beckoning. She said something I couldn't quite make out, but it might have been, "Come on then, hand it over!"

The rider spoke, his words muffled by the helmet, and then lowered the zip of his leather jacket. He dug in a hand. It came out holding a chrome-plated automatic. Jesus, another gun! He pointed it at her. She screamed. The pistol spat flame and coughed smoke. The percussive explosion hammered in my ears.

Biker fired again.

Imelda Bowen slumped forward. Her head hit the steering wheel and stayed there. Freddie yelled, "No!" and scrambled for his door handle. Biker turned his weapon, aimed, and fired a third time. Freddie's right shoulder punched forward, jacket ripped, and he fell through the open door.

The exit door behind the boss and Alex opened. A woman, giggling into her mobile, pushed through.

David yelled, "Get down!" and dived towards her, right arm raised, hand waving.

Alex drew her gun, dropped onto one knee, minimising her profile, and yelled, "Armed police! Lower your weapon."

David bowled the woman to the floor, keeping his body between her and the gunman, who turned towards Alex's shout, ignoring Freddie. His gun moved, barked again. Alex fired, jerked, and tumbled backwards. Blood splattered the wall behind her. As she hit the concrete, her gun flew from her hand, and hit the back wall.

"No!" I screamed, dropped the tablet, and started climbing the exit ramp. Eighty metres away, that's all, but I'd never get to her in time. She didn't move.

Oh God. I couldn't see her breathing!

The walking stick fell from my arm. I tripped, stumbled, and fell. I grabbed the stick and started crawling, keeping down, trying to stay below the killer's sight line.

Biker raised the gun, aimed, and fired in one movement. Concrete splintered two centimetres above David's head, shards and dust speckled his hair. He held tight to the struggling woman, who kicked and screamed, trying to push him away.

Alex sprawled against the far wall. She hadn't moved since the bullet slammed into her chest. Her gun lay in a shallow gulley, a million miles away.

Biker took aim, I screamed "No!" again, and he turned, searching for whoever shouted.

Lights!

Lights behind me, down on the third level.

Through the ringing in my ears, I made out the rumble of a diesel engine in low gear. A delivery van moved slowly, heading towards the up-ramp to the fourth level. Biker stretched taller in the saddle. He had to have seen the van.

With the panel van blocking the up-ramp, only the down ramp remained clear.

Calm as you like, Biker faced forward and stared at me as I tried to scramble to my feet, walking stick in one hand, the other on the floor, pushing. Thankfully, the tablet had fallen into a shadow.

Biker transferred the gun to his left hand and fired another shot at Freddie before resting it on the handlebar grip. He operated the clutch lever with his pinkie and ring fingers, hit the starter, and the bike's engine roared.

Still staring at me, he kicked the bike into gear and wrung the throttle. He revved the engine three or four times and released the clutch but not the front brake. The rear wheel spun. The tyre squealed and a thick cloud of black smoke bloomed behind him. Biker's cheeks bunched and his crow's-feet deepened.

The bastard was smiling. Smiling at me!

He released the front brake and pulled a wheelie. Twenty-five metres later, he dropped the front wheel. It bounced and the bike slowed.

The killer stopped the bike fifteen metres from me, balanced on the lip of the down slope. He closed the throttle. The growling motor quietened to an animal purr. The smiling eyes stared straight at me, taunting. He raised the gun and aimed it at my face.

"Get out of my fucking way, son," he called, his accent pure Belfast hard-man. "I don't have a problem topping cripples."

His finger tightened on the trigger.

Chapter 38

Friday 11th October

I cowered, raised my free hand in surrender, and leaned so heavily on the stick, it bent under the weight.

"Please don't shoot. I didn't see nothin', honest."

Even to me, it sounded high-pitch and pathetic, and I didn't have to act scared. Staring down the barrel of a gun for the second time in a few hours did something strange to my voice-box.

"Look at me, son."

I raised my eyes and stared through half-closed, fluttering lids.

He flicked the gun to the left, showing me which way to move. I shuffled to the inside railings, still leaning on the stick, making my movements slow, deliberate. Wincing every time I moved my left leg. Oh, I must have been a pitiful sight. So harmless, I could barely stand.

"Don't shoot me. Please don't."

Behind the killer, David finally managed to convince the woman he wasn't an attacker. He raised his fingers to his lips and pushed her into the stairwell. Then he turned and edged towards Alex and her gun. I kept my head lowered, trying not to let the information show on my face.

Biker had plenty of room to pass, but took his time. No doubt seeing me as a coward and no threat. He sniffed, put his gun away, and zipped up his jacket.

David reached Alex, checked her pulse, and nodded at me. Still alive! Thank God. David edged toward the gun. A few more seconds, that's all he needed.

Biker waved me away, contempt in his eyes. Then he opened the throttle and burned rubber again, on his way to freedom.

No! Damn it!

Anger flared. The murdering bastard shot Alex and the Bowens and dismissed me as through I were nothing. Fuck that. He wasn't leaving. No way.

As the bike flew past, I dived forward and sideways, and jabbed the end of the stick into his front wheel. It tore from my hand, whipped round, and jammed against the forks. The rear wheel lifted, the motorcycle bucked, and Biker flew. He smashed headfirst into brickwork, slid down the wall, and landed in a crumpled heap. The bike continued down the ramp on its side, throwing up a shower of orange sparks.

David sprinted towards me, Alex's gun in hand. "Call an ambulance. Alex is hurt but alive. I've got this bugger."

An empty pocket reminded me David still had my phone. I picked up the tablet, hurried to Alex, and knelt, keeping the bad leg stretching out to the side. "Alex, are you okay?"

"Yes," she said, eyes open, fixed on me. "My arm hurts and I hit my head. Where is the boss? What happened?"

"Later. Where's your phone?"

"*Hjälp mig att sitta?*"

"Sorry?"

"Help me to sit."

"No, stay where you are. Your arm's bleeding and there's an ugly bump on your head."

"Stop fussing. Go and see to … DC Bowen. He might be still alive. I shall call the ambulance."

There wasn't as much blood as I'd feared, but her left shoulder didn't look right and might have been broken or dislocated. I helped ease her upright, leaned her against the brickwork, and draped my jacket across her shoulders.

"You know where we are, right? Brent Cross car park, fourth level." I took the mobile from her pocket and she took it. "Dial 9-9-9."

"Phil, I am fine. Take this." She opened the flap of her jacket. She had another gun tucked into her waistband. The revolver Hook had given me.

"How the hell did you get this?"

She waved her good hand. Now was not the time.

"Bowen may be armed. Take no risks. Go."

I accepted the revolver, checked the load again—one spent shell, one empty chamber—and swapped hands. For some reason, it felt more comfortable in my left. Weird. I'm a righty.

"Okay. I'll be right back. Shout if you need me. Freddie can bleed out for all I care."

My half-walk, half-stumble to the BMW didn't take long. As I approached, I slowed and raised the gun. Alex was right, of course, I could have been walking straight into a bullet. I was a sheriff in one of those old black and white movies moseying up Main Street ready to face the black-hearted gunslinger. How they didn't wet themselves every time, I'll never know.

I needn't have worried. Freddie hadn't moved from his position on the concrete and lay in the shadow of the car's open door. A large pool of blood circled his head, but his chest still rose and fell. Tears squeezed from his closed eyes. What were they for? The pain, his dead wife, or his lost freedom? I didn't know and didn't really care. After the damage he'd caused, I'd waste none of my sympathy on the bastard.

When I reached him and patted him down for weapons—coming up empty—he opened his eyes and stared at the revolver.

"Imelda? Is she …"

One look inside the Beemer gave me the answer. Imelda's vacant eyes stared into nothingness, and the back of her head didn't look natural. The bullet had taken away part of the crown and splattered it over the grey leather upholstery. Bone, blood, and bits of white matter painted an abstract pattern inside the driver's compartment. If I tilted my head to the right and squinted, I might have been able to make out a Rorschach inkblot.

In life, Imelda Bowen played the part of slowly disintegrating wife. In death, she had … actually disintegrated. Sometimes, there is such a thing as poetic justice.

"Yes, Freddie," I answered, keeping my tone professional, trying not to turn my nose up at the gore and the smell. "She's dead."

He let out a pathetic animal groan. While his eyes were closed, I set the tablet to voice record.

"I told her we should just run, but she wouldn't listen. Never listened to me. Needy, she was. Always wanted … more. More than I could give her on a policeman's salary."

"What were you doing here? Who's the guy on the bike?"

He lifted his head, winced, and dropped it back into the blood pool. "Did he get away?"

I turned.

David had taken Biker's right hand and attached it to the railings with a pair of handcuffs. He took care not to jostle the killer and used both his hands. He must have put the gun away after he'd confirmed Biker's incapacitation.

"No," I told Freddie, "we've got him."

"Good. Evil animal deserves all he gets."

"Who is he?"

"Didn't you … recognise him?" His eyes closed and his head rolled to one side.

"Alex?" I shouted and turned my head. "Did you get through?"

She held up the phone. "*Ja.* The ambulance will arrive soon. Is he alive?"

"Just about. Imelda isn't. Boss, you okay?"

"No problems here. You?"

"Fine. Recognise the biker? He had a Northern Irish accent."

David shook his head. "Can't see his face through the scratched visor and I'm not removing his helmet. Better wait for the paramedics."

"Can you check on Alex? There's a nasty bump on her head, and I think her arm's broken."

He raised a hand. "I was on my way."

Before he left the killer, David grabbed the man's foot and bound it to the railings with one of the black cable ties he always carries. A resourceful bloke, my boss. I'm trying to learn from him, but his jackets always seem as roomy as a magician's coat. Mine aren't.

A hand grabbed my ankle and I looked down. Freddie tugged on my trouser leg, beckoning me closer. I knelt beside his head, trying not to grunt as the movement stretched my scars. On the plus side, flexing my knee didn't hurt so much. I leaned close but kept the gun well out of his reach.

"Phil … you know … how they treat cops in prison. Shoot me … Please? You can say I grabbed for the gun."

I snorted. "That isn't happening, Freddie. You have questions to answer and I'm no murderer. Who's the biker?"

He blinked slowly, seemingly struggling to keep his eyes open. "You really … don't know?"

"Don't start that again. I only saw his eyes. Who is he?"

Freddie's pupils dilated as he lost focus. He smiled. A sly smile that made me want to smash his face in, or go back on my word and use the revolver. He'd thought of something to sell as leverage. Nuts to that, I wasn't buying.

Leaning close to hide what I was doing from the boss and Alex, I pulled the gun, cocked the hammer, and pushed the muzzle into his cheek hard enough to force his head around. He squealed. The smell of blood cooling on the dirty concrete, and the sight of his matted hair sticking in the semi-congealed ooze churned my stomach.

"Tell me all you know and I'll pull the trigger."

Freddie's eyes widened. "Promise?"

I nodded, and eased back a little on the muzzle pressure. "Who's the guy on the bike?"

"Brendan McGuire … Brendan Padraigh McGuire."

"What?"

Paddy M? No wonder I'd recognised the bugger's eyes.

Jesus wept!

I'd seen enough photos of IRA members in my time. Paddy M, the nationalist movement's top bomber and assassin from the '70s through to the early '90s. A wanted man since 1976, the official line had it that the Loyalists had 'disappeared' him around the time of the Good Friday Agreement. The last report I read marked the Paddy M case as Unsolved/No Action Necessary.

Vomit tried to force its way up from my boiling guts, but I swallowed and put up with the burning aftertaste.

Less than ten minutes earlier, I, DS Phil Cryer, the Gimp, had been on the nasty end of a gun wielded by one of the worst terrorists that poor, benighted country had ever produced. And I'd taken him down with a walking stick.

How about that? Maybe the name, Lucky Cryer, wasn't that far off.

"He used Imelda. Paid her to befriend me when I was working for ATU27, the anti-terrorist unit. I've … I've always been hopeless around women and when someone as beautiful as Imelda smiled at me … I … was lost."

I took another look at the corpse in the BMW. Nothing beautiful about her now.

"She worked for Paddy M?"

"Yes. Oh, God. I didn't want to do anything bad. At heart, I'm a good … an honest man." He coughed and looked away. "Say something, Phil. Please?"

He wanted me to agree that he was basically honest? Fuck that. No way I was going to say anything to make his life easier, not after what I'd seen at the safe house. It wasn't up to me to offer a salve to his conscience.

"I am. Honest, I mean. But do one single thing wrong … turn a blind eye … take a bribe … and you're theirs forever."

"The Alzheimer's. Your idea or hers?"

"Imelda's and Paddy M's. They wanted me to join the OCTF. It has a broad remit, more potential information to sell, but they only had vacancies for DCs at the time. Imelda's … illness was the best excuse we could come up with for my taking a drop in rank and pay." He coughed and his mouth creased into a grimace. "It's not like we needed the money."

"How did she keep up the pretence all that time? Must have been a hell of a strain."

"No, she started off as an actress. The role of her life, she said. … Loved playing it. Only supposed to last a few months, but Paddy M kept demanding more information and Imelda kept demanding more money. Oh, God. Imelda, my wife. She's really dead? What am I going to do?"

More tears fell as he stared at the corpse. I pushed on before he broke down completely.

"How did you recruit Hannah?"

Freddie dragged his eyes away and focused them on mine. "Hannah? Where is she?"

"I'm asking the questions. You're answering them. Go on. Time's wasting."

"Okay, okay. I didn't recruit Hannah, she approached me." He snorted. "You wouldn't think to look at her, but she's a gambler. Cards, roulette, raindrops running down a window pane, anything. She hides it well at work, but doesn't know when to stop. Weak willed, you know?" He paused for breath.

I added a little pressure on the gun. "Go on, Freddie. Don't stop there. This is riveting stuff."

He was having trouble swallowing. "Like most gamblers, Hannah isn't very good at self control. Made some bad choices. She … ended up owing tens of thousands to a bookie acquaintance of Paddy M. He forced her to seek me out and I helped her to join the NCA. Altered her CV enough to make her look worthy of a grunt job on Bee's team. She isn't a bad cop, but I've been carrying her on the team, protecting her. She has her uses though. Hannah turned out to be pretty handy with … certain aspects of Paddy M's business affairs. A natural. Enjoys the wet work, too. If you see what I mean."

"Did she kill Richie Juno?"

"No. That was one of Paddy M's other … contractors."

His arm shot up, reaching for the gun, but I slapped it away. The wound in his shoulder, close to the neck, opened and dripped more blood. It might end up doing the job Freddie wanted from me. Only one visible wound though. From what I could tell, Paddy M's second shot had missed.

"And Richie?"

"I didn't have anything to do with his death. You have to believe me. I overheard him making an appointment to speak to Knightly and told Imelda. She told Paddy M and he … he had Richie killed. I don't know by whom. Honest"

"Honest?" I punched the tablet's 'stop record' button. "You piece of crap. Shut your whining and say goodbye."

Freddie closed his eyes and smiled again. I squeezed the trigger. The hammer fell on the empty chamber. The *click* made him jump. I rose to my feet. Even without the stick, it wasn't too difficult. Maybe I was getting better.

Freddie opened his eyes as I stuffed the revolver into my pocket and his face crumpled.

"But you promised," he wailed. The tears fell again.

"Yes, I promised to pull the trigger. Never break a promise, me."

I so wanted to pull the trigger again, I really did, but the difference between his sort of cop and *my* sort is *we* stay within the law. Our rules don't allow us to act on revenge, no matter what the provocation.

"You'll do your time and I hope you'll enjoy every second of it."

The growing wail of approaching sirens didn't quite drown out his reply, but it wasn't worth repeating.

Chapter 39

Friday 11th October

The emergency vehicles arrived in a convoy led by a Vauxhall Movano equipped for riot control—including bull bars and a protective grill covering the windscreen. Behind it, five police cars, all fully loaded, and two ambulances parked on the third level.

David and I held up our warrant cards as seven officers, armed heavily enough to wage war and wearing full body armour, exited the Movano. They fanned out in a 'V' formation behind their leader, an inspector. He ordered his men to secure the area and take charge of any weapons. With one hand still holding up my ID card, I held out the revolver, handle first. A burly sergeant took it from me and handed it off to one of his men. He squinted hard at my ID, checked that my face matched the photo, and only then lowered his weapon.

"All secure here, DS Cryer?" He took in the scene, his eyes resting on Freddie's prone figure.

I nodded and thudded against the nearest column, light-headed, and weak-legged.

"You okay, mate?" the sergeant asked.

"Not really. It's been a long night." I scratched the itch on my nose. "I haven't searched the BMW yet, but Mrs Bowen isn't going anywhere and this arsehole's no danger." I pointed at Freddie. "Gunshot wound to the neck or shoulder. All that blood's his."

The sergeant waited while two of his people searched the BMW. One, a dark-haired woman, opened the boot and reached inside. A second later she straightened and held up a tartan rug. "Sarge, you might want to take a look at this."

The sergeant raised a hand to tell me to stay put and hurried to his subordinate. He peered into the boot, used his finger to run a count, and then looked at me. "Any idea why these people have ten miniature telephone boxes?"

It took me a second to register the question and about a minute more to stop laughing long enough to answer his question. "Yes, Sarge," I managed to say, hysterical tears rolling down my cheeks. "I rather think I do."

The bloke must have thought I'd cracked. There I was, pissing myself, when this guy expected to walk into a fire fight. I mentally slapped my face. Hysteria can get people locked up. Or worse. "DS Cryer, what's the … What's going on here?"

After taking a quick peek in the boot, I explained where the telephone boxes came from and what they were made of. I didn't pick one up in case I couldn't put it back down again—temptation can be a terrible thing. Ask Hannah and Freddie.

"If I were you Sarge, I'd mount a close guard on this vehicle and contact DCI Bartok from Paddington Green. He's been looking for those little beauties."

Seemingly assured of my sanity, the sergeant gave two officers sentry duty and then pointed at Freddie. "Who's he?"

"DC Frederick Bowen, of the NCA."

"What?" He glowered at me and waved at the lead ambulance. "Officer down. Get over here quick."

I raised my hand to hold him back. "Before you go thinking I'm the most callous bastard you've ever met, let me add that this man's a cop killer and a thief, and was working hand in glove with the arsehole in the motorcycle leathers. My advice is to treat him accordingly."

The sergeant looked towards Paddy M, who still hadn't moved. With any luck, the fall had broken his bloody neck.

"And who's he?"

"Him? He's also a killer. Shot Mrs Bowen, shot Freddie, shot my colleague"—I nodded towards Alex—"and fired at my boss, DCI Jones. He's the distinguished-looking guy talking to your inspector. I wouldn't waste your sympathy on these three."

I kept Paddy M's name quiet for the time being. No telling what that sort of revelation would do for the situation. Certainly wouldn't help keep tempers even.

"Since you put it that way, I won't." The sergeant's scowl softened as he took in the carnage. "Looks like you've had an interesting evening. Sure you're okay? You look a bit peaky."

"Not surprising after the night I've had. Don't have any water, I suppose?"

"Eddie?" he called to one of his men. "Fetch DS Cryer a nice fresh bottle of Peckham Spring from the van." He winked and, despite everything, I had to smile.

The tall constable, who now had the revolver—its fourth keeper of the evening—trotted off to the Vauxhall. He returned with two paramedics and a bottle of water, which tasted as good as anything I'd ever drunk.

The paramedics started working on Freddie, and I spoke quietly to the sergeant. "Make sure he's handcuffed to the stretcher and put him on suicide watch, okay?"

"Will do, Sarge."

"My name's Phil."

"I'm Ray. Nice meeting you."

We bumped elbows. Armed police officers don't shake hands when on call.

"Can I leave this with you, Ray? My boss is looking a bit edgy, and I want to see how my colleague's doing."

"Yeah, go ahead. We've got this covered."

Without the stick, I took my time descending the ramp and reached Alex and the boss as a second pair of paramedics loaded her onto a trolley. She had a foam collar in place and a padded brace on her arm. Her colour had improved, and she turned her cool blue eyes towards me.

"Phil, please tell the boss this is unnecessary. I can walk."

I held her good hand. "Do as you're told, DS Olganski. I'll be with you as soon as I can find a bunch of flowers."

"Thank you Phil, but I prefer grapes, please, or chocolates. *Blommor* ... flowers, are not my style," she said, trying to hide a grimace as the paramedics tilted the stretcher.

"Grapes it is, then."

I released her hand and the paramedics rolled the trolley towards one of the ambulances. The sign on its side panel read Queen Anne's Hospital. Not far away and with a good reputation. They'd look after her.

David continued briefing the inspector, and I stood behind them, watching three different paramedics work together to remove Paddy M's bin lid.

One man braced the killer's neck in his cupped hands, while another peeled back the plastic padding inside the helmet and eased it clear. The first man then held Paddy M's head steady, while the third worked a spinal board under the body. A slick operation, they might have just saved the ex-terrorist the humiliation of having someone else wipe his arse for the rest of his days.

"...and given what we have lying in a puddle of blood over there," David added, turning towards the upper level, "you'd better notify the Met's Anti-Corruption Unit. They'll be in charge of the investigation. Despite the Home Secretary's sanction, this is outside my jurisdiction. I've more than enough work of my own to deal with."

"Boss," I said, moving to his side, "sorry to disturb, but I need a word. It's important."

He looked at me, no doubt surprised and annoyed by my interruption.

"Inspector Malone, this is my second-in-command, DS Cryer."

"Evening, Inspector."

"Good evening, Sergeant. You made a bit of a mess of that lovely motorbike."

"Shame that, eh?" I said and half-turned towards the spot where Alex had been lying and tilted my head. The boss took the hint.

"Thank you, Inspector," he said. "I'll be here for a while if you need me."

A question flashed in Malone's eyes, but he looked at the boss, said, "Thank you, sir," and turned on his heel, heading up the ramp towards the Bowens' BMW.

"Well, Phil? Is DC Bowen still alive? That what you wanted to talk to me about?"

"He is alive, but ... No, boss," I said, scratching my chin. "This whole case is bigger than we thought."

His sigh told me he expected the worst, and I wasn't going to disappoint.

"Not certain of the protocol here," I said, keeping my voice down, "but we'll need to lock off this crime scene and contact HOATU, the Home Office Anti-Terror Unit."

"Thank you, Philip. I know what HOATU stands for. What did Bowen tell you?"

"The biker's name. It's Brendan McGuire. Boss, we've just captured Paddy M!"

"No! It can't be." He spun around and stared at the killer, eyes wide, nostrils flared, breathing hard. "He's dead. The Loyalists got to him in '97."

He bent at the waist, tilted his head to improve the angle, and peered closer at the former terrorist.

The ambulance team carried on with their task of fastening the webbing straps and securing their patient to the spinal board while David looked on. I started to move, but he raised his hand to keep me away—his fingers trembled.

I waited for an explanation, but he said nothing until the paramedics hoisted their patient onto a collapsible stretcher. As they lifted it and locked the wheels in place, David straightened, fists clenched, lower lip trembling. He stood for a moment, closed his moist eyes, and took a deep breath. A moment later, he turned haunted eyes on me. My heart lurched as I read his pain.

"You were right. That's Brendan McGuire," he said, in a voice so soft and quiet I could barely hear him. "Phil," he whispered, grabbing my arm, "that man murdered my wife and baby boy."

Numb, I had no response.

That one statement answered so many questions I had about David Jones. Why he kept himself to himself. Why he had so few close friends. He carried such a burden, no wonder he looked so damn sad all the time.

I tried to imagine how I'd feel if I lost Manda and my babies but gave up. That way led to madness.

When the ambulance drove away with Paddy M, David leaned against the railings, grasping the handrail for support. I stood at his side, close but not touching, ready to help if he needed me, but not forcing matters.

We stood together in silence. I didn't prompt. He'd tell me more if and when he wanted to. I stared through the gaps between the concrete pillars and watched falling rain backlit by the coloured lights of Brent Cross.

"Her name was Siân," David said at length, his eyes damp and unfocused. "Siân Mair Savage. We met in 1975, when I was on summer secondment in South Wales. We were married three months later."

He looked at me. His face registered sadness and pain, but something else, too—lost happiness.

"Yes, Phil. I can guess what you're thinking. Three months? Not long, but we were kids. Impetuous, but … I … I don't really have the words."

He stopped talking and lowered his eyes. I thought he'd reached the limit of his verbal self-evisceration, then he looked at me again.

"What you have with Manda, I should have had with Siân. But one of that bastard's bombs killed her." He pointed over his shoulder to the fallen motorbike. "April 1976. We were in London, taking in the sights. Siân was twenty-six weeks pregnant. The doctors tried to save my boy but he was too small. His name was Paul."

"Paul? Bloody hell."

"At least I got the chance to hold him."

Another question answered. In the maternity ward, when Manda and I asked if we could name our newborn son David, in his honour, the old man refused. He suggested Paul as a better alternative.

"You don't have to tell me this, boss. Not now."

"I know, but I've been keeping it to myself for so long … Siân and Paul deserve better, but …"

David's voice faded to silence and he closed his eyes. I waited for more, but he pushed away from the handrail and straightened his tie. And that was that; the old man was back.

"You'd better call the HOATU," he said, voice firm, controlled. "The sooner they arrive, the sooner I can send you home to your family."

I reached out and he let me touch his arm. "You okay, boss?"

"Yes thanks, son. I'll … survive. I think Manda would like you home sooner rather than later. And don't worry, next time you invite me for dinner, I'll bring the photos I have of Siân and Paul. I'll tell you both all about them. That okay?"

"Yes, boss. We'd like that very much."

David took a spotless white handkerchief from an inside pocket and wiped his eyes.

"This place is filthy. Grit in my eyes."

"Yeah, me too."

Chapter 40

Sunday 13th October

Friday had passed in a blur of visits to Queen Anne's Hospital interspersed with endless interrogations by faceless HOATU spooks.

David and I refused to speak to them until Alex came out of surgery. The bullet—a through-and-through—nicked a muscle inside her upper arm, tore some blood vessels, but hit nothing major. The surgeon expected a quick recovery and a return to full mobility. As I diagnosed, she did dislocate the shoulder. The doctors admitted her overnight to monitor for concussion. She complained the whole time that everyone was fussing too much and she should be 'released from this prison'. Even David's infamous dead-eyed stare couldn't calm her down.

Billy Hook endured a five-hour operation to rebuild a shattered femur with titanium pins, nuts, and bolts. Surprisingly, his CT scan showed an actual full-sized brain, but no permanent damage. I didn't wait around for his recovery, but left a message that I'd check in on 'the new Gimp' as soon as I had a spare moment.

Then I spent hour after interminable hour with the spooks answering the same questions over and over. Eventually, David pulled rank and forced them to let me go. In exchange, he offered to stay in London until the medics discharged Alex and made himself available for their questions instead.

Ryan and Ben got off lightly. One long interview each and they were allowed to leave. Both elected to keep vigil with Alex, whose room ended up looking like a fruit and chocolate stall.

On a promise to return to London on Monday for further debriefing, I made it home a little before midnight on Friday night, exhausted, bleary-eyed, but completely delighted.

Seeing my kids asleep in their beds again after all that had happened in Watford and Brent Cross made me blub, and I didn't hide my tears from Manda either.

Yep. Big softie, that's me.

On Saturday morning, Manda and I woke early, but stayed in bed. We cuddled, drank coffee, chatted, cuddled some more, and watched BBC News on my tablet until Paulie demanded his breakfast. A small item at the end of the national bulletin made me smile. It mentioned a minor incident in a Brent Cross car park in the early hours of Friday morning.

Apparently, a number of local residents and late night shoppers called the police claiming to have heard gunshots. Armed police units and three ambulances arrived at the scene within minutes to find an injured motorcyclist who had fallen off his bike as the result of a mechanical breakdown. In a press conference held on Friday evening, a spokesman for the Metropolitan Police calmed fears by assuring the public the episode had nothing to do with terrorism or gang warfare. The spokesman attributed the shots to the motorcycle backfiring twice and the sounds echoing off the walls. He claimed that the down ramp of multi-storey car parks were notorious for this acoustic phenomenon.

I didn't think such stage management possible in the age of twenty-four-hour news coverage, but the HOATU spooks, it seemed, maintained a tight control over the national and local media. No doubt the conspiracy theorists would have something to say on the matter, but at least the cover up meant I didn't have to mention my brush with death to Manda.

A major upside.

Jamie joined us at a little after nine, and I powered down the tablet.

She'd lost another tooth since I started with the NCA. Damn it, I love playing the Tooth Fairy, but missed the latest one. When she lost the first tooth, we agreed a sliding scale—one pound for molars, fifty pence for incisors, and bicuspids counted as molars. My daughter negotiates a tough deal and would never let me forget the details. As if I would.

Manda left to prepare a full English breakfast—a special treat for the homecoming hero. Alone in my bedroom, Jamie looked at me, her deep blue eyes serious.

"I missed you, Daddy," she said, giving me a hug and an Eskimo nose rub.

"Missed you too, my angel."

"Have you finished your work seconding?"

"Seconding? Oh, you mean secondment? Yes, nearly. Just a couple more days to write my reports, but I'll be coming home nights." She squealed as I tickled her tummy. "Why don't you go help Mummy in the kitchen? I need to make a quick call."

She scooted off and I called the boss for an update. He answered from the waiting room in Queen Anne's Hospital.

"Alex is fine," he said. "The doctors have discharged her. We'll be on our way home as soon as the hire car arrives. I've ordered a sporty Megane."

"Excellent. Is she there?"

He handed Alex the phone. "Hello Phil. Can you tell the boss if he doesn't stop his fussing, I am going to scream."

"And David Jones is going to let little old me order him around? Oh yeah, right."

The image of her lying on the dirty car park floor in all its high-definition horror returned to haunt me. Bloody eidetic memory.

"Come stay with us while you recover. Please."

"Oh, Phil, that is generous, but I have a friend who is a nurse. She will take care of me."

We spoke for a few more minutes and I ended the call after inviting them both to Sunday dinner. Alex declined, David accepted.

I dressed and was halfway down the stairs before realising my walking stick was still wrapped around the forks of Paddy M's Yamaha. The knee still ached, but so much less than it had before I started at the NCA. A little stiffness, that's all. No worse than the cramp I used to suffer in the days after the first rugby match of the season.

A breakthrough. I couldn't stop smiling.

#

Late Sunday afternoon and mayhem reigned in the Cryer household. Paulie, wailing upstairs in his cot, fighting his afternoon nap, Manda baking—David loves her *Men-Only Lemon Drizzle Cake*—and Jamie jumping up and down, literally.

"Where is he, Daddy? He's late."

"He'll be here, angel. Don't worry and don't go mad when he arrives. You know what he's like."

"Yes, Daddy. I'll be good," she said, adding one of those patient smiles she's learned from her mother.

The doorbell chimed and, before I could finish heaving myself out of the recliner, Jamie scrambled to the front door. She peered through the letterbox before opening it as I taught her and jumped into David's waiting arms.

"Uncle David, Uncle David, you're late. I've tidied my room and helped Mummy in the kitchen, and I've been a good girl. Honest I have, and I got all my spellings right on Friday. Fifteen out of fifteen."

"You are my little genius, poppet." He hugged her for a moment, eyes closed, and then brushed a lock of blonde hair from her face. "Let me look at you. Prettier than ever. Afternoon, Philip. Mind if I come in?"

"Better had," I said, leaning against the doorjamb to the front room, trying not to smile. "You're letting in the cold air."

Manda called from the kitchen, "In here, David. Kettle's on. As is the oven."

Still carrying Jamie, he stepped over the threshold, a shopping bag swinging from his free hand. I don't think he's ever visited without bringing something for Jamie and now Paulie, but he doesn't come all that often, and won't spoil them.

"Smells wonderful, Manda," he said. "Where's young Paul?"

"Just dropped off to sleep, but he'll be up for his supper soon."

We trooped into the kitchen, and David offered Manda the carrier bag. "A little something for the kids and a bottle that needs to see the inside of the fridge."

Manda delved into the bag and removed two book-shaped packages—each beautifully wrapped—and a bottle that looked suspiciously like Champagne, gold foil around the wired cork and everything. Jamie's eyes bulged at the presents, but she didn't ask, even though I knew she was desperate to reach for hers and start tearing at the wrapping paper.

Manda held up the bottle. "What are we celebrating?"

David shrugged. The sadness behind his eyes was still there, but didn't seem to cut so deep.

"Tell you later," he answered, setting Jamie down on the breakfast counter. "Jamie, would you like to open your present now?"

She beamed. "Yes please."

Manda handed her the larger package and she started trying to peel back the sticky tape, her impatience growing.

"It's okay, poppet," David whispered. "I don't mind you ripping the paper."

In seconds, the wrapping was off and the torn paper fell, but David caught it halfway to the floor. He folded it into a neat square while watching Jamie's eyes light up as she read the title of a leather bound edition of *The Hobbit*.

"Uncle David, this is way cool. Thank you so much. Will you listen to me read it at bed time?"

David looked at Manda and then at me. "If your mum and dad say it's okay."

Jamie sighed. "Don't be silly, of course it'll be okay. Isn't that right, Mummy?"

Manda nodded. Neither checked with me. Fathers are so often ignored.

"Excellent," he said. "So, Philip. After your holiday down south, I daresay you'll be keen to return to some real policing?"

"Yes," I answered with feeling. "I've an appointment with the FMO on Wednesday afternoon. Fingers crossed."

Jamie raised her arms and David lowered her to the floor. "I 'spect you grownups want to talk now? Mummy, can I go to my room and start my book, please?"

"Yes, but quietly. Paulie's sleeping. I'll call you when dinner's ready."

"You'll come earlier next time, Uncle David? So we can go to the park? I'll push Paulie's pram if you like. I am strong enough. Aren't I, Daddy?"

"It's a deal," David said and she ran up the stairs, book hugged tight to her chest, and closed her bedroom door with barely a thump. He turned to Manda. "You don't mind me giving her *The Hobbit*? I checked the reading age with the woman at the shop and she suggested it's okay for a girl her age. Not too scary and none of that princesses and fairies fluff. I thought it would be an intelligent read for a pocket genius."

"She'll be fine. It's a beautiful thought and she'll take good care of it." Manda pointed him into a stool and cleared a space in the fridge for the bubbly.

"I know she will. Doesn't even crease the spines of her paperbacks."

Manda held up David's plastic bag. "Did you know there's a big envelope in here?"

The boss glanced at me before answering. "Some … family photos I found when clearing out my garage. I'll show you later."

Manda put the bag to one side, but I could tell she was desperate for a look-see. Inquisitive soul, my wife. Would have made a great detective.

I joined David at the breakfast bar and perched on the second stool. "So, what's the Champers for? What are we celebrating?" I asked, changing the subject when I saw his eyes start to glisten.

Manda turned, tray in hand with the fixings for tea and coffee. "Yes, you were going to tell us. Come on, out with it."

"Okay. How about a toast to the successful end of a difficult case? Or the fact that the doctors moved Brian Knightly out of intensive care this morning? That enough? Oh, and I nearly forgot. I talked to the Deputy Chief Constable this afternoon. Disturbed his golf round. Crying shame. Turns out he's filled Big Jock's spot on the team."

The final sentence stabbed like a knife through my guts and definitely wasn't a reason to celebrate, but I managed a nod. "That's great, boss. Do I know his replacement?"

Manda handed him his tea and me a coffee, and remained quiet.

David tugged at his earlobe. "I rather think you might." He raised his cup. "Congratulations, Acting Detective Inspector Cryer—glad to have you back on board. Careful, Philip. Don't spill your coffee."

The End

Please Write A Review

If you liked this book and, since you reached the end, I sincerely hope you did, please tell a friend—better yet, tell the world by writing a review on the book's Amazon page. Even a few short sentences are helpful. Please spread the word.

Also, if you fancy a chat, I would love to hear from you. You can email me at my website here or follow my Facebook page here.

Sign up to my Newsletter here to receive notifications of future releases and special offers (such as subscriber-only price reductions, free novels, prize draws, and free additional content). Never fear, I won't inundate you with mail.

Acknowledgements

My heartfelt thanks go to Michaela Miles for her unstinting help during this project. Whether beta reading, copy editing, proofing, web design, or supporting my mood swings, she's always ready to offer a kind word and a helping hand. Thanks millions, my cariad. Although we've never met in person, I love you.

I also heap thanks and praise on my alpha readers from the Scribophile community who helped by reviewing my early drafts. Thanks in particular to: Susan, Randy, Helen, Chris, and Steve—you know who you all are. Thanks millions guys.

By the way, dear reader, they bear no responsibility for any errors within this text—the fault is entirely mine. ☺

I also have to commend my longest-serving friend, David Ilic, who risked damage to his camera when taking this author's headshot.

Biography

#1 International Best-seller with On Lucky Shores, Kerry J Donovan was born in Dublin. A citizen of the world, he now lives in a cottage in the heart of rural Brittany with his wife of forty years, Jan. They have three children and four grandchildren (so far), all of whom live in England. An absentee granddad, Kerry is hugely thankful for the advent of video calling.

The cottage is a pet free zone (apart from the field mice, moles, and red squirrels).

Kerry earned a first class honours degree in Human Biology, and has a PhD in Sport and Exercise Sciences. A former scientific advisor to The Office of the Deputy Prime Minister, he helped UK emergency first-responders prepare for chemical attacks in the wake of 9/11. This background adds a scientific edge to his writing. He is also a former furniture designer/maker.

Contact him:
Website: http://kerryjdonovan.com/
Twitter: https://twitter.com/KerryJDonovan
Facebook: https://www.facebook.com/KerryJDonovan

Author's Notes

First, let me reiterate the opening statements (above). This is a work of pure fiction. None of the characters or situations exist outside of this author's misfiring mind or outside the pixels/pages of this novel. Although, having said that …

The National Crime Agency *does* exist and its headquarters *are* in Tinworth Street, London, SE11 5EF, but their operations, as described in this novel, are fictitious. The buildings and their internal structure were conjured in this author's febrile imagination. Although electronic 'cleans rooms' like The Cage do exist, I have no idea whether the NCA employs such systems. Again, I invented this device for reasons of plot. Let me say here and now, that the NCA is no more prone to corruption than any other large organisation and I wouldn't like to suggest anything else. This is a work of fiction. It is made up. That's it.

Now for a word about my mate, David Jones, and his team. First, let me say to all readers who make a study of the UK Police Services, I know that the Midlands Police Service doesn't exist, nor does its headquarters in Holton. The organisation with responsibility for policing Birmingham and the surrounding region is the West Midlands Police.

You might ask why I felt the need to invent David Jones' force but kept the name of the NCA based in realty. Simple really. David, is of a vintage that might have given him an association with the happily defunct and notorious West Midlands Serious Crime Squad—they of the infamous Birmingham Six and other monstrous miscarriages of justice. I wanted to keep David Jones well away from that issue.

And another thing …

As a reviewer once pointed out, back in the 1970s, Midlands police recruits are likely to have completed their basic training at the West Midlands Training College at Ryton-on-Dunsmore, which now offers specialist training courses for existing police officers only. Currently, training also takes place at the charmingly named, Tally Ho Training Centre.

In my defence, as is the defence of any writer of fiction, I needed a way for David Jones and Brian Knightly to have met in the dim and distant past. I used the public's perception of Hendon as being the Police's version of the British Army's officer training college in Sandhurst, instead of inventing a whole new back story for the meeting. I hesitate to suggest that I used 'artistic licence' for fear of sounding awfully pretentious. This author does not consider himself to be an artist, more a teller of campfire tales.

Hopefully, that clears up some of your questions. If you have more, please feel free to contact me either through my website, or my legal representatives, here.

Please Write A Review

If you liked this book and, since you reached the end, I sincerely hope you did, please tell a friend—better yet, tell the world by writing a review on the book's Amazon page. Even a few short sentences are helpful. Please spread the word.

Also, if you fancy a chat, I would love to hear from you. You can email me at my website here or follow my Facebook page here.

Sign up to my Newsletter here to receive notifications of future releases and special offers (such as subscriber-only price reductions, free novels, prize draws, and free additional content). Never fear, I won't inundate you with mail.

Acknowledgements

My heartfelt thanks go to Michaela Miles for her unstinting help during this project. Whether beta reading, copy editing, proofing, web design, or supporting my mood swings, she's always ready to offer a kind word and a helping hand. Thanks millions, my cariad. Although we've never met in person, I love you.

I also heap thanks and praise on my alpha readers from the Scribophile community who helped by reviewing my early drafts. Thanks in particular to: Susan, Randy, Helen, Chris, and Steve—you know who you all are. Thanks millions guys.

By the way, dear reader, they bear no responsibility for any errors within this text—the fault is entirely mine. ☺

I also have to commend my longest-serving friend, David Ilic, who risked damage to his camera when taking this author's headshot.

Biography

#1 International Best-seller with On Lucky Shores, Kerry J Donovan was born in Dublin. A citizen of the world, he now lives in a cottage in the heart of rural Brittany with his wife of forty years, Jan. They have three children and four grandchildren (so far), all of whom live in England. An absentee granddad, Kerry is hugely thankful for the advent of video calling.

The cottage is a pet free zone (apart from the field mice, moles, and red squirrels).

Kerry earned a first class honours degree in Human Biology, and has a PhD in Sport and Exercise Sciences. A former scientific advisor to The Office of the Deputy Prime Minister, he helped UK emergency first-responders prepare for chemical attacks in the wake of 9/11. This background adds a scientific edge to his writing. He is also a former furniture designer/maker.

Contact him:
Website: http://kerryjdonovan.com/
Twitter: https://twitter.com/KerryJDonovan
Facebook: https://www.facebook.com/KerryJDonovan

Author's Notes

First, let me reiterate the opening statements (above). This is a work of pure fiction. None of the characters or situations exist outside of this author's misfiring mind or outside the pixels/pages of this novel. Although, having said that …

The National Crime Agency *does* exist and its headquarters *are* in Tinworth Street, London, SE11 5EF, but their operations, as described in this novel, are fictitious. The buildings and their internal structure were conjured in this author's febrile imagination. Although electronic 'cleans rooms' like The Cage do exist, I have no idea whether the NCA employs such systems. Again, I invented this device for reasons of plot. Let me say here and now, that the NCA is no more prone to corruption than any other large organisation and I wouldn't like to suggest anything else. This is a work of fiction. It is made up. That's it.

Now for a word about my mate, David Jones, and his team. First, let me say to all readers who make a study of the UK Police Services, I know that the Midlands Police Service doesn't exist, nor does its headquarters in Holton. The organisation with responsibility for policing Birmingham and the surrounding region is the West Midlands Police.

You might ask why I felt the need to invent David Jones' force but kept the name of the NCA based in realty. Simple really. David, is of a vintage that might have given him an association with the happily defunct and notorious West Midlands Serious Crime Squad—they of the infamous Birmingham Six and other monstrous miscarriages of justice. I wanted to keep David Jones well away from that issue.

And another thing …

As a reviewer once pointed out, back in the 1970s, Midlands police recruits are likely to have completed their basic training at the West Midlands Training College at Ryton-on-Dunsmore, which now offers specialist training courses for existing police officers only. Currently, training also takes place at the charmingly named, Tally Ho Training Centre.

In my defence, as is the defence of any writer of fiction, I needed a way for David Jones and Brian Knightly to have met in the dim and distant past. I used the public's perception of Hendon as being the Police's version of the British Army's officer training college in Sandhurst, instead of inventing a whole new back story for the meeting. I hesitate to suggest that I used 'artistic licence' for fear of sounding awfully pretentious. This author does not consider himself to be an artist, more a teller of campfire tales.

Hopefully, that clears up some of your questions. If you have more, please feel free to contact me either through my website, or my legal representatives, here.

OTHER WORKS

CRIME THRILLERS

The DCI Jones Casebook: Sean Freeman

The DCI Jones Casebook: Raymond Collins

The DCI Jones Casebook: Ellis Flynn

The DCI Jones Casebook: Cryer's View

ACTION ADVENTURE

On Lucky Shores

FANTASY THRILLER

The Transition of Johnny Swift

SHORT STORIES

The Collection

Printed in Great Britain
by Amazon